FULL CIRCLE

Mike Seabrook

Full Circle

THE GAY MEN'S PRESS

First published 1997 by GMP Publishers Ltd,
P O Box 247, Swaffham, Norfolk PE37 8PA, England

World Copyright © 1997 Mike Seabrook

A CIP catalogue record for this book is available
from the British Library

ISBN 0 85449 242 9

Distributed in Europe by Central Books,
99 Wallis Rd, London E9 5LN

Distributed in North America by InBook/LPC Group,
1436 West Randolph, Chicago, IL 60607

Distributed in Australia by Bulldog Books,
P O Box 300, Beaconsfield, NSW 2014

Printed and bound in the EU by The Cromwell Press,
Melksham, Wilts, England

Author's Note

This story is entirely a work of fiction, though I have no doubt that such things did happen occasionally.

For the incidental description of the mythical prisoner-of-war camp, its facilities, daily routine, staff and inmates, I am most grateful to Yehouda Mindel for his detailed and painstaking descriptions of his own time as a prisoner of the Germans.

I am indebted to Peter J. V. Elliott, Keeper of Research and Information Services at the RAF Museum at Hendon, for help with the technicalities of the Handley Page Halifax bomber, and to Richard Riding, the editor of *Aeroplane Monthly* magazine, for the same, and for lending me his copy of K. A. Merrick's book on the plane, published by Aston Publications Ltd. The staff of the Imperial War Museum were unfailingly patient and helpful with numerous queries.

My friend Paul Beale was most helpful with RAF detail, especially its uniform and insignia; and Pierre Duboz, Alain Czak and Hedwig Dobbs all helped with a number of those small points of detail which matter so disproportionately much.

Finally, as always my profoundest debt of gratitude is to my wife, Perviz. In particular she ensured that the snippets of German that appear here and there were correct, and translated passages from 'Das Lied im Grünen' [The Song of the Green Countryside], by Friedrich Reil, Schubert D917; but in general her contribution was, as always, so great that it is beyond measuring here.

My sincere thanks to all of them for their various contributions. It's a weary old cliché, but it has to be said, because it's true, that if any errors or shortcomings remain, they are no fault of theirs, but mine alone.

Part One: Journeying

Part One: Journeying

I

HALIFAX bomber KX968:G *Betelgeuse*, of 858 squadron, Coastal Command, lumbered steadily through the great bank of cloud that covered most of Biscay and the Channel as far as the Thames.

They had answered a call just before dawn from a patrolling Liberator to help in dealing with some motor boats refuelling a U-boat, but had had to abandon the mission when they had been attacked by a pack of ME-109s that appeared out of nowhere and harried them until they found the cloudbank and took cover in its sodden grey cotton-wool embrace. A few minutes later the outer port engine had started oozing thick, bubbling oil, then heavy, greasy black smoke, and the pilot, Roy Dean, had got it shut down and feathered just in time to stop it from bursting into flames.

The plane also had a ten-inch hole in her port wing, she had lost most of her electrics, and her entire instrument panel had been blown to bits by a chance burst of cannon fire from one of the marauding Messerschmidts. Dean had been leaning out of his seat to take a tin mug of coffee from the engineer at the moment when the stream of shells thrummed through the air where his head should have been. He had gone cold when he had turned back and realised the narrowness of his escape, and felt inclined to take the feeling out on someone. With a full load of 13,000 pounds of bombs burning a hole in his pocket, he had suggested that they find something to drop them on, and the rest of his crew had assented vigorously.

"Any idea where we are?" asked Tim Cherry, the wireless operator.

"Fed up, fucked up and far from home," grunted Dean. "Otherwise, no. My instruments are shot to hell."

"Time always seems to go twice as slow in clag," grumbled Cherry.

"It's not the time, or the clag," said Dean, with a faint smile. Cherry was the youngest of them, and the newest aircrew member at their home base at Bovingdon, and his enthusiasm and impatience caused considerable amusement and irritation. "It's you, always wanting to get out and push the moment the old girl drops a gear. Any ideas, Brian?" he called over his shoulder to the navigator.

"We were still over sea last time I got a sight of anything but this cotton wool," called back Brian Hales. "But that was a while back. I reckon we're somewhere about on a lat with Le Havre. Best I can do."

Dean sat in thought for some moments. "I'm gonna take her down a bit," he said at last. I'd like to know how low this cover goes. Stand by." There was a change in the drone of the remaining three engines, and the long, cigar-shaped plane suddenly inclined forwards at a steep angle. "Whoa, there, Neddy," came Dean's voice, and the angle abruptly flattened considerably.

Down they went, and down, and down, until every one of them was unconsciously braced against some part of the airframe, waiting for the spine-jarring, tooth-rattling crash as they hit water. And still the plane kept up its steady descent. Without realising it they had fallen into a dead silence. The only sound in their enclosed world of damp grey candyfloss was the muted rumble of the engines. The seven men were barely breathing.

They realised that only when the plane burst through the base of the mass of cloud and into the half-light of dawn. The drone of the engines turned to a full-throated roar, and every one of them suddenly let out his breath in an explosive hiss. Immediately afterwards there was a ragged cheer, mingled with ejaculations of astonishment. The heavy grey swell of the Atlantic heaved gently no more than a hundred feet below the belly of their plane. Dean flicked a bead of sweat off his forehead with the tip of a gloved hand, blinked twice to reaccustom his eyes to daylight, and set about finding the coast, and a landmark for Hales to use to find their position.

Before they had been out of the cloud for ninety seconds, however, he had seen something else which sent everything else instantly from his mind. "Well, well," he muttered. "Here's a bit of luck, then." And he chuckled aloud in his gleeful surprise. "Brian," he yelled, making the rest of them jump out of their skins. "Forward, old man. Target for you."

Hales came hurrying forward from his cubbyhole, ready to take up his secondary role as bomb aimer. "What've you seen?" he demanded, looking up at Dean from the top step of the stairwell to starboard of the pilot's perch.

Dean gestured ahead and slightly to port, and at the same time there came a fusillade of delighted cheers and laughter from the front gunner in the nose turret, the engineer in his cubbyhole aft of the pilot and Cherry below him, as they all saw it at the same moment. "Ho-HO," he heard Cherry cackle. "It's your birthday, *mein Kapitan.* Come and GET it!"

Hales had been unable to see a thing so far, and dropped hastily down the stairway and into his cushioned bubble at the foremost point of the belly of the plane. He saw soon enough, and his lips tightened into a hard, fixed grimace. Little more than a couple of hundred yards distant, and directly ahead, were two fully surfaced submarines, with three small motor vessels fussing busily round them. "Getting bloody saucy, these buggers," murmured Keith Topliss, the nose gunner. "Coming up for air in daylight now. Can't have that, now, chaps, can we?" He switched his heavy Vickers machine gun from the safe to the ready setting.

"Ready?" called out Dean. Hales fought down all the usual feelings, steeled himself, gulped and swallowed. "Ready," he called, and his voice was as steady as that of his pilot. The Halifax went into a shallow dive, and opened its attack.

* * *

As he did every time they engaged the enemy, Brian Hales was coping with his own personal crisis of conscience. Surely the last irony, he was thinking, as they thundered down towards their target, who apparently even yet, through some freak of acoustics, had not heard or seen his danger. There must be men everywhere, in every theatre of the war, engaged on its every evil duty, of sufficient compassion and imagination to see what they did plainly for what it was, and to hate what they did. But how many crews could boast a *bomb-aimer* with a conscience? he wondered to himself.

Reason told him that he was anything but alone, that almost everyone involved in the slaughter knew exactly what he was about, and hated every moment of it. He doubted if a sane man could feel otherwise, except when he was too busy being bored witless or frightened shitless to have time to spare to think about it at all. Which, of course, accounted neatly for just about all of most fighting servicemen's time, he reflected wryly. But he couldn't keep his mutinous mind from considering his own small group of comrades aboard the *Betelgeuse.*

Roy Dean was the senior among them, with more than forty

missions under his belt already. Hales had occasionally tried to draw him on his feelings about the war and what they currently did for their living, but Dean would never unbend enough — not with Hales, anyway — to reveal his true feelings. So effective was the mask behind which he concealed his emotions, indeed, that Hales could not say with any degree of assurance that he thought about the matter at all. He felt pretty sure that Dean was too intelligent and thoughtful a man not to have serious feelings; but if he had, he had clearly decided that they were not for discussion.

Tubby Barrell, he did know, lived somewhere close to the outer frontier of the nervous system's spectrum of endurance. But he, too, had chosen reticence as the best way of dealing with feelings that ran clean counter to everything to which he had to apply his mental and bodily skills each day: apart from the daily necessities of communication — ordering his food, reporting the unwelcome presence of enemy fighters and so on — he simply never opened his mouth at all except to say something sardonic out of the corner of it. As for the rest of them, they were mere kids, of whom Cherry was fairly typical, and were far too taken up with the excitement and adventure of it all to be expected to be reflective. Hales dismissed the matter from his mind and settled down over his bomb sight.

They drew nearer and nearer, until, now, he could clearly see the individual figures of the U-boats' crewmen busying themselves about the decks of their vessels. And in the moment when he registered the fact, he saw also that they had been seen, or heard. Each tiny figure turned a white face in the direction of the Halifax thundering down on them, and all began a frantic scurrying dash towards the hatches and conning towers. "Ready, Brian?" came Dean's calm tones from above. "Ready," he replied, and his voice was as steady as his captain's.

They had made the first run before the seamen could get to battle stations, and Dean had put the plane into a steep climb out of danger. They could all feel the fuselage of the aircraft shuddering as they roared towards the low cloud ceiling. Tubby Barrell's four heavy Brownings could be heard chattering busily as he sprayed the four vessels with fire as they climbed away. The gunfire ceased, and was replaced by Barrell's voice. "Good shootin', Brian, old scout," came his lazy drawl from the tail turret. "Bang on, old man. Gratters!"

"What's the score?" came Dean's voice.

"Direct hit on one of the U-boats," Barrell answered, craning his neck to scan the scene of devastation they had created out of orderly calm. "She's crippled. Goin' round in circles, by the looks of it. An' one of the motor boats has disappeared. Direct prang there. Other U-boat's roundin' up survivors an' — I say, Roy, she's preparin' to dive. Clearin' the decks, by Jove. An' the other motor vessel's scarperin', too. Better get back for another go, if we're goin' to, old man."

Dean obediently hauled the plane round in a tight turn and commenced another screaming dive on their prey. Hales swallowed once to subdue his rising gorge, then settled once more over his sights, and forgot everything except what he was doing. This time Dean ran even lower, until Hales could see the individual white crests of foam on the heavy swell, a mere fifty feet below. The undamaged submarine had got its gun into operation, and there was a bit of flak as they made their approach, but Dean threw his giant craft around, dodging and weaving, and they were on their target and past it without damage before the gunner had a chance to line up. Hales released his remaining cargo of high-explosive bombs, and rolling off to one side of his cushion to get a wider-angle view, saw that he had been highly effective in creating further carnage. Great clouds of dense, oily black smoke were billowing from the crippled submarine, and even as Hales watched, the bows of the stricken boat rose out of the water at a steep angle and it slid rapidly beneath the surface, spilling crewmen into the swell. The second motor vessel was an inferno, with patches of oil also burning furiously on the surface of the sea about her. There were upwards of twenty bodies in the water. He could not see how many of them were alive.

The plane banked, enabling Dean to look down on the scene. "Let's pull outa here," he said. "Good shooting, Brian."

Hales acknowledged, but otherwise said nothing as he continued watching the scenes of feverish activity as the plane banked and began climbing once more. He had time to see the undamaged submarine come nosing back to the oil slicks and assorted flotsam where its partner had sunk. He watched as the numerous survivors were hauled unceremoniously aboard and thrust down hatches; one man was staggering about on the U-boat's foredeck with his clothes on fire. Hales saw two sailors hurl blankets over him and then roll him on the deck before thrusting him down through one of the open hatchways. The last thing he saw was the sole surviving craft of the four they had surprised slipping beneath the waves as she crash-dived. Then there was nothing but a burning hulk, an oil slick and a few bits of floating detritus to indicate where several sailors had lost their lives.

It was only as they roared laboriously in a steep climb for the beckoning cover of the cloud that they saw the pack of Ju88s approaching. The first they knew of them was a sudden crackle in their headsets, Tubby Barrell's voice sounding sharp and urgent, almost ruffled for once. "Bandits, two o'clock," he snapped. "Range five hundred..." he broke off, and they heard the sharp, vicious rattle of his Brownings. At the same time there was a sound like a gigantic sheet of calico being savagely torn asunder, and a long spray of cannon fire ripped a pattern of holes down the entire length of the starboard side of the fuselage. The nose and dorsal turrets had opened up by now, and their little enclosed world had shrunk to a deafening cocoon of machine-gun fire.

Then suddenly, there was a five-second pause, in which they heard Topliss's voice on a note of triumph. "Tally one to me," he was crying exultantly. "Leader, too." They could just hear the altered note of one of the aero engines, and those of them with windows saw the leading Ju88 peel off from the pack with a thin ribbon of smoke dribbling from its engine cowl. At the same moment they also heard a very different sound from one of their own engines, rising suddenly to a high, tortured whine, then emitting a fast, staccato series of loud bangs as it backfired, and finally cutting out altogether. "Outer starboard engine gone, skipper," shouted Hales, spotting the flames belching from the wing as he wormed his way back from the nose blister to his place aft of it, beneath the pilot's feet. Dean gritted his teeth and had no time to reply, continuing evasive manoeuvres while still taking the shortest route for the inviting safety of the cloud.

They reached it, just about, with their remaining two engines labouring heroically; but the end came quickly. Only a few seconds after they had plunged into the comforting invisibility of the thick grey cloud they heard the 'whump' of an explosion from the port wing, a flat, barking sound that sounded deafening even with the muffling effect of the cloud, and a moment or two later the inner port engine was a mass of flame and oily black smoke. "We're gonna hit the drink," came Dean's voice, sharp and urgent. "Repeat, we're hitting the drink. Get cracking." He took the plane into a shallow dive, while the rest of the crew did what they could to anchor themselves against anything solid and cushion themselves against the impact. Seconds passed, and then the bomber, now half enveloped in flames and pouring a trail of heavy smoke, shot from the cloud ceiling. Already a long way behind, the pack of Ju88's saw them heading for the sea, and turned away on other business, satisfied that they had made their kill. A long minute or two later, a split second before putting down, they heard him say "Here it is. Brace yourselves."

When the *Betelgeuse* finally put down he did his best to level off his angle of impact so as to glide onto the surface of the waves as nearly as he could; but it still hit with a tremendous, back-breaking concussion. The aircraft weighed little under twenty tons even after shedding its massive payload of bombs, and there was a heavy swell running. She put down parallel to the swell, slamming into a huge wave which, even though it was running the same way as the doomed plane, halted her as if she had hit a mountainside. Roy Dean died in that moment, his neck broken by the whiplash effect of the impact. The rest of the crew were all hurled forward from their hurriedly contrived points of refuge, curling themselves up and grabbing at anything they encountered to stop their headlong tumble. None of them apart from the pilot was seriously injured in that helter-skelter dervish dance of whirling limbs and bouncing bodies. That was the first minor miracle. The second was that despite the modular construction of the Halifax, whereby it was constructed in a series of sub-frames which tended to snap apart at the joins in any heavy impact, on this occasion the plane remained, providentially, in one piece.

In the winking of an eye they entered, once and finally, a world of water. In the instant when they hit the churning maelstrom of Biscay all the calibrated systems made by men to regulate and impose order on creation twinkled and went out. Time in particular rolled over and telescoped, and none of them could have said afterwards whether their escape from the ruined hulk of the plane that had been taking them home to safety and the familar order of things had been accomplished in seconds or half a day. Reason, when it eventually reasserted itself, told them it must have all been over in a few minutes; memory told a different tale. Within seconds they all felt as if they had never known any other environment but water.

It roared and thundered at them, it was on them and over them and all round them, an immeasurable elemental force without brain or reason but endlessly malevolent and contemptuous, world without end, a demon giant with a hundred heads and a hundred thousand tearing, clawing hands, water green and black and silver, frothing maniacally as it tore and gored them, intent on tossing them into other worlds, a different one every second. Intent on *killing* them. Its playmate was the wind, another screaming colossus, sucking the very breath out of their chests and flinging it from them, leaving them gasping and frantically sucking on holes in the air for breath. Words were flung headlong from them before they had formed. Their hair, limbs, the sodden rags of their clothing were caught in the middle of a playful tug-o'-war between the two insatiable titans, whipped this way and that, torn brutally off their bodies one instant and slapped against their protesting skin the next. It was a vast, unimaginable wind; it was dwarfed by the water so that they scarcely noticed it.

Hales had stumbled forward to find Roy Dean's body. He fell as he reached him, sprawling prone and lying for a moment, all the breath driven from his body. A glance at Dean's head, lolling at an unnatural angle, eyes staring, told him that his pilot was beyond help. He grabbed at stanchions and the pilot's chair and hauled himself to his feet, adjusting as best he could as the fuselage of the plane bucked and pitched crazily back and forward in the swell. He propped himself against the seat for a moment and peered through the window. No sign of the dinghy. He staggered aft and found the escape hatch aft of the rear spar, manhandled himself up the ladder like a monkey, and wrenched frantically at the handle. It refused to move. Unheard in the roaring, slapping frenzy of sound from the monstrous beast outside the frail refuge of the plane and the innumerable jets of water hissing and squirting into the plane from a thousand entry points, he cursed the maintenance crew for every known species of lazy bastards; scrabbled desperately at the handle; switched his violent, insane flood of cursing to himself as he remembered it turned anti-clockwise, twisted it again and felt it give easily and smoothly.

He grabbed one of the emergency packs on the wall of the fuselage and took a moment to thrust it inside his shirt, beneath the flying jacket. Then he got the hatch undone, wriggled upwards and got his head and shoulders through it.

There was a single moment of appalled, shocked protest as he popped up from the comparative calm and protection of the fragile hull. The razor-edged wind raked and scoured him. Freezing spray flailed him, soaking through his heavy flying jacket and underclothing in seconds, and the vast force of the sea buffeted the plane under him, vibrating it like a twanging piece of elastic and thrumming through his own being via the soles of his feet still on the rungs of the escape ladder inside, his elbows on the fuselage, through every inch of his body and, as it felt like, through his very soul as well. He took a deep breath, and gagged as the wind tore it out of him before he could take it down. Instinctively cupping his nose and mouth in an armpit he breathed again, trying to do it calmly. Swallowed hard, gulped, and twisted himself out through the hatch. Fighting the wind and spray he launched himself as carefully as he could down the curving side of the fuselage, and landed in a crumpled heap — but land, at least, he did — on the port wing, huddling up against the hull and trying to take stock.

He peered out from his pathetic remnant of shelter, looking for the dinghy he had released. A wall of green, froth-stained water met his eyes, blurring crazily in and out of focus as the spray filling the air was flattened against his eyeballs. With the uncanny ability of the mind to go off into all manner of ridiculous fancies at the most inappropriate moments, he found himself observing, in wonder, that the pads of water this created against his eyes made lenses, which threw everything into and out of focus as the wind and the motions of his eyeballs altered their focal length.

The wall of water bore down on him, a towering, fearsome force of nature that must surely fall in on him, like a house dropping on him, and crush him out of existence in a fraction of a moment of earthly time. And then, incredibly, it was gone. It did not pour itself over him in an annihilating crash. Just, one moment it was there, looming terrifyingly above him, and the next it was not there any more. Instead, he felt himself swept aloft, as if on a platform powered by some unimaginably powerful pump or engine; and suddenly it was if he could see for miles. In the brief moment before he went plummetting down again into the next trough, he got a split-second's glimpse of a bright yellow, button-sized dot of hope and security in the angry, hostile universe into which he had been hurled. The dinghy, floating a few brief yards away to port; and two thrashing, flailing forms already almost up to it. All of a sudden the bottom dropped out of the world, and he dropped twenty feet in a tenth of a second, but in that moment he saw one of the forms heave itself over the fat roll of the side of the dinghy and flop down into the body of the tiny craft. As he went down his mind dislocated itself once more, and he found himself remembering a hump-backed bridge near his home when he had been a child. Crossing that bridge in a car he had always felt the disconcerting, but, when you got used to it, by no means unpleasant, sensation of leaving his stomach behind. It had felt exactly like that when the sea dropped him. "Wandering in your bloody mind, Brian," he told himself, angrily, and prepared to take the fateful step.

How swiftly the human mind accustoms itself to changing circumstances, his rebelliously independent mind insisted on remarking as he made his single preparation. Five minutes ago (five *minutes?* five hours? a lifetime or two maybe) I'd have said the inside of the old bus was a fair definition of hell. A minute or two on that wing joint and I wouldn't have swapped inside the plane for Claridge's. And now... He eased himself onto his backside and waited for the next sea to hoist him aloft. As he soared he blinked his eyes fiercely to clear the water from them, and glared in the direction where he had seen the dinghy. Yes, there it was, still in the same spot, with at least two people in it... he was dropping down a lift shaft once again. In the momentary lull in the motion when he nestled right in the trough of the wave he edged himself back towards the trailing edge of the centre plane. Clutching desperately by his fingertips to almost non-existent handholds between the flaps and the main plane, he perched, too busy to fear death, and waited. The next sea tossed him into the air once more. On the crest of the wave, he slid off the wing. His timing was almost perfect: a second or two earlier and he would have been safe, sliding down the glassy wall on the dinghy side of the swell. As it was, he hung on just a fraction too long, and was dropping again as he slipped into the water. As the water swept him away his head jolted sharply back, slamming smartly against the wing of the plane as it disappeared, and he was unconscious so quickly that he never even registered it as everything went black.

* * *

Luckily, he had been seen. Hurled as he had been into a new dimension and a new existence, with time going in and out of focus, he had spent little more than a single minute, measured in earthly time, perched in the angle of the plane's wing and the fuselage. In that time Tubby Barrell had fought his way through the smashed and twisted remains of his rear gun bubble and along the main corridor of the plane, seizing one of the crash axes as he went. Reaching the hatch through which Hales had escaped a few seconds before, he found the ladder already gone, slewed off the wall at a drunken angle. He wasted no time trying to do anything about it, but instead, checking swiftly that he was over the main plane, launched a ferocious assault on the flimsy skin of the Halifax with the axe. In no time he had a large hole gaping ready, allowing in the swirling blast of the wind, drenching cascades of spray and occasional gouts of chill water that slapped against him so that he felt as if his legs were under attack from a large and malevolent seal. He was about to abandon his axe and step out onto the wing when he heard cries behind him.

Turning, he found Tim Cherry. The boy was bedraggled, his eyes huge with shock, and he was bleeding freely from a jagged slash across one side of his face, but he was still on his feet and had a first-aid pack in one hand and a bottle wedged tightly under one arm. Behind him Neil Simmonds, the flight engineer, was scrambling as fast as he could from his cubbyhole. "Roy's bought it," he yelled as he spotted Barrell. "I've seen the dinghy. Let's get out of this coffin."

Barrell saw Cherry look through the hole he had made with the crash axe, and saw his Adam's apple bounce as he swallowed. He wasted no time. He slipped the bottle from beneath the boy's arm, thrust it into his shirt, did the same with the emergency rations pack, and finally hustled Cherry roughly through the hole into the howling gale outside. Then he gestured with an arm to Simmonds, indicating to him to go out onto the wing first. But Simmonds hung back, making an identical 'after you' gesture. Barrell glared ferociously at him, but he didn't press the matter. In the racing seconds as he passed into the frenzied world outside he seized Simmonds's arm, drew him close and roared into his ear, "Brian's outside — saw him go in the oggin. Think he's okay. Others baled out?" Simmonds wagged his head up and down in an exaggerated nod of assent. Barrell disappeared through the hole, took firm hold of Cherry, waited until Simmonds joined them on the pitching plane, and, still guiding Cherry with one hand on his elbow, picked his moment with care and pitched the two of them headlong into the swell.

It carried them high into the air, and a moment later he was swimming as strongly as his heavy, saturated flying gear would allow him in the direction in which he had caught a momentary glimpse of the dinghy.

In the few minutes it took the three of them to fight their way to the bobbing dinghy all three of them died a dozen times. In his first moment in free fall in the glittering world of bubbles Cherry chose the wrong moment to breathe, and swallowed several pints of water. He instantly sicked the lot straight up again, and it cascaded back through his mouth, nose and even, he had a weird feeling, through his *ears*, together with gouts of vomit, snot and blood from his nose, which had smashed hard against some unyielding part of Barrell's body. He felt as if he had become water, dissolved into water. He breathed again, swallowing more water, but, blessedly, got some air into his shrieking lungs, and suddenly felt a wild, insane sense of triumph. A moment later he was swimming.

Almost before he'd had time to comprehend what was happening to him he felt strong hands clutching him by the scruff of his flying jacket and his half-belt, and he was being yanked high out of the torrent and over the bulging side of the dinghy. He came inboard inelegantly, sprawling on his belly in a slopping puddle of oily water and retching great gouts of watery vomit into it. A hand smote him heavily in the small of his back, and a voice yelled "All right?" at him. He gasped, thrashed convulsively in an effort to turn onto his back, managed it, and nodded vaguely in the direction of the face looming above him. The face disappeared, and a few moments later Simmonds flopped over the smooth rubber side of the tiny dinghy beside him. "Where's Tub?" he asked, making his meaning felt more than heard. Cherry did his best to shrug and spread his hands, then gave himself in earnest to efforts to heave himself into a sitting position. Together they peered over the top of the rubber wall. "There!" howled Simmonds to the others, pointing frantically back in the direction of the Halifax.

Twenty yards off they could see the bright orange of Barrell's Mae West, bobbing and flouncing down the side of another mountainous wave. He seemed to be struggling with some kind of burden, and a second or two later they all saw that it was the form of another man, also wearing a Mae West. From the strange, filletted aspect of the other man, they realised that he was either dead or unconscious. "It's Bri-urrghh" yelped Cherry. The words turned to a retching gurgle as a flying mass of spray slapped him hard in the mouth and a lot of it went straight down his opened throat; but they had all got a brief sight of a smear of tow-coloured hair, and knew that Barrell's short, stocky body was all that stood between Hales and drowning. They watched, silent and, if they had known it, not breathing, as the little gunner fought his way coolly through the water towards them. They saw him find the rope trailing from the dinghy, which had been attached to the valise containing emergency rations, paddles and the other small trinkets of survival. He clutched it, raised it above his head and took a moment's rest; they saw his mouth open and close. In the same instant they all stopped holding their breath and yelled. They heard a vague confusion of words. It was all whipped instantly out of their mouths and into nothing by the wind, but Barrell had seen, and a moment later he resumed struggling towards them, resting every couple of strokes and allowing the two Mae Wests to keep them afloat.

At last he got the two of them in reach. Willing hands reached out to them, clutched; they were snatched violently away, tearing fingernails from hands already chilled to the bone and purplish-blue from the cold. They clutched again, grasped, took hold, and at last Barrell could relax for a moment, relieved of the terrible, dragging dead weight, as Hales's lolling form was hauled over the side. Another few seconds and Barrell himself was sitting in the dank, smelly puddle in the dinghy, being slapped on the back in an almost hysterical access of congratulation and joy. "Well, we're not dead yet," he bawled above the sound of the sea.

For some time they were kept fully occupied with the simple business of getting used to being in the dinghy. The mere fact of not fighting the unequal conflict with the titanic forces on which they were cast adrift was blessing enough. As a measure of energy and ability to focus seeped back into them, reinforcing their resolve, they began to apply themselves to making their position a little less miserable. There was no baler, but they used flying boots and the binoculars case to keep the dinghy as dry as possible; they rigged up the little awning, and took turns to avail themselves of its vestigial shelter, keeping Hales tucked as far into its protection as they could. They were all seasick, adding a final touch of humiliating misery to their state. They forced down a makeshift meal from the ration packs, blessing young Cherry for his forethought in snatching up the almost untouched bottle of brandy from the wreck of the Halifax. They had managed to get a little of the spirit down Hales's throat, and in time he had come to, wondering where he was, but able, after a while, to remember, with a shudder, what had happened. They had watched sadly as the Betelgeuse had broken up and sunk under the unrelenting buffeting of the waves.

After that, with Hales slipping in and out of consciousness, the others strove desperately to paddle the unwieldy little craft somewhere in the direction of home. They took short turns with the paddles, and fought the ocean until every muscle in their bodies screamed for relief — to no avail: wind and tide were united against them, sweeping them relentlessly down on the unknown shoals and terrors of the Brittany coast. "For you, ze varr iss over," muttered Barrell; and as if guided by providence, the next time they were heaved up to the crest of a great wave, they all saw it at the same moment: low and fast in the water, a sleek, dark grey destroyer, coming straight towards them.

Three-quarters of an hour later they had been fished out and were in captivity. Four of them were locked in tiny cabins. Cramped, feeling vilely sick from the stale, fume-laden air, but towelled down and blessedly dry in coarse grey blankets, and too prostrate with exhaustion, reaction and simple relief from the constant fight against the elements to feel anything much for the time being, they were carried at a brisk twenty-five knots towards Le Havre, captivity and an uncertain future. Simmonds, as the senior able-bodied crew member, was being questioned in passable English by the Second Officer about their mission. Hales was receiving rough and ready but capable treatment for concussion, shock and exposure. As he slid once more into a warm, hospitable cocoon of unconsciousness his lips moved and he muttered a few words. The grey-haired medical rating attending him bent over him, under orders to take careful note of anything his patient might say in delirium. As he listened, screwing up his face in concentration, Hales obligingly muttered the same words again; but the rating was no wiser for having heard them. "Well, Ronnie, you've got your wish after all," was what he heard. Hales was asleep.

II

THEY had met at a party a year before the war. It had been given by a much-loved veteran playwright, who knew Hales slightly, and had befriended him when he had come to live in London a year or two before. Otherwise the party had been thronged with actors, who seemed to spend half the time trying to impress each other with tales of theatres they had played, sums they had earned and whom they had been to bed with in recent months, and the other half giving waspish impersonations of other actors. They talked in a sort of shrill code which initially held Hales and Ronnie spellbound and quickly ended up by boring them with its unintelligibility and exclusivity, making both of them feel like the only two outsiders amid a gathering of people speaking an unknown language.

They had naturally gravitated towards each other, and quickly realised that Ronnie was only there at all because the veteran playwright had taken a colossal fancy to his dashing good looks when they had chanced to meet in a pub a week before. The playwright spent half of *his* evening enchanting his entourage of gorgeous young acolytes, and the other half escaping from them to make dazzling efforts to persuade Ronnie to slip off to one of the innumerable bedrooms with him. After an hour or so they were bored brainless. Half an hour later they had exchanged glances, looked quickly round, observed that the guests, and more importantly the host, were preoccupied with their own groups, and slipped unobtrusively out. In the time it took a taxi to take them to Hales's small, scruffy flat they were in bed together, and within a fortnight Ronnie had moved in. Within a fortnight more he was running Hales's affairs for him; and Hales, with his somewhat passive personality, and bowled over as he was by Ronnie's overwhelming good looks, presence, competence and energy, was happy to let him.

For the next year they were idyllically happy, building a small, shabby paradise in the dingy confines of Hales's flat and the atmosphere of impending doom as the storm gathered outside their small private world. The trouble began as it became apparent that war was looming inevitably and monstrously before them. They spent hours, endlessly digesting the news and discussing possible solutions, but always at the bottom of it there lurked a shadowy, shapeless threat: something that threatened them, certainly, but which they did not discuss, but rather banished hurriedly from their minds; but they both knew that one day it would rise from the shadows and be discussed, because it would have to be.

It was all to do with their attitude to fighting. Ronnie's views were clear-cut, passionate and unequivocal: he was never going to be anything other than a conscientious objector. Hales, though drawn to the notions of pacifism, was far less certain about it, and dithered.

This was in itself anathema to Ronnie's impulsive, decisive mind. "You either are or you aren't," he was to snap a hundred times over the next few awkward months; and his patience rapidly grew very short with Hales's troubled "It's not as simple as that," or whatever other ambiguous response he might murmur. The uncertainty as to what course of action he might choose infuriated him still more.

They began to quarrel. From there the descent was sharp and painful. Within a short time it seemed as if every conversation turned with increasing rapidity to What Are You Going To Do When The War Starts? An acrimonious note crept into their most trivial conversation, and they spoke to each other less. Acrimony turned to anger, then to bitterness. Both took to going for long, solitary walks through the streets, restlessly seeking a way out of their increasing despair.

Oddly, the physical side of the relationship intensified, as if they were seeking somehow to say in the wordless language of bodily affection what they could not find in the charity of their hearts to say rationally in words. But it didn't help to find a solution to their problem. Ronnie deployed every argument his agile mind and persuasive tongue could find, and Hales parried them all with a mute obstinacy that drove his more mercurial, impatient partner frantic with the frustration born of impotence. Beneath it all lay the single, immovable fact, that on the one subject that looked more important than all others, Hales was thinking for himself and declining to be managed, and Ronnie could not accept it. He moved out — and was back within a week, asking to be forgiven and taken back and finding Hales just as desperately ready to do both. But in less time than they had been apart they were back where they had been before he had stamped angrily out. They could not live with each other, and they could not, for the moment at least, live without each other.

Over breakfast during one short interlude of calm they started discussing something of substance without, for once, the usual sense of gathering black clouds. Ronnie observed, musingly, that it was odd how neither of them had even considered finding someone else. "I love you," said Hales simply, and a little hopelessly; and was promptly startled to see two large tears form in the corners of Ronnie's eyes and roll slowly down his cheeks. Ronnie, unbearably moved by the simple statement, and more by the utter ingenuousness that prompted it, had choked over his toast and run from the room in great distress. Hales had followed him hesitantly, only to come to a dead stop as he heard him being horribly sick in the bathroom. He had crept back to his breakfast, knowing that it would have been catastrophic for Ronnie to find out what he had overheard. When Ronnie had come gingerly back to the table he had asked Hales to pour him some tea, and not another word had been said on The Subject for several days. It had provided them both with a much-needed respite from confrontation. But, ultimately, it hadn't done much good. Nothing had really changed.

It came to a head on the day Hales's call-up papers arrived. He had picked up the envelope and gone back to the breakfast table with it in his hands, staring down at it in a kind of trance, and Ronnie had known immediately what it was. "Well come on then, man," he had cried impatiently. "Open the bloody thing, don't sit there waiting for it to sing to you." Hales had glanced up, smiled faintly, and slit the envelope open with an unused table knife.

"It's what I asked for," he said in a flat, lifeless tone after scanning rapidly through the official letter. He glanced up at Ronnie and saw that he was poised, motionless, in the middle of lifting his cup to his lips. There was a bottomless well of pain in his expressive blue eyes. "I've got the RAF," said Hales quietly. "Not fighters. Bomber Command. Report to RAF Bovingdon. On Monday."

Ronnie had come to life, slowly lowering his untasted tea. His head dropped slowly into his hands, and his shoulders started shaking. Hales stared at him for a long time, at a loss to know what to do, and with nothing to say. At last he got up, went round the table, and hauled Ronnie out of his chair, pulled him close and hugged him without a word. They had stood like that, with Ronnie's sobs rising fast to a tempest and equally quickly subsiding to a gentle, despairing rocking motion against Hales's shoulder. When they had ceased altogether the two of them separated, and in an almost comic simultaneous motion, picked up their cups, drank deeply, made simultaneous grimaces of disgust at the dank cold tea, and started for the kettle in the same moment. They prolonged breakfast, making the most of the moment of calm, both seeing things in a clearer perspective than either had been capable of in the past months. Afterwards they went by spontaneous instinct to the bedroom. But after that the arguments started once again, in earnest.

"God dammit, you're going to be a murderer, man," Ronnie cried at one point.

"If I'm going to be a murderer," Hales defended himself mildly, "half the population's going to be in the dock with me — and half the rest in the next court for aiding and abetting us."

"Christ!' Ronnie screeched in anguished frustration, "you don't cast guilt or innocence by reckoning up *numbers*, for Christ's sake. Ninety per cent of the population" — he put an ugly emphasis on the word, making a nasty, sneering imitation of Hales's tone as he had said the word — "believe in hanging, but you don't change your mind about *that* just because the bloody government tells you it's legal, do you? No, you don't," he supplied himself when Hales had no answer. "You don't, because you *know* — whatever the government says, *you* know it's wrong, utterly wrong, a barbarity, and that nothing they can say can make it right, can legitimise it. So how can you sit there and tell me it's any different dropping high explosive on people? They're still people..."

Later, "What have you got against German people?"

"Nothing," Hales said, again mildly, prompting an anguished bout of head-clutching from Ronnie.

"Well there you are, then," he spluttered when he regained the power of speech. "You wouldn't go shooting, or knifing, or dropping bombs on your own commanding officer, and you might well *know* he was a grade one shithouse, an ideal candidate for a violent and painful death. Yet this thing you wouldn't let God himself order you to do to a known first-class bastard, you're quite happy to go and do without a momentary qualm to perfect strangers — perfect strangers who are probably perfectly decent people, just like you and me — people who love Beethoven and read Goethe, just like you — and all because the fucking government *tells* you you can? Says it's all right?"

Hales talked hesitantly of Hitler and the Nazi party, Jew-baiting and the recent reports of genuine atrocities committed against Jews and other minorities — "including people like us", he added sombrely at one point. "Haven't you heard what they're doing to people like us?" Ronnie brushed the point impatiently aside.

"You can say what you like," he snapped brusquely, "you're still trying to defend the indefensible, dropping bombs on ordinary people. For God's sake, man, d'you think it'll be fucking *Hitler* manning the piddling anti-aircraft gun or the factory or the railway yard you drop your bombs on? Do you really, seriously think the Nazi party themselves will be out there in the front line, doing anything dangerous? Cor... They're... the Nazis are *politicians*, for Christ's sake. Politicians don't fight wars, Brian, they *start* them. Every fucking war in human history was started by politicians, and waged and finished off by other people. Ordinary people. People like you — people like the ones you're going to drop bombs on. Christ, man, they're adepts at fighting to the last drop of other people's blood. *Your* blood..."

And later, "There's no such bloody thing as a just war..."

"Some are more just than others," Hales answered, wearily.

"Not a defence," Ronnie snapped.

"I'm not saying it to defend myself," Hales said, more wearily still. "I don't need to defend myself..." — which at least had the consequence of shutting Ronnie up for a while. Hales closed his eyes and wished he was anywhere but where he was, just to be out of range of the angry tones of censure and reproach.

From that time onwards they lived together like a long-married couple whose juices and vitality had long been sapped by the gales and reefs of marital strife, who had stayed together for years after they should have gone their separate ways 'for the sake of the children', and now remained together because they had drained each other's energy until neither had enough remaining to get up and go. Hales pointed this out to Ronnie in an odd moment of amiability between storms, and Ronnie had replied with some of his old sparkle. "There's no human duty so under-rated as the duty to be happy, my boy. Stevenson." And after a pause he had added, "I don't think it can possibly be an accident that the word 'marital' is an anagram of 'martial'." And for a brief moment they had found themselves laughing together. Just like old times: they both had the same thought simultaneously. It killed the laughter instantly.

* * *

Of Ronnie's courage there was no doubt. It was of the kind that is confident and serious enough to come clean about its inconsistencies. He openly admitted his admiration and respect for those, including several of their own acquaintance, who had served in Spain — while conceding without hesitation that his own refusal to fight had applied equally to that most emblematic of all lost causes. When the time had come for his tribunal to assess his claim for exemption as a conscientious objector, he had been questioned at length by the Chairman. Most of the applicants appeared to have been processed at the same startling pace as drunks at Bow Street: the tribunal seemed to have a formula for deciding which were serious and which were camouflage jobs, and the cases were whizzed past at a breathless pace. Ronnie, for some reason, seemed to arouse the curiosity of the Chairman.

On the face of it he appeared about as unhappy a choice of Chairman as it could have been Ronnie's ill luck to have come up against: spherical, red-faced, with vast white moustaches that looked almost like a cartoon symbolising the constituency of retired-colonel England, and a habit of blowing gustily through them which reinforced the caricature; a clipped military manner which he delivered in harrumphing upper-class tones added to the effect, and heather-mixture tweeds half an inch thick completed it. If two people could have been selected as species designed by creation as natural antagonists, Ronnie and the Chairman seemed made for each other. It was a marriage made somewhere in Linnaeus.

The application began inauspiciously, with Ronnie making a short prepared speech disputing the tribunal's right to sit in judgment of him, while Hales, who had managed to swop his leaves in order to accompany him, sat wincing in the public gallery. For a while thereafter the proceedings followed the same pattern as the other cases, until the Chairman asked if his objection was made on religious grounds.

"No," said Ronnie promptly. "I have no religion."

"Hmph!" grunted the Chairman. "Atheist, I s'pose?"

"Not at all," Ronnie snapped. "Atheism is at least as arrogant and insupportable a posture as faith. I'm an agnostic, as we all are, if anyone told any truth about these things." At the end of this short homily he stared aggressively at the Chairman — who took him rather by surprise by producing a faint, hastily smothered smile.

"My objection is political," Ronnie said without being asked.

"Oh?" the Chairman responded mildly. "Perhaps you'd like to explain."

Ronnie had been very happy to explain. He began by declaring that he would not do at any government's behest that for which the same government would have hanged him the preceding day. This had the rather surprising effect of eliciting another faint smile from the Chairman. It was quickly erased when Ronnie elaborated the declaration into another of his set-piece harangues, which sent the watching Hales into further attacks of wincing embarrassment.

Eventually the Chairman glanced ostentatiously at his watch, and asked Ronnie to bring his remarks to a conclusion. Ronnie obligingly produced a carefully scripted purple passage denouncing war, militarism, conformist casts of thought and, in very thinly veiled cipher, empurpled ex-brigadiers encased in Harris tweed who blew through their moustaches and sat on tribunals. By which time Hales was shifting uneasily on his exquisitely uncomfortable wooden bench, his toes curled up inside his shoes with embarrassment and anguished expectation. It would not have surprised him to hear his lover sentenced to the Tower of London for the duration of hostilities.

Instead, the Chairman asked Ronnie if he would be willing to perform any duties in the war effort other than full military service. "Oh, yes," said Ronnie immediately — and Hales was almost certain that he identified the expression that flitted across the Chairman's countenance as one of disappointment. "Oh?" he asked. "Such as what? Would you work in a munitions factory, for example?"

"Certainly not," snapped Ronnie.

"Medical work?" suggested the Chairman, throwing Ronnie a lifebelt. "Ambulance driving in one of the theatres of war, that kind of thing?"

"Rather than commit government-licensed murder, yes," conceded Ronnie. "But for preference I'd rather go behind the lines."

Everyone looked puzzled at that. "Behind the lines?" spluttered the Chairman. "That suggests not merely exceptional bravery, but exceptional *military* bravery. Kindly explain what you mean."

"I'm willing to undertake war service," said Ronnie slowly and distinctly, "on the strict proviso that my service consists of undercover assignments to assassinate the politicians who started this war. By this I mean," he went on, "that I am willing to accept an assignment to go to Berlin in an attempt to kill Hitler, Himmler or any of the others." This time, Hales thought to himself with a sudden brief access of hope, there was no doubt about the expression of genuine amusement on the Chairman's face. For a moment he looked a positively jolly red-faced ex-brigadier.

The entertained expression vanished with Ronnie's next words, however. "I will only accept a commission to undertake this task on one condition," he announced.

"How typical of Ronnie," thought Hales wearily, "to manage to imply both senses of the word 'commission'. He might be a conscientious objector, but it would be as an *officer*."

"I see," murmured the Chairman, ominously quietly. "And what might this condition be, pray?"

"It is," said Ronnie, "that having performed this service to mankind with their politicians, I be permitted to carry out the same service with ours." And without giving anyone the chance to say anything further he had sat resolutely down.

* * *

"We have been favourably impressed by Mr. Hetherington's eloquence in his own cause," said the Chairman, opening his brief remarks. "In particular we are entertained — "

"Oh, God," thought Hales. "He's had it."

He had.

" — by his novel and ingenious proposal to shorten the war..."

And from that point it had been, especially to the agonised Hales, mercifully brief. Ronnie's application was dismissed. He had been asked the conventional questions, had formally refused to serve with any branch of the armed services, and been committed to prison.

He served his time without a word, forbidding Hales to visit him, but writing regularly. His letters had been uniformly cheerful, bright and, beneath their surface glitter of charming, superficial banter, devoid of anything serious, affectionate or even sympathetic. He chattered brightly of people he had encountered in prison, talking excitedly about a brilliant young musician named Tippett, whom everyone admired vastly, and seemed to regard as an inspirational figure, and other celebrities in the small world into which he seemed to have immured himself. But of himself, of his relationship with Hales, there was never a word, a hint or a reference, direct or by suggestion. Hales completed his training then flew his missions, missed him inconsolably, but felt a growing sense of having lost him, and could not begin to understand how it had happened, what he had done wrong or how to begin to put matters right between them. All he felt, at bottom, was a deep and increasingly desperate sense of missing Ronnie and wishing he had him back beside him.

And then, without warning, Ronnie came out. No one ever explained to Hales by what process of assessment, or by whom it had been decided, that his debt to society had been paid off, but there he was, slipping quietly into the flat one Monday morning while Hales was, by an astonishing chance, on a rare weekend's leave. They had said hardly a word, just slid silently and comfortably into bed, where they had spent most of the day. And, by some process that Hales never sought to query until much later, but simply put down as miraculous or semi-so, and accepted with gratitude and humility, all was right between them. Or so it seemed. But something had changed. There was a hard edge to Ronnie that had never been there — or, at least, never been visible — before, a cold, bitter side to his personality that took the form of occasional bouts of what seemed to Hales almost like hatred — hatred of himself, and also of Hales.. During these attacks his normal mien of sardonic, sceptical irony metamorphosed into a kind of unrelenting, person-ally directed sarcasm against Hales and everything to do with him, in particular the side of his life to do with the RAF, that was quiet but almost savage in its cruelty. Hales bore it in silence, ascribing it to bitterness accumulated in prison — 'I guess everyone must be affected by prison, become bitter and a little bit twisted by it,' he rationalised to himself — and coped with the deep, bitter hurt as best he could, dredging deep into his own private reserves for salv-ing balm.

It was during one of these attacks, when they had hardly spo-ken two words to one another from when Hales had let himself into the flat on Friday evening to the afternoon of the following day, that they were invited to a party. The silence had become op-pressive, certainly to Hales and, he suspected, to Ronnie too, and by some kind of unspoken consent they had walked through the blackout to the nearest pub. There had been a noisy party there from the nearby hospital, with exhausted doctors and nurses snatch-ing a brief moment of relaxation and letting a lot of tension escape in superficial gaiety. A few moments after they had slipped through the door one of the doctors spotted them and came over. Hales was instantly on his guard, knowing that he was a former flame of Ronnie's, from whom he had parted only shortly before settling with Hales himself. However, the doctor, who seemed pleasant and friendly to both of them without distinction, only wanted to invite them, discreetly, to a party at his own flat the following night, the Sunday.

"It won't be anything much," he said. "Just a few drinks and a bit of music, a chance to unwind and get some of the tension out of your system," he went on, patting Hales sympathetically on the shoulder, while Ronnie looked on radiating a glacial hostility. The doctor glanced from Hales to Ronnie, seeking to include him in the invitation, but after one quick look at his expression quickly looked away again. "Do come," he murmured to Hales, and flitted off to rejoin the party.

It seemed that he had kept at least half an eye on them, how-ever, for a while later when Ronnie had gone off to the lavatory, he came over to Hales, glancing furtively and, Hales thought, more than a little fearfully, over his shoulder in the direction of the door through to the gents'. "Try to make him come to my little do," he had said urgently, looking a little embarrassed. "I can see he hasn't changed. He used to get these fits on him," he elaborated, "and it does him good to be taken out of himself. You don't mind my saying that, do you?" He was visibly anxious as he asked it, and equally visibly sincere. Hales felt a sudden feeling of warmth, sympathy, even a kind of solidarity in adversity, towards him. It was, he reflected, a notably kind, indeed generous impulse that had drawn him from his group to offer a word of sympathy. Moved by the sudden warm feelings of gratitude, he responded in kind. "We'll be there," he promised, and the young man, with a final rapid glance in the direction in which Ronnie had departed, smiled briefly, and was gone.

Sunday had been little better than the Saturday; but they had gone to the party, after a considerable amount of persuasion from Hales, and once there the atmosphere lightened a little. By tacit agreement they had separated, joining different groups and talking about nothing very much, both deriving a certain amount of much-needed lightening of tension from doing so. Then, after they had been there about an hour and both drunk enough to dispel the first layer of inhibitions, the door had burst open and a bright, glittering and slightly drunk young man barged gaily in, who proceeded to take the party by storm. It was this youth who had precipitated the final, bitter confrontation between Ronnie and Hales.

Like Hales, he was an airman. Unlike Hales, he was in uniform, looking boyish, very dashing and, Hales instantly recorded, not merely beautiful, but beautiful in a particular way, to which Hales was and had always been extraordinarily susceptible. He was as high as one of his own kites when he arrived — on benzedrine or something of the kind, Hales thought — which made no difference to Hales whatever. The moment Ronnie drifted off to find a bottle with something remaining in it, Hales strode swiftly and purposefully across the room, cut ruthlessly in on the group that had gathered round the new arrival and engaged him in conversation.

In less than five minutes he had him to himself, the rest efficiently shut out by the bristling rampart of RAF jargon with which they immediately encircled themselves; in less than half an hour they knew more about each other than any pair of long-established lovers in the room — the simple fruits of shared experience of the wholly extraordinary, of that which was outside the ken of anyone else present; and in less than an hour they were strolling together through the streets, holding hands like two children taking comfort from each other's presence to ward off evil spirits that might be lurking in the dark. Ronnie was not even a distant memory to Hales in that blissful short time under the mild night sky. Hales was already in love.

III

FOR days, for whole weeks it seemed, they had lived on trains. Clanking, rattling and wheezing through the grey, interminable hours of daylight, thundering with an entirely different note through starless nights, the black engine lurching ahead in a cocoon of its own sound and fiery orange-red glow. They bounced, jolted and swayed along endless miles of boredom, where everywhere presented the same nightmarish landscape of blackened, ruined industrialised hell. The occasional figures they saw seemed like stylised caricatures, dragging out a strange, alien way of life as they went about their mysterious business. The racketing of the train dimmed and faded into a faint background music that was constantly there, not heard but more absorbed through soles of feet and aching, protesting backsides and spines, punctuated by strange shouts, guttural commands, an occasional bark of a laugh, which always seemed as if it had been shut off by the closing of a valve.

Periodically great billowing curls of smoke would pour back from the engine as it grunted and laboured up some anonymous hillock, rolling through the slatted sides of the cattle trucks and choking them for a few minutes before disintegrating into wisps and curls hanging in the air behind them. Now and then another train would rumble past them in the opposite direction, and they would receive a blast of hot air, smoke and steam, laden with glowing sparks that stung their skin ferociously and seared their throats. At frequent intervals they were halted, herded off the train and made to wait about in knots of steaming, stamping, shivering misery on some deserted grey platform or beside some remote siding, ordered about, cursed and occasionally booted or helped along with the butts of rifles by young soldiers in heavy grey overcoats and coal-scuttle helmets. The soldiers looked as miserable as the prisoners, and little better fed. Then, after an hour or so of mysterious, apparently pointless eddying about they would be barked and gun-butted into more cattle trucks on other trains.

Once they were shunted into a siding and sat there for several hours. That was the worst time of all, an interminable interlude of waiting, without knowing what they were waiting for, wondering if the next step was to be the arrival of lorries with machine guns mounted behind the tailgates, and a hail of bullets followed by a mass grave in some nameless wood. Grim stories of prisoners of war meeting such a fate had often been the subject of ill-informed gossip in happier times, home safe in England. In fact all that had happened was that after they had sat in the siding for what felt like most of a day, a train consisting of an engine hauling a single coach had gone roaring past at high speed in the opposite direction. A few minutes later their driver went tramping alongside their vast train of trucks, complaining softly and obscenely to himself, and a few moments later they were clanking back onto the main line and on their way again. The few of them who understood some words of French told the others that the single-coach train had been taking some high Nazi official from somewhere to somewhere else, and the delay had been simply to allow it unhindered passage. They also relayed the substance of the train driver's soliloquising, which got a laugh and cheered everyone up a little.

Every so often they were herded off the train in the middle of nowhere and given a scanty ration of grey bread and tough, stringy meat; there was usually a tap dripping forlornly on the isolated platform where they were fed, with water for cracking throats and a rudimentary wash for the wounds that many of them carried, and they were permitted the luxury of urinating or defecating on a patch of bare, oil-impregnated waste ground. It was primitive, the chill wind froze their hindquarters where they squatted, there was nothing to clean themselves with but mangy handfuls of dead or diseased-looking vegetation, but it was better than on the move, when they made use in rotation of a hole torn in the planking of the floor of the trucks, and where there was nothing to clean themselves with at all. Once, blessedly, they were marched in ragged order a hundred yards down a deserted village street and into a football club's changing rooms beneath a tiny concrete grandstand. Inside they were left to themselves, with only a couple of glowering soldiers at a time, who looked as if they had drawn lots for the job and lost, pacing up and down at each end of the large, barn-like room. There were rough blankets on the floor, and though the building was perishing cold, the relief from the winds that cut through the cattle trucks made it seem like paradise. Best of all, they were allowed to crowd into the communal shower baths and wash in passably hot water.

So they lived and stank together, sweating by day and freezing in the autumn nights, wrapped in a miasma of their own communal stink, so enshrouded in each other's and their own bodily odours that they ceased to notice either. The rare moments when they were not in motion, and the rarer ones when they were allowed off the train, allowed them a blessed opportunity to stretch cramped limbs, but they had never a moment of solitude, and were grateful for the lack of it, too desperate for the comfort and reassurance of each other's company to want it even for a moment; too scared, too bowed down under the misery of defeat and too apprehensive about their uncertain future even to recall the human need to be alone for a while. So they progressed across France in an erratic, zig-zagging course, forever the least important cargo on all the trains in the country, always first to be signalled into a siding to let others pass, always last to go through, comfortless and forgotten, but always heading more or less eastwards, and everywhere picking up more and yet more scrawny, ragged and forlorn comrades in arms for whom the war had come to this.

Thus the trip from Le Havre to Paris, which might have taken seven hours on a bad day in peacetime, took them four and a half days. When they reached it the city seemed little more than a long blur of endless grey suburbs that all looked the same, and the overwhelming impression was of a place even greyer, danker and more ill-used and depressed-looking than everywhere else. The sight of the Eiffel Tower rearing its gaunt length in the far distance like some prehistoric monster was somehow the most depressing vision of all. They turned their faces from it as their train clanked by, and many of them wept, without really quite knowing why the sight moved them so. Paris passed in a hundred mind-deadening waits, a thousand leaping, jolting points changes and a momentary vision of a skyline against a sunset; and still they rattled on, ever eastwards.

Like all the others huddled and squashed in around him, Brian Hales passed the nightmare journey as best he could, taking advantage of every shift in the cramped, overcrowded occupants of the truck to exercise and flex his aching muscles, sharing a precious cigarette from time to time, getting used to being perpetually hungry, thirsty, more uncomfortable and, most of all, more bored than he had ever dreamed possible, progressively ever more dirty and enveloped in his own stink, and wondering how much longer he had to live. Like the others he spent as much of the time as he could manage escaping into the blessed refuge of sleep; and when he slept, he remembered. Remembered the young airman he had met at the party, and remembered far, far beyond him, back to where it had all begun. As he slept, burrowing deeper in the warm, comforting safety of dreams and recollection, far from the terrors, aches and pains and humiliations of the train, he smiled, a faint but radiant, private smile, tugging at the corners of his mouth and eyes and easing the tension and weariness from his face. He was smiling as the train crept into a siding in a vast marshalling yard full of sidings, sheds and activity, hissed grey steam and squirted water, and finally fell silent for the night.

* * *

It had begun when he was thirteen and a half and Peter Butterworth was sixteen. He had been punting a ball about with a few cronies in break one morning and the ball had flown far into the next pound of the quadrangle — by unwritten but rigid convention reserved for members of the upper school, and strictly *verboten* to juniors. The etiquette regarding the division of the quad was unwritten. School rules, on the other hand, on the subject of running in densely populated areas, were very clearly written indeed. Hales had hared after the ball without a thought in his head for either, at the precise moment when Butterworth chose to walk round a corner of the School House building. Butterworth was two and a half years older and three inches taller; but he was lightly built and graceful, whereas Hales, even at thirteen, was square-rigged and powerful for his age. He was also carried along by the momentum of his headlong rush after the ball. Butterworth was bowled over, Hales rebounded several feet from the force of the impact, and the two of them finished in a sprawl of arms, legs and school uniform.

"I... I'm sorry," muttered Hales, sitting up and feeling slightly sick. He sat up, trying to rub several places at once, principally a badly gashed knee that was protruding through a gaping rent in his trousers. Knowing how jealously the upper school guarded their privileges, he fully expected to be booted without ceremony back to his own territory. The older boy too sat up and made a gingerly exploration of the various points at which he felt damaged. Then he looked, a little dizzily, at his assailant. Hales saw a black cloud of indignation pass over his face, confirming his apprehensions. Then, to his great surprise, the other boy looked at his gashed knee, by now bleeding profusely, and his frown cleared. "Better get something done about that," he said mildly. "Come on, I'll take you to the first-aid box. There's one in the Prefects' Room."

"Nunno, I'll be all right," he had replied, embarrassed. "It's only a graze." But he was still feeling sick and a little dizzy from the collision and his crashing fall to the unyielding hardcore of the quadrangle, and had not felt inclined to hurry to his feet, now that the prospect of a booting appeared to have faded. Butterworth pulled him up and led him off anyway, ignoring his protests. They went through the corridors of the senior end of the school, where Hales had rarely gone, and eventually stood before the Prefects' den. Butterworth knocked, at first lightly, then with a firm, confident rap. When there was no answer he boldly pushed open the door and led Hales into the sanctum. In that moment he became a hero to the young Brian Hales.

He stood looking about him, his damaged knee forgotten in his keen interest in these glamorous and forbidden precincts. It was a small, cosy room, dominated by a broken-down ping-pong table, which stood in the middle, barely a square inch of its drunkenly canted surface visible beneath a litter of essay paper, cricket boxes, rugby balls, scarves, half-eaten sandwiches and other debris. Hockey sticks and sports bags hung from a row of pegs that ran along one wall, while blazers, jock straps and every other kind of garment were strewn about the floor and the half a dozen battered and threadbare armchairs. It was, Hales felt immediately, the most comfortable room he had ever been in, wholly masculine and reassuring.

Butterworth crossed the room and reached a green metal first-aid box down from a shelf, and set about making businesslike repairs to Hales's knee. He worked quickly and efficiently, without fuss. Hales was surprised, and vaguely impressed, by the gentleness with which he cleaned and dressed the wound. By the time he had finished they were already friends.

It had been an unusual friendship in the rigidly hierarchical society of a boys' school, where differences in age were treated like sacred charms far up into the senior echelons. Lofty members of the Upper Sixth might legitimately talk to their immediate juniors in the Lower Sixth, but beyond that the convention was absolute: you moved among your peers; lower boys you passed by as the idle wind which you respected not.

Butterworth was a lone wolf and a law unto himself. He was utterly immune to the blandishments of fashion. In a school where prowess at games was the universal currency in which everyone's relative worth was reckoned, he was, at his own casual, dismissive

estimate, a duffer at rugby and a total dead loss at cricket; and for
the cult of games he expressed excoriating contempt, openly jeering
at 'hearties', whom he dismissed, in their hearing, as 'brainless as-
semblages of superfluous muscle'. Sustaining such heresy on the wave
of his own kind of excellence, he went his own way — which was to
be quite overtly and outspokenly intellectual, in his diligent application to the classical languages and their literatures and his
unconcealed love of them. By the time he reached the Sixth Form
he had made a beginning on textual emendation, and acquitted himself without discredit in a couple of donnish exchanges in the pages
of the *Classical Review;* he also produced, for his own amusement,
an uninhibited translation of the *Frogs* of Aristophanes that left the
classical staff of the school simultaneously scandalised and bursting
with pride. And over the next two and a half years he contributed
as much as anyone and more than most to Hales's education, gently
ridiculing his adolescent certainties, unobtrusively introducing books
and ideas into his path, and talking, endlessly talking and laughing
with him, sometimes instructing him in his surreptitious way, but
most of all, always there, and never too busy to spare time for his
young friend.

When Butterworth was in his scholarship year, by this time
himself a Prefect and contributing his twopennorth to the squalor
in the chaotic room where he had ministered gently to Hales's
wounds, Hales was in the Lower Remove. He had filled out and
was already a good way towards being the good-looking young man
who would take Ronnie by storm a few brief years later. He was
neither a 'blood' nor a scholar, performing adequately but without
distinction at both games and work while Butterworth was gliding
effortlessly to an open scholarship to Trinity; but Butterworth exerted to the last a quiet, civilising influence over him, stiffening
Hales's diffident, uncertain disposition and bringing out such tal-
ents as he had in work and even in the despised games. Hales, for his
part, had come, within a month of making Butterworth's acquaintance, to regard him as an oracle, the fount of all wisdom.

The compliment was not undeserved. Peter Butterworth was
unspoiled by celebrity, and remained a wise and sensible boy, gentle
and affectionate; and Hales was aware, in a vague way which he
never sought to put into words, of how good his friend was for
him. He never knew, because Butterworth never said so, that
Butterworth was in love with him. It didn't matter unduly, because
they were both conscious that there was love between them, of a

kind; but both felt instinctively that it was not something that ought to be put into words, for fear of spoiling the bloom. Butterworth yearned in secret, but he was too scared of losing what he had to articulate the more that he desired. So he kept his yearning to himself and waited, hoping. Why he directed such devotion to such an apparently mediocre object he could not have said, except that there was something distinctly appealing about Hales's diffidence, something almost coquettish, though anything of the kind would have been the last thing to enter Hales's honest, straightforward head.

In the end it was not a great surprise to Hales when Butterworth decided that his moment had come. One summer afternoon, when they had known each other for about six months, they were walking after school across the vast, shaggy golf course through which the school cross-country teams ran, talking as always about anything and everything that came into their heads, Butterworth imparting knowledge and Hales absorbing it. After several miles they were in need of a rest. Butterworth turned abruptly off the grassy walk between two stretches of fairway and pushed through a light screen of bushes. Hales followed him into a small, light clearing. They stripped off their blazers and ties and sprawled on the light, springy grass.

A discussion of cricket turned into a light-hearted argument, spiced with laughter and mutual schoolboy abuse, and then into horseplay, ending with them rolling breathlessly together on the turf. Though Hales was already rather the stronger of the two, Butterworth was still quite a lot bigger, and used his long, wiry limbs to wrestle his friend into submission. He sat triumphantly on his chest, propping himself on his hands over Hales, so close that he could feel his pants of breath on his own face. Impulsively, without stopping to realise what he was doing, he bent forward and kissed Hales. At first it was a timid, hasty peck; but when the younger boy made no protest or attempt to wriggle free he slid down, took him in a long, hard embrace and kissed him again, full on his lips, spending all the bottled-up passion of six months and an expressive, affectionate nature in that first, rapturous contact.

They stripped quickly, urgently, without words, with a sense of inevitability about it that they were both clearly aware of. After that they found time almost every day to go somewhere private to masturbate together, giving and taking mutual pleasure which in Butterworth was raised to the higher powers of ecstasy. Again, he kept the deeper, darker currents of his feelings to himself, sensing that it would be dangerous to let them too far out of their captivity deep within him.

Then, one day a few months after their first sexual contact, they had gone wandering one evening through the woodland that ran for miles from the far side of the golf course, carrying on, as always, an animated discussion. They talked about fungi, which were sprouting in profusion in the moist autumn woods, birds, and the occasional small animals that they heard scuttering about in the underbrush. They were both conscious of the usual undertone of sexual arousal, and the pleasurable anticipation of its imminent gratification; but they were good enough friends, and easy enough with each other that it didn't obtrude itself or cast too oppressive a foreshadow as they strolled. From time to time one of them would say something that demanded a physical response, and there would be a brief scuffle, or they would chase each other among the trees. Then they would saunter on, laughing, getting their breath back, savouring the poignancy of friendship.

They turned off by tacit agreement at a well-known clump of birch trees and headed into a circle of rhododendrons, escaped decades ago from a nearby baronial estate. In the middle of the clump was an irregularly shaped grassy clearing, just big enough for two boys to stretch out in the dappled light. They undressed without haste, looking at each other's bodies and taking pleasure from seeing each other's arousal. But this time, instead of going into his usual clinch with his young partner, Butterworth had held him in his arms only briefly, looking down from his superior height into Hales's face with a great tenderness in his mild brown eyes, and then he had slid slowly down his body, flicking out his tongue to lick Hales's smooth white chest. He paused to lick and tease his small brown nipples with his tongue, then sank to his knees in the damp grass. Then, gently but with a firm, determined certainty about him, he ran his tongue up the length of Hales's small, very hard penis, and slipped the tip into his mouth.

For a few moments Hales was so surprised that he was transfixed. By the time he had registered the amazing, shocking thing his friend was doing to him his blood was already running cold from the pleasure of it. His entire body was tingling and trembling from the hitherto unplumbed depth of sensation. He lifted his chin and gazed glassily up at the gently waving birch and beech leaves high above the dark ring of rhododendrons. Then he closed his eyes, letting the late sunlight make a warm, red curtain of their lids, and gave himself up to the incredible, blissful new sensations flowing in a powerful beat, like the tide, from his genitals.

Butterworth teased and fondled every fold of him with his tongue, sending wave after wave of electric shocks through him. Then he released him, to run the tip of his tongue and then his lips up and down the length of his erection, round his small, tight scrotum and back to the tip again. At last, feeling the rhythmical throbs in his friend's body coming closer and closer together, he took him back deep into his mouth again, feeling the tip of his penis thrusting urgently against his palate, and sucked him hard until Hales, with a long, gasping moan of relief, spirted a stream of semen that seemed to go on and on, flowing round every corner of his mouth and trickling down his throat. Butterworth relaxed, suddenly becoming aware that his entire body had been tensed like a coiled spring, and made small, gentle licking motions with the tip of his tongue against Hales's softening penis, wishing only that the moment could go on and never end. He wished with all his soul that they could be captured and frozen in that moment for the rest of time, like two flies in amber. In fact, being the wise and practical boy he was, he swallowed, savouring the unfamiliar taste, and let Hales go.

Hales stood for a few moments, observing closely as the feelings of bliss ebbed and ceased. Then he looked down at the top of his friend's head, resting in the faint dark fuzz of his incipient pubic hair, the fair hair tousled against his white lower belly. Moved by a simple instinct of gratitude, he ran the fingers of both hands through the fair, straight hair. "Stand up, Peter," he said after doing this for a while. Butterworth, sensing what was to come, rose shakily to his feet, trembling all over. Hales dropped briskly to his knees before his friend.

* * *

After that, though, it was never quite the same between them. Something fragile had been broken, and could never be reforged. They were still friends, and they still pleasured each other frequently, sometimes in the same way as they had among the rhododendrons. The pleasure was so great that they were both keen to renew it, though for different reasons. But where Butterworth was a solitary youth, with few acquaintances and hardly any friends, more than content with the one passionate relationship, Hales was a much less complicated spirit, with many pals in his own year. While Butterworth was bookish and reflective, Hales was an enthusiastic joiner of any cliques and coteries going, a ready participant in whatever rags, mischief and antics anyone might happen to suggest to improve the shining hour. As time went by he began to hear what his cronies had to say about 'people like that Butterworth', as he overheard on more than one occasion. When he considered the sort of things they would say if they knew what he got up to with his friend, his blood ran cold. So, gradually, never fatally but damagingly enough, a chill crept between them. They saw less of each other by degrees, and when they were together there was a guardedness between them in place of the old careless openness.

Butterworth saw, quite clearly and early, what was happening, and was sensible enough to realise that he could do little or nothing about it. He got on with his work, moving methodically towards his scholarship, continued to devote a necessary minimum energy to the avoidance of cricket and rugby, and spent many of the hours between grieving quietly and alone, grasping whatever his young beloved still saw fit to offer him, and being grateful. He had enough sense of his own dignity to know that he was never, whatever he felt, going to grovel or beg for favours from Hales.

He made an exception to this once only. A few days before he was due to leave the school he sought out Hales, now a hefty and, ostensibly at least, a considerably more self-confident sixteen-year-old, in morning break. "Come for a walk with me tonight, Brian," he murmured in his ear, while Hales, having the grace to feel no little of a heel for doing it, could nonetheless not help shooting a swift, covert glance round his pals. But they carried on booting their ball about, drifting away with the tide of their game, to Hales's somewhat guilty relief. Butterworth had seen the nervous sidelong glance and diagnosed it correctly. "Just one last walk across the golf course, Brian," he said softly, without a trace of pleading. "For old times' sake. I shall be leaving next week, and I'd like to have a last time with you. We've been good friends..."

Hales felt a sharp stab of guilt and shame scorch through him. He was aware that he had treated Butterworth shabbily, even brutally, when all he owed him was gratitude for giving him friendship, loyalty and pleasure without limit or reservation, and for teaching him a great deal. He realised — dimly, but the realisation was there — that his friend had been a profoundly civilising and shaping influence, and had made a contribution to his growing up that he might never expect to fathom, let alone repay. All this came to him in a series of frissons of feeling, wild, formless, inchoate and inarticulate. It left him feeling nothing he could have expressed but a vague but extremely uncomfortable feeling of mingled guilt and sadness coupled with an overwhelming sense of impending loss. It was all over in a few instants of time, but it had been strong while it was passing through him, and it left its mark. He looked levelly at Butterworth, with a sadness in his face that Butterworth had never seen before. It made him look older, turned his ordinary, boyish face, for a few seconds, into one of transcendent beauty. Then it was gone, and it was the face of Hales the schoolboy, whom he still loved, looking at him with much of the old affection.

"Of course I'll come with you, Peter," he said, and for one last time all the old affection and easy friendship was back in his face and tone.

The walk was not a great success. Though they were both trying — perhaps too hard — they could not re-establish the old rapport. And when Butterworth tried to take Hales in his arms and kiss him, Hales wriggled awkwardly in his embrace, and blushed hotly. Butterworth saw how things stood, and sighed as he released his friend, feeling his erection collapse precipitately into his pants. They turned back then, by unspoken agreement, both sadly aware that something had just come to an end. In that moment a great deal about Brian Hales was revealed to Butterworth, in his difficult and uncompromising self-vision; and something in him writhed briefly, whimpered, and died. When they reached the point where Hales had to turn one way for his house and Butterworth went the other way for his, they stood facing one another, not knowing what to say or how to go about saying it.

Eventually Butterworth stuck out a hand, and Hales, feeling a conflicting cocktail of relief, shame, sadness and a vague, indefinable regret, took it, shook it awkwardly and then held on to it for a moment, as if not knowing how to let it go. They were both rather glad when they turned their respective corners and passed out of each other's sight.

With his friend departed for home and then Cambridge, Hales quickly and assiduously diverted his energies elsewhere, feeling relief that potentially dangerous emotions could now be left safely dormant in their cage, where they could not betray him, bringing risks of losing him face among his widening circle of friends.

It would be some years more before Hales would understand that there was a simple, not specially important but fundamental difference between himself and other men. When it came he was able to draw on unsuspected reserves of resilience and inner strength to deal with the knowledge, and the immense additional pressures from outside, without collapsing under them. It was then that he finally knew and acknowledged his full debt to his friend; and then, too, that he savoured fully the grief that comes from first acquaintance with the bitterest, most poignant of betrayals: betrayal by oneself. But all that was to come. For the time being he took away from his relationship with Peter Butterworth one legacy that would echo and resonate through his life: he was never afterwards proof against a certain kind of looks. The lethal cocktail required a combination of masculinity with prettiness: a gracefully built boy, all blue eyes and clean blond hair, would ever afterwards set off images in Hales's mind of golden days when youth seemed impregnable and school and the companionship of boys seemed as if it might never end, when the sun was always bright and the breeze always cooling; and Hales would be lost.

IV

IT was while their German guards were bedding the train and prisoners down for the night that the astonishing, unimaginable thing happened.

They had been allowed off the train, one van at a time, to ease their limbs and take water from a couple of standpipes beside a smoke-blackened brick hut that stood, with no obvious purpose but looking dirty, squat and as if it belonged, after the manner of little brick huts in railway yards everywhere, in the middle of the vast expanse of tracks, signals, rolling stock and puffing, hissing engines. When it came to Hales's truck's turn they piled off enthusiastically and scampered or hobbled, depending on the state of their legs, across the fifty yards to the pipes. The water was icy cold and tasted very faintly of soot; but it was like ambrosia to their starved, scorched throats. Several, heedless of the risk of chills or worse and the impossibility of getting properly dry, stripped down on the spot and washed rapidly, extracting tiny fragments of soap from unlikely corners of their uniforms and persons.

When they had had their allocated ten minutes they were rounded up by the guards, prodded back across the open space to the train and herded back aboard their cattle truck, now smelling considerably cleaner for a few minutes' airing in the cold evening wind. The guards saw the last of them swing up and inside, slammed the sliding door on the side of the van closed, and moved on to the next one to give its occupants their turn.

For a moment there was a dead silence while they all waited, hardly daring to breathe lest they should call undue attention tothemselves, and sure the guards would remember in any case and come hastening back. They had all noticed the unbelievable omission, though they could scarcely credit the evidence of their ears: between them, the guards had forgotten to lock them in. "Talk normally," said somebody urgently, after a minute or two had passed. "if we're unusually quiet they'll smell a rat for sure." Answering murmurs of agreement came from all corners, and a buzz of conversation sprang up. Like all staged conversations it began falteringly, but they soon settled down and the talk became more natural, dwelling on the bloodiness of the war, the especial bloodiness of being taken prisoner, and the fathomless, immeasurable bloodiness of their present circumstances.

Soon they were left to themselves, with just a couple of guards pacing up and down the great length of their train to keep an eye on them. Judging their safety by the approaching or fading scrunch of the guards' boots on the cinders, granite and slag that made up the surface of most of the enormous marshalling yard, the inmates of Hales's van set about an urgent whispered conference over what to do. Oddly, they broke down more or less on service lines: the airmen present, of whom there were five, were strongly in favour of their all making a break for it, trying to escape but in any case doing as much damage as they possibly could before they were recaptured. Most of the army personnel, however, were on the side of caution, arguing that if everyone tried to escape the net result would be that no-one would. This faction thought the attempt ought to be restricted to a small group of volunteers, small enough for their absence not to be noticed until the next count, at least, while the remainder covered up for them and made it as difficult as possible for the guards to make any enquiries.

In the end it was put to a vote, and the army, being much the more numerous, won without a count: the airmen would make the attempt alone. Everyone made way for Hales and the other four RAF prisoners to edge their way to the cover of the centre of the van for a council of war.

"First of all, we've got to know where we are," said the grey-haired major who had been chosen as their leader and spokesman for their van in all dealings with the Germans. Clandestine enquiries were passed along the train, and an answer quickly came back. Someone with a smattering of French and German had overheard a gang of French railwaymen talking, and thought they were at or near a town called Montbeliard. A few moments later a second message was relayed along the train, and for a while served only to confuse the issue: someone else had overheard a gang of repair workmen, probably the same one, and declared confidently that they were near a town by the name of Sochaux. Yet a third communicant relayed the information that though he didn't know exactly where they were he was sure they were close to the river Rhine.

"Hmph!" said the elderly major, stroking his moustache and squinting hard at the floor of the van. "Sounds as if we're just about as far from home as we could be in France. Just about to cross into Germany, too, by the sound of it. Well, gentlemen, you must decide for yourselves whether to make the attempt. I don't need to tell you how slender a chance you have. But if you do decide to make a break for it, it seems to me that you've got a plain choice. You can either take the long road, and try to make it back to England, or you can opt for a much shorter distance and try for Switzerland. The road to England will be a lot longer, perhaps more gruelling, but in the long run, I think, less dangerous, with less risk of capture. You may be able to make contact with the Resistance. That, I think, will be more likely if you head westwards. Then there's Switzerland. I suspect you'll find it's a *much* harder road, and it's almost certain to be heavily guarded. On the other hand, if we're roughly where I think we are, it really is a *very* short distance to the border; and you should be able to find a way across the frontier in dense cover: it's all forest and open country hereabouts."

They chose unanimously to head for Switzerland. Various voices contributed miscellaneous bits of advice, most of it wildly impractical. When he was satisfied that there was nothing more to be said, the major took over once more, drumming the route into their heads by the simplest method of endless repetition. "None of this is much use immediately," he muttered in conclusion, "since we don't know where you're starting from. But if you can find out where you are in relation to Basle, or Belfort, you should be able to follow what I've said. Otherwise, you're on your own, gentlemen. Good luck, and God speed..." There was a murmured chorus of "Good luck, chaps" from the entire company, followed by an awkward, difficult silence. Hales felt his stomach turning and rising slowly and inexorably up his gorge, and fought it down in a furious silent internal battle. He found himself wishing fervently that the moment to make his break would come, and even more fervently that he had never been such a congenital, ditch-born imbecile as to volunteer to try to escape in the first place. He fought off a shudder, but couldn't suppress it.

The grey-haired major was crouching next to him, and felt it. "Are you sure you want to go through with this?" he asked, instantly all concern. "It's still not too late to change your mind, you know..."

"No, no, sir", Hales hissed at him, "I'll be all right. Just tension. Waiting's the worst part, I dare say..." He felt a hand rest on his upper arm and briefly squeeze his biceps. "Good luck," came a whisper, and then it was time to go.

The moment had come when both guards were farthest from their van. Willing hands eased the sliding door open, hearts coming into mouths when the pulley wheels screeched angrily on the oil-starved runners. In the general cacophony from the myriad nocturnal repair and maintenance jobs going on all over the giant yard, however, no one was noticing an odd extra shriek of tortured metal, and after a long pause inside the van the escapers dropped silently to the ground. The others watched them as they instantly scattered. Hales dropped slightly awkwardly from the van, and had to pause for a few agonising moments to rub an ankle that had almost turned beneath his weight as he landed. He broke into a stumbling, hobbling run, however, and headed for the nearest piece of cover. The others had already vanished.

As things turned out no one actually suffered the humiliation of recapture before managing to break out of the yards; but the two pairs were picked up before they had got beyond the boundaries of the town. They were pounced on with great glee by army patrols and put on following trains the next day with much chaffing and joking, and remarkable good humour.

Hales had better fortune. He was in slightly better condition than the average aboard their appallingly cramped van, and after the first few halting steps, when he had shaken the brief but agonising hints of cramp from his tortured muscles, he found that his legs responded well to the unaccustomed hard working.

He ran, darting, half crouching, and shooting fearful glances in all directions, for about fifty yards, and reached the cover of an apparently endless train of heavy freight wagons. There he rested, cowering between the two end wagons, pumping in breath and rubbing the shrieking muscles of his calves. After a minute or two the circulation was something closer to normal, and he spared a couple of moments to pop his head out from the comforting shadow of the freight cars to look about him and take stock of his situation. He could still see the train on which he had until so very recently been suffering such vile privations, and found himself feeling an almost wistful sense of regret for the security it represented. He knew that to indulge such feelings would sap what little scraps of resolve he had mustered in no time, so he thrust them resolutely from him and forced himself to think as coldly and clearly as he was able.

It seemed that he would be able to get as far as the perimeter of the marshalling yard, at least, without too much difficulty. There were very few people about, and the busy yard afforded plenty of cover. He took a deep breath, fought off a momentary feeling of faintness, and stepped boldly out of the friendly shadow of the trucks.

Nobody took the slightest notice of him. He half-turned, raised a hand briefly in the direction of his erstwhile captivity in case anyone was still watching his progress, and passed out of sight. After a few yards he became aware that he was scuttling along in a half-crouch that would be an instant give-away if he was observed by any of the railwaymen ambling here and there. With a conscious effort he straightened up a little, slowed his pace and tried to copy the round-shouldered, resentful trudge of the railwaymen he could see here and there. He recalled from the numerous snatches of conversation he and others aboard their train had overheard that most of the railwaymen were almost certainly Frenchmen pressed into the service of the occupying Germans, and it crossed his mind that if he were to wait for a passing gang of permanent-way men or freight loaders and throw himself on their mercy, it might be the fastest and most efficient method of finding his way into the helping hands of the Resistance.

It was so bright and inspiriting a thought that he slipped into the cover of another train of wagons to give himself a minute or two to consider it. After a moment's thought, however, he rejected the idea on the grounds that if he chose wrongly he would suffer the ignominy of being put back onto his train without even having got out of the yard; and though he recognised that the objection owed more to obstinacy and pride than to common sense or logic, he felt that it was a moment to follow instinct. A fleeting picture flitted inconsequentially into his mind of Roy Dean, climbing down from the cockpit of their Halifax as they had come limping home, badly shot up and almost out of fuel, at the end of a particularly fraught mission shortly before their final crash into the unwelcoming waters of Biscay. The others had swept him aloft and carried him into the debriefing on their shoulders, yelling their fervent congratulations — which were, in truth, nothing more than their heartfelt thanks to him for getting them back alive. Afterwards, when the first hysterical release from fear was over, they had all had a comforting bowel movement and Hales and Dean were de-electrifying themselves in the mess, Hales had tried to thank him seriously.

"Nothing to thank me for, old boy," Dean had said, sipping his hot Oxo and sketching a taut, white grin. "There's a time for thinking, and there's a time for following your instincts, however bloody daft they may seem. We came back on pure adrenalin. Eight times out of ten you make it. The other two... bye-bye, blackbird; and that's all there is to it."

"Is that what they mean by 'flying by the seat of the pants'?" Hales had asked, feeling a sudden glow of understanding flush through him. "You got it," Dean had said laconically. "Have another Oxo, Brian, and welcome to the club." He had stood up, stretched luxuriously and gone to get more hot Oxo, leaving Hales realising that he had grasped something immensely important. It was, he realised, the moment when he had truly understood his own job for the first time.

He felt a sudden, utterly unexpected bolt of sorrow, a flash of compassion and regret for the sadness and profligate waste of the war, go lancing through him. It passed out of him almost like a sob, and then it was gone. He spared a last moment's memory of Roy Dean, who had been his friend. Then he gritted his teeth and, following his instincts, stepped out from his temporary cover and plodded on his way towards the perimeter fence of the yard.

He advanced by short stages, proceeding jerkily from one bit of cover to the next, taking frequent short rests to spare his muscles, which were already beginning to pain him in a grim, unremitting ache. He thought that if he remained at liberty as far as the following morning he was going to have bad trouble getting mobile at all after a night's sleep. "If I get a night's sleep," he reminded himself grimly. However, he managed in this stop-start way to cover several hundred yards, and then he had a piece of good fortune. He had paused in the shadow of a small brick hut. Crouching beside the grimy wall he idly tried the door and found to his astonishment that it was open.

He ducked quickly inside and drew the door hastily to behind him. The first thing he noticed was the extraordinary difference in temperature once he was inside with the door closed against the wind. Outside it had been cold. The effect was disguised to some extent by the fact that it was a brisk, dry cold, but it was a brutal, bone-chilling cold that got down into the depths of the body with astonishing rapidity; and although the wind was light and blew only intermittently, when it did blow it did so with a deadly razor edge that did as much to sap the will as to chill the body. Inside the little hut it was almost pleasantly warm, so great was the contrast of a few degrees and the relief from being shielded from the wind.

He groped in his uniform for a match. In the dim light it cast he saw that he was in some kind of stores shed, full of stacks of fishplates, coils of electric cable and all manner of other railway impedimenta. There was also, he found to his unutterable joy, a set of sloppy, filthy overalls and, better still, the remains of some rail-wayman's lunch. It was only a couple of stale crusts of bread, a slab of coarse greyish cheese with a semi-circular bite out of one side, and a large raw carrot, but he wolfed it ravenously, and thought it was among the most memorable meals he had ever partaken of. There was also a dirty bottle, which had once contained some kind of spirit but now held three inches of dirty brownish fluid which was, he found, cold tea. He washed the makeshift meal down with it, and swore to himself that he had never tasted anything as good.

A few minutes after he had finished his unexpected supper his stomach registered a protest at a meal of such unaccustomed size, and for some time he suffered griping pains that almost doubled him up. After a while they eased, however, and he stood up, stooping slightly beneath the low, angled flat roof, found another match, and set to explore his surroundings. There was nothing else worth stealing, but when he had edged his way to the rear of the little hut he found there was a narrow empty space between the last of the stacks of fishplates and the end wall. It was wide enough for a man to lie down in comfort, and, wonder of wonders, the cinder and dirt floor was covered by a thick double stack of filthy empty coal sacks.

Hales suddenly realised that he was weary. Not merely tired, but tired beyond the power of any known language to express. He looked down at the sacks, and the luxury of lying fully extended and able to stretch his limbs was so tempting that he cast all caution, indeed every other thought at all, to the winds. He strewed the sacks in a thick layer over the bare bit of floor. Then he enjoyed a luxuriant stretch, moaning softly to himself with pleasure as his joints crackled, and struck another match to look at his watch. It was ten minutes to eleven. He had had long practice, in the seemingly prehistoric era of his flying days, at setting a kind of internal alarm clock. He had only to focus his mind on a clock face with the hands set at a given hour, and he would, he knew, unfailingly wake up at precisely that hour the following morning. He dropped the match and trod on it, lay down and stretched out, drew the last of the sacks over him, and concentrated on seeing a large round clock showing two o'clock. He had scarcely had time to summon up the image before he was deep in a dreamless, exhausted sleep.

He woke with a start. After a few moments of panic-stricken wondering where he was, and what had happened to the other prisoners, he remembered. He stretched, taking his time over it and savouring the pleasant electric shocks of flexed muscles, then lay back in his cocoon of smelly, coaly sacks, and took stock of his situation. Although his limbs, and especially his legs, had stiffened and were torturing him most agonisingly, he was immediately conscious of feeling better than he could remember feeling for what seemed like forever. His next feeling was one of ravenous hunger, but he was used to that, and dispelled the feeling by the simple expedient of forcing himself to thrust it from him and resolutely forgetting about it. Next came a second burst of panic as he became aware that he could see his surroundings. It was daylight, and somehow it was getting into his little hut. Swallowing and steeling himself in readiness for whatever frightful shock awaited him, he looked at his watch — and almost groaned aloud.

His unfailing mental alarm had failed him, and done so in style. It was twenty-five minutes past five, and he had slept for nearly seven hours.

He thought fast. The prospect of spending an entire day in the little blockhouse was not by any means unpleasant, and he might have decided there and then to grant himself such a day of recovery, but for one thing. He was hungry, not with just the everyday, routine hunger that had become normality in the short period since his capture, but ferociously, agonisingly ravenous, so that he knew that if he didn't eat very soon it would drive him to give himself up. It was, he recognised, as simple as that.

He threw off the upper layer of sacks, stood up and stretched once again. He cast a regretful, almost affectionate glance round his night's abode, stacked the sacks in the two piles in which he had found them, looked about him once more to say goodbye, and popped his head out of the door. At close to eleven o'clock at night there had been few people about. Now, at half past five, there was no one at all. He picked up the ancient overalls and put them on over his uniform, wrinkling his nose in disgust at the overwhelming reek of oil, grease and coal that they exuded. He added a greasy cloth cap with a soft peak. Someone, presumably, he thought, the owner of the overalls, had left a small canvas bag, stiff with the accumulated grease of years, full of tools. It occurred to him that it would make a plausible-looking camouflage, and he slung it over his shoulder. As he was on the point of making his final departure he noticed a short, light crowbar, shaped like a burglar's jemmy, standing against the wall of the hut in the corner nearest the door, and thoughtfully picked it up. It might, he thought vaguely, make a more than half-useful weapon if he had to fight off any challenge.

At last he was ready and there was no putting off the decisive moment any longer. Casting a last glance round his cold, dank yet immeasurably comforting little sanctuary, he peered unobtrusively out of the shed, took a deep breath and exhaled it sharply, and stepped out into the unknown dangers of the outside world.

V

THE first thing he noticed was the sky. Though it was a dank winter morning and the dawn was yet some hours distant, the entire sky was lit up from below in a somehow deeply ominous, satanic orange glare, and he spent a puzzled moment or two wondering why he had failed to notice the same thing the night before. The reason, he quickly understood, had been pure adrenalin: he had been so entirely preoccupied with the excitement of the escape from the train and the crazy zig-zagging flight that had ended in the little blockhouse that he had been in no condition to observe anything, about his surroundings or anything else. Now, however, he could see clearly that this, wherever it was, was a place of some considerable heavy industry. He assumed there must be some kind of munitions work going on here, and immediately decided that he ought to head away from the source of the glare in the sky, even if it took him for a brief period away from his ultimate goal of Switzerland, in the east. The last thing he wanted, he thought, was to begin his attempt for liberty by heading straight into a part of the town that was most certain to be fully peopled at all hours, and where there were certain to be Germans, at that. He halted in his steady trudge towards the perimeter fence of the marshalling yard, and squinted into the sky, turning slowly in a circle to examine it in all quarters.

The trouble, he found, the moment he made the attempt, was that it was impossible to determine from which side the furnace glare extended upwards into the night sky. It seemed to be coming from both sides at once. He stood for a moment, apparently a railway worker on the night shift taking a moment to glance up to where the stars would be if they had only been visible. Then he shook his head and gave up. Maybe it was some trick of the light, or of the atmosphere. Maybe there were two, or more than two, separate factories, or mills or whatever they were to throw up such vast and fearsome palls of glare. He shifted the shoulder strap of the bag of tools, which was already weighing uncomfortably heavily on his weakened frame, took a new grip on his jemmy, and resumed the slow, steady plod that he had already discovered to be the most comfortable method of proceeding.

He came surprisingly soon to the high chain-link fence of the marshalling yard. It was a formidable affair; but, in common with most English males, Hales had spent a sizable slice of his boyhood as an avid trainspotter. The thought flitted into his mind that where there was a marshalling yard, there were engines to be seen and, if the local railwaymen were at a safe distance, to be clambered into; he had never once yet known a marshalling yard fence that didn't have a hole in it somewhere; and he suspected that French boys were no less resourceful than their English counterparts in finding such holes if they existed, or in making them if they didn't.

The thought brought an accompanying grin as he started along the wire; and a few yards later it was followed by another, broader one, as he found the proof of his theorem. Good old trainspotters, he thought to himself, and was surprised at the sudden lift the thought gave to his spirits, out of all proportion to the size of the victory won. He slipped through the boy-sized hole in the wire and started up the uneven pavement that ran alongside it, slippery with dew, on the outside. After a few yards he realised that he could hear whistling; a few yards further still he realised, to his still greater surprise, that the whistler was himself. He smiled to himself and went on his way. But he didn't stop whistling.

As he plodded through the narrow streets he was aware of a subdued noise that was ever present with him. It was almost more of a vibration than a sound, but he could hear it, a deep, as if subterranean rumble. He tried to analyse it, and decided it must be the noise that went with the glare in the sky: it was the unending throbbing of heavy machinery. He also saw that as he kept turning towards the east he was heading inexorably towards the source of both the glare and the rumble. He shrugged slightly to himself, shifting the toolbag from one shoulder as he did so. There was nothing much he could do about it now, he thought.

Before long he came into plain sight of the source of the *son et lumière* display. He turned once more, eastwards as usual, and found himself in a very short narrow street of cobbles and small houses, no more than half a dozen on either side. At its far end the street entered a T-junction, and as Hales reached it he saw that on the far side of the much larger way there ran a heavy metal fence that would have dwarfed the one enclosing the railway yard. It ran, unblemished and gleaming steely blue-black in the industrial half-light, for as far as he could see in either direction. Beyond it, in one direction, were great stacks of indeterminate shape and size, each stack neatly covered with a black tarpaulin, gleaming under its covering of dew. In the other direction were vehicles — literally acres of them, standing in silent, serried lines under the lit-up sky, throwing out red, orange, yellow and coppery glints from the occasional bit of bright metal. They were like an incredible, colossal, forgotten army, the ordnance of an army of ghosts, stretching far away into the distance — somehow terrifying, in their immaculately drawn-up ranks and their terrible silence.

He impatiently shook off the faintly eldritch feeling, made a rapid and inconsequential decision which way to continue, and started off along the fence to the right. Shortly both fence and road veered sharply to the left, and as he rounded the turn he saw the works, the source of the sub-lit glare in the sky and the sound that thrummed in his ears but also, he had distinctly observed, through the soles of his feet. With it went a whole new cacophony of sounds: a clangorous symphony of metal on metal, thumping, pulsings, occasional voices raised in unintelligible shouts, and underlying it all, a steady 'whump-whump-whump' rhythm, unending and inhuman, the heartbeat of the giant works. He plodded on towards the vast black mass until he came level with a set of enormous wide gates. They were slightly open, and in the middle, set where it would be on the street side of the gates when they were closed, was a small cubicle in which he could see a couple of soldiers. They were wearing helmets in the distinctive pattern of the German army.

So too, Hales noticed in dismay, were two other soldiers, who appeared at that moment round a bend in the street ahead, and were now approaching on the far side of the gateway. Clearly, he thought, they were a routine German patrol. So far they had taken no notice whatsoever of the nondescript railwayman plodding towards them; but as he drew abreast of the gateway he saw one of them nudge his colleague and gesture in his direction. The two of them exchanged glances, and their entire demeanour became subtly more alert.

A whole cascade of visions tumbled one after another in front of Hales's mind's eye in a fraction of a second. He saw himself held up, asked to produce his papers; explanations were demanded in halting French for why he was breaking the curfew; and then... then the discovery of his RAF uniform beneath his greasy disguise; there were guttural exclamations of surprise, warning and triumph... and then gun butts, and... and what? Handcuffs? The Gestapo? *That* thought was enough to make him conscious of a cold, decaying feeling about the heart and set the base of his testicles crawling. In the space of a couple of instants everything he had heard about the Gestapo unreeled in his mind. He imagined dank, dripping basement rooms with bare tables and rubber truncheons, the sound of screams from somewhere down a dimly lit stone-floored passage... There was an almost irresistible urge to turn and run; but that, he knew, would be the end. Suppressing the urge with a mighty effort of blind will, he pulled himself together, and felt the power of thought return like blood flowing back into limbs released from a tourniquet. Hoping fervently that his titanic efforts to keep control of his legs had not shown in any change in his dogged, resentful gait, he turned in at the gateway and trudged towards the two soldiers in the gatehouse.

They scarcely bothered to glance up from their game of cards as he drew abreast of them and sidled towards the wicket gate beside their gatehouse. Hales gave a silent yell of jubilation as he realised he had made it past the first real test. And then, as he shoved the wooden door to open it sufficiently to pass through, he had to turn half sideways on to the gatehouse. There was a side door, open, and one of the soldiers inside was lounging against a wall, looking down at his cards. He had only to raise his eyes and he would be gazing directly at Hales.

How long did it take to push a sticking door open and slip through? Less than a second, surely? He got the door open, with a low scraping sound on the oily concrete. The soldier glanced idly towards the sound... and at that moment the press stud holding the upper part of Hales's dungarees snapped open with a 'pop', releasing a flap of the coarse denim material to flop open... and revealing a section of neatly tailored jacket in the unmistakable cut of a service uniform. Powerful arc lights had been rigged up to bathe the gateway in bright white light, and in the brilliant cross-glare they produced the colour was equally plain: the distinctive hue of the delousing ointment used to repel the assaults of crab lice; otherwise, RAF blue.

Not that the colour mattered, Hales felt himself think as he saw the startled look of recognition leap into the soldier's eyes. In that frozen instant of calm before who knew what broke loose, he realised clearly that the mere fact of a neat service uniform showing beneath his stinking rags was enough, more than enough, in itself. But the thought had scarcely broken the surface of his consciousness before it was stillborn, and Hales was through the door and running.

There was a yelp of "Hi!" from behind him as he squeezed desperately through the inadequate space, followed immediately by further guttural shouts and the sound of running feet. Somewhere a bell began to ring. Hales broke instinctively to the left, spotted a doorway brilliantly lit in a huge expanse of wall by the furnace glare from within, and darted towards it. He ran in a crouch, instinctively dipping and weaving like a snipe in flight. He covered the twenty yards between him and the stencilled rectangle of fiery orange light in a few seconds, shot through the doorway, slipped to one side of the opening so as to be out of sight from outside, and forced himself to halt and look about him, clawing the treacherous flap of overalls back onto its press stud as he did so.

The building was, he saw, built on the lines of an aircraft hangar, a simple construction of corrugated iron sheeting that seemed to stretch forever in all directions — especially, he noticed, upwards. It was set up as one gigantic machine room, and the whole vast edifice pulsed and vibrated to a hundred cross-rhythms set up by the huge assortment of machine tools it contained. There were machines of every imaginable size and shape, all painted a dark green drab, and all making their own contribution to the deafening symphony of sounds to which the great shed danced. In the first few breathless seconds Hales took in a large, squat machine in front of him that was making a high-pitched whine, punctuated by a low, rumbling bom-bom-bom-bom every few seconds. A few feet away was a tall, thin machine that made a horrid steely ker-swishing sound, like a fingernail drawn down a blackboard. A few feet in the other direction was a long box-shaped device that contributed a continuous soft 'dunka-dunka-dunka'. And somewhere not far away there was something that dwarfed all other sounds: a huge, rhythmical pounding that seemed to shake the very earth. Everywhere there were small electric motors, varying from the size of a large coconut to titans the size of a small motor car. They looked like a giant's strings of beads.

Hales knew he had no time to spare taking in his surroundings. The cries and the sounds of booted feet were already terrifyingly close outside. He took a swift glance round, then darted down the access path that ran along the wall. There was a shallow bend a few yards along, and he darted round it before there were any signs of pursuit. Once round it, he paused again to take another glance round.

It was almost his undoing. A confused chorus of shouts broke out at the door from the yard, with one stentorian bellow that rose clear above the cacophony in the giant shed. *"Da! Da druben!"* Hales took a swift glance over his shoulder and saw grey uniforms racing his way. He bolted down the nearest walkway between ranks of throbbing, clanking and whining machinery and disappeared. As he set off he suddenly realised that he still had the heavy bag of tools slung over his shoulder, weighing him down and bashing clumsily against his hip with every pace he took; he was also, ridiculously, still lugging his jemmy, which seemed to be heavier with every stride he ran. He slipped the clumsy bag off his shoulder as he ran and let it fall, and flung the jemmy aside. There was a clang, and some machine immediately started screaming on a very different note. *Done something for the war effort,* he caught himself thinking as some corner of his mind registered the change, and to his own surprise he found himself grinning. A strange, dislocated feeling of sheer exultation took hold of him, and he found himself surging with energy, rejoicing in the simple pleasure of being free, being chased and being ahead of the pursuit. He charged onwards, watching for openings in the narrow gangway between the long lines of machines performing their inscrutable purposes.

Yells broke out behind him, and then there came the sound, cutting effortlessly above all the clangorous sounds of the factory, of a rifle shot. His heart missed a beat as he waited for the searing bolt of pain as a bullet crashed into him, then realised that the impact would have come well before he heard the report. Instead, the shot was followed instantly by a chorus of cries which sounded, to Hales's racing mind, like several people yelling recriminations at one another. At all events, there were no more shots. He dived down another side gangway, and felt an enormous surge of relief and excitement when he saw another doorway at the end of it, a simple black rectangle of the night outside.

Other people had become aware of the untoward events in the shop. He could hear cries from all sides now, and as he spied the doorway at the end of his gangway two men in overalls appeared directly in his path, halfway between him and his goal. As far as he could see they were unarmed, and he instantly made up his mind that there was nothing for it but to try to knock them out of his path. Sparing a split second to curse himself roundly for having discarded his weapon, he streaked onwards, heading straight for them. As he came up to them, however, to his immense surprise they separated, one moving out of his way to either side of the gangway. As he sped between them he caught a brief tang of the ubiquitous heavy oil and grease. He took a lightning look at the two of them. Both were elderly men, in their sixties, he thought, and both had lined, ill-shaven faces with the same greyish, weary, undernourished look about them. Both were lit up in great beaming smiles, which made the two old men look almost beautiful; and both were waving him on enthusiastically, flapping their arms towards the black opening. He caught a couple of words, flung behind him as soon as they reached him: *"Allez-y, mon pot..."* from one side, and a simple *"bonne chance..."* from the other.

Flushed with yet a further top-up of the same insane exhilaration, he swept down the alleyway and shot through the doorway into the darkness beyond, where the air outside met him like a douche of cold water in the face, refreshing him instantly and bringing a blessed moment of calm. He slowed a little in his headlong dash, but kept running, waiting for his eyes to adjust to the comparatively stygian darkness of the yard.

As the power of sight began to return he saw that he was in the vast storage yard that he had looked in on from outside the wire. There were lights, slung on a network of wires that formed a sort of thin spider's web above the vast yard; but they were few in number and cast only a feeble light for a radius of a few yards here and there.

Still, there was enough light for him to navigate by, and he headed straightaway for the nearest of the huge tarpaulin-covered stacks. He was safely concealed in its comforting black shadow by the time the first cries issued from the machine house. He watched as first one, then a second and finally a group of helmeted figures appeared in silhouette in the doorway, then slipped silently down between the stacks in search of somewhere to hide.

Taking care to run on the balls of his feet and trying to make no sound on the yard surface of roughly pulverised clinker, he flitted from stack to stack. As he went he felt the earlier feeling of exhilaration ebbing rapidly away, to be replaced by an oddly equal and opposite sense of mounting despair. The more desperately his eyes flicked from side to side, from one giant stack to the next, the more hopeless his plight seemed. There was not only nowhere big enough to conceal an average-sized kitten, there was not even a single differentiating feature to enable him to tell one of the great piles of whatever the hell it was that the tarpaulins concealed. It looked as if he was doomed to be hunted up and down interminable ranks and files of stacks until he was finally cornered, then to be tamely recaptured, questioned and, no doubt, given a good kicking for making a bloody nuisance of himself before being ignominiously gun-butted onto the next passing train heading for the prison camps. The feeling filled him with gloom, and almost without realising he was doing it, he slowed to a normal walking pace.

With the end of his frantic racing pace, which he had sustained for far longer than he'd had any right to, he reflected, there straightaway came back the power of rational thought, and with it came a slight lifting of the sense of foreboding and despair. He pressed himself as far as he could into the heavy tarpaulin covering of the stack in whose lee he was sheltered, seeking the deepest, most impenetrable heart of its black shadow, and forced himself to think. He was still doing so when the first pair of soldiers came down the gangway he had just turned off. They were creeping down the aisle in gingerly fashion, at the half-crouch, their rifles held ready to fire, the long, thin bayonets gleaming evilly in the faint glow from the nearest light. Hales stopped breathing as they crept past.

As the faint sound of their muttered conversation died away in the distance the answer to his problem of where to conceal himself came to him. When he had pressed himself into the canvas of the tarpaulin he had felt it give, offering some idea of the shape of the load that stood underneath its cover. Kneeling on the sharp clinker, he felt along the base of the stack, and found that the tarpaulin was secured by an occasional pin, like a tent peg, driven roughly into the ground every ten feet or so. Cursing himself once more for having discarded his jemmy, he worked on the first pin he found, and after a lot of furious scrabbling and heaving, at a cost of several gashed knuckles, he managed to work it out of the ground.

This left just enough slack in the tarpaulin to allow him to slip under its skirt and roll up beside the foot of the stack within. By feeling along the stack he discovered that the load was made up of large high-explosive shells, presumably destined for the artillery units of the German army. They were stacked in layers, the lowest resting on a heavy wooden pallet, the shells in the layers pointing in alternate directions, prevented from rolling by small wooden wedges; and there was just enough room between each pair of pallets for a man to slip down between the two and rest. He slipped his fingers under the bottom of the tarpaulin and drew it to as near to its former position as he could, laying the peg aside within the cover of the canvas. Then, satisfied that he had done all that could humanly be done to cover his tracks, he wriggled his feet and legs in towards the centre of the stack until he was resting on the ends of the two pallets where the planks projected out beyond the points of the lowest layer of shells. It was surprisingly comfortable, and in defiance of all his firm resolutions to lie there only until he was sure the pursuers had given up and gone, in a few minutes he was asleep.

He was wakened from his uneasy, jittery sleep by the sounds of the search continuing in the yard. He had no idea whether he had slept for five minutes or five hours, but he felt a little refreshed, and judged that it must have been at least an hour or two. The voices that had awoken him faded into the distance, and when it was silent once more he eased himself out of his cramped lair and cautiously lifted the edge of the tarpaulin. His brief glimpse of the outside told him that dawn was close. The indigo of the sky was streaked with pale, greyish light, and the furnace-like glare from the factory was much less pronounced. He pressed the skirt of the canvas flush with the ground once more and wormed his way back, an inch at a time, into the comparative security of the stack of munitions. There he risked striking a match to look at his watch, and found that it was just after eight in the morning. He twisted himself round to get his head close to the tarpaulin and listened for further sounds of the hunt.

After some time he heard voices approaching, and listened for all he was worth, the trip-hammer beat of his heart thudding in his ears.

Hales had very good French — a fact he had carefully kept to himself throughout his interrogation after they had been captured, and also throughout the interminable journey through France on the prison train. He could not have said why he did so, except from a vague but powerful instinctive feeling that the less he did to draw attention to himself the better it was likely to be for him.

Now, however, he quickly gathered that the German troops had co-opted gangs of workers from the factory and organised them into search parties, working in pairs to quarter the whole vast area of the yard.

"Haven't got a clue who he is," one of the men was saying as they came properly into earshot, "and neither have the Krauts. That fat bastard of a sergeant was saying it was someone with a uniform on under his overalls, but I don't know…"

"I heard there were some got off one of the trains last night," put in the second voice. "They got most of 'em within a few minutes, apparently, but one or two of 'em got away. But you can never trust anything the Krauts say. Their intelligence is about as reliable as the gear we knock out for em here…" They both chuckled.

"Bloody good luck to him, I say," resumed the first voice, "if it was a prisoner. Hope we don't find him."

"It's all balls anyway," grunted the other speaker grumpily. "All this, I mean — getting the whole bloody lot of us out here when we should have buggered off home an hour ago, chasing our tails round this place hunting for him, when you know and I know he's found that bloody great hole in the fence and cleared off hours ago — if he ever existed at all in the first place. I shouldn't be surprised if it was just some off-duty copper or fireman or something of the kind, sloping off home after seeing his bit of crumpet. As for us finding him here, if it *was* some prisoner making a run for it, we've got more chance of poking butter up a wildcat's arse with a red-hot knitting needle…"

"Well, don't get het up about it," consoled his partner. "We'll be finished in half an hour and they'll let us piss off home. I don't think even the Krauts are really expecting to find him still here…"

"Well, good luck to him, if he does exist," said the other voice for the second time.

"I bet he doesn't and never did," the first man repeated sourly.

"Let's drink his health, anyway. Got a fag?" Hales heard the two of them lean against the tarpaulin over the stack in which he was concealed. They were less than five yards away. There was a sound of a cap being unscrewed from a bottle or flask. *"Bonne chance, mon vieux, qui que tu sois,"* said one voice, and then *"À la tienne, Riton."*

"À la santé du con qui paye," said the other speaker, and there were drinking sounds. Then a match scraped, and the rank scent of caporal tobacco drifted along to Hales's nostrils, choking even thinned and at a distance. He waited, scarcely breathing, while the two of them finished their fag, had another swig from the bottle, and at last made up their minds to resume their perfunctory efforts at searching their section of the yard. They moved off, still complaining about their enforced extra duty, making contemptuous jokes about the Germans and dismissing their task as a pointless waste of time. Hales noticed that they kept their voices low, however, and deduced that there were still at least some German soldiers about.

He lay motionless until the two grumbling voices had faded out of sight, then allowed himself the luxury of stretching and flexing his agonisingly cramped limbs. Then he eased himself back into the dark womb of the stack of shells, feeling more encouraged and optimistic than he had since the wild, adrenalin-induced excitement of the previous night. He eased his body into as comfortable a position as he could find, and settled down to wait until he reckoned the hunt would be abandoned as pointless — at least half an hour, he thought, judging by what the two unwilling members of the pursuit had said. He occupied the time by going through the points of encouragement in his mind, checking them off on his fingers.

First, it was comforting to know that the local French people were very much on his side. He had no idea whether their natural sympathy for him would be translated into anything in the way of practical help if he was caught, but it meant that if he was taken by Frenchmen rather than Germans there was at least the possibility of appealing to them. Perhaps he could ask to be handed over to the Resistance, he thought. He knew very little about the Resistance movement, but he had heard some inspiring tales of their heroism, including the saving of many crashed airmen, back in the impossibly distant days in another lifetime when he had been a flier himself.

Of still more practical encouragement was the knowledge that no one was really taking the hunt for him seriously any longer. If even the Germans privately thought he was probably long gone, it augured well for his chances of at least getting out of the great yard without being captured; and it made reaching Switzerland seem a good deal less of an impossible dream, too.

Finally, most cheering of all, was the news that there was, somewhere, a hole in the high perimeter fence through which he could make his escape. He would not, at least, have to rely on finding a gate or door left negligently open, or, worse, try to break, dig or climb out — worst of all, try to fight his way out. He lay in the comforting darkness, now distinctly lighter as the gathering daylight penetrated the canvas, turning the pitch blackness to a greenish, faintly submarine twilight, and tried to work out which way he ought to head when he finally broke cover.

He knew there was no gap in the fence where he had walked along the road beside it the previous night. That left the opposite side of the yard or the far end, about a mile distant. He decided that he would head for the nearest point on the far side. Having made up his mind, he reviewed his decision and found no obvious flaws in his reasoning. He decided that there was nothing else he could profitably try to decide now in any case, and tried to make his mind a total blank so as to give himself the best chance of getting a last bit of rest before the next leg of his ordeal.

VI

HE continued to hear occasional voices for some time. At length, however, the last of them faded and there was a long period when he heard nothing except the constant subdued thunder of the factory, pouring out deadly trinkets of warfare. It was an effort to venture out from the dark reassurance of his hiding place, but he had worked out that if the giant works was producing munitions at such a rate, it was more than probable that the stocks piled in the yard would be moved at a similar rate, which meant that any security he felt beneath the tarpaulin was almost certainly illusory, and that he was in reality in a trap — quite likely a death trap, at that, if he should be caught there. Back at the airbase they had heard blood-chilling stories of what befell fugitives who were caught by the Germans in disguise. As he passed his last few minutes in hiding he strove to collect his thoughts and to rationalise his objectives.

They came to very little. He had to get clear of the factory and its constant shifts of watchful German overseers. He then had, very quickly, to find somewhere that really was safe, where he could lie up until nightfall. And then he had, at the earliest possible moment, to contrive to get himself delivered into the hands of the Resistance. If he couldn't achieve that, he recognised, he was finished. He worked his way to the skirt of the tarpaulin, eased it clear of the clinkers and listened for several moments, straining his ears for the slightest sound above the thrumming of the factory. In the end, satisfied that it was as safe as it was ever going to be, he wriggled out from under the canvas, stood up and stretched himself, and waited a few moments for his eyes to accustom themselves to the light of morning. Then he flitted to the corner of the stack and peered cautiously out along the main thoroughfare.

There was no one and nothing in sight. He swallowed hard, and dashed across the path, pressing himself gratefully into the canvas cover of the next stack. After a moment he cat-footed his way to the next corner and repeated the procedure.

By this jerky, leap-frogging progress he gained the far perimeter fence of the yard. The last row of munitions stacks were close to the fence, leaving a gap scarcely wide enough for him to scurry along. He rested in the lee of the last stack in his file, breathing hard and longing for a cigarette, while he wondered which way to go in search of the hole in the fence he had heard the French workmen speaking of.

He could see that the narrow path between the last row of stacks and the fence was little used, for there were tussocks of coarse grass working their way up through the clinker here and there. He imagined vaguely that a gap in the fence would be less likely to escape notice if it was near the works itself, so, taking another deep breath, he slipped out into the narrow pathway and began running along it as fast as he could, away from the looming colossus of the machine house, towards the far end of the huge yard.

He was slowed down by the frequent necessity to squeeze past where the stacks had been dumped closer than normal. It was never more than a few inches difference, but it meant that he had to stop and edge through sideways, and once he was forced to clamber up a few feet to where the stack canted slightly away from the fence, scramble over it and drop on the other side. He had to do his best to avoid direct contact wih the fence, in case it set up vibrations along its length that might be seen elsewhere, and paid a price in frequent barked elbows and ribs against the unyielding hard edges of the shells piled under their protective canvas on his left. By the time he found the hole in the fence his entire left side felt like raw steak. He also had an agonising stitch in his side brought on by the strenuous activity; he could feel the pulse pounding in his temples, and his heart was thundering alarmingly. He spotted the place where the heavy chain-link was torn away from one of the stanchions, however, and offered up a brief prayer of thanks to providence for having guided his instincts right.

Hales glanced back towards the machine shop through which he had raced earlier that morning. He'd had no idea that he had run so far, but already its glowering squat bulk was diminished to the point where he could see it as only one small part of a truly enormous spread of factory buildings. They stretched as far as he could see, all ugly, practical buildings without pretensions to beauty, elegance or fitting into their surroundings. All were painted in camouflage colours, and every window in each of them was painted out with a heavy wash of dark ink-blue, giving them all a peering, sightless look. He turned away from them with a sigh; stepped over to the stanchion where the fence was torn away, and eased the chain-link aside to make a gap wide enough for him to slip through. A second later he was striding along the narrow, cobbled street on the other side of the wire.

For some time his way lay through a maze of identical little streets, between small houses inhabited, he guessed, by the workforce from the factory. Once or twice a door opened, and his heart came up into his mouth; but the first time it was only to reveal a woman with a towel round her head like a turban, and with a series of mats to shake out over the street, and the second time a young woman came out into the street and set off along it with a shopping bag in her hand. She shot a rapid appraising glance his way, and nodded quickly to him. He returned the nod, and she turned away indifferently. Otherwise no one took the slightest notice of him, even when his way began to take him towards the town centre and a few people began to appear around him.

He kept away from the centre, more by instinct than anything else, always taking the lesser of two roads at a fork, always veering away from the central area that he glimpsed occasionally at the far end of a street here and there, seeking always the quiet, the suburb, the shabby rather than the brighter, the run-down and poor seeming over the more prosperous. At length, when he estimated he had put a good mile between himself and the factory complex, he decided that he had to risk trying to get something to eat. He had been aware of the hunger clenching his insides to a knot for some time, but since escaping from the factory yard he had passed several houses from which cooking smells had been drifting into the street, and they had driven him almost frantic with the need to eat. The moment the thought entered his head he was assailed by a ravening hunger; at the same time he became aware that his entire tongue and mouth were so parched and dusty that he could not have raised enough saliva to spit.

He had a little French money: they had had a whip round on the train, and scraped up a few francs one or two of them had found or somehow got hold of, to give him and the other escapers a start. He halted at a street corner, looked furtively about him to be sure there was no one in sight, relaxed and groped beneath his overalls and into the pocket of his uniform trousers. He counted the greasy, creased notes and the handful of coins with hands that refused to stop trembling despite his angry efforts to force them to a halt. Eventually, however, after several clumsy attempts and one or two dropped coins, all was ready. He had more than enough to pay for a meal and a glass of wine. He thrust the money into the outside pocket of the overall trousers, and plugged on, his eyes flicking this way and that as he kept alert for a café — or for the first sign of a German patrol.

He found a café-bar within fifty yards, a tiny, mean-looking place with a single window disclosing neat little tables and chairs within. He peered through the window, shading his eyes against the reflected light from outside. As far as he could see, the place was empty. He shuffled over to the narrow door and hesitated. But the need to eat was greater than all his fears. "Oh, well," he muttered to himself, "shit or bust," and pushed open the door.

Inside the little café it was spotlessly clean, belying the meanness of the appearance of the place from outside. The tables were covered with neat squares of red-and-white check material, there were knives and forks laid at some of them, with wine glasses that had been polished until they shone. The ashtray on every table was similarly gleaming and spotless. He slid behind a table in the farthest corner from the door, where the shadows were deepest and he was pretty sure he could not be seen from a casual glance in through the window.

The legs of his table scraped as he made room for himself behind it, and a moment later a thin, scrawny elderly man with extravagant moustaches appeared behind the tiny counter. They exchanged pleasantries, and he found that although it was as yet long before lunch would normally be served, the man could offer him a hunk of cheese, some bread, and he thought he had a morsel of sausage. He winked at Hales as he said this. "The Krauts don't know quite as much as they think they do," he murmured as he went shuffling off to prepare the meal. Hales noticed that he used the same word, *les schleu*, for the Germans as the two railwaymen he had heard talking outside his makeshift shelter in the factory yard. In his mouth, as in theirs, it was full of contempt, spoken like a swirl of spittle. Hales drew considerable comfort from the observation.

"You're not from round here," said the man in a low voice as he brought a small carafe of heavy red wine. "Working up at Peugeot, I suppose?"

Hales nodded, busying himself pouring a little of the wine into a glass. A couple of minutes passed, seeming like an eternity as he sought to parry the old man's attempts at passing the time of day without saying more than was strictly essential. Eventually, to Hales's thankful relief, a voice called from somewhere in the bowels of the building and the man went off, returning in a moment with a large plate. On it was a thick triangular hunk of coarse orange cheese and a broken-off length of a *flute* of bread. There were also half a dozen thick slices of some coarse local sausage of a mottled dark blood-red and white colour, and two dark brown individual sausages, square in section and about the size of a fountain pen. "We had a couple of *gendarmes,* said the old man with a grin, indicating the two dark sausages. That's what we call 'em round here. *Bon appetit.*" And to Hales's relief he went off behind the counter and into the back room, leaving Hales to eat ravenously.

He forced himself to eat slowly, fearful of bringing on a crippling bout of indigestion if he wolfed it as he felt inclined to do. Even so, he seemed to have finished his meal in a couple of minutes, and occupied himself in chasing the few crumbs from the bread round the plate, picking them up with a wet fingertip and crunching them with delight. He drank the rest of his wine, which, though coarse, was excellent, and then drank off the water from the pitcher the old man had unobtrusively left for him. As if he had been watching the performance, the proprietor reappeared, asking if Hales wanted coffee. Hales found that he wanted a cup of coffee more than he had ever wanted anything in the world.

"It's only the Krauts' ersatz shit", said the old man apologetically. It's all we can get." Hales nodded his understanding. "You haven't got any cigarettes, I suppose?" he added tentatively. Greatly to his surprise the old man grinned. "Oh, yes," he said wheezily. "I'll bring you some." He disappeared again.

When he returned he brought a little cup half full of dark liquid that steamed most appetisingly, and smelled more or less like coffee. Beside it he laid a paper packet of Gauloise cigarettes. Hales broke the packet open and shook out one of the rank, loosely-packed cigarettes, noticing that it had the dull yellow *mais* paper. He groped in his overalls for a match, but had to slip his hand through the gusset inside the pocket to feel in the pocket of his uniform jacket. He could feel the old man's eyes on him as he did so. However, nothing was said until he had got his cigarette lit. He drew the first drag down gratefully — and immediately had to take the cigarette out of his mouth to give way to a paroxysm of coughing as the rank, bitter smoke hit his lungs.

He coughed until his eyes were streaming, but eventually got it under control, and by dint of smoking it very carefully was able to enjoy the remainder of his cigarette. The old man had by this time seated himself quietly in the chair across from Hales. He watched in an amicable silence while Hales finished his smoke, and courteously went and refilled the water when Hales coughed again. Only when Hales had sat back and stretched himself from sheer delight at the small pleasures of a semi-full belly and a smoke did the old man speak.

"There's been a lot of talk about a prisoner of war escaping," he said delicately. Hales stiffened in mid-stretch, then came fast out of it and sat hunched on his chair, almost like a coiled spring in his sudden wary anxiety. He eyed the old man closely, wondering whether to leap for the door and bowl the man over as he went. The old man clearly read his intentions, for he held up one hand, palm outwards in the universal sign for peace.

"It's all right," he said in a murmur. "I'm no collaborator." He paused as he said it, and Hales thought for a moment that he was actually going to spit on his spotless floor. He refrained, but his feelings could not have been clearer. Hales relaxed a little. "No, we're French here," went on the old man. "And we heard a lot about this man, an English air-force man, apparently. It seems he and some others got off one of the prison trains in the yard up yonder..." he gestured vaguely to the east. "The others were all picked up in no time, before they got out of the railway yards, but this one, he got away. Led the Krauts a merry dance, too, by all accounts. We get the night shift from Peugeot's in here when they come off," he added by way of explanation. "Apparently this prisoner got spotted by a Boche patrol, and they chased him halfway round the factory. Ran 'em ragged, it seems." He laughed, an old man's laugh, somewhere between a wheeze and a cackle. "Of course, I don't know whether you're interested in our local gossip... but it struck me that this chap'll need help..."

"Oh... what... er... what sort of help would he be looking for?" asked Hales cautiously.

"Oh, well," the old man mooted, blowing through his moustaches, "he'll want to be put in contact with the local Resistance, don't you think...?"

For some minutes they fenced their way delicately round the subject, both too cautious and cagey to be first to come out plainly with what was in both their minds. Hales gave in first. "Do you know anyone in the Resistance?" he asked abruptly.

The old man peered hard at him in silence for several long moments. Then, without warning, he reached down and twitched Hales's denim overalls aside, revealing the cool airforce blue uniform jacket beneath. "You'd better come with me," he said, speaking even more softly than before. He waited while Hales came out from behind his table, then led him behind the counter and into the main part of the building at the rear. They passed through a small living room impossibly over-furnished with knick-knacks and ornaments and into a narrow back corridor that ended in a 180-degree turn into an even narrower staircase. There was a tiny entrance-way, and a back door that appeared to lead into a small back yard. The man led Hales to the foot of the stairs and stood aside to let him pass, gesturing to the stairs as he did so. "Wait here," he said, urgently. "I'll be back in two shakes." He turned away without waiting to see whether Hales obeyed his instructions, and disappeared into another room at the other end of the short corridor. Hales watched him disappear, then sat down on the bottom stair but one, slewing himself half sideways to squeeze himself in on the ridiculously narrow space between the wall and the spindly, frail-looking banister, and waited to see what his fate was to be.

After a moment he heard voices below, one of them female, followed by footsteps, then a further murmur of talk and a sound of bustling about, doors opening and closing, and finally a profound silence. It was broken by the distinctive shuffling tread of the old man, who reappeared, hurrying as best his age and his arthritis permitted and carrying what looked like several old coats over his arm. "Come on," he hissed, beckoning to Hales and opening the back door. Hales followed him out into a small, square yard. There was an ancient mangle, a stack of crates that had held bottles, and an astonishing quantity and variety of the everyday debris of an inn. The man led him quickly across the yard, which Hales crossed in four rapid strides. At the far side there was a solidly constructed brick shed. The proprietor produced an enormous bunch of keys from the pocket of his ancient grey flannel trousers, selected one and unlocked a heavily creosoted wooden door. Hales followed him into the darkness within.

A feeble electric light went on. In its dingy glow Hales saw that the shed was crammed from wall to wall and from the sanded concrete floor to the sloping asbestos roof with piles of every imaginable kind of junk. Tottering piles of mouldering newspapers and magazines stood several feet high. On top of one of them a rusty parrot cage stood in permanent and drunken danger of falling off. Another pile was topped still more riskily by an elderly wireless set, and yet another by a huge fish tank with a great crack disfiguring the front glass. He glanced round curiously, and saw an ancient gramophone with an enormous trumpet, a horse collar complete with a set of hames and a huge knotted tangle of tack. There were rickety garden chairs and a giant sunshade; piles of flower pots and odd gardening tools, several old paintings in heavy Victorian gilded frames from which the gilt had long worn off and been replaced by mildew, boxes of dog-eared books. A rusty magic lantern was perched on what looked to Hales's townsman's eye like a chaff-cutting machine. Most surrealistically of all, a human skeleton, held together by piano wire, dangled from a hook high up on the rear wall. There was a powerful musty odour of decaying paper, which fought for supremacy with a pungent hint of the presence of mice.

The old man had not waited for Hales to exhaust his amazement. He squeezed his way between the stacks of seed boxes and other heavier junk that stood towards the back of the shed, and disappeared from sight. Hales followed him hurriedly, and found him heaving on a heavy wooden trapdoor in the concrete floor. "You can stay down here till nightfall," he said as he straightened up. Hales peered down the hole revealed by the lifting of the door, and saw a flight of stone steps leading down into some form of cellar. "Down you go, quickly," urged the man. Hales turned and backed gingerly down the steps. Another light went on, as dim and inadequate as the one in the shed above, as he descended.

There were only seven steps, but they were extraordinarily deep, almost a foot for each riser, and with perilously narrow treads. The cellar beneath was tiny, and Hales was glad that he was of no more than average height: had he been a full six feet he would have had to stoop slightly to avoid hitting his head on the ceiling. It was comparatively bare, with only a couple of heavy wooden chests pushed back against the walls, and Hales could see straightaway that it was at least dry and reasonably sanitary. To his relief, he could see no immediately obvious signs of rats. It was also surprisingly warm, with none of the usual dank, bone-piercing chill of cellars. "Wait there," called down the old man. Hales waited standing on the stairs, halfway out of the trap door in the shed floor. A minute or two later there were puffing noises and the man returned, squeezing his way between the junk and lugging with him a great truss of straw.

"Here," he said, "take this down there. Spread it on the floor. It'll stop the cold from coming up through the concrete and giving you a chill." He motioned for Hales to move out of the way, and dropped the straw down the trap. He followed it with the old coats he had brought from the café. "Wrap yourself in these if you get cold," he said. "I'm sorry, it's all we have... but I think you should be comfortable enough. I'll bring you some food and water, to keep you going, and a litre of wine, eh?" He grinned conspiratorially at Hales, who understood just what the little old man was risking in all this, and was grateful enough merely for being helped at all. He gave the man a big smile, and thanked him effusively. The man waved him into silence. "It's nothing," he said dismissively. "You were fighting the Krauts..." Hales noticed once again the use of the word *schleu*. "It's our duty to do whatever we can to help, and that's all there is to it. Now, you get yourself as comfortable as you can with that straw and the blankets, and I'll get you some things. Would you like something to read? You're going to have to stay there all day, and maybe longer. I'll have to go and see some people this afternoon."

"I'd be very glad of a book, if you could leave the light on," Hales admitted, then obeyed his orders and descended once more to spread his bed of straw and shake out the elderly coats. There were also, he found gratefully, a couple of blankets, as the man had said. They were old and smelled musty, but they were very thick, and large enough for him to be able to wrap himself right round in them if necessary. It's not much, the old man had said. By comparison with anything I've had lately, Hales thought to himself, this is going to be like the Savoy Hotel. He spread the blankets on top of the straw and lay down on them to see how they felt. The straw was plentiful, and apart from one awkward spot on the point of his hip he found himself surprisingly comfortable. He cast his mind back over the last few days, wondering when he had last spent a truly comfortable night in a bed fit for a human being. It was, he realised, the night before his final mission in the *Betelgeuse*. It seemed like another lifetime, separated from this one by several more, all of them unpleasant.

His ruminations were interrupted by the return of his benefactor, who peered down through the trap and hissed to him to come up. "Some wine for you," he said, thrusting a large china jug into Hales's hands. Hales took it carefully down and set it on the floor a safe distance from his makeshift bed, where he could not upset it if he stirred or flailed in his sleep, then went back up. He took also a similar jug of cold water, disposed of that equally carefully, then went back for a glass and a battered, dirty copy of *Madame Bovary*. He tried to express his immense gratitude, but the old man would have none of it, insisting that he was only "doing his bit". "I'll bring you something to eat a bit later," he said. "You rest now. I'll be off to talk to some people about you this afternoon, and I'll come and tell you what they say later on. There's a light switch down there. You'll see it at the bottom of the stairs. The other one's here." He showed Hales the switch, set in the wall just below the trapdoor. "Now I should try and get some sleep if I were you."

"I shall", Hales promised gratefully.

The old man turned and started to shuffle out of the shed, then turned back before Hales had had time to lower the trapdoor. He bent and thrust his head through the opening, and gestured towards the far corner of the cellar. Hales slewed round dangerously on the ridiculously narrow stair, and saw that there was a drain in the corner, where the floor sloped slightly down from all sides to a simple round hole in the concrete, innocent of any kind of grating. *"Pisser"*, said the old man laconically, with a faint twinkle of a grin in his faded blue eyes. "If you want the other thing, well..." And he gestured once more to the drain, then at the straw. Hales, who was of a fastidious nature, grimaced, and was immediately assailed by a burning need to do precisely what his mind had told him he would not do at any cost. He fought the feeling for a few difficult moments, realising that it was all auto-suggestion, then burst suddenly into a short bark of laughter. The old man's twinkle broadened into a proper grin, which lit up his old, tired face and made him look momentarily a lot younger. Then he turned and was gone.

Hales lowered the trap door awkwardly, dropped back to floor level and once more settled himself on the piled straw. He found that he was going to need the blankets, so he wrapped them loosely round himself, drew the old coats over the whole lot, and settled, truly comfortable and warm enough for the first time in what seemed like forever, and opened the paperback book. He was sound asleep before he had read half of the first page.

VII

HE slept, woke, wondering for a few desperate moments where he was. Ate ravenously from the slender provisions the café keeper had left him. Used the drain in the corner. Slept again, and awoke to find the old man shaking him vigorously. He wondered muzzily why the light in his cellar seemed twice as bright as it had before. Urged on frantically by the old man, he shook his stiff limbs into motion and went hurriedly up the concrete steps. He realised about the light as he pushed his head blearily through the hole left by the trap door. It was brighter because it was now pitch dark outside. He let the old man scramble ahead of him and lead the way across the cluttered little shed, while the cold air in the yard outside smote his reeling senses like a douche of icy water. He glanced up at the night sky as they hurried as best they could across the yard, and saw an astonishing profusion of stars: more by far than he had ever been aware of before. The thought traced its way across his mind, slowly enough for him to register its passing, that for perhaps the first time he could see why the galaxy was called the milky way. But there was no time to follow up the thought. The old man was already tugging urgently at him.

"Come on, come on. They're here for you. They're here."

His mind started functioning again with a jolt as he remembered, and suddenly started racing ahead. His stomach turned slow convulsions as his imagination began playing over all the unformulated dangers that might lie before him that night. He swallowed desperately, fighting against the rising of his gorge, and plunged on after the old man.

They skirted round the building, looming black against the astonishingly bright starlit sky, and followed a narrow flagged path round its bulk. In the street outside was an ancient car, soft-topped, flimsy looking and belching clouds of smoke. But its engine was running quietly enough, Hales noticed. He squinted at it as the two of them dashed across the rough stone setts of the footway, and thought he could see one dim shape within.

"This is Henri. Go with him and do as he says," wheezed the old man, winded from running. He pulled open the nearside door of the old car. Inside, as he was already scrambling in, Hales saw a short, squat man with a seamed but clean-shaven face, wearing a navy-blue beret and smoking a caporal cigarette. "Good luck, Monsieur," whispered the old man. Hales felt him press something soft into his hand, then the door was closed silently but firmly on him. They were already in motion while he peered closely to see what the old man had given him. It was a soft packet of Gauloises. For some reason he found himself almost unbearably touched by the small gesture, puny though it was, and he felt his heart clench within him, and his eyes filled momentarily with tears.

He didn't have much time to spare for sentimentalising, however. The squat man was hauling the old car round right-angled corners of the narrow streets of the little town at such a pace that it was all he could do to keep himself from being thrown about all over the front seat. He fought his way into a defensive posture, jamming himself hard up against the door and the cracked, creaking blue leather of the bench seat, and tried to get a fingernail under the wrapper of the packet of cigarettes.

A hand came out from the driver's seat, and he felt a cigarette being slipped into his hand. "Better not try to open it now," came a low voice. A large cigarette lighter of ancient design followed the voice. He lit the digarette, drew on it deeply and thankfully and returned the lighter, squinting in the darkness of the car to try to get a look at his companion. "Thanks," he said. "Thanks very much. Where are we..."

"Don't talk now," said the driver, swinging the car dangerously round another corner. The voice was crisp and distinctly commanding. Hales had enough sense to obey it, and resumed trying to get a glimpse of the man in the occasional fleeting moments when the starlight entered the car and rested on his face. Within minutes, however, the journey was over. The car came abruptly to a stop in yet another narrow, unlit side street. Hales saw that it was even darker than most of the streets through which they had come, and the houses, though still small, were slightly less mean than those in the earlier part of the brief journey. They also boasted small front gardens. He supposed that they were in an outlying suburb. The driver reached across him and shoved the door open for him. "You get out here," he said in a low voice. "Wait in the garden of this house, the nearest one. Get down out of sight, and *don't* show yourself, eh? Someone'll be along for you any time. Good luck, friend." Even as the final words reached Hales, who was already stumbling across the footway towards the garden the driver had indicated, the car was in motion, continuing on in its previous direction. Hales saw the door slam to as the vehicle picked up speed. Seconds later it had vanished round a bend in the street.

Feeling more alone than he had ever felt, he thought, in his life, Hales felt his way along a low, dusty hedge that made a rough demarcation between the street and the tiny garden. His feverishly groping hands found a wooden gate, and after a moment of panic when he couldn't find a catch of any kind he found that too. Remembering the essential need for silence, he felt it over carefully, found out how the simple mechanism worked, opened it and slipped through into the garden.

It was a simple square patch of threadbare lawn, with two tiny flower beds in the middle. He closed the gate again gingerly, went onto the lawn, and settled himself down with his back against the hedge to wait. The whole of the garden and the street beyond was in the deep shadow of the house, and it was so dark that he could see nothing of his own body. That, at least, afforded him some small comfort. He was aware, at some level, that he was feeling very frightened — more frightened, he thought, than he had ever felt or imagined he would ever feel; but he was also aware, at a level much closer to ordinary consciousness, of a tremendous, surging excitement. There was nothing in his experience with which he could compare it: not even anything on missions had brought his adrenalin into such a sudden, dam-bursting rip tide as this. He sat hunched into the little garden hedge, simply feeling his own pounding pulse, and observing the experience. He suspected it was not one he might feel often again, and thought vaguely that it would probably be a good thing if he did not. For the moment, however, as he realised with a slight start, he was almost enjoying the sensation.

He could not have said afterwards how long he sat there in the shadow waiting for his next unknown rescuer. Probably it was less than five minutes, but in his state of excitement it could have been half an hour. In the end, however, his ears picked up the sound of a vehicle approaching. It was the first sound he had heard since the other car had disappeared from sight up the street, and he traced its approach through the small streets close by. He heard it turn into the street where he lay up, and a moment later it drew quietly to a halt right behind him. There was no sound of a door opening or closing, nor of footsteps, but he felt, rather than saw, a figure appear through the gate. It loomed over him, and he had once more to fight down a feeling of profound fear, even though he knew, as far as he could know anything, that the unknown person was there to help him and, with luck, deliver him to safety.

The figure stooped over him, nothing more than a patch of deeper blackness against the blackness of the deep shadow in the garden, and he felt a hand on his shoulder. "Monsieur? Come," hissed a voice, and he was disconcerted to hear that it was female, and sounded also to be very young. He hadn't expected to be helped by girls, though the thought was instantly blotted out by the realisation that for the French, under occupation, it was everybody's war, and that there was no earthly reason why it shouldn't be a woman, of any age, who took a part. "Come *on*", hissed the voice again, the urgency coming through clearly despite the fact that it was almost inaudible.

He scrambled to his feet and allowed himself to be led by the cuff of his overalls back to the gate, which she had left open. It was gently closed behind them, and he was run across the narrow pavement and into another vehicle. This one was much larger and newer, and seemed to be some sort of delivery van. He slid into the passenger seat, and smelled a powerful odour of onions and other vegetables. The door was eased shut on him, and a moment later the girl got in at the other side. He caught a brief glimpse of her after a moment, when she lit a cigarette. She was about nineteen, thin, with a triangular, foxy face covered in freckles, a sharp chin, and thin, mousy coloured hair drawn back in a pony-tail. He got a fleeting glimpse of her every few moments as she drew on her cigarette, and began to make up a picture of her: thin, pale lips, no make-up there or elsewhere, as far as he could see; a strong, straight nose, and, he was certain, a pair of small, humorous eyes, grey or blue he thought, though he never had a chance to find out, beneath straight, unplucked eyebrows.

"You're... er... you're taking a terrible risk, aren't you?" he said. Even as he said it he realised how fatuous it sounded. "Sorry," he burbled on. "I didn't mean it how it sounded. But.. well... I mean..." He tailed off, ridiculously, in confusion.

"Because I'm a girl?" she said, making it more of a statement than a question. "Of course I'm taking a risk. So does everybody. Except the ones who work for *les schleu*," she added thoughtfully. There was a world of contempt in the last word. He thought she was going to relapse into silence. Then she spoke again, her voice low but hard, with a steely tang of emotion in it. Thinking about her afterwards, as he did often, Hales thought he identified it as mingled pain and ferocious, concentrated fury. "I've lost my brother and my fianceé. They took the real risks. I've got less to lose." The bleakness in her tone made him feel curiously small, insignificant and vaguely ashamed.

"I'm very sorry," he said, and the simplicity of it made it the right thing to say.

"You get back to England," she said, glancing over at him in the darkness. Her tone was audibly a shade warmer. She had heard the contrition in his own voice, he thought — and diagnosed it correctly. No one's fool whatsoever, he added to himself.

"You're an airman, aren't you?" she asked. "That's what they said you were."

"Yes. Bombers."

"You're a pilot?"

"Navigator. And bomb aimer."

"Drop one for me," she said. And then, after a short pause, "How many Boches have you killed?"

He thought about it, but had no answer. "I don't know," he eventually had to say. "There's no way of telling. Several hundred, I suppose." He'd never thought about it in this close-intimate way, and didn't want to. "How many have you killed?" he added, trying to turn it into a joke.

"Sixty-one," she said. "So far." There was really nothing to be said to that, and he concentrated on watching her as she threw the van rapidly round corners, though nowhere near as rapidly as the previous driver. He saw that the houses were now much larger and farther apart, and there were patches of rough open land here and there. He ventured a question. "Where are we headed?"

"I don't know," she said.

"You... you don't..." he left it unfinished.

"No," she went on. "Of course I don't. I only know the bit I've been assigned. I'll be dropping you in a moment. It's all a matter of cutting the risks down to a minimum. It means none of us has to have you for too long, or go too far from home — it's after curfew, don't forget — and so none of us knows anything if we get caught. If the Gestapo question me, all I know is that I was ordered to pick you up where I did, and to drop you where I'm going to. I don't know who else is involved, or anything else about you. Not," she added thoughtfully, "that the Gestapo'd need more than that."

He didn't like to think too far along *that* line, and said so. She, however, had clearly thought about it to a conclusion, to her own satisfaction. "I'd probably be all right," she said, sounding as if it didn't matter much to her one way or the other. "I'd say I'd been with my boyfriend, and there's someone permanently ready to confirm that story if he's ever questioned. It might not work, in which case it would be unpleasant. But... well, it's war, isn't it?" Once again he found himself reflecting that this was real war, war to the death, involving everyone, in a way that the people back home could not begin to understand, or even to conceive of. He tried to imagine some of the more portly and consequential people of his acquaintance talking in these matter-of-fact tones of being questioned by the Gestapo, and not believed, as being 'unpleasant' — and found that he wasn't equal to it. It required more imagination than he possessed.

As he was thinking on this track the girl slowed down, and he could see her peering anxiously through first the windscreen and then the side window, evidently looking for some landmark. After only a few seconds of this she saw what she was looking for, and slowed still further, to a crawl. Then she turned sharply off the road between two large houses, and halted with the nose of the vehicle almost buried in a clump of thick gorse bushes. "You get out here," she said. "If you work your way round this patch of gorse you'll find there's a clearing in the middle. Wait in it, and there'll be someone to pick you up in a few minutes. They'll get you into Switzerland, if anybody can. Good luck, Monsieur. Don't forget to drop that bomb for me. For my brother and my fiancé."

"I won't forget," Hales said humbly, thanking her profusely. She waved him into silence. "It's war," she said simply. She drew the van door closed without making a sound, reversed onto the road, and disappeared back the way they had come. Hales stood breathing the night air, looking up at the stars, then, admonishing himself, turned to the patch of gorse bushes, and started looking for a way in to the clearing. Having found it at the cost of a few gashes from the wicked spines, he lay on his side in the long grass of the little glade, his back propped against a silver birch sapling, and waited to see what, or who, happened next.

He heard the car coming while it was still some distance away, and crawled out from his lair to meet it, peering cautiously from the cover of the nearest gorse bush to the road. It came slowly along the road he had recently travelled with the girl, looking strangely menacing with its lights out. It turned off the road as it came level with Hales's hide-out, without any hesitation, suggesting that unlike the girl the driver knew exactly where he was looking for.

Like the one that had picked him up at the café for the first brief leg of his journey, this car was an old model, but was by far the fastest of the three vehicles in which he had ridden, a rakish Citroen saloon. A figure spilled out of the front passenger door before the car was at a standstill, and as Hales rose to his feet the figure came fast towards him in a half-crouch. "Monsieur l'Anglais?" came a soft call. Hales advanced quickly to meet the man. Once again his arm was taken and he suffered himself to be half led, half hustled up to, and into the car.

This time there was another difference. Instead of a solitary driver, this car was almost crammed with people. The driver was an oldish man, in his sixties. The passenger who had come to fetch him, by contrast, could have been no more than seventeen or eighteen. In the back was a third man of indeterminate age somewhere beyween the two. Hales's throat constricted momentarily in surprise as he saw that the two who were not driving were both cuddling gleaming, deadly-looking black machine guns. He had little time to think about it. The moment he had been thrust into the back seat the car was moving off, picking up speed rapidly as it turned back the way it, and Hales before it, had come. It followed the road they had travelled before only for a few hundred yards, however, then turned off into a *route départmentale* that wound and twisted a switchback course up a steep scrub-covered hill away from the town — the direction, as far as Hales could judge, that led to Switzerland.

His companion in the back noticed his eyes returning at frequent intervals to the evil-looking sub-machine gun. Hales saw his face crease in a grim smile. "No guns up to now, eh, English?" he said with the beginnings of a throaty chuckle. Hales gave him a pale sketch of a grin in return. "No need to take unnecessary risks," the man said. "They didn't need 'em, whoever they were."

"We do," contributed the elderly driver over his shoulder, without taking his eyes off the road as the car jolted and bounced its way up the steep incline. "*They* weren't likely to run into road blocks or the Gestapo. *We* are. Oh, shit!"

He had spoken only too prophetically. As the car slewed fast round a bend they all saw, concealed round the next twist in the road, a full-scale road block — a number of vehicles with pencil-slit headlights. The driver braked fast but expertly, bringing the car down from its dangerously high speed to a halt in quick time without any screech of brakes, without any skidding and accompanying squeal of tyres on the dusty road surface, without, in fact, any sound at all. He performed a lightning three-point turn by making use of the wide scrubby verges on both sides of the road, and immediately cut the engine as the car began to freewheel down the steep gradient. "Easy, nice and easy," muttered the driver. "We'll see if they've seen us before we do anything dramatic."

"We were lucky," said the man with Hales in the back. "If they'd been careful and put their block behind the high bit of the hedge, we'd never have seen it."

"We weren't meant to see it," said the youth in the front, speaking for the first time since he had come to find Hales in his gorse bush.

"Of course we weren't," said the driver. "Luckily for us the *schleu* make more fuck-ups than their reputation admits..."

"They saw us," remarked the man in the back, who was twisted round in his seat, constantly scanning the road behind them through the small rear window.

"Shit," said the driver mildly, starting the engine as he did so. The car suddenly burst into life and leapt forward. As it did so Hales slewed in his seat and was in time to see something some hundreds of yards behind similarly leap forward. "There's at least two vehicles," he reported, squinting in a desperate effort to see clearly. He thought he could see one jeep-like vehicle, and one low-slung staff car.

"Right," said the driver imperturbably. "We'll see 'em off if we can get into the side streets. Sorry about this, English," he went on, as if he was apologising for the brief postponement of a casual appointment for a drink in a favourite bar. "We'll have to take you back to square one." Hales mumbled something reassuring, and continued squinting through the back window. The car continued its hazardous, bouncing, rocketing course down the hillside. But the two pursuing vehicles were, Hales could now see quite clearly, slowly but consistently gaining on them. He reported the fact. "Steady," said the driver. His voice was steady and comforting.

They hit the road at the foot of the hill at about fifty miles an hour, and the driver had it steady and roaring at full throttle along towards Hales's gorse clump before Hales had even realised they had turned almost at right angles to do it. Before they reached the gorse, however, they switchbacked off the main road, and were suddenly back among the houses of the outskirts of the town. They plunged into the maze of residential streets at breakneck speed.

Even so they were not quite quick enough to throw off the pursuit. One of the following vehicles continued along the main road; but someone in the other, which unfortunately happened to be the fast-looking staff car, saw them, and it turned off after them and followed fast through the streets. The driver, who was evidently the commanding member of the group, began talking to Hales, after checking to make sure he understood the rapid flow of French. "I'm going to drop you, with Sylvain here" — he jerked his head sideways to indicate the boy in the front passenger seat — "to guide you. He'll take you to a safe house here in town. We'll give the Boche a bit of time to let the dust settle, then we'll have another go at getting you out." He paused. "We'll get you out next time, too. I'm just worried about this flow of information. They're one step ahead of us too often for my liking lately."

"You've been infiltrated?" asked Hales, suddenly fearful for such magnificently brave people, in his mind's eye suddenly seeing visions of them dying unspeakable deaths at the hands of the Gestapo torturers in some dank subterranean dungeon. "I don't know," muttered the driver, "but I fear so, yes. Still," he went on after a pause, "we'll find him. We're getting close, I think. Now then," he said briskly, changing back to businesslike arrangements. "I'm going to slow down to walking pace shortly, when we hit a small square. Sylvain and you'll jump out, he'll lead you to the safe house, while we lead them off, try to throw 'em off the scent, and stand 'em off if we have to."

Hales did his best to express his gratitude to his rescuers, but they were all too preoccupied with thoughts of what was to come. They squirted in and out of a series of complicated manoeuvres in the side streets, designed to throw the pursuing German vehicle off the scent for a few moments, and finally the car slammed to a halt in

81

a tiny square. The youth in the front was out before the car was still, and Hales was not far behind him. By the time they had tumbled out of the car and found their feet, the car was already vanishing fast out of the opposite side of the square in a snarl of exhaust and a brief scream of tyres.

Meanwhile Sylvain had already grabbed him by the arm, and was hurrying him forwards as fast as they could go, towards a small bridge spanning a narrow, oily canal running through the centre of the square. The sound of the pursuing vehicle was gathering volume as it roared closer and closer through the streets through which they had just come. And as they drew level with the bridge a patrol of German soldiers came doubling into the far side of the little square.

Sylvain saw them at the same moment. He seized Hales's arm and dragged him with a single prodigious jerk off the pavement, down onto the towpath that rose from beside the still black water of the canal to emerge into the road where they were passing. Hales flailed his arms to keep his balance as they flew down the steep muddy incline, just managed it, and the next second the two of them were running as fast as they could and still keep their footing on the squishy quagmire of the old towpath. Offering up a silent prayer that the patrol had not seen them at the same instant as they had seen the patrol, he gave himself up to haring along in the wake of the youth Sylvain, and concentrated wholly on not flying head first into the canal. In less than a quarter of a minute they were lost between the dilapidated rear walls of the myriad small factories and works beside the waterway.

After a few hundred yards Hales had to pause. He bent over double, thrusting his hands on his knees, and took in air in great gulps. Sylvain danced agitatedly up and down, looking anxiously back the way they had come. "Come *on*," he hissed fiercely. "If they saw us..." His voice trailed off in a sighing gulp. He grabbed Hales's shoulder and jolted him upright, at the same time spinning him round and pointing back along the towpath. Hales's heart sank. Round the last bend, running in a steady, mile-consuming, inexorable jog-trot, the German patrol appeared. There was a loud guttural yell of *"Halt!"* As Hales summoned up the last shreds of his will-power and started running behind Sylvain once more, the flat report of a rifle shot resonated along the natural echo chamber formed by the sunken canal. A moment later there was a 'ping' from somewhere much closer, high above them, and the whine of a ricocheting bullet. "Come *on!*" cried Sylvain once more. "Not far to go now. Only a few metres... come *on!*" Hales gritted his teeth, and careered after him as fast as his failing wind would allow him to go.

VIII

HALES could distinctly hear the sounds of pursuit getting louder, and as he followed Sylvain round a curve in the towpath he risked a quick glance over his shoulder. It confirmed his fears: the onrushing grey uniforms were visibly closer, less than a hundred yards behind them. There was another yell of *"Halt!"* and as he disappeared from their sight the sound of another shot came eddying along towards him.

He was flagging badly now, with every breath dragged into his labouring lungs a ferocious effort of will. He was almost doubled up by an agonising stitch, which sent a jagged skewer of pain through him with every movement, and brought with it an almost unbearable need to double up. As he staggered round the turn a hand came out and seized his elbow, and Sylvain hustled him along a few yards further. Just round the bend there was another little hump-backed bridge looming above them, and Hales dug deep for a last reserve of stamina to climb the steep ascent to the road above. But the guiding hand suddenly hauled him with surprising strength, not onwards along the rising towpath but aside, towards what at first sight seemed to be a vast, unbroken expanse of factory wall beside the towpath. At the last moment Hales saw a narrow slit of deeper darkness in the blackness of the wall. Next second they had plunged into the opening. Squeezing crabwise along a tiny alleyway behind his guide, he realised that they were in fact in the space left between two separate factory buildings. It was little more than a foot wide, and he found himself wondering, even as he plugged despairingly along, what could conceivably have possessed the builders to have left a space at all, instead of simply constructing the two buildings with a single party wall.

The thought vanished as fast as it had appeared, however, in the titanic effort it now required of him to pant along the alley. Fortunately for Hales they had little distance left to cover. The alleyway turned sharply to the right, taking them finally out of any possible sight of the Germans, and a few yards later it emerged into a road onto which the factory that had been on their right fronted. Sylvain was waiting for him as he came puffing out of the mouth of the alleyway. He held Hales back while he peered each way, and Hales had a blessed moment's respite when he was able to double up, easing the pain in his side and dragging down a single great shuddering breath. Then they were off again.

Once again Sylvain grabbed Hales's arm and pushed him off in a new direction, along the street, away from the canal bridge; a short way along its unlit length, they dived into yet another alleyway, this one a little wider, so that Hales was at least not obliged to run along half-twisted sideways. They scurried along this for perhaps fifty yards, then Sylvain again took him and steered him out into yet another of the apparently endless series of identical streets. This one was lined with small houses, and after only a few yards Hales felt himself being yanked off the pavement and down a path beside one of them.

The path brought them into a tiny square of back yard, and there, to Hales's inexpressible relief, Sylvain halted. He slipped behind the cover of the house, dragging Hales with him, and drew him close against his own body. "Shhhh! Silence!" he hissed, in a barely audible whisper. "Listen!" Hales found himself clamped so closely against him that he could feel Sylvain's heart, thumping from his exertion. Sylvain kept a strong, lean arm round him to keep him from moving, and Hales could feel the intensity of him as he listened, his entire body expressive of the straining of his ears. A few moments later they heard sounds drifting towards them from somewhere back the way they had come. *"Les schleu,"* hissed Sylvain in his ear. The sounds continued for a few seconds, then faded. "We've lost them," Sylvain breathed. "Let's go." Hales's heart sank at the thought of yet more running, but his fears were unfounded.

Sylvain unclamped his arm from Hales's chest and turned away. Hales saw that they had been huddling beside a small outside porch, a yard square, built of brick to waist level and glazed above, around the back door of the house. Sylvain dug in his pockets and produced a bunch of keys, selected one and unlocked the door into the tiny kiosk. The same key apparently did duty for the back door as well, and a few moments later Hales found himself standing inside the house. Sylvain slipped past him and locked the two doors, and they were able to be still and gulp in air at last. Hales, utterly done up, leaned his backside against the wall and folded himself double, clutching his abdomen to assuage the now ferocious stabbing pains of the stitch, and listened to the faint 'plop' of large drops of sweat dripping onto the floor from his hair, forehead and the tip of his nose.

When they had recovered their wind somewhat, Sylvain took Hales's hand and led him silently up a narrow flight of stairs in almost pitch darkness. Hales felt himself being propelled through a door, and pushed into sitting on what felt like a bed. He saw Sylvain silhouetted momentarily against the deep indigo squares of windows, which then disappeared to the accompaniment of a faint whirring sound. A moment later the light went on.

Hales sat for some moments with his eyes screwed up, totally blinded by the sudden flood of bright light — despite the fact that the bulb was of a low wattage, and cast deep shadows even in a small room. When his sight returned he looked about him, intensely curious to see where his adventures had brought him.

He was indeed seated on a bed, a rather sumptuous double one that struck Hales as oddly out of keeping with the small size and spare fittings of the room. There was a small bedside table with a lamp and a paperback book on it; a double wardrobe, another small table between the two windows — both of which, he now saw, were covered by heavy blackout curtains — with a hard chair neatly pushed beneath it. There were some writing things on the table. Otherwise, the room was bare. The carpet on the floor was worn but of obvious quality, and the walls were covered with paper in a heavy floral pattern. Sylvain stood watching Hales's reactions to the room, a faint smile on his face. "Well, we got rid of the Boche," he said at last. Hales looked up at him, and saw him clearly, in a good light, for the first time — and drew in a sharp breath, with a sudden shock of recognition that was closely akin to pain.

There, in all essentials, stood his ideal of perfection: Sylvain was a slim but firmly built young man, standing about five ten in his now unbooted feet. His hair was fair and abundant, fine enough to fly about his head and form a ragged halo when he moved about, yet thick enough to curl just a little and to keep its shape in a shaggy mop. It also dropped over his forehead in a heavy fringe, meeting his firm, slightly darker blond eyebrows. His eyes were a darkish blue, almost royal blue, and sparkled and twinkled in accordance with their owner's mood. His forehead, when he blew or brushed his hair aside and it could be seen, his nose and his chin were all firm and clean of line and his skin was fair and unblemished.

Hales stared at him for several long moments as he stood before him, and found himself instantly wondering what his genitals were like. Sylvain returned his stare with a faint smile and without embarrassment, or any other any visible emotion. After a few moments Hales closed his eyes and opened them again quickly, to make sure he wasn't dreaming. Satisfied that the vision of perfection was real and wasn't going to go away he gave himself away to a stare of frank admiration, in which dispassionate appreciation of the boy's comeliness was mingled with unconcealed and anything but dispassionate desire in equal parts.

Sylvain allowed the inspection to go on for several moments. Then he laughed and said "You need a shower. Come on, it's through here." He put out both hands to Hales, who took them and allowed himself to be hauled to his feet. "This way," said the boy, and led him from the room, along a couple of yards of passageway and into a tiny bathroom. There was no tub, simply a walk-in recess with a raised concrete rib to keep the water in and a heavy rubber curtain to draw across. Sylvain gestured at the cubicle and then at a large carved chest, covered in patterned material, which stood against the wall at the far side of the small room, beneath the blacked-out window.

Everything that had happened to him since the *Betelgeuse* had ploughed into the heaving green maelstrom of Biscay — the insensate boredom and racking privations of the interminable train journey, and then the adrenalin-jetting excitements and the ever present sense of squirming terror since his escape — had conspired to warp and blur his sense of what was normal until he no longer had any such conception; he had forgotten how badly he craved, and how desperately he needed, the simple luxury of a hot bath. Yet in the simple act of walking into a bathroom and seeing the means of making himself clean he had felt all his former sense of conventional humdrum normality come flooding back. In that instant he forgot his sudden access of yearning for Sylvain that had ignited so utterly unexpectedly in the bedroom, and every other feeling with it, except the sudden desire to stand, if possible for several hours, under a stream of hot water with large quantities of soap. Without any further urging from Sylvain he crossed to the chest and began stripping off his clothes. Sylvain slipped unnoticed from the room.

When he was standing naked under the shower and had worked out how to make it function, it was all he might have hoped, had he bothered to waste time hoping. He stood with his head back, allowing the spray of droplets to patter against his closed eyelids, the soft skin beneath his jaw, his throat, periodically twisting himself and stretching luxuriously to allow the blessed stream of warmth and cleansing to search out another hidden area of his skin and work its benevolent wonders there. He swore a private oath as he soaped himself and luxuriated in the triple sybaritic pleasures of its delicate perfume, its soft feel against his rank, much-abused skin and its simple cleanness — that he would never again, as long as he lived, take the fact of a readily available bath for granted.

Once, for a moment, the sense of something a little out of place obtruded itself on his pleasure-taking: he found himself wondering where Sylvain might have procured soap of such quality. He would, he found himself thinking, have expected the ordinary French citizenry to be relying on coarse, gritty carbolic substances such as they had had to use at the RAF station. But the thought was as evanescent as the soap bubbles in which he was sheathed, and disappeared as quickly as it had come. Without realising he was doing it, Hales started humming to himself, and the humming soon gave way to singing, until before long he was singing lustily: 'Bye, Bye, Blackbird', 'A Nightingale Sang', 'The White Cliffs of Dover', and, somewhat surrealistically, 'God Save the King'. He was halfway through 'Do Ye Ken John Peel?' when the shower curtain was drawn back, rattling on its big brass rings, and someone stepped softly into the shower cubicle behind him. "I was going to wait," said Sylvain softly in his ear, "but you looked as if you were going to be there all day, so I decided to come anyway."

Hales felt two arms go round him from behind, and at the same moment felt the firmness of a strongly erect penis pressing into the skin of his lower back. He felt himself go hot and cold in rapid succession, and tingled all over. All this happened in the instant of turning slowly round in the loosely prisoning arms. The sparkling royal-blue eyes were sparkling on overtime through the heavy tendrils of wet fair hair. The lips of the generous mouth were curved in a faintly ironic smile, which broadened as Hales turned round, to expose a row of regular white teeth. Sylvain flicked the tip of his tongue over the teeth, then curled it sensuously up over his upper lip. "You've got the soap," Sylvain said. rubbing himself slowly against Hales's stomach. "So soap me." Hales obeyed, wondering what he had done to earn this answer to his unspoken yearnings in the bedroom.

He rubbed the soap over the whole of Sylvain's body, leaving him covered with a fleece of bubbles. Finally, saving the best for last, he rubbed the tablet furiously to make a handful of lather, and began a slow, feather-light massage of the large, swollen penis. But

Sylvain gently pushed his hand away. "Not like that," he said. "Not here. I shan't be able to hold it, and it'll be a waste." Hales felt a mighty wave of feeling surge through himself at that. It throbbed through his own distended penis, prickled its way up his spine; the tiny hairs on the nape of his neck stood on end in miniature regiments, and he felt slightly sick, all in the same fraction of a second. All manner of hot and cold flushes and throbbings started up elsewhere in his body at the same time.

He shifted in Sylvain's arms, which had remained loosely draped round his shoulders throughout, and put his own round the boy's neck. "How did you know... about me?" he ventured.

Sylvain laughed, a merry, bubbling chuckle of a laugh. "You made it pretty plain," he said, "the way you were looking at me in the bedroom just now. I thought you wanted to eat me alive."

"I shouldn't mind, at that," murmured Hales, taking a proper firm hold on him and working his pelvis softly against Sylvain's. "All right," said Sylvain simply, disengaging himself. He completed washing himself swiftly and stepped out of the shower, seized a towel and began rubbing himself dry in long, hard strokes. "Come on," he said gaily. "You can get back under the shower later." Hales followed him. He had forgotten that he was still an escaping prisoner, and far from out of the wood. He had forgotten the Germans, forgotten danger, forgotten even the war, the colossal, brooding shadow that had loomed over every thought and feeling for the last three and a half years. He slipped into the bedroom. Sylvain was lying on his back on the bed, stroking himself gently up and down, and looking up at Hales with his tangled hair pushed back to show the smile of naked invitation in his eyes. Hales lay down beside him, taking care not to bump against him, and put his arms out. Their lips met in a long, slow kiss. After a while Sylvain twisted in the hard grasp of his arms. He slid a hand beneath the pillow and brought it out holding a small box, which he proffered to Hales. "Cream," he said. "You first."

* * *

They made love all night and most of the day that followed. There was a brief interval just before noon, when Sylvain had slipped gracefully into his clothes and gone out, returning with a bag of onions, a few carrots and, to Hales's surprise, a small quantity of good mutton. He had busied himself in the kitchen downstairs, from which very shortly a wonderful aroma summoned Hales from a dreamy semi-doze. He realised that he had not smelled cooking like that since his final mission, or, he thought, a good while before, and he went flying downstairs to see what could be producing it.

Sylvain had worked some small culinary miracle, he found, with the scanty resources he had managed to procure, and when he summoned Hales to sit at the small kitchen table and eat the stew he had put together Hales ate it ravenously. Fighting simultaneous urges to lick his plate and to burst into tears, he declared it the finest meal he had ever eaten. Sylvain focussed a long, concentrated stare on him, a strange gaze of mingled fondness, a curious kind of sadness that Hales even in the overheated emotion of that moment found himself trying unsuccessfully to analyse, and something else, some wistful quality of regret, that he couldn't even identify. And then the look was gone, replaced by his usual insouciant grin, and the moment was gone with it, a small, fleeting incident compounded of almost nothing, yet one that was to return to haunt Hales long into the future. For the present, though, he dismissed it as Sylvain said, almost merrily, "If I'd had something a bit less mean to work with I could have really given you a feed. Still, we have to make do with what we can get these days."

Hales sat licking the last globule of thin gravy off his lower lip before it ran down his chin to be wasted, and rhapsodised about the meal again. Sylvain grinned and refused to take him seriously, preferring to pull his leg about *rosbifs* and their degraded palates from being forced to eat English cooking from infancy. When the meal had gone down, helped on its way by a couple of glasses of coarse but passable red wine , Hales wanted to sit and talk. He asked Sylvain a variety of questions, about his work, about his family, what he had done before the war, even tried to touch on the Resistance, but Sylvain would not let him settle on anything, flitting from topic to topic with some casual joke or simply shaking his head and becoming flighty and flirtatious. After a short spell of this kind of tennis they looked steadily into one another's eyes for a moment, and without a further word both turned and made their way to the stairs.

Back in the bedroom they fell on each other hungrily and repeated the performance of the morning. Afterwards they lay in each other's arms, savouring each other's presence and the easy-going, intimate silence that sometimes comes to soothe and comfort birds of passage who have got to know one another as lovers for a while. Eventually they drifted into a light sleep, curved to accommodate the angles of each other's body. Hales dreamed of men who pursued him relentlessly with dogs all day and flashlights all night, stretched him naked on a cold metal table in a dungeon for questioning, and beat his flesh with thin metal rods. He woke to hear the echoes of his own scream dying away; but it was only in his imagination. Sylvain lay curled up trustingly in his loose embrace, his fair hair spread over the pillow in a halo, his breath cool against Hales's cheek, sleeping like a little boy. Comforted and reassured, Hales slipped back into the cradling arms of sleep.

*　*　*

"I've had my instructions," said Sylvain late that evening as they ate a light supper. "I'm to take you to a café and leave you. You'll be picked up there and they'll try for the frontier again. Don't worry," he added sympathetically, seeing the unease grow instantly in Hales's eyes. "They'll make it. If anyone can get you across the border these boys can. They've done it often enough. Now come upstairs and give me something to remember you by." Two hours later they slipped out of the house, flitting like darker shadows in the moonless night round to the front, where Sylvain had brought a small soft-topped car to wait for them. They got in and he drove it almost silently through the narrow streets. Hales recognised one or two landmarks from their adventures of the previous night, but was soon lost. After only a few minutes Sylvain drew up outside a tiny café-bar in one of the streets near the canal. "Go," he hissed quietly. Leaning across, he gave Hales a quick, unexpected kiss on the cheek. "I shan't forget you, Brian, *mon petit anglais*. Good luck." Hales stumbled out of the little car and it immediately slid away from the kerb and within seconds was out of sight round the nearest corner. Hales stood for a moment, staring after it into the profound darkness, wondering how his brief idyll had come to so abrupt an end. Then he pulled himself together, mentally shook himself in readiness to face the renewed dangers and excitements of normality, and pushed open the rickety door of the café.

He seated himself in a dingy corner and, after a long wait, was served a cup of unpleasant ersatz coffee by an unsmiling, unspeaking woman. "Wait here," was the only sentence she uttered before disappearing through a door behind the counter, not to emerge again. Hales drank the bitter mess with a grimace of disgust, and waited as he was bidden. He tried to comfort himself with memories of the blissful moments under Sylvain's shower, and tried to imagine he could still smell the faint perfume of Sylvain's soap, though in fact it was submerged beyond hope of survival under the obliterating reek of his familiar greasy overalls. He had, however, helped himself, at their owner's invitation, to a pair of Sylvain's socks and, the most refined luxury of all, to a pair of his underpants. He had been surprised at their quality, and could feel them now, cool, soft and blessedly clean against his skin.

When he had been waiting almost half an hour the door was pushed quietly open. Hales, who had fallen into a semi-doze in his corner, roused at once and half rose from his raffia and cane chair — only to subside again with a small, stifled groan of dismay. Instead of the expected moustachio'd and leather-jacketed figures of the Resistance cell who were to escort him across the border into Switzerland and safety, the new arrivals were two troopers and a grey-haired officer in the grey uniforms of the German army.

Hales had not the ghost of a chance of escape. They were across the small, dingy room in a matter of seconds. Having first very efficiently patted him down to satisfy themselves that he was not carrying any sort of weapon, the two soldiers took up position several feet distant to guard against any sudden attack, their weapons trained rigidly on Hales. He saw that they even had their bayonets fixed. The officer came up to his table — and, to Hales's immense surprise, slid onto the chair across the table from him. His hand was on the butt of his Mauser service pistol, but he had not drawn it. He removed his cap and placed it with noticeable care on the table, brushing a hand across the surface first to ensure that he was not laying it in any puddles of spilt drinks. Then he gazed levelly across the table at Hales. He was a pleasant, ordinary-looking man of middle age, with a mildness about his grey eyes. They were also, Hales thought, very worldly eyes, and desperately tired ones. "Please take off the overalls," were the first words he said, not unkindly, after seating himself. Hales, puzzled but recognising that he had no choice but to obey, did so, not at all sorry to strip off the evil-smelling rags that had been his constant companions for what seemed like a very long time.

"Thank you," said the officer in the same pleasant, matter-of-fact tone. "You will kindly identify yourself." Hales rattled off his name, rank and service number just as they had been indoctrinated to do by endless repetition during basic training — 'as per the Geneva Convention', as it was invariably accompanied, world without end.

"I must ask you some questions," went on the officer, taking a packet of cigarettes from his jacket pocket. He offered Hales one, and he took it gratefully. It tasted unpleasant, but he smoked it down to within a quarter-inch of the end. So, he noticed, did the German. He waited courteously until Hales had stubbed out the last remnant of his cigarette, then rose, picking up his cap and putting it on his head as carefully as he had laid it on the table. "Now you will come with me to army headquarters for questioning," he said. Hales followed him, and the two soldiers fell in behind. As he passed throiugh the door Hales took a swift glance over his shoulder, looking for the surly proprietress of the café; but she was nowhere to be seen.

Outside he was bundled into a grey staff car, and a few minutes later they drew up in front of a large building in a central square with municipal building written all over it. The Germans hustled him unceremoniously up a broad sweep of steps, through a dusty hall, along a corridor smelling strongly of floor polish, and into a large office full of grey filing cabinets and littered with soldierly impedimenta. The officer seated himself behind a heavy, ornately carved desk that had once, Hales surmised, been the property of the local mayor, and drew a pad towards him. He waved the two soldiers away, and they withdrew. The officer waved a hand negligently at another chair across the desk from his own, and Hales, surprised, dropped into it.

The questioning was thorough but not relentless; the officer, in keeping with his behaviour throughout, courteous and even affable. Hales, who had been fearing gun butts and worse, even went so far as to relax a little; but he strove to preserve an air of aloof detachment, and to give no answers beyond the impersonal, parroted routine of his name, rank and number. After a while, however, he began to be beguiled by the easy-going kindness of the officer, who announced himself as Captain Schollmeyer, and unbent sufficiently to declare at one point: "You must be sick of hearing my name, rank and number, Captain Schollmeyer. But I assure you, I have nothing else to tell you. I haven't been spying, I've seen nothing, encountered no one, achieved nothing. I don't even know where I am."

"I don't doubt it," said Captain Schollmeyer wearily, pushing back the spectacles he had put on and rubbing his eyes. "My problem is what to do with you. Officially," he went on conversationally, "I'm supposed to hand over anyone we find in disguise to the Gestapo as a suspected spy..."

Hales felt a cold clutch of terror round his heart at *that*, but the captain was already speaking again. "But..." He lowered his voice, more, Hales thought, from instinct than anything else. "But I don't like doing that, ever, if I can help it, and I'd certainly rather not do it now. Still, I don't suppose those stinking old rags of overalls would count as a disguise," he mused, murmuring more to himself than to Hales.

After a good deal more of the same, Schollmeyer made his decision. "There's a train in this evening with prisoners bound for one of the camps," he muttered. And, suddenly brisk again, "Come on, up with you." Hales could see the relief in his face. Relief at having made his decision, Hales supposed; or possibly relief at having been able to find a way of dealing with his problem that did not involve the Gestapo. "Come," said the captain, rising to his feet and looking, Hales thought, wearier than ever, despite his apparent satisfaction at having come to his decision. He picked up one of several telephones on the desk and after a short wait spoke briefly and tersely into it in rapid German. A few moments later the same pair of troopers came in, and the party moved off at a rapid forced-march pace back through the corridor, back through the dusty, deserted hallway and out into the bitterly cold air. Two bored sentries at the top of the steps snapped to attention and threw up sharp salutes, which Schollmeyer returned even as he hurried past them and down to the staff car already waiting at the foot of the sweep.

They piled into the car once more and set off through the streets at a cracking rate. After a short drive, Hales began to realise that he was recognising parts of the town through which they were hurrying, and in the end, as the car slowed up and began threading its way through a great area of criss-crossing railway tracks, he saw with a strong sense of irony that they were back at none other than the large marshalling yard where he had first dropped from the cattle truck and begun his attempt at escape.

They bumped and jolted their way across the great yard, slewing this way and that as they crossed innumerable tracks, Schollmeyer swearing now and then as they had to jerk to a halt to let a shunting engine go rumbling fussily past with a row of wagons, until at last they reached a row of long trains standing side by side with locomotives blowing off steam and smoke at their heads. The car lurched to a halt for the last time, and Hales was ordered to get out. He did so, feeling acutely aware of the deadly edge on the wind that cut across the yards. He thought regretfully, almost fondly, of the extra layer of covering his oily overalls had afforded; but he had little time for such reflections before the two soldiers, at a rasped command from Schollmeyer, began prodding and jostling him forward towards one of the trains.

The party stumbled to a halt beneath the looming bulk of the rearmost wagon. Captain Schollmeyer rapped out another command and the two troopers swung themselves up on the frame of the truck, manhandled the heavy sliding door open and dropped back to the ground. Hales turned towards Captain Schollmeyer, and had just enough time to mutter a few words of brief but sincere thanks. Schollmeyer nodded brusquely, but made no reply in words, and before Hales could catch a glimpse of his face in the familiar glare from the nearby factories, he was half helped, half thrown, aloft and forwards, and found himself sprawling half in and half out of the truck. Helping hands came from all sides and dragged him inboard. Almost before he was fully inside the two German soldiers had sprung up one more and were slamming the door closed. It rumbled to on its oiled runners and shut with a booming clang. "Well, we weren't expecting company," said a voice in English, "but welcome all the same. It isn't much, but we like to call it home."

IX

HALES had caught up on a lot of much needed sleep over the past day or so, so he was able to get through the inevitable process of getting to know some of his new companions and giving an account of his adventures. The prisoners in his truck, who seemed virtually indistinguishable from the group with whom he had travelled previously, listened in silent fascination as he told his tale, suitably edited when he reached the part of it dealing with his stay with Sylvain. When he had finished he was slapped on the back, offered congratulation and commiseration in equal measures — and something he appreciated a great deal more, a couple of cigarettes — and allowed to rest. A precious fragment of floor space was found for him, a wisp of still more precious straw spread; they produced a serviceable heavy greatcoat, formerly the property of a prisoner who had died early in the journey, and he was left alone with his thoughts.

He smoked the cigarettes one after the other, then lay down as comfortably as his hip bone would let him, and gazed through the crack between two of the slats in the side of the wagon. At some point during the night he drifted into a light, uneasy doze. He was awakened when the train clanked and banged backwards and forwards, rattled over numerous sets of points, and got slowly under way. After what he estimated was about an hour's run they sat for what seemed like an eternity at some signals. When they at last moved off once more the regular rumbling of the wheels took on a hollow, drumming note that was new, and he could tell they were on a bridge. He tried to look out, but all was deep blackness. From the length of time they were on the sounding board of the bridge, however, he felt sure they must be crossing the Rhine. They were entering Germany: inside the Third Reich. At that moment of grim realisation Hales curled up as tightly as he could in his corner, and fled into the refuge of introspection.

With little else to think about, he turned to the question that had been worrying him ever since the German patrol had come quietly into the tiny café where he had been caught. Had he been betrayed, and if so, by whom? He knew he would almost certainly never know the answer to the question; but he could not keep it from occupying the forefront of his mind, try as he might to think of something, anything, else. He knew, when he thought about it rationally, that the patrol might very well have been carrying out routine activity when it entered the café. It might, indeed, have come in for a five minute respite from the dank, chilly streets over a cigarette and a cup of acorn coffee. But it had seemed somehow too neat, too convenient, too preordained. The Germans had manifested not an iota of surprise to find a British airman there — which ought, he thought, and he didn't think he was flattering himself by it, to have been a pretty fair capture. On the contrary, they had looked exactly how he would have expected them to look if they had been expecting to find him in the café. The more he thought about it and relived those few moments in his mind, the more certain he felt that they had known — all this quite apart from one of the Resistance members' expressed belief that they had a spy in their midst. He lay on the floor of the truck, feeling the steady 'lend us a bob, lend us a bob' rhythm lulling him into a semi-stuporous condition, somewhere halfway between sleep and wakefulness, and not at all unpleasant, and considered the evidence he had. And the more he thought about it, the more his suspicions came to rest on his partner in bliss of the previous twenty-odd hours, Sylvain.

The more he thought about it, the more he realised also that all such speculation was idle and, in every meaningful sense of the term, useless. He would never know the truth, he could never know it, because there were too many imponderables. If Sylvain was in the Germans' pay, why had he expended all the fearsome effort of the night before, escaping the patrol that had pursued them along the towpath of the dank little canal? Why had he not simply turned on Hales the moment the other Resistance members had whizzed out of sight, held him up, and handed him over to the patrol then? He could have saved himself — both of them, for that matter — a lot of pain about the rib-cage, and much stress, while achieving the same result as he had by betraying Hales into the hands of an identical German patrol twenty-four hours later.

Other small things came popping up to the surface of his consciousness: the high quality of Sylvain's soap, and of his socks and underpants: he had wondered, with a small nagging sense of uneasiness, how the boy had obtained such luxuries, but had dismissed it as paranoia brought on by the unrelieved sense of being hunted of the preceding few days. But how *would* an apparently undistinguished boy (except in looks, Hales acknowledged with a faintly guilty stirring of bodily pleasure) get hold of two of the very things that whole populations were doing without, unless by collaboration with the one group of people who quite easily could, and routinely did, have access to such items?

And what's *this*, answered counsel for the defence, if not rampant, galloping paranoia? If Sylvain was to stand condemned on the strength of some perfumed soap which at any time before 1940 would have been the veriest commonplace in any halfway decent *pharmacie* in France, and on a few pairs of underwear of which the same could be said, then who might 'scape whipping? And yet...

...and yet, one small part of his troubled mind insisted on repeating, there was this nagging feeling, not of certainty, admittedly, but of deep and undiminished suspicion, that his recapture had all been too easy.

He drifted in and out of the same uneasy sleep as the train pounded its noisy but slow way eastwards, and every time he came briefly back to the surface it was to hear one or other of the two disputing voices in his head pressing home its argument. And then, at last, as he awoke once more, to see the first streaks of grey luminescence in the eastern sky, his natural common sense reasserted itself, and the matter resolved itself in his mind, putting him out of his misery and permitting him the last small luxury of a deeper, undisturbed sleep as the train rumbled on the final hundred miles or so of its journey. The voices for the defence and the prosecution had talked themselves out, and from some dark recess of his mind, the last lurking haven of common sense and balance, a judge was giving his summing-up.

"What the fuck does it all matter?" the dry judicial tones asked him. "What's the truth? The truth is that you don't know, you can't know, therefore you never will know, but is even that the real truth of the matter? No, it isn't, and you know it. The real truth is that you don't even care what the truth is. All you really feel conscious of is being glad it's over and you're back on this train, freed from the necessity to think for yourself, freed from the unceasing, minute-by-minute, moment-by-moment necessity to keep yourself concealed, from the never knowing who is to be trusted and who is not. For you, the war is over... his mind skimmed, fast as light, back to Tubby Barrell — was it old Tub? — to someone, anyway, saying that in a mock German accent, in the wild moments as they fought the elements for control of the tiny dinghy after the old *Beetle Juice* had pancaked.

In that moment, in the dark confessional of his private thoughts, Hales admitted the truth to himself: if there was a traitor about, there was only one who mattered: he, Brian Hales, was convicted in *in camera* proceedings at the bar of his own private self-knowledge: guilty of being glad that for him the war was indeed over, and that he was as happy to spend the remainder of it as a prisoner as anywhere else. Somewhere safe.

It was, at any rate, a satisfaction to have sorted out what mattered from what didn't. He took a last look at the pastel colours of dawn seeping upwards into the fading indigo of the night sky like inks soaking into a blotter; drew a dead man's greatcoat more closely about him, curled up on his bit of straw and went to sleep.

He dreamed not of his young companion or his own miserable suspicions of him, not of the privations and hardships of the war, nor even of the alarms and excursions of the last few days. Instead, he found himself slipping down into a deep well of memory, back to the evening of the actor's party. That night, too, had been characterised by deceit and betrayal, the recording part of his mind whispered nastily into his ear; but it no longer had the power to hurt. He and Ronnie had been at an impasse anyway, and it had needed a decisive act on the part of one of them to bring it to an unmessy conclusion. The surgeon's knife: one of Ronnie's favourite expressions, he heard himself murmur in his dream; but only, as with so much with Ronnie, a form of words. It had had to be he, Brian Hales, who turned it into anything more. He saw himself once again, in a clarity that seemed to come from some kind of amber-coloured stage lighting, slipping away from the gathering with the glittering young fighter pilot on his arm, leaving Ronnie not even knowing he had gone...

* * *

The young pilot's name turned out to be Michael Ayres, which the indefatigable coiners of nicknames who were to be found everywhere in the RAF had corrupted, via 'Ayres and Graces' to 'Gracie', thus embodying a fond reference to Gracie Fields and at the same time a sly acknowledgement of his sexual practice, which he scarcely made even the most perfunctory efforts to conceal. "Listen, sweetie," he said without bothering to lower his voice as they walked past two policemen chatting on a street corner, "I'm going to be dead within months at the most, more likely in days. The life expectancy of fighter pilots is now something approximating to that of sub-alterns in the first show. If I can come to terms with that, with knowing my life expectancy and measuring it in hours, I'm not likely to come out in a fit of the vapours because I'm a naughty little queen who prefers boys' botties to women's parts, am I now?" He had beamed a ravishing smile at the two policemen, who had given up any pretence of being engrossed in their own conversation, and were listening in shamelessly.

To Hales's surprise, the two burly, grizzled policemen had smiled with unmistakable fondness right back at Ayres — responding, Hales took it, to something in him that was so elemental, so unaffectedly lovable, but mostly so rigorously and unanswerably honest that it could not be denied. He had felt something of that moving in himself, a sudden access of love, compounded of naked, unselfish admiration, desire to serve and... what was it? Respect, that was it. It had hit him with such force that he had almost staggered in his stride beneath its onslaught. "You know something, Mi... er, Gracie," he had said. "If you asked the Archbishop of Canterbury to go to bed with you, he'd say yes. He wouldn't be able to refuse you."

Ayres had grinned at him and blown him a kiss. "Can't say I've ever aspired to a bishop," he had said with a chuckle. "Did manage a Bishop's *son* once, though. Llandrindod Wells or some ghastly place in the back of beyond. Not that I knew he was the bishop's son until later on, of course. Just a pretty youth I'd chosen to fag for me. *He* said yes, all right", he added, smiling beatifically at some private memory of the occasion.

They had walked for hours that night, the conversation never rising above this level of flippancy because Ayres refused resolutely to allow it to do so. Hales had tried assiduously all evening to turn it into something po-faced and important, and his new friend had laughed at him unceasingly, until he had finally given up and gone along with the play and the banter. It had only been later, Hales had realised with a gloomy understanding of his own fatuity and inadequacy, that he had come to set a true value on the play and the glittering small talk. Later, and too late.

So the ill-assorted pair had strolled through the darkened streets, talking and falling silent, talking again. At one point the sirens had gone, but by common, tacit consent they had ignored them and continued walking, brushing aside the angry efforts of an elderly ARP warden to coax them into a shelter. At one point Ayres had turned to Hales and said "I hope I'm not being a dreadful disappointment to you. I mean, I imagine you wanted to come to bed with me..."

"I'm happy just to walk and talk," Hales had said. "Happy just to be with you," he had added in one of the very few contributions he had made to the conversation that had been at all felicitous — that had not, indeed, been fatuous.

"Good," said Ayres. "I mean, we'll go to bed all right, just a bit later. I just have to walk off this tiredness, you see, before my next tour."

Hales had halted in his tracks and turned to stare at him. "Your next... Why... When are you next...?" he had said, too surprised to stammer it out whole.

"On stand-by in two hours," Ayres had said.

"But... but you're not fit to... you're in no condition..."

"It's us or nobody goes up at all," said Ayres, with a brilliant sketch at a smile. "Somebody's got to go."

He had been scrambled three times later that morning, flying 'by the seat of his pants', as they said, but flying really on a potentially lethal cocktail of reflexes, adrenalin, benzedrine, alcohol, nicotine and sheer drummed-in familiarity and routine. Mercifully his squadron-leader had still had enough of his own senses about him to recognise how close to final collapse Ayres was. He had gone to see the wing commander about him, and Ayres had been peremptorily grounded when they got home from the third dog-fight, late that morning. He had dug deep and found a last shred of self-possession sufficient to enable him to drive his snarling little racing car home, then come up the stairs to his flat where he had left Hales, stumbling with the fatigue he had at last been able to release, and just had time to tell Hales the news before falling into an impenetrable slumber from which Hales could not rouse him for twenty-four hours.

When he had finally surfaced, Hales had been waiting for him. The moment he saw signs of returning consciousness he busied himself in the kitchen, preparing as appetising a breakfast as he could put together, and Ayres woke to a fragrant aroma of bacon and eggs. He had been unable to find a grapefruit, but he had by some oddity of chance managed to find a small melon, and served it up sprinkled with some ancient powdered ginger that he found lurking at the back of one of the kitchen cupboards. Ayres stared up at him for a moment, with blank unrecognition in his blue eyes. Then his memory clicked on, and he smiled: not the brilliant beam of the night before, a rictus donned as a mask to hide the weariness and exhaustion, but a real smile, altogether more human and friendly.

He had eaten the breakfast with appreciation, talking animatedly but without the forced brilliance of their forced march through the streets on the night they had met, while Hales had to give a sketchy account of the walk and what they had talked about. Ayres had been so close to the end of his tether that his memory of the evening had deserted him: it was as if their meeting at the party and everything that had followed it had taken place while he was in a coma.

He became greatly distressed when he understood that Hales had left a partner at the party to leave with him. "You must go to him," he said immediately.

"No," said Hales with equal force. "It was over anyway." And he had to give an account of his troubled relationship with Ronnie.

"He needs you," said Ayres.

"I don't need him, and I don't think he needs me," Hales replied. "He needs something, but it isn't me. Whatever it is, it isn't me. Whatever it is he needs, I can't give it to him. I haven't got it to give." Ayres looked at him doubtfully, but he had let it pass. "I shall have to get myself up again," he said with an abrupt change of subject. Hales looked at him in horror. "You can't be serious", he had protested. "You need six months on the ground, at least. You need that much just to pull yourself together. In fact, you need that long a holiday."

Ayres smiled at him, a sweet smile of mingled resignation, affection and gentle admonishment. "Brian, Brian," he chided, "you know better than that. How can I take a holiday when the others are all going up umpteen times a day risking their necks? Besides, if I don't go up again PDQ I shall never go up again at all, you know that. You do know, too: you're in the same line of business yourself, and you know very well that if you're pranged you have to get into the air again at the first moment possible. No, I'll report for duty tomorrow, if Wings'll have me. And he will."

He had gently ridiculed all Hales's protests, and Hales had not pressed them much: he was airman enough to admit the force of what Ayres said. His woebegone expression was too much for Ayres, however, and he had playfully pulled him down beside him, pitching the breakfast things on their tray onto the floor beside the bed. Hales had capitulated and allowed himself to be played with, caressed and finally seduced into a love-making that washed him clean of his worries and brought the ultimate wartime balm of forgetfulness. But when they were both agreeably sticky, sweaty and exhausted, and trembling on the verge of sleep, Ayres had returned voluntarily to the subject, speaking as off-hand as if they had never dropped it and the hours of strenuous sexual play in between had never intervened. "You see, old dear, if I don't go up straightaway, I shall get too attached to this way of life. There's only one thing I really want out of life now: for the bloody war to be over, and I can't have that. I couldn't leave the rest to carry it on and go skulking around down here, and nor could you. You couldn't leave your pals to keep on taking that flying cigar of yours up, and you know it."

This being the literal truth, there was nothing more to be said. They drifted into a deep, easy sleep in one another's arms, at peace and fulfilled and, for a little while, content.

A couple of days later Hales had returned home to collect his belongings. He had put the moment off as long as he could, but he could not borrow clothes from Ayres, who was in any case rather smaller, for ever, and in any case Ayres was insistent that he owed Ronnie at least an explanation for his disappearance. Hales, dreading it, had gone.

Their flat had been deserted when he got there, and packing his things took little time: they all fitted comfortably into his two suitcases. He had just manhandled the heavy cases into his car when Ronnie arrived. They greeted one another awkwardly, speaking in the restrained, exaggerated politeness of couples who have fallen out. Ronnie suggested a drink, and Hales reluctantly followed him back into the flat.

The explanation had quickly turned to recriminations, and from there it was downhill all the way, into bitter raking over of old scores, the long memories of love and love thwarted coming into play as effectively as usual. There followed tearful scenes of pleading from Ronnie and grim, thin-lipped resistance from Hales, who knew that if he gave way to pity and allowed himself to be blackmailed into giving in this time he would despise himself; and finally it descended to mere abuse, intensifying to a screaming match as they both helped themselves rather too liberally to the ample supplies of American whisky that Hales had procured from a friendly USAAF store-basher somewhere.

Ronnie had finally fallen into a drunken sleep in an armchair, in the midst of half pleading, half demanding for the umpteenth time that Hales unpack and stay at least overnight, and Hales leapt at the opportunity to let himself silently out of the flat. He eased the door closed and crept down the stairs to the street, feeling dirty and furtive, disgusted with himself for having allowed himself to be inveigled into a sordid shouting match but even more disgusted with Ronnie for casting all semblance of dignity to the four winds and resorting to crude moral blackmail in a hysterical attempt to cling on to a lover whom he had himself already more than half rejected.

A few days later, he found a letter waiting for him at his airbase. It was a brief note from Ronnie: in oddly formal, stiff English, he apologised for having behaved so indecorously, and wished him well for the future. "Please don't worry about me," he concluded. "I was overwrought that night, and more than a little drunk, even before I got back and found you there. I shall be all right, and I know you will be also. Try to survive this bloody war without getting shot down. Maybe we shall see something of each other after it's over, but maybe we shan't. No good trying to foretell the future. Just take care of yourself, and try to remember the good times. I shall. With love, Ronnie." Hales had read it through grim-faced until the last words, which had undone him. He blinked fiercely to repel the tears that were trying to squeeze themselves from the corners of his eyes, and glanced about to make sure no one noticed. The moment was soon over and in the usual chaos of getting off on the day's mission it was soon forgotten. He never saw Ronnie again.

For the next few months he lived on an emotional switchback with Ayres, alternating between times when he felt that he was truly one of life's favourites, basking in a bliss such as he had never known before, and intervals when he thought there were no greater depths of fear and depression to be plumbed. These came, simply enough, every time he knew his coruscating young beloved was in the air.

Ayres had indeed reported for flying duty the following day, and been welcomed back with the customary off-hand pose, which concealed profound relief at having an experienced member of the squadron restored to the active list. The losses were past the critical point, and every flier with any significant number of flying hours in was of a value beyond calculation.

So when Ayres was with him, Hales enjoyed an all-round sense of wellbeing beyond his power to express in words. The mysterious chemistry between them gave a tincture of golden adventure to every small thing they did together; physically they ascended to a plane of sexual ecstasy that left them satiated, feeling more than anything else a profound sense of gratitude to a merciful providence for bringing them to each other; most of all, every moment they passed in each other's company was fun, sometimes boisterous, often hilarious, sometimes a quieter, more contemplative kind of fun, but all combining to make life a joyous affair.

Yet over all of it hung the great looming shadow of fear, that it was all but a brief interlude before unimaginable catastrophe. Everything they did, all the fun they had, all the small things of love, every aching crescendo of passion, was sketched against a sombre backdrop of the statistics of pilots lost, especially fighter pilots.

It never occurred to Hales that he, too, was a member of a threatened species, performing a profession that was, in statistical terms, impossibly perilous. If Ayres suffered the gnawing hours of unimaginable fear as he lay alone at nights when Hales was on a mission, he concealed it better than Hales did. When Hales slipped quietly back into the flat and into bed after a night flight Ayres was always there to receive him gratefully, with soothing words and the freedom of his golden, supple body. When it was Ayres who returned after an outing in his Hurricane he more often than not found Hales an emotional wreck, twitching neurotically and hardly able to speak, let alone give any attention to the small matters of physical love. They made love, certainly, but it tended to be of an anguished, clinging kind, too desperate and frantic to be either ecstatic or soothing; and it was Ayres, once again, who had to do the calming down and the consoling. It all left Hales feeling wretchedly guilty and inadequate, and nothing Ayres could say could persuade him to go easy on himself, to give himself a chance.

In a way this proved a blessing when the inevitable end came. By chance this was a day when they were both in the air on daylight missions. Ayres's squadron had been escorting bombers over the continent on one of the earliest of the daylight raids over the Ruhr, while the *Betelgeuse* spent an interminable but rather successful day prowling around Biscay. They had found two submarines on the surface for refuelling and repairs, and crippled one and sunk two out of the three motor boats attending them before being driven off by a hurriedly summoned squadron of Messerschmidts. As they had fled from what Roy Dean had cheerfully referred to as "a bit of a firework display" in the form of a storm of cannon fire from the MEs, Hales had, as usual, taken little part in the jubilant yuk-yukking; but at least he had been kept busy enough to have no time for worrying about Ayres.

They had given the furious pursuing fighters the slip in low, scudding masses of cloud, and were on their way home to base, feeling ready for a night of it in the mess, when, quite by chance, they had stumbled upon a tremendous prize: Hales had thought he got a glimpse, far off, of a long, rakish grey shape in the heavy seas, and since they still had a few bombs burning a hole in their pockets, Roy Dean went to investigate. As they approached the weather conditions suddenly turned nasty, which though it did not make flying any easier, had provided them with a providential measure of cover. Then, suddenly, they found themselves under a barrage of ack-ack fire which it had taken all Dean's experience, skill and cold nerve to outfly. But they had seen the kill: a heavy cruiser, apparently on her way from one of the Brittany ports to help the U-boats in harrassing the convoys running the terrible gauntlet of the north Atlantic between Liverpool and America, and in so doing providing Britain's last life-line for supplies, armaments and enough foodstuffs to remain in the war.

The crew of the *Betelgeuse* had thought they'd seen every trick of unconventional flying in Dean's repertoire, but that late afternoon of dirty weather and high triumph he had shown that he could still surprise them. They had made three runs at the cruiser. Each was utterly different from the others, and none would have been found in any tactics manual. The first two were screaming dives, from which he pulled out at angles that subjected the airframe to stresses the others would have sworn would tear it apart, in order to present the smallest possible target for the ship's gunners. At the same time he flipped the heavy, cumbersome plane through a series of ducking, weaving manoeuvres, avoiding the almost solid wall of fire from the ship's massive armaments by whole series of miracles.

For the final run, by way of variety, he had ducked *beneath* the cruiser's ferocious retaliation until he was almost skimming the foaming, wind-whipped crests of the vast seas. They had to have the wipers going to clear the screens of sea-spray, so low had they gone in; and as they came roaring in on the aft quarter of the great vessel her lean grey bulk had seemed to rise like the side of a mountain out of the churning sea, looming and towering over them until they all had the same sickening certainty that they could not avoid running straight into her side.

Then, at the last second — or, as the rest of them would all swear later as they shakily gave their accounts of the action back at base, some time well after it — he had lifted the plane in a rearing climb that had every bolt and rivet of the fuselage screaming and creaking under the colossal stress, and lifted her a matter of feet above the stern of the cruiser. All Hales had to do was open the hatches and let the bombs fall out. He could not have missed if he had tried. "Only thing I was worried about," he said as he gave his account of the run, trying not to let the shaking of his hands show in the beer in his glass, "was that we might get caught in the blast ourselves. I reckon one more ounce of stress and the old girl would've torn herself apart. Never seen anything like it. Or imagined anything like it. I thought I was joining an air force, not a flying circus." But he had grinned across at Dean, who was busy giving his own comically understated version of events, with affection and genuine admiration, not unmixed with gratitude for getting him home alive, and the others were already raising their glasses and chorusing assent.

It was late, and the celebrations were breaking up, when the telephone rang and Hales was called to it to take a message. It was from a friend of Ayres, who knew of his relationship with Hales and was sympathetically disposed. The message itself was short to the point of curtness. "You Brian?" asked the other airman laconically. Hales admitted that he was. "Message for you," came the voice.

"From Gracie. He asked me to get in touch with you and give you the word if... if anything ever happened to him." Hales went cold from the tips of his earlobes downwards. "Go on," he said, steadily enough, feeling the slightly drunken elation drain out of him as if a vast plug had just been pulled from its socket.

"Pranged, I'm afraid," said the voice. The young airman was speaking softly, his voice becoming slightly husky with emotion. "He... he asked me to be sure to let you know if it ever happened to him. He wanted you to know as soon as possible, from him rather than indirectly. I'm... I'm very sorry to be the bearer of such bad news." There was a long pause, followed by "You're all right?"

Hales pulled himself together. "Oh... yes, yes, I'm okay. Thank you. Thank you very much for... for letting me know. I really am grateful..." He muttered a few further platitudes into the receiver, reassuring the caller at the same time as he wondered why he should have to reassure anyone just then — and who was going to reassure him, later on.

He had no recollection afterwards of how he had got home that night, or when. He guessed he had got a lift from one or other of the rest of the crew; but he never got round to checking, and before very much longer he'd had his own spill and been captured. The next thing he remembered was staggering under the shower and standing there while it ran first cold, then icy, the roaring sound and beating sensation of the droplets hitting his head feeling as if someone was trampling on him in cleated boots.

Nor could he say afterwards how he got over it. All he knew is that he did, that Ayres's friend, a young leading aircraftman by the name of Schofield, became a close friend in their shared grief, and that eventually, after a period that surprised him by its brevity, he *was* over it. Once over the worst, he coped more by shutting the period with Ayres out altogether. He recalled trying to offer some stammering explanation of this to Schofield, and of his being perfectly charming about it. And very shortly after Ayres had bought it, Hales had almost bought *his*, and had been too occupied thereafter to have any time to spare for thinking about Ayres or anyone else.

He woke with a jerk, jolted back to consciousness by a lurch of the train, and found that the jumbled dreams of Ayres had somehow cleansed his mind. In the moments when he had been able to think about his lover since the brutal news of his death, it had been a messy torment of unexorcised grief, aching regret at opportunities lost, when he had failed to extract the maximum joy from some small adventure together, and remorse at having been, as he felt bitterly conscious in his own mind that he had been, the weak, dependent half of an unequal partnership. He had relived every time when Ayres had come home after a mission, bone-weary but too electrified from tension to sleep, and instead of finding solace and comfort in his lover's arms, had instead had to be the one to do the soothing, talking Hales down from his half-hysterical pinnacle of fear and self-reproach. Now, in the odd clarity of mind that the dream on the bucking, jolting floor of the train had brought with it, he saw, with a clarity that had always eluded him in more normal times, that Ayres had been happy to take on the additional burden. Some people, he supposed, were made to be givers and healers, others were made to provide them with patients to heal and recipients of their need to give. For the first time since he had met Ayres, he found himself able to consider him dispassionately.

"Maybe I've just accepted that he's gone," he muttered to himself. One or two of the other prisoners around him stirred from their awkward and uncomfortable positions, sitting with their heads on their knees, or lying in knotted shapes on the board floor, and glanced towards their new companion. They saw that he had apparently muttered something in his sleep — a very commonplace thing indeed in that half-mad world of recent horrors and ever present fears — they compassionately turned away and left him to whatever private ghosts he had to exorcise.

His mind came to rest at last on almost the last time he had been with Ayres, one of the many good moments, a moment when they had laughed themselves into a fit in the car later on, and the love-making later still had been calm and contented. It had been a moment typical of Ayres, who had been above all else kind of heart and had hated to see anyone suffer. It was a good way to remember him, an episode typical of the man and his startlingly original style. He curled up again and gave himself up to affectionate remembrance.

They had both had a rare weekend's leave, and had gone driving without any particular destination in mind, stopping at small country hotels, drinking beer when they could find it and whisky when they could not, eating country meals with vast enjoyment of the things that were not to be found in towns or on airbases, and savouring the simple pleasures of being together, away from the war and its all-pervasive giant shadow.

It was, Hales thought, as fine a way of remembering a departed lover as any. As the train rattled its way through endless miles of heavy pine forest, he heard, over and over again, in his head and echoed in the drumming of the wheels, one of the last things he had heard Ayres say: "I only want one thing out of life: I want this bloody war to be over..." It is over for me, he thought to himself. And I'm glad. It was the last thing he thought before he fell once more into an uneasy sleep.

The next time he awoke it was full daylight, and the train was fussing about on points, shunting backwards and forwards. Eventually it found the right line and continued rattling through the interminable forest; but after only a few miles it slowed to a walking pace, and finally chuff-chuffed its way to a halt. After a wait they heard sounds of heavy bars scraping against the sides of the trucks, and the rumble of the sliding doors being opened. There was a hubbub of voices, with cries in German sounding stridently above the general clatter.

"I think," said someone slowly, "I *think*, gents, that we're there."

Part Two: Eugen

Part Two: Eugen

X

FOR some time, as usual, they waited. Gradually, however, the sounds of banging and crashing and the shouts approached their truck at the rear end of the long train, and at last they heard the heavy wooden bar being raised from its brackets on the side of the truck, and full daylight suddenly came flooding into the rattling, insanitary hovel on wheels that had been their home, and grey uniforms appeared in the opening.

The soldiers came hustling into the truck, barking orders and urging the prisoners towards the opening. They scrambled out and dropped to the ground alongside as quickly as they could, amid a chorus of groans and curses as they forced their cramped, tortured muscles into unaccustomed activity. Several of their number were wounded or injured, some quite seriously, and had to be helped to stand or half-crawl across the wooden floor. Somewhat to Hales's surprise several of the Germans lent an occasional hand, assisting some of the more seriously injured with here a hand under an elbow, there an arm unobtrusively slipped round a waist or shoulder to lighten the jolt of the five-foot drop to the iron-hard ground beside the train. Only a couple, he noticed, helped with swinging blows of their rifle butts, and on a couple of occasions he saw other soldiers curbing those with a sharp though softly spoken word or a restraining hand laid on a grey-overcoated shoulder.

They were all offloaded within a few minutes, and stood in an uneasy group, blinking a little in the full glare of the thin winter sunshine, looking at the many similar groups standing all the way up the train and wondering what was going to happen to them next. Their breath hung above the groups in clouds of white vapour, slowly rising and circling and gradually forming ragged shapes and dissipating in the frosty air. Within moments of descending from the trucks they all began stamping their feet, and there was an occasional curse as someone's boot landed on some hapless fellow-prisoner's foot covered only in bandages.

With considerable efficiency the guards brought about some sort of order in the milling groups of men, arranging them in ragged lines, checking off numbers and examining the condition of the wounded. Men were moved from one group to another as they were sorted according to some unguessed-at system, and about a quarter of their number were herded briskly up the train and prodded back aboard the leading half-dozen vans.

"Officers all going off to their own camp," muttered one man. "Gentlemen's bleeding club more like," another grunted sourly. Hales and the others in his little group just had a chance to say hurried farewells to a handful of their companions before other soldiers came tramping rapidly along the train, closing up the sliding doors in the sides of the wagons and replacing the bars, and the train, now three parts empty, emitted a screeching whistle and a series of gargantuan belches of steam and smoke, and went clanking off, slowly picking up speed as it trembled slightly in the distant haze and disappeared round a curve in the track. Hales watched it until the very last wagon had gone clanking out of sight, and felt oddly desolate and lonely when he finally had to tell himself that he could no longer hear the faintest distant echo of its friendly, familiar sound. It was only then that he noticed the depth of the silence that now enveloped them. He looked about him, and began to take an interest in his new surroundings.

They were, it seemed, in the middle of nowhere. They were grouped near the top of a vast bluff of rough terrain which rose up out of surrounding forest like the bald spot rising from a monk's tonsure. There was nothing approximating to a station: just a roughly but solidly constructed makeshift platform of sleepers laid along a low structure of scaffolding. There was a small blockhouse affair, which might have been a guardhouse — though what purpose there might conceivably be for guards there was beyond Hales's power of imagination — or a hut for equipment. Otherwise it was an anonymous point on the lonely railway line, indistinguishable from any other spot in the high heathland above the forest. The ground fell away quite sharply from their vantage point on all sides, and below, all round for the full 360 degrees he could see the tossing canopy of fir forests, stretching away endlessly in every direction. At its nearest point, he estimated, the forest began some two or three miles below their high vantage point.

Here, where they stood stamping and waiting for something to happen, the terrain was rugged and broken, but possessed of a certain wild beauty for all that. It was a country of thin grass and thorn scrub, broken by small stands of trees dotted about here and there. There was whitish-grey outcrop stone everywhere, breaking the surface in weathered, seamed bluffs and shoulders and miniature escarpments. Here and there on exposed surfaces patches of half-melted snow gleamed an almost preternatural silvery white, and the sky was a pale, thrush's-egg blue, flecked with small white curls of cloud jockeying their way across it. The dominant feature, though, was the wind: a thin, mean, fast-moving wind with devilry in it and a keen razor edge. It keened in the thin grasses and whined round the jutting bumps and ledges of outcrop stone; it howled across the natural ridge of the permanent way, and penetrated in moments into the innermost recesses of their clothing. Hales was aware of being, already, profoundly glad when his inspection of his surroundings was interrupted by a sudden sound of grinding gears as a couple of battered canvas-covered trucks arrived from somewhere behind them. At the same time there came a sharp order to move off. A moment later they were on the move.

The motion afforded some small relief from the bitter chill of the wind, but it was indeed scanty, because they were tied to the pace of the slowest among them, the less badly crippled. A few of the most seriously wounded had been separated from the rest by the soldiers, and were apparently to make the journey, wherever it was to take them, in the trucks. Many others, however, were forced to go on foot, and had to walk it as best they could, helped, in some cases half-carried, by the able-bodied. If anyone began to stride out and put any visible distance between himself and the main column, he was immediately called back by snapped commands which, though they were in German, left no doubt of their meaning. And so the ragged mockery of an army proceeded, at something between a saunter and a stagger, to their new home.

Their route took them in a very gradual descent of the tonsured hillock, and they wound their way slowly round the bald patch as they descended, until they were on the slope facing roughly, Hales thought, south-west. There was a little relief from the ever present wind when they got to that side, but not much: it still scythed its way into the last fold and recess of their inadequate clothing, still razored their stubbled cheeks and left them feeling as if they had been shaved with a blunt, nicked straight razor and douched in stinging acid lotion. They tramped on and endured it as best they could, complaining and swearing bitterly as they stumbled and trudged and trudged and stumbled their way along the rough tracks that were all there was to guide their footsteps.

They had been trudging for what seemed like hours, but was actually, according to Hales's watch, no more than fifty minutes, when they first caught sight of a dim, haze-distorted collection of what looked like buildings. Hales and his group at the rear of the long column were alerted by a ragged cheer from those at the front; and a moment or two later they became aware that the pace had picked up appreciably. They stepped out themselves with a distinct sense of rising hope — not, admittedly, hope of anything that would be very pleasant; but it was, at least, hope that they might soon be able to take their weight off their sore, suffering feet, get their screaming bodies out of the devilish wind, and perhaps even, Hales thought with utter, unconditional longing, a mug of hot tea.

Half an hour later the blurred collection of vague shapes still looked as far off as ever, and they were tiring rapidly.

"Christ, I 'ope they've got the kettle on when we get there," said the man beside Hales. "Or the boozers are open. I could murder a pint." Hales grinned. "Tea'd do me better," he said, with feeling, shivering and drawing the dead man's overcoat more closely round him. "This bloody wind cuts straight through you."

They trudged on in mingled misery and resignation until they reached a great shoulder of heath-covered rock bulging out of the hillside, which afforded them a little shelter from the biting wind. The officer commanding their escort of soldiers rapped out a series of orders, which one of the troopers translated into rough English. "Break for cigarette. Five minutes. Stay in your order of march. Sit down."

The entire crocodile of weary, stumbling men promptly flung themselves down on the short, wiry grass and groped for cigarettes. A moment later there was the low rumble of several dozen men swearing as the wind playfully scotched their efforts to get their cigarettes alight. They managed, however, and Hales drew gratefully on his cigarette and took a closer look at his companions. "They say you escaped," ventured the man who had spoken before. Hales turned on his side and found the man watching him with obvious interest.

"Well, I didn't really," he said, grimacing. "I'm here, aren't I? But I had a go for it." The other man looked impressed. "Good effort, even if you was unlucky," he said. He pressed for details, and Hales told him something of his adventures. Before he had got far there was a blast on a whistle from the head of the column, and they were urged back onto their feet once more and resumed stumbling across the heath towards the distant camp. Hales carried on with his account, speaking out of the side of his mouth and carefully keeping his eyes on the rough, tussocky conditions underfoot. When he had concluded his tale the other man whistled softly. "Christ, you *did* have some rough," he said, and Hales could see genuine admiration written all over his face.

"It was nothing really," he said, embarrassed. "More a matter of luck than anything that I got as far as I did. I hadn't got the first clue what I was doing, and it was only a series of accidents and coincidences that kept me from getting caught long before."

"Oh, well," said his companion, "the experience'll be useful. You'll get away with it next time."

"There's not going to *be* a next time for me", said Hales emphatically, with a shudder.

The other man turned to gaze at him in astonishment, half checking in his stride to do so. "No next time...?" he repeated in great surprise. "You mean you aren't going to try to escape again?"

"Not if I can bloody well help it," said Hales, wih great feeling. He glanced at his new friend's face, and gave a faint involuntary grin at his expression of surprise. "Have you tried to escape yourself?" he asked slily. It was below the belt, unquestionably. But Hales wanted more than anything else to shut the man up, and in that he quickly succeeded. The man's face fell visibly. "No. Not... not yet. Why?"

"Nothing. Don't mistake me, I'm not being critical, not in any way at all. But I think it's something that... something that maybe you don't... *can't* really understand until you've been there yourself. You see, by the time I got recaptured, I was *glad* to be. I was so weary, and at the end of my tether, I wasn't fit to be on the run. I was... I was just... so tired... So tired..." He fell into a meditative silence. His preoccupied expression was so forbidding that the other man, after a quick look at his face, decided not to break in on his thoughts. They plodded on in silence.

His introspection was broken some time later, as a ripple of talk broke out further up the line. His partner nudged him in the ribs. "We're getting close," he said, with a faintly apprehensive glance at Hales's furrowed brow and set face. Hales came out of his brown study with a start. "Eh? Oh. I'm sorry", he replied. His contrite tone did much to wipe the doubtful expression from his partner's face, and his faint smile did more. He followed the other man's gesture, and saw that the last lap of their difficult cross-country trek had indeed brought them a great deal closer to the camp. He peered ahead into the haze with interest, and found he could now clearly discern a high perimeter fence of rolls of wire, with high wooden structures towering high above it at intervals. Within there were many large structures that looked like huts; and they could see a blur of activity, still as yet tiny, ant-like forms and motion, but getting closer now with every awkward pace they took.

They found also, with relief, that the going was now a lot easier: the terrain had levelled out, and the rough goat-track of a while back had become a much better trodden path. Their spirits rose, and they strode along with almost a swing in their step. "Well, we'll be seeing if they've put the kettle on as you asked," Hales grunted, feeling a sudden parching in his throat as he envisaged mugs of hot tea to lay the dust of the track in his throat. The two of them looked briefly at one another, and grinned. It did much to restore the companionable atmosphere between them in which they had started out, and which his curt observations on the subject of escaping had spoiled.

At length they came down onto a well-flattened area, criss-crossed with tyre tracks made by heavy trucks, the grass worn away by the constant passage of people and vehicles. There were barked commands from the head of the column, repeated down the line by the grey-coated guards striding along beside them every twenty yards or so. The guards, too, were evidently glad to have come to the end of the arduous trek across difficult country. Hales and his partner stood on tip-toe and craned their necks like everyone else to see ahead. At the head of the column they could now see quite clearly the rolls of wickedly barbed wire that made up the outer of what looked like several perimeter fences. In it were set a pair of enormous gates, little more than lightweight wooden frames inset with more wire. There was a strongly built guardroom set into the fence on either side of the gates, and everywhere in the vicinity of the gates there was a bustle of busy activity.

An interval followed in which they did another spell of standing about, followed by another bout of shuffling, counting and taking of names. At last, after what seemed an interminable wait, they began moving forward again, and a little while later Hales and his companion passed through the gates and into the camp.

The fences they had seen from a distance turned out to be three in number. The first was the dense profusion of heavy rolls of razor-wire. Inside that was a strip of muddy grass twenty yards wide. As they tramped past it they saw wooden signs bearing the words ACHTUNG! MINEN, above and below skulls and crossbones. Then they passed another fence, as high as the outer one, but much simpler, consisting of close-mesh chain-link. This was liberally decorated with further notices bearing the legend GEFAHR! 20,000 V. "Huh!" said Hales's friend with a chuckle. "It's the amps what kills you, not the voltage. Prob'ly no more than two 'undred and forty, if not 'undred and twenny. Still, they'll know what it needs. Say whatever else you like about Jerry, 'e's on the efficient side." He saw Hales's raised eyebrows at this show of expert knowledge, interpreted it correctly, and grinned. "Sparks, that's me. 'lectrician in civvy street," he said simply, and went on to introduce himself as "Melford. Les to me friends." Hales returned the confidence.

They passed another twenty-yard chicken run, and at last through the final set of gates. The third and final fence was again of chain-link, with rolls of razor wire on either side at the base and overhanging the top on the inner side.

As they passed within there was a roar of welcome from a great assembly of prisoners, all in uniform, many of them ragged but all looking reasonably healthy, standing in a densely packed crowd on a wide, dusty area between the final fence and the nearest of a great array of large wooden huts. The ground here had been compressed by the endless passage of booted feet, until it was almost shiny, and here it seemed as if every man in the camp had come to greet their new companions.

The thunderous cheer seemed to wake the German guards up: they instantly formed into several small squads which set about driving back and dispersing the reception committee. Meanwhile, the newcomers' hopes of hot tea faded quickly. Other guards manoeuvred them into a regular rectangle of ranks and files in an oversized parade, and there they remained.

Eventually numerous new grey uniforms appeared, and at last an officer wearing the red tabs of a major or colonel, Hales wasn't sure which, came striding onto the parade-ground, accompanied by a detail of troopers carrying a makeshift dais. They set it down in a central position before the prisoners, standing easy and griping out of the corners of mouths, and the officer climbed with dignity up the three steps and surveyed them. "Pep talk," said Hales's companion from beside him, and there was a world of disgust in his tone.

117

The despised pep talk duly followed, but it was mercifully brief, and consisted mainly in repeated exhortations not even to think about trying to escape because escape was, A) impossible and B) pointless, as there was nowhere to go if an attempt succeeded. "This camp is very high," the officer, who identified himself as Colonel Edwin Schumann, went on in good English. "It is very cold up here, especially in winter, like now. If you managed to get out of the camp you would freeze to death before you could reach anywhere from which to make good your escape. Here there is nothing to eat, not even water to drink, and the nearest town is forty kilometres distant — that is about twenty-five of your English miles. So be sensible: your war is at an end, and you will do well to recognise the fact. You will be well treated here, according to Geneva Convention — unless you misbehave, in which case it may be necessary to take reprisals to point out to you your error..."

Consorting with German women, he told them, was a capital offence. He droned on for a short while more about Red Cross parcels, the rules concerning the writing and receiving of letters, the availability of the camp doctor, and then about the procedure for making complaints, which elicited a good deal of stifled hilarity in the ranks of the new prisoners. With that he ended abruptly, saluted, stepped smartly down from the dais, and strode back to the hut from which he had emerged. The same troopers picked up the dais and ran it back to the hut from which they had brought it.

After more waiting about they were sorted into four lines, and the lines began slowly shuffling into the nearest and largest of the wooden huts. When Hales's turn came he entered the hut, and a wave of pleasurable warmth rolled over him. He shivered involuntarily in pleasure, only to have the smile wiped off his face as the delightful sensation of being warm, for the first time in what felt like living memory, was followed instantly by a murderous attack of hot-aches. He crossed a wide space of boarded floor to one of a row of desks, rubbing various points where his muscles were crying out in protest, and stood before a bespectacled clerk. To his astonishment he saw that the clerk was wearing what looked like French Army uniform, and his impression was confirmed when the man spoke, in English with a strong and unmistakable French intonation.

"You're French?" he said without thinking, speaking French. The clerk looked up at him sharply, then nodded and smiled. The pleasure in his face at hearing his own tongue was unmistakable.

"Prisoner of war," he said laconically. "First wave. Before the fall."
The smile disappeared from his face as if wiped off with a duster.
"And pressed into service here at the *acceuil*," he added wryly, and
flashed Hales an ironical moue that vanished almost before it had
appeared.

He pulled up a huge, dusty, old-fashioned ledger book and took
Hales's names, service details and the dates of his being taken prisoner and arrival in the camp. "Are you suffering from any illnesses?"
he asked. Hales shook his head. "Any known allergies?" Again he
shook his head. "So you're fit for work?" asked the clerk. As he did
so he glanced rapidly from side to side and, seeing that no one was
taking the slightest notice of them and that the nearest German
trooper was yards away and staring idly into space, quickly pulled a
face at him. Hales strove to read it, then took a chance. "I can't see
very much," he said very softly. "Lost my glasses somewhere along
the way." The clerk nodded. "Make sure you tell the MOs", he said.
"They'll certify you unfit for work. They'll also promise to get you
a pair of glasses, and forget all about it the moment you're out of
sight." He nodded briskly, switched off his agreeable expression and
replaced it by one of blank officialdom, and waved Hales past the
desk.

He advanced past the clerk's desk and through a door at the far
end of the hut, which led him straight into another, equally warm,
smelling faintly clinical and divided into a series of channels, separated by makeshift walls of taut canvas tentwork. Hales walked
straight ahead and into the lane ahead of him. After a few feet it
suddenly widened out into a small 'room' with a desk, behind which
was seated an elderly, grey-haired man in German uniform with a
stethoscope round his neck and tired but gentle eyes behind gold-
rimmed glasses.

A swift but apparently efficient medical examination followed,
after which the doctor asked if Hales had anything to tell him. Hales
dutifully told him about his lost spectacles, and the medical officer
scribbled on the card he had been filling in. *"Leichte Arbeit drei,"* he
muttered, and Hales, trying to read his scrawl upside-down, could
identify the characters LA3. He caught the MO's eye and raised his
own eyebrows interrogatively. "Unfit for work," said the MO curtly.
"It means, actually, restricted to light work, but here there is no
light work. Therefore you will not work. For the moment. You
will be provided with a new pair of spectacles very soon, then you
may work. Until then, exempt. Thank you. Good day." He nod-

ded, then gestured with a motion of his head to indicate that the interview was at an end and that Hales should leave by the continuation of the canvas corridor. He did so, opened a door at the far end, and found himself back with the other members of his group, and back in the cold outside air again.

They stood around for some time, stamping their feet and clapping their arms round their chests and shoulders in an effort to keep out the renewed onslaughts of the biting wind. Eventually guards arrived, and they were chivvied off between lines of big, solidly constructed wooden huts. From time to time as they arrived at a hut men would be detached by the guards from the head of the column, sometimes in ones and twos, sometimes in larger groups of up to ten or twelve at a time, and pushed in the direction of the door. By this means Hales quickly found himself at the head of the line, and was one of only three to be separated at the next halt. Followed by the other two, he climbed up three broad wooden steps and stood before a closed door. Moved by he knew not quite what spirit of decorum, he knocked, three firm raps with his knuckles, before pushing the door open. The three of them stepped across the threshhold and surveyed their new surroundings. And so Hut F9, Stalag XLVII, became his home for as long as it should please the fates that the war should last.

XI

THE next few weeks passed surprisingly quickly as he settled into the routine of the camp. One long wall of Hut F9 was taken up by triple-tier bunk-bed units, where they slept with their feet towards the central gangway. On the opposite side of the hut there were tables and upright chairs, where they ate their meagre meals and whiled away their ample free time on endless games of cards, Monopoly and whatever other diversions they could devise. Mostly, they talked: almost all of it amounting to nothing more than endless discussion, monotonous, wholly without point or relation to any reality, of their hopes, dreams and plans for What They Were Going To Do When The War Was Over.

Halfway along its length the hut was broken by a row of wash basins, solidly assembled and simply but efficiently plumbed, that ran the width of the building, one basin to each three-bed unit. Two huge black cast-iron stoves, constantly almost red-hot, kept the hut, large though it was, comfortably warm. Within a few days Hales was mildly astonished when he realised that the ceaseless shivering, the uncontrollable chattering of teeth and the bone-aching misery of constantly being cold, which had become drilled into his conception of normality during the long train journey across France and Germany, was no more than a rapidly fading memory.

They began their day with *Appell*, when they were drawn up in ranks on the compacted-earth parade area and counted. Then they returned to their huts and prepared communal breakfast for the whole hut from the latest batch of Red Cross parcels, taking the duty in rotation and vying with each other in grumbling at each cooking team's efforts. After breakfast most of the prisoners were marched off under heavily armed guard to work. Many of them made up foraging parties in the surrounding forests, gathering dead wood and brush and felling trees to feed the stoves of the hutments. Others spent long and weary hours preparing small areas of flat terrain, back-breaking work consisting mainly of picking up and removing the huge numbers of stones that made up most of the ground in that mountainous region of thin soil and unyielding rock, in optimistic efforts to get land ready for vegetable growing when the spring came. Others, selected for their pre-war trades of carpenter, plumber, electrician, glazier and so forth, were assigned to the small and mundane but unending and essential tasks of everyday maintenance of the camp.

Hales and the comparatively small number of prisoners exempted from work were free to idle their days away as they pleased, and dispersed to join friends from other huts to play chess, cards and other games. They were joined by the working parties for the long evenings and at weekends, when, to Hales's surprise, work was in abeyance. Some formed energetic PT groups, and afforded the others much raucous amusement as they spent hours jumping up and down and flapping their arms in and out in baggy knee-length shorts improvised by the camp's five professional tailors.

Impromptu classes were formed, and anyone with any special knowledge or accomplishment pressed into service as instructors. Men took the opportunity of equipping themselves with the rudiments of trades — always "so's to be ready after the war's over"; anyone who spoke a language was urged to teach it, while others taught chess, history, mathematics, anything to help pass the time, boredom being the common, universal enemy. Hales's fluent French was swiftly spotted, and from the middle of his second week in the camp he ran a lively and enthusiastic class of beginners, which rapidly had him clutching his head in anguish at the appalling assortment of accents on display, and another, smaller but infinitely more rewarding class of advanced pupils who plodded methodically but enjoyably through whatever French classics they could get hold of from the Red Cross, sharing battered copies of Flaubert and Hugo, Stendhal and Merimée. He tried taking them on occasional forays into Verlaine, Rimbaud, Baudelaire and Gide, but quickly abandoned these when he found that most of the pupils found the poets distastefully decadent and, worse, outspoken about matters normally taboo among the more reserved Anglo-Saxons who made up the majority of the prisoners, so that the poetry classes had a tendency to turn into furious arguments about what a dirty-minded bunch the French were.

They all spent time on getting their service uniforms into the best condition possible, the smallest tears or other blemishes neatly mended by the tailors, discoloured spots carefully restored to the appropriate colour with a remarkable assortment of improvised dyes. The condition of one's uniform, Hales and the other new arrivals quickly learned, was an important emblem of morale, and as such was taken very seriously indeed. They had an iron in his hut, obtained by some devious means via the black market, and it was in constant demand. The oldest inhabitant of their hut, a leathery and terrifying company sergeant-major, instructed the others in the mysteries of securing razor-like creases by the judicious use of soap, and a blinding polish on the toecaps of boots and shoes with a tiny dash of spirit (stolen from the camp MO's stores) and a spoon. "Bit of orange peel'd be better'n anythink," he declared mysteriously. Hales never found out what that meant.

Hales quickly formed a close bond with the other two men in his bunk unit. The bottom bed was occupied by a giant, raw-boned pilot with red hair and a Scottish accent so thick that he was sometimes almost unintelligible. "Ah sheed hae a neem lak Sandy McMurrrdo," he said as he introduced himself and his middle-bunk comrade to Hales soon after Hales was shown his place above them. "As ut uz," he went on, twinkling, "ah'm plain Bill Shepherd. Pleased to meecha." Hales found himself grinning amiably at the enormous man, and marvelling at his ability to invest words with more R's than seemed possible. He even contrived, Hales noticed, to insert R-sounds into words that did not actually contain any. "Ah'm Canadian," he added, twinkling still more, "but that's nae muir nae an accident o burrrth." Hales found himself grinning still more widely.

Hales and his two fellow newcomers completed F9's comple-
ment, so they all found themselves sleeping on top-tier bunks, the
prized bottom beds and the second-best middle ones having long
been annexed by older hands. The other occupant of their unit was
also Canadian, and also an airman, a thin, stooping youth of twenty-
one named Ray Lacey, and they made up the only all-air force unit
in the hut. On this account they immediately became known as 'the
feathered friends'. The self-styled Sandy McMurdo was the leader of
one of the forestry units, and regularly astonished his fellow prisoners and their guards alike by performing prodigies of physical
strength. He was ferociously proud of his Scottish descent, and on
one occasion he decided to stage a caber-tossing competition, which
he won on a walkover as the only man capable of lifting the huge
log he selected as the caber, let alone tossing it. Lacey, however, was
in poor health, having contracted a serious lung infection on the
way across France. His dry, racking cough was a familiar sound in
the camp, and he was excused all work, so he took it on himself to
act as Hales's guide, showing him the ropes, taking him on walking
tours of the entire camp, which took in every remote nook and
cranny, and bringing him up to date with the latest gossip.

With such ample free time to themselves in the long winter
evenings, the new arrivals quickly became acquainted with their
twenty-seven hut-mates, and within a short period they had got to
know the widely differing personalities in the hut, and the friend-
ships and enmities, the natural leaders and the naturally led, the
flamboyant and the mousy, and the strengths and fallibilities on
hand. During the first few days there was a certain amount of quiet,
unostentatious exchanging of places between huts.

"Isn't that *verboten*?" asked Hales as they watched one such
move being made under the eyes of the guards while he and Lacey
sauntered about on one of their informal patrols of the entire camp.
"Sure it is," said Lacey in his soft drawl. "But the squareheads turn a
blind eye. They know it's only done to nip fights in the bud, and
the Krauts know it's as much in their interests as ours to get them
stopped off before they get properly started. Matter a morale, you
foller?" Hales saw that plainly enough: in the hothouse atmosphere
of the hutments full of bored prisoners, with all its potential for
introspection and resentments, the smallest enmity could easily fes-
ter and flare up into outright quarrelling, and ultimately, perhaps,
open violence, and that would be catastrophic for them all. The

Germans too had a vested interest in good morale and good order among the prisoners. So the camp regulated its own temperature with the tacit blessing of the guards.

On one of their explorations of the remoter parts of the camp soon after Hales arrived, Lacey took him into the special compound reserved for the Russian prisoners. This was, he told Hales, officially 'off limits' to the other inmates, but no one bothered about enforcing it. The Russians, he went on, were not covered by the Geneva Convention, so they were supposed to be kept separate, with officers and other ranks billeted together. To Hales's surprise, Lacey showed an easy familiarity with many of the Russians they encountered, and several of the Russians showed great pleasure when they saw him coming, their flat, Slavic features coming alive with pleasure as they hastened up to greet him. He was still more surprised to find that Lacey spoke passable Russian, enough at least to exchange greetings and bring the Russians up to date with the gossip of the rest of the camp.

"Picked it up since I got here," he explained briefly when Hales asked him about his unexpected accomplishment. "It's very useful to know a bit of Russki, and to know them. For a start they've got the only real medics in the camp — 'cept the squareheads, a course. If you ever get anything really wrong with you, come and ask to see Ustinov or Oblemov. They're the two MOs here, and they're good doctors, too. Only for Christ's sake don't let the Krauts know you're seeing em — that's one thing they *don't* like."

"Could either of them give me an eye test, d'you think?" asked Hales immediately. His lost spectacles had become a much more serious matter since he had started taking his classes, and the German camp doctor had been good for nothing more than vague promises of an eye test and prescription 'soon'. Lacey had spoken in Russian to the prisoners with whom he had been swopping stories of various common acquaintances' recent doings, and in moments they were being ushered hurriedly and with many covert glances round to one of the huts. Inside the stove was blasting heat into the room at such power that the hut was almost unbearably hot, and Hales was streaming with sweat within seconds of entering. Lacey led him to a tall, lean man sitting at one of the tables and dealing with a short queue of the flat-featured peasants who seemed to make up most of the Russian contingent. He was thin almost to the point of emaciation and clearly bone-weary, but his features were fine and his eyes very penetrating behind steel-framed spectacles. Lacey spoke animatedly to him for some moments. The man turned and looked at Hales, appearing for a moment supercilious. The impression was false, as he showed a moment later, when his gaunt features were transformed by a brief but brilliant smile.

He got up and went to a large cupboard, rummaged about in it, and emerged wearing a triumphant smile and bearing an optician's eye chart. The letters on it were cyrillic, but they solved that problem by the simple expedient of having Hales copy them as best he could onto paper, and within ten minutes he had a presription for spectacles. He thanked the doctor, who turned out to be Oblemov, and promised, through Lacey, to come to see him if he was ever in need of proper medical examination. He also agreed, gladly, to help the Russian by providing occasional contributions of such things as soap, which were even more hard to come by for the Russians than for everyone else. "It's the Geneva Convention again, see," explained Lacey as they threaded their way back through the Russian compound to their own part of the camp. "They're not signatories to it, so they never get Red Cross parcels, or letters or anything at all. So anything you can spare them is worth a fortune to them. Help 'em if you can, Brian. That Oblemov's nothing short of a saint, you know, him and Ustinov. They're working themselves to death, but they're keeping their people as fit as they can." Hales swore to give up something from his parcel whenever he could spare it.

"But how do I get these glasses?" he then asked, turning to the question that had been bothering him ever since they had left the harrassed Russian to his peasant patients.

"Easy," Lacey replied casually. "Black market. I know who to see, and I'll let you know how much they'll cost you." He glanced sideways, saw Hales's eyebrows raised in surprise, and grinned. "There's always the odd Kraut who's amenable to a little bit of business on the side," he said with a chuckle. The chuckle was summarily interrupted as he was suddenly bent double by a racking fit of coughing. When he eventually got it under control and stood straight again, wheezing and gasping for breath, he found Hales standing over him, watching him helplessly in mingled alarm and dismay. "You ought to get that seen to," he said, feeling bitterly conscious of how useless the words sounded.

"I know," gasped Lacey, his voice almost inaudible as he fought to draw breath into his tortured lungs. "That's what Oblemov was telling me just now. I'll see the Kraut MO. Have to." He leaned on the hut they were passing and gradually got some colour back into his face as the fit subsided.

It was the last time Hales had the pleasure of his jaunts with his friend. The next day Lacey did visit the German medical officer, and the following week saw the periodical visit of a mobile X-ray unit. Lacey was ordered to attend, and when the results were seen he was summoned peremptorily to the German doctor. Within minutes he had been sped to an especially large hut that stood on its own, at a distance from the remainder of the camp. It was further distinguished by being painted white. Hales had been watching from a distance and seen his new friend being whizzed off, and he made enquiries among the other inmates of F9. His heart sank when he was told that the white hut was the isolation quarters for prisoners diagnosed as having tuberculosis and other deadly and highly infectious diseases.

After that he had to hold occasional conversations with Lacey through two separate fences of barbed wire strands, ten yards apart. Their talks were always interrupted by Lacey's stentorian fusillades of coughing, but he never seemed to get any worse, though he didn't get any better either; and he was never the same irrepressibly bright and cynical character again, seeming depressed and downcast by his enforced isolation from his friends, his network of contacts and his ingenious methods of fixing things. However, he did manage to do two last favours for Hales, even at a distance and from isolation in what he insisted on referring to as 'the leper colony'. He bequeathed him his middle bunk, a small but potent gesture which Hales found almost unbearably touching; and he told Hales who to approach to get his glasses via the black market. Hales saw the man to whom he was directed later the same evening, and was told in brisk, businesslike tones that the spectacles would cost him one tin of coffee, large, and would be delivered one week from delivery of the same. It turned out to be a prediction of perfect exactness, and thereafter he found his French classes vastly less of a burden to himself; but every time he closed his French novel, dismissed his class of eager pupils and took off the new glasses to put them back into their case he found his thoughts straying towards Lacey and their short time together. It was always with great sadness.

The prisoners were allowed to write as many letters as they wished. Hales had few relatives, but he wrote to his parents and to as many uncles, aunts and cousins of all descriptions as he could think of, instructed by older hands that the more people he wrote to the better the chances were of getting parcels of food and clothing organised back home. The letters themselves were almost ludicrously innocuous affairs, since they had to be handed over to the Germans for censorship and were then censored all over again by the British authorities when they reached them, in case anything might be unwittingly disclosed that could be damaging to morale at home. He also wrote to his few close friends, and with those he attempted to be more open about the war, trying to tell, in the heavily guarded code they all employed, a little more of what had really happened to him, and asking if anyone had had any news of his former colleagues from the *Betelgeuse*. In the first batch of letters he wrote he sent one to Ronnie; but he never received a reply, or found out whether it was because his own letter never reached its destination or because Ronnie was still unforgiving.

After a long interval the letter-writing began to pay off, in the form of a welcome succession of parcels of clothing and other small items. Hales had long since discovered that everything and anything was of enormous value, either for itself or as currency. He contributed the odd item to the communal weal, and was a proud shareholder in the clandestine radio they managed to assemble a few months after his arrival. This was a common enterprise of the whole camp, and was gradually put together by the numerous radio operators and those who had been electricians in peacetime from an extraordinary collection of parts obtained from the Germans on the black market. Once assembled the radio moved from place to place under cover of night, and a runner came from whichever hut was running the set at the time and delivered a daily bulletin to every other hut. The radio was the one item that roused the Germans to really vigorous activity in their strenuous efforts to find it; but they never caught up with its movements, and the prisoners derived immense satisfaction from being able to keep up with the progress of the war — or, at any rate, the heavily censored version of it that they were able to hear on illicit broadcasts from the BBC and other stations from the free world.

For some time after his arrival Hales was in an odd condition in which he was conscious of almost feeling happy. In common with all the prisoners he had four blankets which, although thin, were quite sufficient, combined with the heat efficiently provided by the two big stoves, to keep him warm at nights, and generally he slept well. In the lonely moments when he woke during the night and had to deal with his fears and uncertainties, with only the steady breathing and rhythmical snoring from the other sleepers to keep him company, he would comfort himself by nightmare recollections of his tribulations during his absurd escape attempt, and the scheme never failed to bring him relief and, usually, to put him back to sleep.

The Germans left them almost entirely alone, and the weather was mercifully mild. From time to time it rained, and when it did it did so in heavy, saturating downpours, in which the rain fell in torrents, thundering on the roofs of the huts and trapping them indoors for days on end. Occasionally it was varied by a few flurries of snow, but there was only one severe snowfall. They made the most of it, staging a contest to see which hut could build the largest and most magnificent snowman and pelting anything that moved with salvoes of snowballs. Some of the German guards thus greeted laughed, and one or two of the younger ones even ventured to return the fire, though only briefly and after much nervous glancing over their shoulders. Some, on the other hand, took it in the worst possible spirit, repaying snowballs with gun butts; and when some reckless spirit suffered a rush of blood and narrowly missed the camp Commandant they all paid by the confiscation of the next round of Red Cross parcels, and went hungry for a week. All the same the snow provided a welcome interlude, but it was brief, being supplanted after only a few days by the heaviest and most unrelenting downpour so far, which washed it all away and left all the thoroughfares of the camp impassable morasses of mud and slush. For a couple of weeks after that even the daily bulletin from the camp radio was in doubt, and failed to materialise for several days on end.

Hales was lying sleepless in his bunk in the middle of one dark and stormy night when he became aware that others were awake as well as himself. He heard only two fragments of murmured conversation. First came one voice, from somewhere down at the far end of the hut. "Race yer, Ginge," it said, and was followed by a chuckle from someone else. There were faint rustling sounds, followed fairly swiftly by a faint gasp. Then a second voice said, in tones of unmistakable satisfaction, "I beat yer then." There was another laugh, from both speakers this time, and then nothing more. Hales lay grinning to himself in the darkness, and began to reflect on the fact that it was by now several months since his thoughts had strayed even momentarily, even in the stillness of the dead of night, anywhere in the direction of sex.

Mostly he put this down to the simple fact that, like everyone else, he was always too hungry to have any energy to spare for such thoughts. They breakfasted reasonably well off the regular weekly Red Cross parcels; but lunch was a miserable affair: they were fed by the Germans, but the meal consisted of nothing more than a small cup of thin soup with tiny fragments of stringy meat (they thought it was probably horseflesh, or possibly goat) floating in it. It was hot, which was pleasant, but it amounted to little more than salty water, and all their efforts to supplement it with grass, leaves and anything the foraging parties could find growing wild in the surrounding country proved worse than useless. The gruel was followed by a loaf of dark, coarse bread between six of them. It was sour to the taste, but they sliced it with extreme care to ensure that they each received slices of identical thickness, and all fell on it and wolfed it ravenously. Then they supplemented these short commons with whatever they had left in their parcels. In the evening the fare was identical, and there was never a night when they did not go to their beds conscious of an aching void in their bellies.

For some time after his arrival he was barely aware of the Germans at all. The prisoners had little or no contact with their captors, and the guards in their turn seemed quite content to leave their charges to themselves, provided that they gave no cause for incident to disturb the even, easy-going life of the camp. As one of Hales's French pupils put it one day while they were enjoying a break from Victor Hugo for a smoke, "The Krauts've got a cushy number here, and they know it. They're all C3 types and old men here. The last thing they want is to draw any attention to the fact. They've got one thing going for them above all else, and that's that there's no danger of their getting themselves shot or blown up." He spoke with a distinct jeer in his voice, and Hales was unaccountably nettled by the complacency in his tone. "You might say the same thing about us," he said drily.

The man looked at him in surprise. "Maybe," he said hesitantly. "But at least we were in action up to the time we came a cropper and got dragged here. We didn't ask to come here."

"Nor did they, I don't suppose," said Hales in the same acid tone as he had used before. "You said yourself, they're all C3s or too old to be in the army at all."

The other man looked hard at him. "I've heard something about you," he said, and Hales could clearly see hostility igniting in his eyes. "You're the one who escaped, aren't you? I heard someone saying you said you were finished with escaping, and that you'd be happy to see the war out taking it easy here."

"What of it?" demanded Hales, irritated to hear that his one short-lived outburst of annoyance had been bandied about the camp.

"Well, it seems a pretty queer sort of attitude to me," said the other man thoughtfully. "I'd have thought it was everyone's duty to try to escape, like they tell us at the meetings."

"What's all this bollocks about 'duty'?" Hales snapped back, finally roused into real anger. "What the hell does anyone here know about duty? Let alone about duty to do the impossible?"

"Impossible? I don't know what you mean. Plenty of the blokes here have escaped."

"Oh, yeah?" scoffed Hales, becoming more incensed by the moment by the young man's blithe manner. "And where are they now? I dare say you can tell me exactly which duties they're on right now."

The youth looked a little abashed. "Well, all right, none of 'em's actually *made* it," he conceded grudgingly. "But plenty've had the guts to try it. Now here's you talking as if it wasn't worth the effort of even trying."

"Well was it?" snapped Hales. "What effort? *Whose* effort? Theirs. I don't mind betting the guards never even had to raise a sweat to recapture them. Just waited long enough for the silly bastards to run out of provisions and start wishing they'd never tried to be heroes in the first place, then send out one man and his dog to follow the scent, and I'll bet they had 'em rounded up in less than forty-eight hours." He glared briefly at the young man and saw from his crestfallen expression that he had assessed the state of affairs exactly right. "In other words," he went on inexorably, "they expended a vast amount of effort, energy and ingenuity, took not one but a whole series of appalling risks, on an undertaking that was a hundred per cent stone-bonk certainty of being a mare's nest, and all for what? To give one German trooper one evening's mild inconvenience. And to do it I dare say he had to involve a large number of others in the risks he took, and put the whole camp at risk of punishment sanctions in retaliation. Haugh!" Hales was fairly snorting with anger by now. "Well, it might be worth all that for a chance to stick something long, hard and pointed up Hitler's arsehole, but to make an empty gesture of trying to escape against hopeless odds in the certain knowledge that you're going to get driven back here on the end of an Alsatian's nose less than two days later... well, you can work out the precise nuisance value of that to the German war effort without any help from me..." He left it at that.

The young man was still staring at him, in a mixture of perplexity and hostility. Hales suddenly saw the expression on his clean young face, observed that he had scarcely begun to shave yet, and finally relented. "You haven't got the slightest idea what I'm on about, have you, son?" he said, just a little wearily as his anger fizzled out as abruptly as it had blown up. "Let me try to explain what I mean."

He stretched his limbs and squirmed around on his chair to find the most comfortable position, drew heavily on his cigarette, and sat trying to get his thoughts into order. "All I'm trying to say," he said eventually, "is that there's no virtue in escaping just for the sake of escaping — no *intrinsic* virtue. Escape only becomes worth doing, or trying, if it has some value. In other words," he went crashing on, seeing the look of dumb incomprehension on the other man's face, "if your escaping can achieve something — for you, by getting you somewhere more comfortable than this, like back home for instance, or in nuisance value — by which I mean *real* nuisance value — to the enemy cause. But for it to have either kind of value it's got to have a chance of *working*. Up here, escape is practically impossible, because of the climate, the cold, the remoteness, the fact that there's nowhere to escape *to*, and a dozen other reasons. So why bother?"

He glanced across once more at the boy's face, and saw that he had not made the faintest dent in the surface of his impenetrable triple armour of ignorance, preconception and self-satisfaction. He sighed, and smiled glumly to himself as he recalled that, at the grand old age of twenty-three, he had rejoiced in the nickname of 'Granddad' at Bovingdon. "Go and ask some of the older men," he said, dismissing the boy with a gesture. He suddenly felt very tired. On an impulse he jumped to his feet, summarily dismissed his class and went stamping irritably out, aware of puzzled and startled expressions all around. As he threw the door of the hut open he heard the young man telling the others why their class had so unexpectedly run into the buffers. He imagined the wide, innocent eyes, and felt a gust of impatience scorch through him. He paused, lit a cigarette from the butt of the other one, and went off, with nowhere in particular in mind, for a walk.

By and by his aimless meanderings led him in the direction of the parade ground and the main gate. He stood there, smoking more than usual and watching the little groups of PT enthusiasts dotted about doing various athletic-looking exercises. After a few minutes he tired of this entertainment and, still conscious of a vague and indeterminate feeling of dissatisfaction and restlessness, continued his ramble, with a vague idea of drifting into the Russian compound to see his friend Doctor Oblemov. To reach it, however, he had first to skirt the wired-off compound in which the German barracks was set. This was a small group of hutments, much like the prisoners' quarters but of stronger and more solid construction, with a concrete blockhouse for a weapons and munitions store, a garage with a huge tank containing fuel for their few vehicles, and a large recreation building with a small bar.

Wandering down the side of this compound, he suddenly came to a dead stop in his tracks, and stood, temporarily enchanted, as he heard a wisp of very well-known music on a piano. In an instant he was transported, away from the camp, from the lowly status of the life-form 'prisoner', from the very war itself; in that moment he realised what it was that was missing from his life: he had heard no music for months, and he had hardly been aware of the fact. But music it was that came to him now, flooding back in huge rollers and combers, bringing back great swathes of memory and association, all set off by the handful of bars of the introduction to a Schubert song, one of his favourites. He stood as if in a trance, which, in a way, he was, and let the words of the song waft from the guards' quarters and wash over him where he stood, oblivious of the cold, of his earlier mood of irritability, of everything but the music...

Ins Grüne,
da lockt uns der Frühling, der liebliche Knabe,
und führt uns am blumenumwundenen Stabe
hinaus, wo die Lerchen und Amseln so wach,
in Wälder, auf Felder, auf Hügel zum Bach,
ins Grüne, ins Grüne...

[Into the green countryside: Spring, gentle lad, calls us and leads us out, carrying our canes clad in flowers, out to where lark and blackbird fly, to the woodlands, the fields and up the hill to the brook, into the green countryside.]

When the song ended he stood, almost holding his breath, to see if the unknown German within was going to play anything else; but after waiting for over ten minutes he was forced to admit defeat, and, suddenly becoming aware of his rapidly chilling extremities,

resumed his walk, at a considerably faster pace than before to restore his circulation. He was not aware of it, but he was singing as
he went, murmuring the words softly to himself:

O gerne im Grünen
bin ich schon als Knabe und Jüngling gewesen
und habe gelernt und geschrieben, gelesen
im Horaz und Plato, dann Wieland und Kant,
und glühenden Herzens mich selig genannt,
im Grünen, im Grünen...

[Oh, how I loved to be in the green countryside as a lad and young man;
there I studied and wrote, read in Horace and Plato, then Wieland and
Kant, and thought myself blessed, my heart glowing, in the green countryside.]

XII

IT was as if the moment of happiness that had taken him unawares
outside the barracks had come especially to give his life a new sense
of purpose. Not that he would have found so apocalyptic a term to
describe it for himself. He had not suddenly soared aloft to take a
God-like view of humanity and the fatuity of its affairs for the small
things that they were, or undergone some mystical transformation.
He had simply been able, for a few moments, to forget the war, the
camp and his own circumstances. The minute of unlooked-for happiness had provided a fresh centre for his small, circumscribed world.
It gave him something to cling on to, something to seek out and
give himself to.

He had always been fond of music, in a casual way. He had
grown up in a house where music was taken for granted as a normal
though not specially important part of life. His parents had had an
ancient wind-up gramophone and a large collection of records, most
of them seldom or never played; but both parents had a mild liking
for light classics and the popular songs of the day.

And so he had grown into his teens with an unreflecting ac-
ceptance of music. The beneficent chance of a music master with a
gift for passing on his own infectious enthusiasm had deepened the
fondness, until it had gradually grown into a serious interest. Drawn

at first by curiosity, then by gradually dawning and slowly deepening affection, he had begun to play the dustier, unplayed records from his parents' haphazard collection, until he had acquired by degrees first a friendly familarity and at last an intimate fondness for the central musical repertoire. It had never crossed his mind, and as yet still did not, that much of the music he loved best was German.

As he progressed through school the attachment had dimmed and eventually become dormant, at roughly the same time as he began to grow wary and self-conscious about his friendship with Peter Butterworth. But it never fully disappeared, and even when his philistine phase was at its height during his final couple of years at school, with Butterworth no longer there to exert his civilising influence, Hales still fled at times of sorrow or distress to solitude and music; and he had remained susceptible to it, too: at odd moments throughout his life he had been stopped in his tracks, much as he had been outside the barracks, by a snatched fragment of melody, or found himself standing transfixed outside some anonymous house or shop or cafe, straining his ears to catch just another bar or two of some well remembered song. Now, when he was at his most susceptible, with the unremitting search for interests to occupy his surfeit of untenanted hours, it was as if music had come back to find him and provide a focus for his life.

For some weeks after hearing the Schubert song he went to the barracks every day, except when it rained, in the hope of hearing something. He was nearly always disappointed, and had to mooch gloomily away after loitering as unobtrusively as he could for ten or twenty minutes, sometimes half an hour. But once in a while he was rewarded, and these rare moments were more than ample compensation for the long periods of disappointment. Once he came within earshot of the barracks in time to hear almost the whole of the Schumann C Major symphony, once some blood-curdlingly fast and virtuoso Beethoven sonatas; and occasionally he heard just the odd Schubert song. It was little enough, but it kept his new sense of purpose alive.

He found that there were several musicians among the prisoners, and that they had formed an impromptu chamber group, which met as often as the weather and work routines permitted to play whatever they could find the music for. There was nothing for the instruments that chance had thrown together, so they simply arranged everything they could lay hands on for their motley combination of violin, flute, clarinet and guitar. But no matter: for Hales the sound of music had become, overnight, the stuff of life, as essential as air and food. He couldn't have begun to explain what had happened to him, or why or how. All he knew was that it had; and he became the most ever-present and appreciative member of the camp quartet's small but enthusiastic audience.

He wrote shameless begging letters to everyone he could think of in England, asking them to send him books on music, and even managed to persuade the radio committee to let him listen, just occasionally, to a few minutes of music when it was broadcast by the BBC or one of the other stations. Once, as a very special dispensation, they even let him tune the set into Berlin, and he lay on the floor where the set was hidden, basking in an entire Beethoven symphony conducted by Furtwängler. He emerged clothed in dust, stiff in every joint but transported, eyed with mingled suspicion and amusement by the radio committee, waiting impatiently to retune the set to hear news of the war.

And so the few weeks after his moment of truth with the Schubert song passed quickly and unusually contentedly. Only one incident ruffled the surface of that period of tranquillity.

He was lying on his bunk one evening, thinking about nothing in particular. It had rained steadily all day, with the fine but penetrative rain that looked little more than a shower but actually made one very wet in no time at all, so he had been unable to go for his daily prowl round the camp. He had heard no music, and felt generally too wretched and sorry for himself to wish to do anything more constructive than to drift in and out of sleep and ruminate — mostly about how greatly he wished the war would end. The working parties had been brought back early as well, and the unaccustomed presence of all thirty of them together in the hut had been getting on his nerves, too, and he had been snappish and short-tempered all day. The others, most of them also fretting in the unusual confinement, had been exhibiting similar symptoms, so that Hut F9 had simmered all day close to a low boiling point of silly, childish argument and squabbling, like a cageful of moody lions. Then, in the mid-evening, there had been a minor commotion at the door of the hut, and a runner came panting and steaming in, with rain streaming off his garments, to deliver a summons. Hales was wanted, he announced, by the Escape Committee.

Hearing his name mentioned in the low murmur of voices from the far end of the hut, he rolled over and took notice at once. Footsteps approached, and the face of one of his own hut-mates loomed in the narrow space between his own and the framework of the bunk above him. "You're wanted, Brian," said the man.

"Wanted?" he queried, wondering who in creation could possibly expect him to venture out into the weather at such an hour.

"Escape Committee", said the other man. "They've sent for you. They want to talk to you." There was a low thrill in his voice. Hales looked keenly at him. He was a very young man, and Hales saw, with a faint smile, that he was bursting with a combination of pride at being the bearer of so glamorous a summons and awe at addressing a celebrity — to which Hales had plainly risen in his estimation by the simple fact of being required to go on such a mission.

The faint smile didn't last long, however. Hales had by this time been in the camp almost long enough to qualify as an old sweat, and was not, in any case, the kind by character to be impressed by committees. He cocked an ear towards the ceiling, registered the regular, unceasing drumming of the rain on the roof of the hut, and grimaced. "Escape Committee?" he growled. "What the hell do they want?" He glared at the boyish bearer of tidings, as if expecting him to offer an instant answer. "Humph!" he went on when no answer was forthcoming. "If they're expecting anyone to escape in this, they can look a lot bloody further than *me*." He rolled off his bunk and swung his feet to the floor, and went clumping off down the hut to investigate, leaving the youth who had brought the message staring.

"What's all this about the Escape Committee wanting me?" he demanded, spotting the messenger from the Escape Committee while he was still half the length of the hut distant. The young man who had brought the summons continued to wipe rain from his hair and face with a towel lent to him by the hut, and waited patiently for Hales to get closer. "Shhh!" came in fierce whispers from all sides.

Hales stumped up to the runner, who was being given a mug of hot tea. "Well?" he snapped ungraciously.

"The Escape Committee," he replied easily "would be glad of your company this evening, to discuss various matters arising."

"Humph!" snorted Hales again. "Silly buggers. Fine bloody night to rake somebody out of his pit. And what the hell do they want *me* for, I'd like to know? They think I'm going to help 'em digging some half-arsed tunnel, or pole-vaulting over the bloody wire? In this?" His voice rose to a squeak of ill-tempered protest as he gestured wildly at the drumming sounds above." He swung round, and was about to stalk back towards his bed once more when a soft voice was heard from somewhere about the mid-point of the hut.

It was that of the acknowledged leader of their hut, a greying NCO of the Engineers. He was a softly-spoken man from Lancashire, one of the few occupants of their hut over thirty, with a bedside manner that would have been worth a fortune to him had he been a Harley Street physician instead of a maintenance engineer from a paper mill. When tempers frayed or there was a dispute to resolve, it was to him that all the other twenty-nine youthful inmates of the hut turned, by instinct and by deference to age and rank, but also out of simple common sense, for guidance and, in the last resort, for command. When the hut had to choose its representative on the unofficial camp council, he had been returned unopposed and by unanimous acclaim. He had been held back only by his inability to speak German from the position of *Vertrauensmann*, or shop steward, the regularly elected representative of the entire camp who conducted any face-to-face negotiations necessary with the German camp authorities. He was, however, generally credited by the other inmates with being the power behind that particular throne — especially by those of F9, who thoroughly enjoyed basking in the reflected kudos of such a belief.

"Brian," came his soft tones, though he was hidden in the dark recess of his bunk (bottom tier, needless to say).

Hales knew better, however ill-tempered he might be, than to ignore that voice. He halted in his surly slouch back to his bed. "Yes?" he called, managing with an effort to keep the surliness out of his voice.

"Better go," came the voice. "You know better than to give *them* a two-fingered salute, lad." There was no urging or coaxing about it: it was a simple statement of fact, which came out in the shape of an order. There was not a man among them who would have thought of regarding it otherwise, or thought for a second on end of disregarding it — disobeying it, as they would have seen it. Hales, though among the least military among them, in common with most of the Air Force prisoners, and certainly the least gung-ho in that hut or, perhaps, in the entire camp, was at least enough of a serviceman to be no exception to this feeling: he would no more have disobeyed the engineer than any of the beardless boys in the hut would have done. "All right, Geoffrey," he said quietly, and resumed his trudge to his bed. He took the RAF greatcoat they had found for him when he had arrived at the camp, to replace the tattered army coat he had inherited from the dead man on the train, shrugged himself into it, and returned to the runner, who was gulping the last scalding drops of his tea with relish.

"Okay, let's go out on deck," said Hales, still simmering with ill humour. "I hope they've got duckboards in their damn-fool tunnel, or it's going to ruin the knees of my trousers." The young messenger giggled like the boy he still was, and led the way out into the rain.

Outside it was already pitch dark, interspersed with brief flashes of blinding white light as the giant arc lamps on two of the machine-gun towers that dotted the perimeter fence moved in their slow rotation across the entire compound. The moment they were in darkness the young messenger slipped a hand under Hales's elbow and led him on the first of a series of short dashes from the cover of one hut to the next. In this manner, dodging the arc light and hugging the protective shadow of the huts, they zig-zagged their way through the camp, which was rapidly becoming a minor quagmire, to the hut that was serving as the Escape Committee's meeting place for that night. They lurked in the lee of the building while the dazzling light swung past them one last time, then stumbled gladly through the door. Hales stood for a moment to accustom his eyes to the light, puny by comparison with the guards' spotlight outside but temporarily blinding him none the less, and blew a spray of cold rain off his upper lip and the end of his nose.

"Sergeant Hales," greeted a voice. "Very glad to see you. Come in and get warm."

He knuckled the rain out of his eyes and peered down the hut. Most of the occupants, he observed with some surprise, were quietly out of the way on their bunks. At the far end of the hut he could see the committee. They were clearly identifiable from their businesslike attitudes as they sat round one of the tables. A deck of cards was arrayed on the table to offer cover in the improbable event of a surprise visit by the Germans, and there were a few men playing desultory games at the tables between the committee and the door, evidently ready to provide cover in the same eventuality. Hales walked towards the group, his steps echoing faintly in the unnaturally quiet hut.

As he drew level with the group round the table a hand appeared unobtrusively and took his greatcoat, which he had shrugged off as he approached. He found himself reminded incongruously of Ronnie's tribunal, when he had had to run a similar gauntlet to seat himself before the white-haired old brigadier or whatever he had been and explain how he would serve only if he could go behind the lines to assassinate Hitler, and then serve his own leaders the same way. There was something, Hales thought, of the same foreboding in the atmosphere, and in the near-silence. He glanced out of the corner of his eye to see who had taken his coat, but the hand and its owner had already vanished, and his coat with them. He had not, he reflected, felt so like a serviceman since his passing-out parade at the end of his basic training. The thought flashed into his mind and foundered equally quickly. He stood, looking down at the committee, and waited.

There were six of them, with one of them unmistakably the leader. Like the engineer NCO in F9 he was an older man, in his late thirties or even possibly his forties, Hales thought, and wore the flashes and insignia of a warrant officer of the Parachute Regiment. His uniform was as flawless, the creases as immaculate as if he had just stepped off a parade-ground drill at Caterham. When he spoke the similarity between him and Hales's own hut leader was again marked in the voice: he too was softly spoken, the voice nicely modulated, but it held the unmistakable note and custom of command.

"Welcome, Mr. Hales. Please be seated," he said with an old-world courtesy that for some reason did not seem remotely out of place. He indicated the single vacant chair at the table with an economical gesture of one hand. A hand of cards lay ready, face-down before it. The leader indicated that he should pick them up. Hales did so. "You've got three Jacks," observed the leader quietly. "But don't gamble on them: you won't win." There was a general chuckle at the mild pleasantry. "Let me introduce you," went on the leader. "My name's Michael Watts. As you see, I'm an RSM. Parachute Regiment. But it's all Christian names here. Call me Mike, please; Michael if you feel you must, but not, please, Mick. Not if you value my friendship. This is..." He introduced the other five men, whose names Hales forgot as soon as he heard them. There were, he discovered, a sapper, an engineer, a corporal electrician from the REME, a Dutch infantryman and, last, a flight sergeant from Bomber Command. He gave Hales a cheerful grin. "Nice to see the crabfats so strongly represented", he said in a strong Yorkshire brogue. "Where'd you buy it?"

"Biscay," said Hales, suddenly gloomy at so unexpected a reminder of the loss of his plane. At that moment a large steaming mug of very welcome tea materialised beside him. He turned to murmur his thanks, but the unseen waiter had disappeared as silently as he had come.

"In the drink," murmured the other man, with a friendly smile of commiseration. "Must've been unpleasant."

"It wasn't nice," agreed Hales. "How about you?"

"Bagged over Holland," said the other. "What kind of crate?"

"Halifax."

"Ah. Strong old horse." He eyed the braid letter N with its single wing above Hales's breast pocket. "Navvy, I see. Who was your driver?"

"Chap called Dean," Hales informed, and was assailed by a vision of Dean as he had seen him last, leaning down with a flask and providentially avoiding a volley of machine-gun fire that had come ripping through the fuselage and out again through the screen. It was so sharp and poignant a reminder of his dead friend that he felt his throat constrict in a spasm of regret. He had to exert all his self-control to avoid a faint whimper of mingled surprise and sudden, almost unassuageable grief that struck him like an unexpectedly big wave striking an unsuspecting swimmer.

"Roy Dean!" cried the Yorkshireman. "*Roy* Dean?" Hales nodded. "You knew him?"

The other man nodded excitedly. "Why yes. Roy and I were muckers. Trained together. Did he get bagged as well?"

Hales sat in silence for a moment, and saw the other's eyes darken as he understood. "All right," he said after a long moment. "He bought it, didn't he?"

"I'm afraid so," said Hales, and watched helplessly as the other man's head dropped for a moment.

"What was it?" he asked eventually, looking up. "Cooked?" His tone as he said it remained even, but his face was rigid with apprehension.

"No," said Hales, gladly. "No, it wasn't that, thank Christ. We hit the drink, hard. He was hitting the anchors for all he was worth, and the impact killed him. Broke his neck, I think."

"Mm. Quick, anyway," murmured the other man, relaxing as he heard it was not the worst. I'm glad to get the straight of it from someone who was there. Thanks."

The others remained silent for their colleague's moment of respect for his friend. Then the leader tapped once on the table and said briskly, "Time to get down to business. Now, Hales — what are we to call you?"

"Brian," he said shortly, still busy with a complex mass of un-expected and unwelcome thoughts about Roy Dean, the *Betelgeuse*, the final plunge into the heaving waters of Biscay and much of what had come after it.

"Very well, then, Brian. We've asked you to come along to-night because we hear that you actually managed to escape on your way to us here. We'd like to hear all about it, if you will, please, and then to discuss how you may be able to help us. Perhaps you'll kick off by telling us everything you can about your escape. We'll ask questions as they occur, gentlemen." He indicated to Hales that he had the table, and sat quietly, waiting.

"Exactly what do you think I can say that may be of any help to you, gentlemen?" Hales asked after some thought. "I don't quite see what I can have to tell you that you can't know as well as I do. Better, in fact, because you've all been here a lot longer than I have."

There was a silence, broken by the leader of the group. "As I said just now, you've had one form of experience that none of us has had, Brian," he said. "You've actually done it. You've had experience of escape; you've been on the run. We'd like to hear about it. How it felt, what difficulties you encountered, and how you sur-mounted them. Tell us about that, if you please."

After a few moments organising his thoughts he gave them a succinct account of his adventures from the moment of disbelief when the train guards overlooked the bolts on their truck to his final anticlimactic recapture, including everything he could remem-ber but carefully omitting any mention of his short but joyous time in Sylvain's bed. From time to time one of them put a question, and they were particularly attentive when he somewhat hesitantly voiced his vague suspicion that he had been betrayed by someone inside the Resistance cell who had helped him. On that they interrogated him intensively, the presiding RSM pressing him particularly hard over his still less formulated doubts about Sylvain.

When he had come to the end of his tale they sat back and looked round the table at each another. After a lot of exchanging of glances, the significance of which, if any, Hales could not guess at, the RSM murmured something into the empty space over his shoul-der. Two of the other men appeared from nowhere, and the RSM courteously requested further supplies of tea. Then, turning back to Hales, he said "Well, Brian, you deserve our congratulations. Fine show. Pity you couldn't make it back, but it was a gallant effort, all the same. Now: what we'd like to do next is to ask your opinion, you being something of an expert witness, as to our chances of organising any kind of escape from here. We've had reports of successful escapes being run from other camps — men transferring here from other places and so on. We've never had a successful attempt from here. Not one. A number have tried, but every man has been recaptured within a few days. Usually less. So, in a sense, you're our most successful escaper so far, even though you didn't make your try from here. Would you care to give us your assessment, based on what you've seen of the surroundings?"

Hales sat for some time in thought, wondering what approach to adopt. He toyed with the idea of telling them what they clearly wanted to hear, partly out of a desire for a quiet life, partly because he suspected that if he told them what would please them most they would let him go so much sooner, and partly because he was, despite himself, beginning to get caught up in the conspiratorial, schoolboy adventure-club air of the meeting.

He rejected the idea finally mainly because it went too much against his nature. He had unconsciously picked up a good many little ways from Ronnie, who never minced his words and rarely opened his mouth unless to say something terse and to the point out of the corner of it, and among them was a directness that many found disconcerting and some downright alarming. Once he had decided that if he owed this absurd committee nothing else he owed them at least the truth, it was more or less inevitable that his way of expressing himself would rub at least some fur the wrong way. Having made up his mind, however, he delivered his verdict quietly and decisively, and it was damning.

"You're wasting your time," he began, and saw all six of them bridle instantly. They said nothing, however, and once started he had no intention of leaving anything unsaid that he judged it necessary to say.

"I have, as you point out, seen something of the surroundings here, and I can tell you with complete confidence that escape is about as near to impossible from here as from anywhere I can imagine." They exchanged expressive glances. "To begin with, we're in Germany here. We're also perched on top of what looked to me as we came here like a sizable mountain, with open scrub country all around, and pine forest beyond it.

"There's no cover to speak of in the scrubland, and none at all in the forest. There's not enough concealment to hide a bunny rabbit between here and the railway, and from what I could see it was the same as far as you could see on the other side of the track. More important, there's no shelter, either. More important still, the nearest town is twenty-five miles away, and you'd — that is, anyone trying to escape — would never get that far. With a spotter plane they'd catch you before you got as far as the forest. Even if by some fluke you got that far — if you waited for foul weather to make your attempt, for example, so a spotter plane couldn't fly — those forests are virtually sterile. With dogs they'd lay you by the heels in hours.

"Then there's the question of the conditions. If it was raining, and it rains half the time here, your mobility would be cut down so much that you'd probably be caught before you got out of the camp compound. And the only time it stops raining here is when it snows, and when it isn't actually snowing it's as cold as a witch's tit. You couldn't travel light enough to travel fast, and you couldn't travel fast enough if you took enough provisions with you to keep alive and even passably fit. You'd snuff it from exposure in twenty-four hours if it turned even half nasty up here — supposing you hadn't been lugged back in with teethmarks in your arse long before then, which in all probability you would have been.

"In other words, gentlemen," he concluded flatly, "forget it."

They digested this in an icy silence. Looking round the six faces Hales could see the deep and angry disappointment scored into their features. He waited in silence. Eventually the parachute RSM spoke. "That's your definite view, er, Brian?" he asked, still polite but with a note of frigid reserve audible in his voice which had not been there before.

"Yes, it is," he said in the same flat, unambiguous tone as before. "I'm sorry," he added, though not troubling to sound very convincing.

"And you've nothing more to say? Nothing more you feel you can — ah — contribute to our little discussion group?" said the RSM heavily, looking at him with freezing disapproval. Hales almost expected him to say something like "If I had you on my parade ground...", but he said nothing at all. The others likewise remained silent, radiating hostility.

Hales looked steadily at him, and then at the others one by one, and his face, which had been set in a stern, unforgiving frown, registering an irritability that he himself could hardly have accounted for, relaxed a little. "I *am* sorry", he said, relenting a little. "But you asked me for my views — my expert views, you said — and I'd be doing you a disservice if I told you anything other than the truth. I could tell you all manner of things that would be closer to what you'd like to hear; but where would that leave you if you sent someone under the wire on the strength of what I said, and he died of exposure, or got taken and savaged by the dogs, or something equally frightful? I couldn't live with myself if that happened, and you wouldn't thank me, even if it didn't turn out to be quite as disastrous as that."

There was another long silence, while the atmosphere grew heavy with unspoken disappointment and chagrin. At length the presiding RSM said, in carefully neutral tones, "So, then, if we were to suggest to you that... that *you* might care to have another go... well, I take it you wouldn't respond very favourably?"

Whatever reaction they were expecting from Hales to that, they had not expected the one that came. Nor, for that matter, had Hales himself. He sat staring at the RSM for some moments, too surprised to say anything. Then, without warning, he let out a roar of laughter. It got hold of him and he sat back in his chair and rocked with laughter, great helpless yelps of it, while the others sat and stared at him in bewilderment, and in visibly mounting anger.

At length the fit subsided and he was able to look them in the face once more without succumbing to another attack. "Not a hope," he eventually managed to splutter. "Not a hope in hell. Listen," he went on, speaking earnestly, striving desperately to convey the urgency of what he was trying to impart. "I have, as you say, tried it already. I had the advantage of being in France, which may be occupied, but that's not the same thing by any means. I had the advantage of speaking the language. There was plenty of cover. Most of all, I was being helped by the Resistance. All that, and I still didn't make it. I was caught in less than forty-eight hours. What chance would I have up here? I speak about enough German to get by, provided no one talks too fast, whereas my French is fluent. I'm no athlete, one leg's still a bit gammy from where I smashed it against some bit of my crate when we got pranged, and I haven't got the slightest idea where we are, let alone which way to go. Work it out for yourselves."

He waited, but they were all apparently too dispirited by his crushing analysis, with its merciless logic, to have anything more to say for the time being. He could see that he had outstayed his welcome. Yet still he felt bound to add the final few hammer blows to their hopes of him, whatever, as he thought wryly to himself, they might have been in the first place. "One last thing, gentlemen." They looked grimly up at him, wanting him to be silent or, better, he thought, to be gone. "The last reason why I've got no intention of trying to escape, gents, is this: I don't *want* to escape. I tried once, because I got carried away in the excitement of the moment, and I'd been pushed out of the train before I had a chance to sit and think the thing out, or even give a moment's consideration to what I was doing and how I might go about it. Actually it was lucky I didn't, because if I'd had time to think about it I'd never have even tried it in the first place. But having tried it once, I've done my bit, I've had my go, and I know when I'm up a gum tree. For me, my old pal said when we hit the drink back there, the war is over. Well, gents, for me, it *is* over, and that's official. I'm quite happy to sit it out from now on. From what I hear it's not going to last much longer now anyway — they're saying we've just given Hitler a very bloody nose in the desert, I've heard that the Russians are holding the Krauts out on that front, and there's even talk of an invasion, now the Yanks are in it with us."

He went inexorably on before anyone could interrupt. "I didn't particularly mind the idea of getting clobbered while we were flying the old kite, because I could at least see the point in it then, and besides, I didn't have any choice about it then..."

"Do you feel that, really, you've got a choice now?" snapped the RSM. "It's every fighting man's duty to try to escape, to try to inflict the maximum damage on the enemy, and if he can't inflict actual damage, then to cause as much disruption and inconvenience as he can instead. Come to that, it's the duty not only of every active serviceman, but of every patriotic Englishman, and everybody else who thinks these Nazi torturers are a plague that ought to be rooted out and exterminated. God damn it, man, how can you dare to sit there and tell us that not just everything we're trying to achieve, but everything we stand for, everything we represent, is mere castles in Spain?"

Hales took a deep breath and turned to face the cold disapproval in the RSM's face. "I said I didn't mind going to my death for the cause while we were doing something identifiably useful," he said, equally cold himself now. "On the other hand, I've got the strongest objections to getting frozen to death trying to bed down in a rabbit hole, or getting eaten by a pack of squarehead dogs, or getting lost up this bloody mountain and running round in ever decreasing circles and disappearing up my own arsehole while the Krauts laugh emselves bloody silly cos they can see I was heading the wrong way in the first place. Finally, I've got the strongest reservations of all about getting captured and tortured in some dungeon by the Gestapo before being shot, or garotted as a spy. I'm sorry, gents, but it's no go. I've no doubt you're thinking of me as unpatriotic if not worse, but I'm sure you'll find plenty of volunteers. You'll have to excuse me if I happen to have learned from experience — or if I just happen to have more sense."

Conscious that he had said quite enough, if not rather too much, and that he had been less than tactful or considerate of their feelings, he rose abruptly to his feet, startling the others. "If that's all, gentlemen, I think it's time to go." He scanned their crestfallen faces, and felt a pang of compassion for them. "I am sorry, gentlemen, really. But you can see, it really is a chicken that won't fight. Good night." With that muttered valediction he went to where his greatcoat was draped over a chair by the stove, still steaming slightly as it dried out, twitched it off the chair and over his shoulders without breaking his stride, and went out. His footsteps reverberated unnaturally loudly on the board floor of the hut as he went, amplified by the dead silence in which he made his exit.

The story of his ruthless demolition of the Escape Committee's hopes and dreams was all over the camp by breakfast the following morning, and he received a great many odd looks from all sides. It was a fine day, so he was able to go on his usual stroll. Without any firm idea where he meant to go he found his steps turned in the direction of the Russian compound, where he had got on friendly terms with the two doctors, in particular with the angular and cynical Oblemov, who had given him the prescription for his new glasses. Oblemov spoke a little English, and Hales himself had discovered, much to his own surprise, that he had some small gift for picking up languages, so that he had very quickly acquired enough elementary conversational Russian to be able to hold a halting conversation. He was astonished when, as he strolled into the hut where Oblemov was attending to a prisoner with a hideous ulcerated sore on his leg, the doctor greeted him with a wave and a dry grin. "Hallo, English. I hear you've been dispelling certain people's foolish illusions."

Hales stared at him in dismay. "Christ, has it reached here already?" he exclaimed in his demotic Russian. "How the hell's it travelled this far?" Oblemov's grey, thin features creased in a derisive grin. "How long you been here?" he said simply. "You should know how news travels in a place like this. It moves by — what's the English word? Osmosis, I think." He sobered quickly. "It won't make you popular, English. No one likes to be told something he doesn't want to hear. And you weren't very diplomatic, I gather."

He stood watching in reluctant fascination as the doctor cleaned the vile-looking ulcer, coated it in some powder, which evidently stung the stolid peasant, who let out a brief, sharp yelp of pain, then dressed it in a freshly washed but second-hand bandage. The soldier went out, thanking the doctor briefly in some guttural language that Hales did not recognise as any form of Russian; but the shy, puppy-like gaze of devotion that he directed at Oblemov from under his knobbly, overhanging brows said more than any words could have spoken. Oblemov slumped into a chair and yelled something very rapidly, in which Hales was pleased to detect the one word, *tchai*, and in a moment an orderly came from a small room at the end of the hut, bearing two glasses of dark, bitter tea, Russian style, to which Hales had taken a liking since he had begun paying occasional social calls on his Russian friends.

They talked for a few minutes, with Oblemov teasing him about the risks inherent in telling children that the tooth fairy was a myth. Then a prisoner came clumping in in huge, ill-fitting boots with the soles flapping loose, to say that someone by the name of Nevsky had been crushed by a tree while out on a logging party, appeared to have several broken ribs, and was spitting blood. Oblemov drained off the scalding tea in a single draught, picked up his bag and heaved his lanky frame out of his chair all in a single movement, and was gone. Hales sat alone in the hut for a while, finishing off his own tea, then ambled out, wondering if he had made trouble for himself by his outspoken and almost contemptuous dismissal of the committee's ideas on escape. But he felt he had been right, and that he had the right, to give his opinion honestly as he saw it. For no reason, and out of nowhere, the thought popped unbidden into his head that he could begin to understand how a dogged individualist like Peter Butterworth must have felt more or less all the time. The thought was a comfort, as he wandered aimlessly in the bright but heatless sun.

XIII

OVER the next few days he gradually became aware that the incident with the committee had made him something of a name among the prisoners.

Among the aggressive patriots it lent further weight to his standing as someone to be left alone, for fear that he might corrupt with his derisive scepticism, already well known, towards the merest hint of the gung-ho.

For others it made him an object for singling out, so that over the next few days he found himself continually being accosted as he loped about the camp on his long walks, by men he had never known before, faces without names among the teeming and ever-multiplying inmates, all anxious to offer shy congratulations on his facing-down of the committee. He began to notice a certain pattern among these unwanted admirers. Most of them were one-offs, solitary like himself, for some reason or for none at odds with the other prisoners. Some were ostracised for their opinions, which ranged from an undiscriminating cynicism involving a refusal to credit decency or honourable motives to anyone at all, through an unpopular over-reasonableness or willingness to see more than one side to matters to do with the war or the Germans, to one half-crazed man who declared out-and-out sympathy with the Nazis, and claimed that the only mistake Britain had made in the war was fighting on the wrong side. He was tolerated, though watchfully and uneasily, only because everyone knew that he had been appallingly wounded, and had been more than half demented ever since.

Others were unpopular for more mundane reasons, for possessing exceptionally acid tongues, for unusually low tolerance for those less keen of intellect or wit than themselves, or from various other causes. At all events, these, outcasts in a company who saw themselves, rightly or mistakenly, as outcasts, seemed to find common cause in seeing Hales as a newly declared champion, and, to his great discomfiture, took the trouble to come up to him and tell him so.

His few close friends treated him no differently from before. Bill Shepherd, the giant self-styled Canadian Scotsman who filled and overflowed the bunk beneath Hales's, treated the incident with the Escape Committee exactly as Hales had expected him to, refusing to take it seriously. He extracted as full an account as Hales could manage of what exactly had been said, and then proceeded to chaff him mercilessly whenever he got a chance about the things he might have said and had forgotten to say or left unsaid out of charity. But his treating the episode as a giant joke did not come as the slightest surprise to Hales, for that was how he treated the Escape Committee itself, and almost every other aspect of camp life.

Ray Lacey, who was still in isolation receiving intensive treatment for his TB, still liked to see Hales whenever he was allowed to, and derived enormous pleasure from their weekly conversations, grinning pallidly at Hales through the wire and across ten yards. They had heard in there about the episode with the committee, and he was able to tell Hales that opinion in the sanatorium hut was divided along much the same lines as on the great outside. Lacey himself was with Hales, he said, which brought out Hales's rare grin — so rare that he himself never knew the power of it.

The most unequivocal declarations of support and agreement came from his friends, the two Russian doctors, who took it in turns to suggest further things he might tell the committee the next time it felt in need of guidance, and poured unending streams of ribaldry, cynicism and crude jokes into his ears, in the intervals between pouring unending ribaldry, cynicism and crude jokes into the same ears about everything else.

Among the majority of the prisoners, however, it had little effect beyond confirming his reputation, already well on the way to establishing itself in the intimate, closed world of the camp, for being his own man, a lone wolf, unclubbable, even anti-social, someone who spoke his mind regardless, indeed fearless, of the consequences, and was no respecter of persons. Among this majority he found that he was eyed with some suspicion from time to time, as being in some way 'unsound', but otherwise largely left alone.

His curt delivery to the committee appeared to have had its effect on them, however. There were no attempts at escape for many months afterwards. When, much later, the summer surprised them all with two months of blazing sun and temperatures in the nineties, they were all too enervated by constant thirst, stringently rationed water and the progressive effects of the ever-increasing shortages of food to think about the horrors of dragging themselves across the scorched, barren countryside. In the autumn a few attempts were made, with the same ignominious results as the few that had been made before Hales's arrival.

Hales continued in his own private routine. He went for his ambles through the camp, watching every small thing that happened, passing the time of day with anyone who was happy to talk to him. He spent a lot of time with the Russian doctors, often taking them some small present from his share of the Red Cross parcels, or his own regular parcels of clothing from his family in England. The Russians, who suffered, as a normal part of daily routine, privations that made his own hardships seem like well-ordered prosperity, were unfailingly grateful to a degree which made him embarrassed and uncomfortable.

The two doctors knew better than to linger over their gratitude, but their terse, almost unspoken mutter of thanks said all that was needed, and the twinkle in their mournful Russian eyes said a great deal more. His little gifts were always rewarded by a fusillade of Russian jokes, of increasing obscenity, and that said most of all. But he knew the precise measure of the value of his small contributions, from when some flat-featured Slavic soldier would nod at him occasionally as he padded his way through their compound. The man would give him a sidelong glance, furtively, as if paralysed with self-consciousness, and mutter a couple of words in some uncouth, almost unintelligible dialect, and then they would pass one another by. But the man would gesture at his feet, to show that he was wearing a pair of socks knitted by a well-meaning but elderly and short-sighted aunt, so that they turned out to be a third too short but three times too wide for Hales's feet. Or a man with a painful and permanent sore throat would jerk a thumb laconically at a woollen scarf rejected by Hales who already had a better one. The smile into which the flat brown face would crease for an instant said all that needed to be said.

They took a shy, but almost proprietorial pride in his gathering command of Russian. It showed in their pleasure when he tried to exchange a few halting words with them, and grew with every step he took forward. His vocabulary grew rapidly, in particular his stock of expressive and inventive Russian obscenities, and he would test himself in competition with the doctors to see who could tell the rudest jokes. The doctors always won hands down, but by the time he was sauntering back towards his own compound the 'new English joke' would already be doing the rounds of the camp, and he would hear it passing from inmate to inmate, mutilated and altered out of recognition in its passage through different dialects, and the pride they took in it warmed him more than a personal tribute from the King and both Houses of Parliament.

He also continued to make his daily detour to listen outside the German barracks, very occasionally rewarded by a few minutes' music. One morning in early autumn, when he had been in the camp for about nine months, he was lucky and heard once again the song that had first rooted him to the spot outside the barracks. He stood transfixed once more, and for the remainder of that day went about the camp alternately whistling the tune and warbling the two or three lines of the words that he had managed to catch as he listened.

He was trying to sing one such line as his stroll brought him out of the hutment area to a point where the deadly rolls of razor wire were a little closer than usual to the nearest huts. There was, for once, not a soul in view. He slowed to a gentle saunter and ambled along, enjoying the mild warmth of the sun on his face, the heady flavour of the music in his head and the unaccustomed solitude, and mangling the words of the song as he ambled. "Im Grünen, im Grünen, am Morgen am Abend in something-thing Stille, entsomething-thing something und something Idylle, und Hymen oft something poetischen Scherz, denn leicht ist die Lockung und something das Herz, im Grünen, im Grünen..." he carolled, wishing he knew all the words, and that he knew what the ones he did know meant, but not caring much.

It was a rare moment of carefree forgetfulness, almost of happiness; and it was interrupted by a chuckle from somewhere behind him. He spun round, feeling unaccountably outraged at the intrusion. Before he could identify its source, however, the chuckle was replaced by a voice. *"Sie mögen Schubert?"* Then for the first time he realised that he had not been, after all, quite alone. There was a lone grey-clad figure, strolling along beside the wire at the same relaxed pace as his own, a few yards behind him. He halted and stared at the soldier, annoyed at having his imagined solitude breached, but mollified by the amiable expression on the man's face. The soldier, seeing his RAF insignia, promptly translated his question. "You like Schubert?" he said in good, almost unaccented English.

Hales stared at him for a moment longer. Then, in considerable confusion, he said "I... yes. I do. How did..." He lapsed into silence. He realised angrily that he was blushing to find that his absurd efforts at singing had been overheard. "You don't know the words very well," the man continued, before he had a chance to say any more. Without waiting for further reply he sang, softly, in a pleasant, light baritone, *"am Morgen am Abend in treulicher Stille, entkeimet manch Liedchen und manche Idylle, und Hymen oft kranzt den poetischen Scherz, denn leicht ist die Lockung, empfänglich das Herz, im Grünen, im Grünen..."* [And morning and evening, in intimate stillness, many a song, many an idyll is born, and Hymen comes often to crown the gay poetic impulse: for it is easy to be seduced, the heart is responsive, in the green countryside...]

Hales stared at him, unable to think of a thing to say, while he sang the remaining verses of the *Lied*, softly, as if to himself. While he did so Hales saw that he was a very young man, not much more than twenty, he thought. Scarcely more than a boy. He was a very ordinary-looking young man, made to look still more so by the uniform. But he had a pleasant young face, with a stubble of very blond hair just showing below the coal-scuttle helmet. He looked as if he had scarcely started shaving. His eyes were blue and wide-spaced, slightly magnified by spectacles, and his expression was as amiable as his voice had been.

When he came to the end of his song he stared levelly and without a trace of embarrassment at Hales. "You like that song?" he asked.

"Yes," replied Hales, who had gathered his wits during the rest of the song. "Yes, I do. It's a funny sort of a poem, from what I can understand of it, but I like the song very much."

The young soldier frowned faintly. "Funny? I don't think so," he said. "It's not a very *good* poem, I think, but it's not meant to be funny."

"I meant funny peculiar, not funny ha-ha," said Hales, and, seeing that the man did not understand, corrected himself. "I didn't mean funny, but that it's an odd poem... er, strange." The faint frown of puzzlement cleared from the boy's face. "Ah. *Ja, ich sehe.* Funny can mean strange, as well as amusing, in English, yes?"

"Right," said Hales.

"Yes, I agree, it certainly is an odd poem. Not very good. But who needs good words with Schubert's music? You are fond of music?"

"Very," said Hales, and the warmth of his tone clearly said all that was necessary to the boy. Equally clearly he approved of the warmth. "I could write down the words for you if you wish," he said. "Would you like that?"

Hales was so surprised by the offer, so friendly, so natural a gesture, coming in so matter-of-fact a tone, from someone whom the severe conditioning of several years had made him think of automatically as an enemy, that once again he stared at the boy for some seconds without a word. But he was recovering his poise, and found his tongue this time before the embarrassment of the other's speaking again. "Why yes... Yes, I'd like to have the words, if... if it won't... er... I mean, if it won't get you into trouble," he finished awkwardly.

"If I don't tell anyone, it cannot get me into trouble, can it?" the youth said, with a faint smile at Hales's confusion.

They stood for a few moments in silence. Then, "You speak very good English," Hales said, meaning it, and this time it was the boy's turn to flush. With his fair, almost transparent complexion and lack of visible hair, it showed as a rich, scarlet blush; but the boy seemed unconscious of it, or at any rate unbothered. "You are kind," he said, and the smile that had been faintly in evidence before showed itself again, less fleetingly. "I hope I speak it well. I am a teacher of English," he went on. "Or rather," he corrected himself, "I *was* a teacher. In a school. That was until I was called up for this — what would you say in English? — for this bloody war, yes?"

Hales grinned involuntarily. "I said it wrongly," said the boy, misinterpreting the grin and looking chagrined.

"No, no, not at all," Hales protested hastily, feeling an oddly urgent anxiety to dispel the mournful expression from the boy's face. "No, you said it quite correctly. It was just funny to hear it come out like that, from a German..." He realised what he had said. "That word again," he said with a mock-rueful smile. "Strange," they said in unison, and this time both of them grinned.

"So," resumed the German. "I was a teacher. And I hope to be a teacher again, when it's over. What were you before this bloody war?"

"Me? Oh, well, I'd hardly begun to be anything", said Hales, and had to explain. "I was training to be a barrister. A lawyer," he elaborated, seeing that the word was new to the boy. "But it takes a long time to... er, to get the necessary qualifications. I was still getting them when the war started."

The boy considered this. "I see. So you will have to resume your studies when it is finished?"

Explaining this to the boy's satisfaction took up several minutes, and the boy glanced hurriedly at his watch. "I must go on with my patrol," he said. "But you can walk with me as far as the end of the row of huts if you wish." Hales did wish. They resumed strolling along the wire, exchanging the small snippets that, coming almost at random, make up the beginnings of every acquaintance. "You had better go down between these huts," said the boy eventually, as they came abreast of the final pair in the row. "It might not be good for us to be seen talking. I have seen you about the camp, yes? You walk every day."

"Yes, when it's not raining too hard", Hales assented.

"I shall be on this patrol this week," said the boy. "If you would like to talk, come tomorrow. I'll have the words of the *Lied* for you, if you would still like them."

"Yes, please. I would," said Hales, turning off to walk down the side of the hut. Immediately he turned back. "One other thing," he said, a little diffidently. he was acutely conscious that he was blushing once more.

"Yes?" said the young soldier, pausing in his stride.

"Your name," said Hales. "I don't know your name."

The boy considered him for a moment. "Schumacher," he said. "Eugen Schumacher."

"Thank you. Are you the one who plays the music sometimes?" asked Hales quickly. He suddenly wanted very badly to know. "In the barracks block?"

"Yes, I play when I'm off duty, and when there aren't many of the others there. Most of them are not interested in music — not the kind I like. They don't let me play it very much. But when I'm in there on my own, yes, I play it often."

"I often come and wait outside there," said Hales, unconsciously adopting the conspiratorial manner of one sharing a secret, "hoping to hear music for a few minutes."

"I know," said the boy, and this time, for the first time, he permitted his grin to appear at full voltage. "I've seen you sometimes. I thought it was for the music. I hoped so. And now," he said, suddenly crisp and businesslike, "you haven't told me *your* name."

"Brian Hales", he said.

"Thank you," said the boy with odd, formal courtesy. And to Hales's astonishment, he clicked his heels together. "Tomorrow, then, perhaps?" said the boy.

"I'll be here," Hales agreed. The boy turned and strode off on his leisurely patrol without a further look back. Hales wandered off on his detour through the end of the hutment, whistling the Schubert *Lied* once more, but unconscious of what he whistled or where he wandered.

XIV

HE spent the remainder of that day in a curiously agitated and rest-less frame of mind, and that night he slept badly, waking often and finding it difficult to settle back to sleep. He got up more than once and padded noiselessly down the hut to get a drink of water, listen-ing to the steady breathing of his twenty-nine hut-mates and the other small noises of the night in a strangely distracted haze of con-fused feeling, as if he was hearing them from some unattainably remote distance. From time to time through the day and during the wakeful stations of the night he found his thoughts turning inward, and wondered "What the hell's the matter with me?", turning the oddly distracted condition of his nerves over and over in a restless search for a cause, and finding all manner of solutions except the right one.

He eventually fell into a heavy sleep of nervous exhaustion at about six o'clock, just as first light was beginning to seep its way up into the sky, and only a brief hour before morning roll-call. When they were due to turn out for *Appell* he was comatose, and had to be rolled bodily and energetically out of his bunk by Shepherd, to the accompaniment of much ribald speculation from everyone else as to what night-time activities could have left him so prostrate. *Appell* and breakfast were a nightmarish vista of weariness, but after he had some food inside him, and several mugs of coffee, he began to re-cover a little, though it was only to find himself in the same nerv-ous, jittery condition of mingled anxiety and anticipation in which he had spent most of the previous day. He still could not have said if he had been asked why he was in so odd a state; but he found a remedy after breakfast: when the others all went off on their vari-ous working assignments, he prowled round at a distance until the camp presented its usual daytime state of semi-desertion, then slipped back into the hut, rolled himself up in his bunk and slept like a stone for two hours.

The tumbling, churning emotions had resolved themselves when he awoke, refreshed and quivering slightly with expectation. He sat up a little dizzily in his bunk, wondering for a few moments where he was and then how he came to be where he was at so unac-customed an hour. Then it all came back to him in a joyous mo-ment of clarity. He looked at his watch in momentary panic lest he was late, saw with overwhelming relief that he wasn't, and rolled out of the bunk, wide awake.

He treated himself to an extra couple of mugs of coffee from a private jar that he had rat-holed in his bedroll, then left the hut and ambled off, apparently with no particular aim in view, as if setting off on one of his customary daily jaunts round the enclosure.

He hadn't gone far, though, before he turned off his route in the general direction of the Russian compound and began heading in a much more purposeful stride for the part of the perimeter where he had met Eugen Schumacher.

As he emerged from between the last pair of huts before the wire his heart was beating unpleasantly fast, his throat was dry and, he realised in some astonishment, he was trembling slightly all over. The shroud of detachment of earlier had fallen from him, and he would have had no difficulty whatever in explaining what was happening to him. He forgot all of that, however, in the first moment of precipitous disappointment as he came out into the twenty-yard rat-run between huts and fence and looked eagerly, anxiously, about him: there was not a soul in sight.

He forced himself to be rational, and, reckoning that being inconspicuous was as wise a policy as he could adopt for the day, slipped back into the cover of the nearest hut. He selected a vantage point from which he had a clear view of the fence in the direction from which Schumacher had appeared on his patrol the day before, sat down in the stringy grass at the base of the hut, and kept watch. After a few minutes he shifted uncomfortably against the unyielding side of the hut and stretched himself out on his belly in the grass instead. Sheltered from the cold wind in the lee of the hut, with the sun pleasantly warm on his back, he settled his chin on the backs of his hands and kept lookout.

He woke with a start, to find the neat grey-uniformed figure of Schumacher squatting on his heels beside him and shaking him vigorously. "Brian... Brian Hales... wake up. Come on, wake up... *ach, lieber Gott,* wake *up,* will you!" he was muttering.

Hales rolled sideways, propped himself on one elbow, looked straight up into Schumacher's face, and smiled. The impatient expression was wiped off Schumacher's young, unshaven face, and without thinking he smiled back. It made him look ten years younger, like a schoolboy, trusting, affectionate and vulnerable.

"I thought I was never going to make you wake up," he said, as Hales rose to his feet, stretched and brushed grass and beads of dew from his uniform.

When he had completed his rough toilet they strolled out into the open. Schumacher slipped a sheet of paper into Hales's hand. He unfolded it and found the complete poem of the Schubert song, carefully indited in a heavy, decisive hand in black ink. He sang the first stanza softly to himself, then folded the paper and slid it into his breast pocket, beneath his single wing. "Thank you," he said. "It's very kind of you. I'm very glad to have it. I can learn the words properly, now." They promptly fell into an awkward silence, neither knowing what to say next. Then they both started to speak at once, and both fell silent, each gesturing to the other to continue, and both declined.

The brief moment of awkwardness was quickly over, however, and the next twenty minutes passed quickly in the kind of small talk, mostly question and answer, of new acquaintances finding out the essential facts about one another, which adds up to almost nothing in the sum of a friendship, yet is among the most crucial of all the stages between meeting and knowing, between acquaintance and friendship, or, as it may be and sometimes is, between friendship and love. That twenty minutes was brought abruptly to a close when Schumacher glanced at his watch. "I must complete my patrol," he said, and by a common instinct they looked sadly at one another, both sorry the moment was over. Neither thought for a moment of attempting to extend it: that was simply not to be considered. But Hales thanked his new acquaintance again, more profusely, for the poem, and they agreed by more or less tacit consent to meet again the next day. Neither of them, at that stage, thought for a moment of suggesting a meeting later in the day, when Schumacher would be off-duty.

But the remainder of that day dragged by on leaden feet for both of them, and when they met the next morning it was a far brighter, livelier meeting than their first. They also contrived, without thinking about it much, to extend it to half an hour. At the end of that time Schumacher had to dash away to make himself visible, and both felt acutely conscious of the wrench of parting in so unsatisfactory a way. Both had the feeling that somehow a measure of formality seemed appropriate to meetings arranged, and conducted, in such difficult and bizarre circumstances. They were both very young.

From the beginning it was an easy relationship, made difficult only by circumstances. They could rarely spend more than a few minutes together at any one time, before Schumacher's duties took him elsewhere. Some days he was on guard duty with one of the gangs out of camp, and they were unable to see one another until evening. At intervals it was his day off-duty, and neither of them had yet devised a way of ensuring a meeting on those days. It was not, as yet, so vital a part of their lives.

They moved easily over the first stages of getting to know one another, and made light work of them. They found within the first few times together that they had a great deal in common. Music, which had taken on a new meaning for Hales in the last few weeks, for Schumacher was a passion. He talked about it in passionate language, lyrical, sometimes apocalyptic, without a trace of embarrassment.

Then one day came a turning point. It was a small thing, but nonetheless it was a moment after which they both knew, instinctively and immediately, that things could never again be the same between them: it was a river crossed, a bridge burned.

They had met by the usual arrangement at the sector of the wire assigned to Schumacher for the week. As he came up to where Hales was loitering in wait he was whistling softly to himself: a gentle, carolling piece that Hales knew but could not place. "What's that you were whistling?" he asked after the usual exchange of greetings.

"Eh? I was whistling?"

"Yes, yes," said Hales. "I know it as well as anything, but I don't know its name." He whistled a snatch of the melody himself. Schumacher's face darkened. "*Ach, du Himmel!* I was whistling that. *Du Menschenskind!* I'm glad it was only you who heard that. I'd have been in trouble if..." He fell silent, and paced for some time in private thought. His face was dark and troubled. Hales walked along beside him, having enough sense to respect the boy's sudden mood of abstraction, but inwardly consumed with anxiety, as well as deeply curious to know the source of the sudden shadow on his friend's young, open face.

"Can't you tell me what it is?" he eventually ventured to say, when the silence had become unbearable — they were still at the stage of finding out about one another in which any silence is unbearable after a very short while. Schumacher half turned towards him, and his eyes were wide. Hales saw in surprise that they were round with fear. "Come on, Eugen," he urged him, "please tell me. Whatever *is* it?"

"That piece I was whistling," Schumacher began hesitantly. "It... I didn't realise I was whistling at all, you see. If I'd been heard by certain people..." He lapsed into silence for a moment, and Hales was preparing to prompt him again when he resumed. "It was one of the *Lieder ohne Worte*." He turned excitedly towards Hales, plainly expecting Hales's face to reflect the fear etched across his own. He saw only blank incomprehension. "The Songs Without Words," he said, as if that explained it all.

Hales still looked question marks. "By Mendelssohn," said Schumacher, evidently in explanation, and watched for light to dawn. It didn't. "You didn't know?" he said, blankly. "No, of course, you wouldn't. I suppose you wouldn't. Well, we are not supposed... we're not *allowed* to play his music. Or whistle it," he added darkly.

"Why not?" said Hales, mystified. "What's the matter with Mendelssohn?"

"He's a *Jew*," cried Schumacher, finally goaded by such apparent thick-headedness into raising his voice. Then he realised what he had done, and instantly looked fearfully over his shoulder, over the other, all round. It would have been comic, Hales reflected later, replaying the incident over in his mind's eye, had the fear that had brought it about not been so transparently real. But it had been: he had *seen* the boy quail, and in the moment before he threw the fearful look over his shoulder his terror had been plainly visible, almost palpable.

Hales murmured soothingly to him until he had calmed down. Then, with many further furtive glances about him, haltingly at first and then with more confidence as he scanned Hales's face to see the effect of his words, Schumacher explained.

"You don't know about... what's been happening in Germany?" he had begun. Hales simply shook his head and motioned to him to go on. Then it had come out, the words swelling to a rush and then into a torrent. Hales had listened in astonishment to tales of Jewish shopkeepers first boycotted, then intimidated and terrorised, and finally their staff, any resolute would-be customers and themselves beaten bloody, and sometimes worse, by gangs of brown-shirted men.

"I had no idea," he said weakly. "I mean, we heard — in England, that is — there were a few reports that a certain amount of Jewish property had been confiscated without compensation, and we knew a lot of Jews were leaving Germany. But they were mostly writers and musicians, intellectuals. Everyone thought it was just

Hitler's opponents. Nobody knew ordinary Jews were being treated like that. And as for people booting them to death in broad daylight... well, it's almost incredible."

"But they were," Schumacher said earnestly. The people doing it were all members of the... of the Party. They were... *Raufbolden* — in English you would say ruffians, I think? People who would have been arrested in no time up to when... before the Party gained control. Then, suddenly, they were legitimate. Jews were kicked to death in front of crowds, and no one moved a muscle. They knew they would be treated the same way if they did. I... I watched it happening myself, once. I went home and cried. I hated myself, despised myself for a coward. But I knew if I had tried to stop it it would have been useless. All that would have happened is that I would have been beaten up myself. Perhaps they might have killed me, too." His voice was shaking. Hales, who had been walking with his head turned, watching him closely, saw a large tear roll slowly down each cheek. He halted, gently but firmly clamped an arm round the boy's shoulders, and lugged him by main force into the protective cover of the aisle between the nearest pair of huts. It was the first time they had touched each other.

It took him a minute or two to soothe the boy back to an appearance of normality. Then they resumed their easy-paced stroll. "But be careful," Hales urged him, detaching his arm and feeling a powerful pang of reluctance as he did so. "You mustn't let anybody see you like that."

Schumacher nodded, and gave him a slightly watery smile of assurance and thanks. Then he completed his brief outline of events in Germany over the past ten years. "They say..." he finished, looking about him still more furtively, "they say... there are places... camps... where Jews are taken in thousands, and... and executed. Killed. I've heard talk of people being shot in batches of hundreds at a time. I've heard of..." His voice sank at last to a whisper, and Hales had to crane his neck and put his ear almost to the boy's lips to hear the next words. "Gas chambers," he hissed almost inaudibly into the ear. "My parents, they live near a place called Sachsenhausen, and once, when I had a weekend pass, they told me that there was one of these camps nearby. But they told me never to mention it, because officially it did not exist. But they said that some of the local woodmen had found mass graves, and talked about it. Next day, they had disappeared, and were never seen again.

"I don't know if these stories are true. I can't really believe that ordinary, decent Germans could do such things, or have any part in them. But... well, one hears the stories, now and then. And Mendelssohn's music... *verboten*," he finished softly. He fell silent. Hales, respecting the evident misery that brought it, and also the equally evident fear that accompanied his talking about such things, forebore to break the silence, leaving it to Schumacher to do that. Eventually, he did. "That's one of the things I can never forgive them for," he said softly, glancing at Hales seeking agreement. "The... the Party," he elaborated, still speaking tremulously, "and what they've done to music. They've taken Wagner and perverted him. They've taken Beethoven, Schubert, Brahms, and bent them to the service of the Party. And Mendelssohn, we're not allowed to whistle his tunes in the street."

Shortly afterwards they had to endure their daily parting, but for once Hales spent little of the rest of the day gnawed by missing Schumacher. He had been given too much to think about by what had been said. One thing, however, did emerge from the recital of terrible goings-on, to afford him a generous dash of comfort. Schumacher would never, he realised, have dreamed of uttering such things, and would never have dreamed in his wildest nightmares of so much as mentioning them, let alone of breathing a syllable of criticism of the apparently all-powerful Party (Hales had observed, with a wry private grin that he took care not to allow Schumacher to see, that he always pronounced the word with a careful capital P), unless he had decided that he could safely place unqualified trust in his friend. It was, Hales decided as he lay in his bunk that night, going over and over the events of the day, a commitment, and one of no small order. He listened to the usual plaintive rumblings of his ill-fed stomach, and turned over with a troubled mind to try to sleep.

His sleep was again fitful. He lay for long periods of the night wondering if the horrors at which his new friend had hinted could conceivably be true, and thought it unlikely. Then his mind would turn to the indisputably satisfactory balance in the personal side of the ledger of his feelings, and a subtle glow of pleasure would steal over him. That, in turn, was promptly replaced by a strong feeling of guilt that he should derive any feelings of comfort or satisfaction in the shadow of the monstrous, almost unimaginable possibilities in the shadowy rumours to which Schumacher had alluded. "Don't be such an insufferable prig," scoffed the down-to-earth, rational side of him. "You can't blame yourself for things that probably never happened. And even if they did happen, you couldn't possibly have done anything about it. Besides, you were *doing* what you could about it. You were sinking Nazi submarines until you were pranged..."

But then he saw again the two large tears that had rolled slowly down Schumacher's smooth cheeks, leaving their trails of faintly glistening dampness in their wake. They had been real enough, hadn't they? And they had been brought on by the recollection of his own witness to an appallingly brutish murder, in which the murderers had gone not merely unpunished but unhindered. That murder had been committed insolently, in daylight, in full view of a crowd of what Schumacher had called ordinary, decent Germans, including Schumacher himself, at the time a mere child, who had wept from shame for having done nothing to prevent or stop it...

...and then he had put a comforting arm about Schumacher's shoulders. Schumacher the man, now, he thought, staring straight upwards into the darkness and the bowed bedroll of the man in the third-tier bunk above his face. There was no disguising or concealing from himself the satisfaction in *that* small part of the day's proceedings, he acknowledged candidly to himself, and turned to sleep once more with his mind feeding quietly off this one undeniable source of pleasure.

Later still that night he woke again, and for a moment had to rack his brains to establish what was unusual about how he felt. Then he identified it: for the first time in months, he was feeling aroused. For months now, all through the long, rainswept winter, rations had been getting shorter, and they had been growing ever more dependent on the regular parcels from the Red Cross for the bulk of their food. Everyone was hungry. Even the most cunning and endlessly resourceful of the 'fixers', grand masters of the arts of scrounging, barter, bargaining and blackmail, were beginning to feel the pinch. The most irrepressible spirits such as Shepherd/McMurdo were subdued by the relentless water-on-stone attrition of constant, ever-present, gnawing hunger. There were no impromptu caber-tossing contests now.

In such conditions no one talked or even thought about sex, or anything remotely touching it. Not only were they too hungry to think about it, but, worse, sex, even thinking about it, used up a certain amount of energy, and they hadn't got it to spare. But this night, Hales awoke fully aroused and thinking very much about sex indeed. For this night it was when he finally conceded to himself what he was feeling for young Schumacher, and knew that he was in love once more.

As the night spiralled slowly into morning he lay, doing nothing about his almost painful condition, and thought about love, and the people he had loved.

He thought first about Peter Butterworth, and wondered what he was doing in the war, if anything. Probably devising fiendishly clever doomsday weaponry in some ultra-secret committee sitting in a bunker somewhere half a mile underneath Shropshire, he thought, and grinned to himself in the dark from a sudden access of fondness. Then he thought of his last few meetings with Butterworth, in particular the very last one, and the thought wiped the smile off his face. He thought of Ronnie, and the miserable conclusion of their relationship. Another betrayal, he thought, not very fairly to himself, but it was a moment for self-awareness. Images of Sylvain flickered briefly in his mental vision, but that had been nothing more than a momentary fling, a brief, urgent moment of refuge from the war and the mental and emotional switchback of constant danger and fear of danger, and the visions faded from his mind as quickly as they had come. Finally he turned to thoughts of Michael Ayres.

Had he been in love with Ayres, he wondered? Or had Ayres, too, been no more than a relief? It *had* been a relief, he was honest enough with himself to admit that. At the time of his all too short-lived interval with Ayres he had been seeking relief as usual from the ever-present slouching monsters of the war and the murderous cumulative strain on the nerves of unending missions, but there had been something else from which Ayres had provided a blessed healing balm as well, in the shape of Ronnie, and his rapidly disintegrating relationship with him. And yet... and yet, a small but persistent voice inside him repeated, he had been truly happy with Ayres, at least most of the time. There had been times when either or both of them had been left with their nerves stretched so taut by the strain of flying out on missions from which they might never return, and by watching so many of their friends fly on identical missions and not return, that nothing short of being knocked unconscious would have soothed them. But in general, yes, he thought, they had made one another happy. Ayres had been an accomplished lover, gentle and soothing but also imaginative and not by any means low on passion. But he had also been great fun, jolly, amusing company, a thoughtful, considerate and affectionate friend, in all, a pleasure to live with. So had he been in love with Ayres? More to the point, perhaps, had Ayres been in love with him? Hales thought on balance the answer was yes to both. Where, he wondered, tossing restlessly again, did that leave him now?

He took stock of his situation. He was a prisoner of war, held in generally fair and reasonable conditions, but held by the army of a nation that had shown itself willing to descend to the most frightful abysses of bestiality on the slightest provocation, or on no provocation at all. The German army by and large respected the Geneva Convention and observed the essential humanities of warfare; but in the last resort, or anything getting close to it, it was the Nazi Party that was firmly in control in Germany. So here he was, with precisely as many rights and privileges as it pleased his German captors to permit him. He was... an echo of Roy Dean's voice popped unbidden into his mind: 'fed up, fucked up and far from home', he heard him saying, some time on that last disastrous mission.

And he was in love with, or very fast becoming in love with, a young German soldier who, though he was, at twenty-three, the same age as Hales himself, looked at any rate as if he had not yet had to start shaving. The boy took an obvious pleasure in his company, was delighted to find, in the midst of the wilderness of war, a kindred spirit with whom he could talk about music and books without having to fear ribald barrack-room piss-taking and arch speculation about his sex, or his sexual habits. They had gone from first, chance contact to almost open friendship in no time at all, and so effortlessly and naturally that neither of them had really noticed the process taking place.

That was all very well, but it was a far cry from any kind of open declaration of love. Schumacher — Eugen, as Hales now always called him: they had been on Christian name terms almost from the beginning — had never come anywhere close to talk of love, or evinced the faintest sign of being physically drawn to Hales. Hales, for his part, had been aware from very early on that he was strongly attracted to Eugen, but he had studiously avoided anything that could even be mistaken for a physical pass, for fear of frightening him off. The truth was, he now decided in the darkness of his bunk, that he doubted very strongly if Eugen would even recognise it if he were to make one. "Or am I crediting him with too much innocence? He's not a twelve-year-old kid?" some devil's advocate within insisted on asking in a quiet, sarcastic tone.

After some time on this fruitless speculation he decided that the only sensible course was to pigeon-hole the question for future resolution. But he was sure of one thing. He was going to have Eugen Schumacher, or make his best attempt, one day. With that he ceased to torment himself with thought, abandoned himself instead to a series of delicious fantasies of how it all might end and, at last, dropped into an uneasy sleep.

XV

WHETHER it was love or not, the daily meeting with Eugen rapidly became an obsession. Hales began to live for the brief moment of intimacy, which he came increasingly to see as a small oasis of sanity and rebirth in a world of whirring, uniform grey monotony. Sometimes they managed to spin it out to half an hour, and those days attained the status of red-letter days, on a par with the arrival of Red Cross or clothing parcels, or the notching up of some triumph of black marketeering.

There were occasional catastrophes also, such as when Eugen was sentenced to two weeks' jankers for being found with patches of rust on his bayonet in a snap inspection in preparation for a visit by some functionaries from the Nazi Party in the nearest city. For the next fortnight he was given the run-around by the Commandant, assigned to all sorts of duties as unpleasant as could be found for him, and for much of the time they were reduced to gazing at each other from a distance, sometimes through the wire as Eugen was detailed to clear the few remaining thickets of small birch and gorse bushes visible from the camp. Generally, however, discipline was fairly slack at the camp, and this they were able to turn to their advantage, so that as the summer went on they were able to find more and more excuses for spending a few additional minutes in one another's company.

When they were together they talked, endlessly, about almost every subject under the sun. Much of it was about themselves, as young men, and particularly young lovers, will, until Hales thought he knew almost as much about Eugen as he knew about himself. Few of the conversations were memorable, but one or two stuck out in his memory. Once, shortly after Eugen's term of punishment postings, they were talking about the duties he had been given for his minor criminal record over the rusty bayonet, and Hales asked, without thinking, why a young and able-bodied man such as

Eugen had been assigned to such relatively safe and undemanding a duty as guarding a camp far from any fighting. Eugen winced, and flushed a little. "It wasn't my decision," he said in tones of protest. "I'm no coward." Hales could have bitten his own tongue off at the root for having wounded his young lover on so sensitive a place, and began gabbling a confused torrent of apologies as fast as he could think of them, but Eugen waved him into silence, and gave him an especially affectionate smile, a potent weapon which, he had learned very early on, bestowed on him the capacity to reduce Hales to a quivering, puppy-like fever of adoration.

"Stop worrying, Brian," he said. "Don't fuss. Of course I know you weren't accusing me of being a coward. I was only saying that I didn't ask to come here. But that isn't to say that I'm not glad I did come here. Not only because I should not have met you if I hadn't come here — though that's a good reason for blessing my draft board, of course..."

He went on to say that prison-camp guard duties were in the main restricted to conscripted men who were too old for the fighting fronts or medically graded C3 or worse, and confessed that his own assignment to such duties was on account of his suffering from flat feet and mild but chronic asthma. Hales scarcely heard a word of the rest of his account, however, after the reference to their own meeting; and he went about for the remainder of that day toasting himself against the warm radiance of his pleasure at the frank admission of affection implicit in the words.

He remembered enough of the rest of it to pick the subject up again at their next meeting, asking anxiously if Eugen was receiving treatment for the asthma, and being briefly and impatiently reassured that it was nothing more than a minor ailment, troublesome and annoying at times but otherwise not to be worried about. "And if it brought me here it's something I'm more than glad to bear," he added. "It brought me you..." Hales went off on another short tour of a world in which moons rhymed with Junes, but came back down to earth this time, in time to hear his friend go on to say, "At least being here I shan't have to kill anyone, given a little luck. I don't know that I could bring myself to kill anyone..."

He went on to ask if Hales had, to his knowledge, killed anyone, and Hales's description of his work as part-time bomb aimer aboard the *Betelgeuse* occupied most of their meetings for the next three days. Eugen was deeply interested, not only in the technicalities of the task but in the feelings it brought in its wake; and he was puzzled and worried by Hales's frank admission that he had never been able to connect his minute but mechanical adjustments to his instruments inside the cockpit of the Halifax with real blood, splinters of bone and searing, unimaginable pain.

This in turn brought in its wake a discussion of the morality of warfare that spread over no fewer than five conversations, until they agreed that they were both sick of the subject and by common consent agreed to turn to something more interesting, such as themselves.

Before that long discussion by instalments was over, Eugen made one remark that caught Hales's attention. "My father used to say something to me when I was a small child," he began. "I never really understood what he meant at that time, but I understand it now."

"Oh? What was that?" asked Hales, interested in anything to do with Eugen's parents.

"He said that when he was serving in his war — he was in the first one, of course — he would much rather have shot his own corporal, or several of his own officers, than any of the Englishmen in the opposite trenches. Not that Vati was ever anywhere near a trench, but it was for an example. I couldn't understand that at all, of course. How could he possibly be willing to shoot a fellow German, I asked, rather than one of the enemy?"

"Very simple, he said. Because he *knew* that his own corporal was a first-class bastard, whereas as far as he knew or could ever know, the Englishman across the mud was just another decent man, no different from himself. That meant that the whole concept of 'the enemy' was a... *ein Fiktion*; how would you say it in English? The same word? Yes, a fiction, I think, is what he meant to say. But, as I said, I wasn't able to understand that concept at all. It is a very adult concept, I think, don't you, Brian?"

Hales stared into space for a moment while he considered the notion, then nodded briskly. "It's a very grown-up notion, yes," he said. "A *thoroughly* grown-up one. But it's the only sane or safe one to hold, if you ask me. I don't think I'd have understood it, any more than you did, if my father had said such a thing to me when I was a child. But I can agree with it now. Look at us, for instance..." The idea sent them both into their own thoughts, not of the happiest: each was privately seeing himself required to kill the other, and finding it, literally, unthinkable.

Eugen's face cleared first, as he dismissed the dark thought from his mind. "I've had some news. It seems the war's not going at all well for us. It really looks as if we're going to lose." His face wobbled a little, reflecting his wavering opinion. "I don't know whether to be happy or sad," he eventually said. "I don't like to think of Germany being humiliated. But it will mean..." almost unconsciously he lowered his voice, and looked surreptitiously about him before going on, "the end of the Nazis... and they're responsible for everything, aren't they?"

"I don't think it's as simple as that," said Hales thoughtfully. "Frankly, I think it's as much our fault as anyone's. If Versailles hadn't been such a colossal injustice, Hitler would never have been able to drum up the kind of support he did. Still..." He closed the subject with a shrug. "Anyway," he went on, brightening, "what's this news you've had? How did you get it, come to that?"

"I've had a letter from my father," said Eugen excitedly. "He says it's disaster. The Russian front is nothing more than a bloodbath, and now the second front has happened. You British and the Yankees have invaded from England, and they've apparently driven us back half way across France in no time."

Hales stared at him. "But how the devil did you get to hear about all this?" he asked in astonishment.

"I told you, I had a letter from Vati."

"But what in the world were your censors thinking of, to let news like that through?" demanded Hales. "I mean, surely your letters here are censored, aren't they? You were complaining only the other day about how annoying it was..."

"Yes, of course there's a censor," said Eugen nonchalantly. "But that's no problem for my father. You remember I told you just now that he never went near a trench in the other war?" Hales nodded. "Well," the young man went on, "he was in the Navy, but actually he never went to sea, either. He worked in some very secret office, making the codes for naval messages. So the first thing he did when I was posted away from home was to devise a simple code for the two of us. Funny, isn't it?" he ended with a cheeky grin, which made Hales's heart throb and contract within him, feeling as if it missed two beats in five for a few moments.

"Funny," said Hales, chuckling himself at the idea of father and son bypassing the censor with such ease. "I didn't think you Germans were supposed to have a sense of humour."

Eugen surveyed him for a few seconds, then grinned again. "Of course we've got one. It's just not the same as yours." With that they changed the subject, and a few minutes later endured the daily pain of parting.

Like every young man in love, Hales wanted desperately to talk to someone about his beloved, to extol his charms, his unparalleled virtues and his uniqueness. The difficulty was, of course, that there was no one to whom he dared breathe so much as a word about even knowing one of the guards. The result was that the more his world came to revolve ever more obsessively around the young German, the more oppressive became the need to bottle up his urge to proclaim his state from the nearest rooftop. It swelled within him until it became like a gigantic bubble of gas and threatened to choke him.

At the same time he yearned more and more desperately to give his feelings some physical expression, yet these feelings too he had to suppress and fight down, for he still did not feel confident enough of Eugen's breadth of mind to feel sure that he would accept an overture, or, if he could not return the physical attraction, that he would at any rate understand it and not resent it. The worst outcome imaginable, that it would horrify and disgust him, and turn his uncomplicated, open friendship to revulsion or loathing, was, in actuality, so far beyond the imaginable that he simply never thought about it at all, at least in his conscious hours. He suspected that it was the mainspring powering a series of frightful nightmares that he began to suffer in his sleep, but there was nothing he felt able to do about it. So he ignored the nightmares as best he could and devoted a substantial part of the vacant hours of each day to planning schemes by which he could introduce his beloved to the idea of some physical expression of his feelings without any risk. But each scheme was more wildly improbable than the last, and none of them was much more than a daydream. His frustration grew apace.

The solution, when it came, was so devastatingly simple that it took him completely unawares, and he was relieved of both forms of internal torment in a couple of days, and in the same quarter.

It began with their first chance to meet on one of Eugen's days off. Hales had set off on one of his lengthy ambles round the camp, feeling both oppressed and depressed at the same time by the knowledge that he had a whole day to endure without so much as a sight of his beloved. As usual, he headed first for the guards' barracks, hoping against hope that he might hear a wisp of music. Even that, he felt, would be some small consolation, knowing that it emanated from one who had become the centre of his private universe. But when he got there and lurked under the looming creosoted wall of the building, it was depressingly silent and devoid of any sign of life.

He usually waited for five or ten minutes on the off-chance of hearing something, but that late morning he was feeling so thoroughly wretched that he turned away almost immediately and began wandering off, without any idea where he was heading. He had gone no more than a dozen paces when he heard a well-known and loved voice behind him. He spun round as if he had been shot, and saw Eugen hurrying towards him. He stood, hardly able to believe his good fortune, and waited for him to come up. It was the first time he had seen him out of uniform. He looked slim and athletic in twill slacks and a heavy woollen pullover, but most of all, it was the first sight of his hair that captivated Hales. It had been shaven almost to the scalp in the ugly German army regulation crop, but the last cut had been a while ago, so that it had grown out a little, to give Hales the combination that had always been fatal for him: blue eyes and fair hair — Eugen's was true blond, a burnished cream rather than yellow.

"Thank goodness I spotted you," he said, and Hales noticed with the exaggerated concern of devotion that even after so brief a trot he was panting slightly. But the words, and the evident delight with which he uttered them, immediately eclipsed all other feelings. "I wasn't expecting to see you today," he said, getting the words mixed up in his eagerness to speak.

"Neither was I," said Eugen. "But one of the medical officers came looking for someone to take a package to someone for him. I was just on my way when I happened to look out of the window, and saw you. I nearly bowled someone over, I came out so fast after you."

Hales smiled inwardly, a sweetly triumphant smile of success, especially success achieved against the odds. "Where are you going?" he asked, falling into step beside him.

"To the Russian enclosure," said the boy brightly. "One of their doctors. Doctor — er — Doctor Ob-something."

"Oblemov!" cried Hales. "Why, he's a pal of mine." A thought occurred to him. "Do you speak Russian?"

Eugen glanced quizzically at him. "Of course I don't," he said off-handedly. "Whyever should I need to speak Russian? I've only got to take this medicine to him." He brandished a small package wrapped in paper.

170

"Oh, well, he may need to ask you something," said Hales elatedly, savouring his opportunity.

"Well, I expect he speaks some English," said the boy, wondering why his friend was making so much of such a trifle.

"No need, my dear," said Hales, and felt his heart come up into his throat as he realised that he had betrayed himself. But Eugen's face showed only pleasure at the endearment. Then it returned to registering faint bewilderment. "But what of it?" he asked. "What does it matter?"

"Only this," said Hales. "I can speak Russian. Oblemov's a chum of mine. You'll need someone to interpret for you, won't you? Obviously you will, in case he asks you something."

Eugen's face lit up readily enough now that it was explained to him, and the two of them walked through the tussocky grass lanes between the huts wearing identical bright smiles. Neither of them realised he was wearing such a smile, radiating happiness, self-satisfied and slightly fatuous, but if anyone had been there to see, the smiles alone would have given their entire game away.

Oblemov was between patients when they presented themselves to him. He was enjoying a rare few minutes in the sun outside his surgery hut when they arrived, his thin body draped luxuriously but inelegantly over a hard chair brought out from the hut. He glanced up sharply at them, his eyes as keen as a starling's behind his slightly intimidating spectacles. "Well, well," he commented drily. "Not one friend but two today. Things are looking up. Who's this, and to what do I owe the honour?"

Hales introduced Eugen, who looked on admiringly at the flow of what sounded to him like rapid Russian. "Tea?" asked Oblemov. Hales accepted quickly, and they went inside the hut. Oblemov went and busied himself in the little odds-and-ends room behind his surgery area at the far end, and Eugen's eyes widened as Hales casually helped himself to two chairs from the waiting area, sat down and carried on a shouted conversation with the invisible Oblemov like an old friend. When Oblemov returned with glasses of tea and waved Eugen negligently to take the other chair he did so, then waited politely for a break in the exchanges of gossip before diffdently offering the doctor his package. "From his MO," said Hales. "Ah!" exclaimed Oblemov, and muttered something in Russian, in unmistakable tones of satisfaction. His grey, creased face creased still further as he directed a smile of thanks at Eugen, who said, in English, "He said the other things will follow very shortly." Hales transmitted the message, and Oblemov turned to the boy and said *"Sehr gut. Danke"*, in German so heavily accented that the words were almost unrecognisable.

After that they sat and held a three-way exchange of camp gossip and snippets of news, interspersed with the inevitable stream of the latest Russian jokes. Half an hour sped by before they realised it, and Eugen began to fidget, and started to look at his watch. "I should go back," he said, but his face told a different story, the regret written all over him. Hales nodded, excused them to Oblemov, and went with Eugen as far as the door of the hut. There he slipped outside with him to say their farewells. "I can come for a few minutes later," murmured Eugen as he turned to return to his quarters. "Oh, good!", Hales whispered in great elation. "Where?"

"Meet me behind the guardroom," Eugen whispered back. "Between Huts A1 and 2. Six o'clock this evening." He half turned to go. Then he turned back, looked rapidly about them, stepped up to Hales, curled an arm round his neck, and gave him a brief kiss on the cheek. It was so utterly unexpected that Hales was cast instantly into a chaotic ferment of consternation, confusion and transcendent happiness, so that by the time he had pulled himself together sufficiently to realise fully what had taken place, Eugen was gone, already out of sight in the maze of huts. He went slowly back into Oblemov's surgery like a man in a dream.

Back at the desk, he slumped back into his chair and accepted Oblemov's offer of more tea with a yelp of gratitude. Oblemov disappeared into his cubby-hole, reappearing with two glasses of steaming Russian tea. He set them down, draped his lanky frame carefully over his chair once more, and fixed a steely grey-eyed gaze on Hales's face. Hales was absorbed for the moment in his own tumultuous thoughts, but when the silence became oppressive he looked up, saw the level, almost stern gaze, and raised his eyebrows. "What is it, doc?" he asked.

For some moments Oblemov continued just looking steadily at him, but eventually he spoke. When he did, Hales saw with relief that all the customary ironical humour was back, making great webs of crow's feet round the keen eyes and stretching the thin lips still thinner across the gaunt jawbones. "Oh dear, oh dear, my boy", Oblemov began. "Are you sure this is wise?" And he sat back and surveyed Hales from beneath his heavy, drooping eyelids, looking, Hales thought, like the most perfect Sherlock Holmes in history. Hales also had a distinctly uneasy feeling that he knew precisely what Oblemov meant; but like any good straight-man he knew he was supposed to supply the feed. He obliged.

"Er... what exactly do you mean?" he asked, and was suddenly furious with himself as he felt himself blushing hotly.

"English," murmured Oblemov in pitying tones, "don't you come the innocent with me. It doesn't suit you. You know quite well what I mean. Are you quite sure you aren't heading for trouble, and biiiiig trouble, at that?"

"I don't know what you're talking about," said Hales forcefully; but he could feel the flush deepening across his forehead and down his cheeks, and he knew beyond a shadow of hope that Oblemov would have seen that, too. He shot a quick, searching look at the doctor, who abruptly gathered his untidy frame together, sat up straight in his chair, and looked steadily across the table at Hales. His expression was now clinical but not unkindly. "Kindly pay me the compliment of giving me the respect that my greater age, the dignity of my calling and my almost infinitely superior wisdom commands," he said, and Hales was sure he heard him suppress a chuckle, "and do *not* treat me like a half-wit. I'm talking, as you know perfectly well, about this entanglement with that boy you just brought with you."

Hales sat back and studied him in amazement. "You know about... about us?" he stammered. "About that?"

"My dear boy, it stood out like the Kamchatka peninsula," murmured Oblemov. "The question is, what are we going to do about it? Or, to be accurate, what am *I* going to do about it? One does not expect the patient to assist in his own treatment — not, at least, when the condition is of this particular nature."

Hales gazed at him in dismay. "What do you mean, what are you going to do about it?" he asked in great trepidation.

"I mean, what am I going to do about it, and you," said Oblemov. "Clearly we must do something. You can't be expected to continue with the present highly unsatisfactory arrangements. No," he went on after a pause for further intense scrutiny of Hales's face, which was by now registering mingled alarm and unhappiness in equal proportions. "Why don't we begin," Oblemov said gently, "by your telling me all about it?"

And so Hales got his longed-for chance to tell someone all about his new love and about his beloved, and he seized it. "I love him, Valeri Borisovitch," he began. "I've been in love before, or thought I have. No..." he reflected for a moment, "that's not fair. I *have* been in love before, but never like this. It's the real thing this time..."

"Good," Oblemov encouraged in his best bedside manner. "It's always best to get the fever out of the patient's system. Then you can tell me what you really think. And feel." Hales shot a suspicious glance at him, wondering if he was giving his scalpel-like sense of humour some exercise at his expense, but he saw nothing but friendly concern, with perhaps just a faint flicker of the usual sardonic humour lurking in the chilly grey eyes. He made a snap judgment, decided he must either place himself entirely in his physician's hands and trust him, or abandon the exercise there and then. He opted for trust, and plunged on.

Half an hour later Oblemov knew all there was to know about Eugen Schumacher, apart from the encoded letters from his father. He sat for some time deep in thought, his eyes almost closed.

"You need somewhere to be together," he said at length. "You can't continue with this absurd affair like this, meeting on the wire and loitering about like a pair of highwaymen, or burglars. You're certain to be seen — you've almost certainly been seen already, but one presumes it was by someone who wasn't ill-disposed towards the pair of you. But sooner or later you'll be seen by someone who is, and it will end in tears. It'll almost certainly end in tears anyway, I dare say," he went on, with something like a sigh, "but I suppose it's too much to hope that you'll have the sense to see that and give it up before it's too late." He sat again in silence, musing, before going on once more. "And after all, why shouldn't two young people have their chance of a little bliss?

"Yes," he said, suddenly becoming decisive. "You must either abandon the whole ridiculous, dangerous business at once, or you must do the thing properly. You've already decided that you're not going to accept any advice that doesn't coincide with what you want to hear. That means you wouldn't listen to your uncle Valeri Borisovitch if he gave you the advice he would give to someone who was still sane. But since you're in a condition in which, as we know from the evidence of the entire passage of human history, nobody could ever remotely be described as sane, I shan't waste good advice. Therefore, you must do it properly. To do that, you must have somewhere to meet, to be together and to be alone. Fortunately, that can be arranged. Come with me." He stood up, looking older, greyer and more tired — and much more forbidding — than Hales had ever seen him before. But as he caught the tail-end of the stricken glance Hales gave him, the steely, grim irony slid from his features, and he looked down for a moment on his young friend with a gentle expression of simple kindness. He observed the look it earned from Hales, and smiled, a little sadly. "I do let up sometimes," he murmured. "Just occasionally. Come, now." And he led the way down the long, echoing hut and out of the door.

Outside it was a fair autumn day, with a fine blue sky flecked with fluffy white cloudlets that raced on the high breeze. The sun was shining, but with little heat, the ferociously hot two months of the mountain high summer already a distant memory. The camp was almost deserted, and there was not a sound to be heard. Oblemov stood looking up into the sky, savouring the tranquillity of the moment. "Ah!" he said softly. "The still hour of the day. This is the moment, young friend, for which we Russians have a special saying. When it is like this, perfectly silent and perfectly still, we say that 'a policeman is being born'." Thus he quite unintentionally spoiled the effect he had been enjoying; for Hales's sudden, unrestrainable yell of laughter dashed the quiet to atoms. Oblemov himself caught the infection, and they stood, howling with laughter, for a full minute or more.

Eventually Oblemov recovered himself sufficiently to stand up straight once more. "Come," he said. "Follow me. The treatment must begin."

XVI

THE hut in which Oblemov and Ustinov fought their incessant war of containment against disease, malnourishment and want among their large and unruly flock was in most ways identical to all the other huts in the camp, but it differed in one particular. At the rear it boasted a small lean-to extension. Strongly built of unfinished logs cut from the nearest forest of pine and spruce, it had a sloping roof of nailed planks covered with some waterproof-looking bituminous material, and in general the place looked more robust than the main body of the hut itself. Oblemov led Hales to this structure, produced a key, and opened the heavy door. He stepped inside, beckoning Hales to follow, and switched on a light. The shack was very small, about eight feet long by six wide, with a bare planking floor. There was no window, and the light was necessary even with strong daylight outside. It smelled strongly of pine resin.

The little place was almost unfurnished. There was a table with two hard chairs, evidently borrowed from the main hut, a small stove with the inevitable tea kettle on the top, and a lot of shelves of rough planking along the wall formed by the section of outer wall of the main hut. These were littered with boxes and packages, bottles and oddments of medical impedimenta. Along the opposite wall, Hales was quick to notice, lay a wide, heavy mattress, with blankets thrown casually across it.

"This place was made as soon as we arrived," Oblemov said. "It was mainly to keep our drugs and medical supplies secure — such as we had of them. If they'd been kept anywhere accessible they'd have been pinched and sold on the black market in ten minutes. Ustinov and I were supposed to take shifts sleeping in here. This is where you and your young friend will conduct your trysts." He turned and directed one of his piercing looks at Hales. "Now tell me you're not pleased with Valeri Borisovitch."

Hales looked about him, taking in the surroundings and, at the same time, what it would mean to him and his bright new love, who had shaken him so utterly to the core a few minutes before. A slow smile spread over his face, and he looked at Oblemov with a world of gratitude and affection written all over him. Oblemov's customary cynical twinkle was swiftly overwritten by a stern, forbidding scowl. "Don't say it," he ordered severely. "I hate being thanked."

"Well, thank you all the same," Hales said in his demotic Russian. "It's perfect. But..." He paused as a snag occurred to him. "What about you and Doc Ustinov? I mean, won't we be in the way...? What about when you need to come in here?"

"Don't worry about that," said Oblemov, dismissing the objection with a wave of a bony hand. "I said we were *supposed* to sleep in here. As it is, we hardly ever set foot in the place, except once in a while to fetch some piece of equipment we use rarely. As for sleeping here, we haven't done that for over a year. Too damned cold. We both sleep over the shop." He jerked a thumb at the wall separating them from the main hut.

"What about your drugs?" queried Hales, looking round at the assortment of boxes and half-empty medicine bottles. Oblemov shrugged. "We've never got anything worth stealing," he said without rancour. "We'd also hear any attempt to break in here, from in there" — he jerked his thumb once again — "and finally... Russians hold doctors in great respect." He hesitated, then went on again, speaking slowly. "Besides... we've got... our own methods, shall we say, of maintaining discipline. No," he said, reverting to his usual brisk way of speaking, "you and your boy will be all right here. And don't worry about Ustinov. I'll keep Gennadi Fedorovitch quiet. Now then, look here." He showed Hales a heavy bolt which they could draw once inside the shack. "You can shut yourselves in with this, and you'll be as snug as two fleas under a cossack's foreskin..." He waited while Hales gave a snort of laughter and had to blow his nose to bring it to an end. "I can't let you have the key, in case we ever have something to protect. But it won't be locked, and the catch will hold it closed. If by any chance you ever find it locked, well, you'll have the satisfaction of knowing we've managed to procure some drugs worth keeping under lock and key. So you should be all right till the war's over."

He turned to lead the way out of the shack, but Hales put out a hand to stop him. He turned back, and without warning Hales threw his arms round his long, bony frame and hugged him. He was dismayed, even as he poured all the fondness and gratitude he felt into the embrace, how little there was of the man. It was like clasping a skeleton. When he released the doctor, he took a step back and surveyed him critically. "You ought to eat more," he said severely, meaning it. Oblemov started to bluster in his customary masterful manner, but for once Hales rode him down. "I can guess what you've been doing. Going without yourself to let others — patients, I dare say — have your rations. But you can't go on like that for ever, you know that as well as I do. I mean, look at you..." He gestured at the spare, skin-and-bones form."

"They need it more than I do," Oblemov said simply. "I make sure I have enough, and that I don't go short of essentials. I keep up my intake of vitamins and trace elements. If my patients go short, they die. I've already lost more since I've been here than I'd expect to lose in a lifetime."

"If I brought you a bit extra, out of our Red Cross parcels — come to that, I expect Eugen could smuggle the odd little something out, too — if we brought you the odd thing now and then, but insisted that you eat it yourself, would you obey?" Hales asked. Oblemov looked at him, and the old twinkle was back in his eyes. "Of course I would," he said. "I'd promise, anyway."

"I'd want to stand over you while you ate it. It's you I love, not your patients." The words were out before Hales could stop himself. In any case, having uttered them, he felt no inclination to withdraw or change them. Just for a moment, Oblemov's face changed, and for one instant he looked terribly old, with an unimaginable world of sadness in the look. It was gone almost before it had appeared across his features, and the usual ironic expression was back in place; but Hales had just time to see that he had succeeded in moving his friend to a level of emotion that he would have deplored with every stringy fibre of his body and every atom of his earthy, sardonic soul. "I'm afraid I couldn't let you do that," Oblemov said. "I think eating is one of the activities that ought to be practised entirely in private. I'd feel constrained to decline anything with conditions attached." He gave Hales a sly grin. "But don't let me deter you. You bring anything you like, and we'll promise to eat it ourselves, a bit later on." And with that he shrugged eloquently, closing the subject.

They went back into the surgery, where Oblemov made more tea and suffered his friend to tell him about Eugen all over again until he was rescued by the arrival of some patients to attend to. Hales thanked his benefactor once again and left to resume his meanderings round the camp. He passed the rest of the afternoon in a haze of pleasurable anticipation, mentally ticking off the minutes until the time came for him to go and wait for Eugen and the promised extra meeting in the early evening.

Long before the arranged hour of six he had become too impatient to wait around any longer, and decided to go and see Ray Lacey, still in purdah in the infectious illnesses compound. Lacey was delighted as usual to receive a visit, and was then the unsuspecting cause of nerve-racking frustration and anxiety when he innocently went on with the exchange of snippets of camp scuttlebutt for some minutes after six o'clock. Before six every minute had dragged out like an eternity for Hales; after it had come and gone the minutes streamed past like as many seconds. Happily unaware that his old friend was straining at every nerve to be gone, and fighting down an ever-mounting urge to look at his watch to see by how many minutes he was late for his meeting with his beloved, Lacey kept him chatting until almost ten past, when he finally decided that it was getting too chilly for him to stay outside any longer, and regretfully took his leave.

Hales considerately marked time for a few final agonising seconds to allow Lacey to get out of sight, then shot off like an arrow from a bow, frantically anxious lest he might find Eugen gone when he turned up. Wild conjectures came crowding into his mind: what might Eugen think? Would he wonder if he had somehow offended

Hales, and be hurt and puzzled? Would he take offence and stamp off in high dudgeon? Worse, would he start wondering if Hales had suffered some mishap, or been taken ill? Might he even go off to Hales's hut to ask about him? Hales went rapidly hot and cold at *that* thought. "No," he muttered to himself, unaware that he was speaking aloud. "No. He wouldn't be so half-witted." Or would he, he immediately wondered. A moment later he hurried round the corner of a hut block — and saw Eugen waiting for him, leaning placidly against the nearest hut and inspecting his fingernails for imaginary signs of dirt.

Hales almost fell down in his relief. He hastened up, and they exchanged greetings which gave no indication, had there been anyone in view to observe them, of the intensity of feeling they represented. They were on the move before the first words had come tumbling out of their mouths. "This way," Hales said as soon as they had got clear of the meeting place.

"Where are we going?" asked Eugen, surprised to discover that they had any particular destination to head for. "I've got something to show you," said Hales, almost crowing. "Something very good for us. Don't waste time wondering what it is, because you'll never guess in a million years." He sounded like a schoolboy. Eugen hurried after him, mystified and anxious to see what had caused his friend to bubble over with ill-suppressed excitement.

When they rounded Oblemov's surgery and reached the lean-to shelter, Hales halted and turned, his eyes shining. "This is it," he said triumphantly, gesturing at the shack as if he had just produced it out of a hat. Eugen looked blank.

"Don't you see?" cried Hales impatiently, "it's the very thing we've needed. The one thing we wanted more than anything else." Seeing that Eugen had still not understood that the shack itself was what he was offering, he threw open the door and almost dragged Eugen into the shack with him. Once inside the pine-scented darkness, he drew the door closed, switched on the light, and shot the heavy bolt. "All ours," he said, waving an arm expansively round him. "Somewhere for us to meet and be out of sight."

For a second time that day Eugen took him completely by surprise. He turned slowly in a full circle where he stood, taking in the drab, bare little room. He did it in silence and without expression. When he was facing Hales once more, he still said nothing; but a wide, open-faced smile spread slowly across his features. Then, still without a word, he took two long strides to the door and switched off the light. "It's fine," Hales heard him murmur. Then there was nothing for some moments but faint rustling sounds. Hales stood where he was, puzzled. After an interval Eugen's voice came again in the pitch blackness. "Put the light on, Brian," it said softly.

Hales stepped cautiously to where he thought the door jamb was and felt for the switch. The light half-blinded him, so that it took him a moment or two to refocus and take in what he saw. When he did so he let out an audible gasp. There before him Eugen stood naked, his hairless body pale gold in the light from the low-wattage bulb above his head. Before he took in the neat proportions, the flawless skin or the lithe musculature, however, Hales's eyes were drawn irresistibly to the central fact about him. It was too flamboyantly, triumphantly visible not to be noticed: he was mightily aroused. The big, smooth penis rose sturdily from a thatch of slightly reddish-tinged golden pubic hair, the foreskin drawn back slightly to give just a hint of the gleaming surface within. Hales goggled at it for some moments. "Christ!" he breathed, temporarily dumbfounded, not so much by its dimensions, impressive though they were, as by the undreamed-of fact that he was seeing it at all.

Eugen smiled at him, a smile full of invitation mingled with undisguised lechery. Hales still stood, staring at him. At last, after what seemed a very long interval, he spoke. "You... you knew," he said stupidly. "You knew I wanted to... to do this with you."

"Of course I knew," said Eugen impatiently. "Did you think I didn't want the same thing? Why d'you think I kissed you when I went back this morning? That was to make sure you knew I wanted it too."

"But how?" asked Hales. "How did you know? I thought I'd kept it completely to myself." Eugen laughed, stroking himself meanwhile. "Kept it to yourself?" he scoffed. "You should just see the way you look at me. Why, I've known since almost the first time we met that you were... that you wanted me. I never said anything because there didn't seem to be any way we could do anything about it."

"*I* never said anything because I was frightened of scaring you off," confessed Hales. Eugen laughed again. "I wanted you from the beginning," he said simply. "Now I've got you."

With that he stepped up to Hales and began to undress him. When the last item of Hales's clothing, his underpants, dropped beside his feet, they slipped into one another's arms, and stood for a long minute in a fierce clinch. Hales was acutely conscious that he was as hard as Eugen: he had never been more *aware* of an erection. He was also conscious of a series of jolts, every time his own penis rubbed against Eugen's. The contact ran through him like electric shock, causing him to catch his breath almost as if he had hiccups and leaving his mouth bone-dry. Meanwhile the sheer physical lust in him rose and swelled till he could feel himself palpably throbbing with it. "Come on," he muttered, his voice thick and husky with the urgency of his desire. "On the bed. Quick."

Eugen released him from his clinch, and they lurched, still half in each other's arms, and flopped down on the mattress. Sweeping the blankets aside, they went straight into another clinch, and this time found each other's lips. The kiss lasted untold passages of time, as measured by the internal clock of gathering lust, until it seemed that it had become a trial by ordeal, to see which of them would be driven to break the embrace first.

It was Eugen who broke. Tearing his own mouth from Hales's, he grasped him hard about the midriff and turned him over in the same single movement. Hales tried to make it easier for him, arching his rump and relaxing. They had no lubricant — though the thought flitted, ridiculously, into Hales's head that there was almost certainly something among the bottles on the shelves that would have served — so Eugen made do with what he had, spitting into his hand and moistening himself with that. When he entered Hales he did so expertly, and Hales moaned aloud for the sheer pleasure of having achieved the goal he had yearned for. Eugen was instantly alarmed, though, and paused in his rhythm to make small questioning sounds. "No, no, don't stop," whispered Hales, hardly able to speak through his emotions. "For Christ's sake don't stop. It wasn't pain..." Eugen, reassured, resumed operations.

Afterwards, when they had changed places and Hales had appeased his own overflowing feelings, they felt about for the blankets and drew them over themselves. Then they felt warm and relaxed enough to talk. Hales started it with a laugh. "What are you laughing at?" asked Eugen drowsily. Hales laughed again. "Oh, just at what a silly arse I am," he answered. "There I was, worrying in case I frightened you off by letting you see how I felt about this sort of thing; and then, when it comes down to it, it's you who takes the initiative. And when we finally get to be in bed together, it's you who takes me first, and you do it like an expert. I was practically *certain* it would be your first time." He chuckled again.

"It was," said Eugen, sweetly.

"Ha-ha-h... whirp!" Hales's chuckle ended in a gurgle. "What!" he cried, startled into raising his voice. "Are you really telling me that was your... I don't believe it."

"Why not?" asked Eugen mildly.

"I... why... well, because... you..." Hales stopped and took a deep breath to stop himself from spluttering. "Mainly," he went on more collectedly, "because you... did it like an expert. I mean, no one could be that... accomplished first time. It's just not possible."

"Well, now you know it is," said Eugen easily. "And I should hope you'd be very pleased, to have such a capable lover." He raised himself on one elbow and looked fondly down at Hales. The teasing note dropped from his voice, and he said, more seriously, "It really *was* my first time, Brian. But only for my body. I've been doing that in my mind since I was twelve."

"Oh," said Hales thoughtfully. "Well, in that case..." He paused.

"Yes?" Eugen prompted him impatiently, when he said no more.

"You've got a lot of catching up to do," said Hales.

"Bitte?"

"Never mind," said Hales, reaching for him.

When Eugen had made a start on the catching up they rolled themselves in the bedding and talked, comfortably, easy in one another's presence. They asked yet more questions, playing the lovers' game, as old as love itself, of finding out everything there was to be found out about each other. How old had each been when he discovered his preference for other boys? What had their schoolboy sweethearts and idols looked like?

At some point Hales yawned and stretched and said casually, "Of course, I'm a damn fool. I could have avoided this bloody show if I'd had my wits about me."

"What do you mean?" queried Eugen.

"I mean that if only I'd had the presence of mind to let it be understood that I was queer — that's to say, like us..."

"I know the word," said Eugen. "Go on."

"If I'd only let it out that I was one of us, they would have refused to let me join the forces," he said, staring a little wistfully into vacancy.

"It is not permitted to be as we are in England?"

"No, it's a serious criminal offence. But you don't have to admit to actually *doing* anything to be excused service in the forces. Just *being* what we are is enough. But then," he mused, lying back with his eyes closed and a smile playing about the corners of his mouth, "I shouldn't have met you then, should I?"

Eugen's mouth came down on Hales's, and closed it for a while. A little later he himself brought the subject back to Hales's imagined exemption from armed service. "So, Brian, what would have happened to you if you had let them know what you were? You would have been..." he groped for the word and found it. "Ostracised, yes?"

"No, I don't suppose so," said Hales indifferently. "Might've been handed a few white feathers, I suppose. But generally there are so many apparently able-bodied men strolling about in London this time round that no one can tell who's skiving, who's on leave, and who's some backroom boy working on government projects in a bunker somewhere. How about here? Could you have dodged the column if you'd told 'em all about yourself?"

A short English lesson followed. Then Eugen gazed at him thoughtfully and said, "You really don't know what's been happening here, do you?" Hales opened his eyes sharply, and paid attention. "Tell me", he said.

"You remember those camps I told you about," Eugen said, instinctively lowering his voice. Hales nodded. "Well, it's not only Jews I've heard about going to them. I've heard there are others, as well. Including... people like us. If I had done what you suggest, I'd have talked my clever self right into the arms of the Gestapo..." He tailed off, rolled away from Hales the few inches that the blankets rolled tightly about them allowed, and lay gazing up at the sloping roof of the shack, his eyes wide and an expression of mingled fear and horror etched into his fair features. It wrung Hales's heart to see the rapid change in his young lover, who had until a moment before shown his real nature as he had never seen him do before, playful and carefree. He set about bringing him back from the lip of whatever abyss he had just stared into. "There, there. Come back to me," he urged him softly, stroking the back of his neck with the tips of his fingers. "I didn't mean it. It was only my tomfoolery. I was just playing the goat. Don't let it upset you, my sweet. Take no notice of me."

Gradually, with endearments and small, infinitely gentle caresses he worked on him, and the evil moment passed. Hales carefully steered the conversation in other, safer paths, and they gradually returned to normality. They made love again, then talked again, until Hales glanced at his watch and they realised in horror that they had been together in the little hut for over three hours, and it was close to half past ten. A panic-stricken interlude followed as they tidied the bedding, flung open the door to air the hut, in which a heavy fug had built up, and hurled their clothes on. Then they switched off the light, slipped out into the chilly night air after a cautious look about, carefully closed the shack, and reluctantly set off for their quarters.

They risked a brief kiss just before Hales peeled off to the left to make for his own hut, and that was that.

Most of his hut-mates were already sleeping when he eased himself through the door and padded in his socks — he had taken the wise precaution of removing his boots at the door — to his bunk. But Shepherd-McMurdo was still awake, and he had to endure a quizzical interrogation and a fusillade of ribald suggestions as to his whereabouts, keeping his end up as best he could, with the whole conversation conducted in low whispers, before he was allowed to turn over and sleep. When he finally did so, he was tired out by a long day of alternating boredom and emotional overload, a long evening featuring a great deal of highly unaccustomed physical activity, and the mere fact that he had crammed more into that one day than he had had to occupy him in the preceding six months. It provided him with the best night's sleep since he had arrived at the camp.

The little shack changed their lives almost beyond recognition. Eugen's days off altered in status from being black days when their brief meetings were impossible, to the highlights of their lives, when they were able to spend hours in each other's company, learning about each other, making the small discoveries that are the lover's stock-in-trade, and, of course, continuing Eugen's crash catching-up course in sex.

Things became noticeably easier as the weeks turned into months: however strict the censorship might be, news of the war flowed in in a constant stream, and nothing could disguise the fact that it was going very badly for Germany, and getting worse all the time. Mightily though they strove to do so, the guards never managed to track down the illicit camp radio; Eugen's father's letters continued to arrive more or less regularly, and no one, seemingly, ever suspected his little code. The arrival, towards the end of the year, of a small contingent of American prisoners brought the most sensational news of all: there had been a plot against Hitler, in which a group of army and naval officers had gone so far as to try to assassinate him. The plot had failed, it seemed, but the fact that it had ever existed must, everyone reasoned, have shaken the morale of the German forces and the civilian population to the very roots.

Shortly afterwards this was confirmed by Eugen's father, who dropped perhaps the greatest bombshell of all when he said that it was popularly believed that the plotters had included none other than General Erwin Rommel, probably the most illustrious and revered man in Germany at that time. "They've given him a full-dress state funeral," Schumacher senior reported, "with some story that he died from some sort of brain haemorrhage. But no one believes that. The talk that he was involved in the plot are too persistent..." The rumour that he had been forced to take his own life, as the only alternative to ending in the clutches of the Gestapo, had cast a black shadow over the whole of Germany, he said; for Rommel had been the one great shining hope for a future for Germany, the only man who might have been able to salvage a remnant of genuine honour from the peace when the war was lost — as everyone now accepted that it would be, must be and, frankly, the old man added in his code, ought to be.

As news of this kind filtered through even to their remote and peaceful corner of the war, it had its inevitable effect on both prisoners and guards alike. Discipline, already comfortably slack, became noticeably slacker. Hitherto the active black market had relied on a few specially favoured and trusted sources among the guards. Suddenly, it seemed that half the staff of the camp were ready to trade, or do small favours, or turn a blind eye to breaches of conduct. "Trying to store up credits against the end," commented numerous prisoners; and Eugen said something similar, lying in Hales's arms late one night in the shack.

Their talk turned more and more often nowadays to what they would do when the war ended. Hales was all for Eugen's turning hiself in to the liberating army, whoever's it might be, and then, after a suitable interval, accompanying him to England. "It's no good trying to think further ahead than that," he argued. "But if it's our lot or the Yanks who get here first we ought to be able to work some sort of flanker and get you somewhere safe. If we can do that, nothing else matters. We'll have all the time in the world then."

"Perhaps," said Eugen doubtfully, after the word "flanker" had been duly translated. "But suppose it's the Russians?" His face crumpled at that thought. The methods of invading Russian armies were the stuff of legend among prisoners and guards alike, and of every guard's nightmares. Both groups contemplated being liberated by the Red Army with undiluted and undisguised terror.

But Hales had an answer for that, too. "It doesn't matter even if it is," he urged. "I'm persona grata with the Russians here, don't forget. Val and Doc Ustinov'll make sure I'm looked after, and I should be able to ensure that you're all right too. As long as our two docs are still here with us, we'll be all right." But Eugen was far from convinced, and Hales had to exercise all his arts and blandishments to keep him from spiralling into a hysterical fugue of panic and despair that evening.

And so, as events in the outside world gathered momentum and the German war effort went crashing in the flames of Dresden and Cologne, they set up tidal waves that penetrated even as far as their placid backwater; as discipline grew ever slacker, the guards resorted to ever greater force, and sometimes ferocity, in retaliation or retribution on the odd occasion when they were forced to put down riotous or rebellious misbehaviour. At the same time food supplies, which had always left everyone more or less hungry, now fell off catastrophically. The prisoners had always relied principally on the regular parcels from the Red Cross for their nourishment, the thin gruel, pitiful morsels of meat and vegetables and sour bread provided by the Germans being welcomed but at the same time despised as being of negligible nutritional value. The parcels had always hitherto arrived regularly, but the present catastrophic conditions in Germany meant that nothing could be guaranteed, and a lot of hoarding went on.

Fights over food began to be a regular occurrence among the prisoners, except in the Russian compound. The Russians, perennially long-suffering, began dying. Hales and Eugen did what little they could, shyly offering small gifts most days, and the gratitude in the faces was more than ample reward. Oblemov looked steadily greyer and more emaciated almost by the day. Even his partner Ustinov, who when Hales had first made their acquaintance had been as rotund and jolly as Oblemov had been lean and hawklike — their patients had always called them affectionately Dr Wolf and Dr Bear — even Ustinov was becoming a bag of bones in a skin that seemed several sizes too large for him. He had taken to holding his trousers up with braces because he would have had to be six inches bigger round the waist to make any use of the innermost hole in his belt.

Eugen, watching as Hales began visibly losing weight, did what he could, pressing him to accept a portion of his own food whenever he could smuggle it out. But it was very little, because the guards themselves were by now on short rations, and eating little better than the prisoners. Reports filtered through that the civilian population in the nearest towns and cities were in still worse case. Eugen's father wrote in cypher that in their village they were still able to eat passably well — "that is, maybe half as well as before the war" — by virtue of living in a fairly remote rural village, where food could be grown and hidden, animals husbanded, killed and salted away, and where the mainly town-bred authorities, SS and Gestapo, could not track them down. But the penalties for such activity were horrendous, and increasing in severity as the noose tightened.

The old gentleman added a postscript: "You will not be receiving any more letters from me, son. The post is so unreliable, and things can only get worse rather than better, until the war is over. I'd rather end now than send letters and not know whether you ever got them." The last few lines of all were not in cipher. "So this is all for now, dear son. Your mother and I pray for your safe delivery, and wait for the blessed moment when we see your face once again after this gateway to Hell is closed again. In the meantime, our beloved Eugen, take care of yourself, and do your duty as you see it. Remember that we love you more than anything, and that all our thoughts are with you every hour of every day. If it is fated for us, we shall see you one day, perhaps sooner than any of us dares to think. Your mother prays for you daily. I can find no comfort in prayer, but my hopes and her prayers come, I think I can properly say, to the same thing. *Auf Wiedersehen*, our son, Your loving Vati."

Eugen read the letter to Hales in the shack on the day he received it, and then cried, gently, silently and steadily for a very long time. Lying as he was, with his head cradled on Hales's bare chest, he did not know, because he could not see, that Hales, looking down at the top of his head, was blinded by the tears streaming just as silently and steadily down his own face; not all of them for his young beloved's sake.

And then, just when they might reasonably have supposed that it no longer mattered much, they were discovered.

XVII

HE knew what had happened the moment he walked into hut F9. There was a low buzz of excited conversation, instantly suppressed. The atmosphere was so electric that it almost crackled as he slipped through the door, and he walked softly down the hut towards his bunk in a silence that could be felt. As he drew near his bed a light went on, dim enough not to draw unwelcome attention from any patrolling guard outside but even so bright enough to dazzle him for a moment. He started, looked to his right towards the source of the unexpected glimmer, and there they were.

Several of the tables from the mess area of the hut had been dragged together to form a makeshift tribunal. Behind them were seated a group of the most senior and influential prisoners in the camp, drawn from all services and various parts of the compound. Geoffrey Singleton was there, the elderly Engineer NCO who was leader of his own hut, looking sombre and unhappy. Michael Watts, the leader of the Escape Committee, and the Dutch infantryman who had been on the committee with him on the night of Hales's unceremonious performance before it. The camp *Vertrauensmann* was there, a scrawny, bespectacled sergeant of the Royal Signals who looked like a bookmaker's clerk in a poor way of business but had in civilian life been Professor of English at one of the new universities. There were three or four others present, including even, Hales saw with astonishment, a representative of the recently arrived group of Americans, a hulking, crew-cut master-sergeant of Marines, who sat stroking a massive square jaw and looking thoroughly puzzled, and said nothing at all.

"Ah, Brian," greeted Singleton, as casually as if he was welcoming a member of a house party returning from a stroll round the grounds to let his breakfast go down. The image was so compelling that Hales grinned faintly. He couldn't help it. There was a suppressed exclamation from one of the others along the table, but he didn't trouble to try to identify its source. Knowing intuitively what was afoot, he summoned up all his reserves of inner strength, which he suspected would be required of him, and looked across at the group as coldly and expressionlessly as he could. "That's me," he said in as light a tone as he could muster.

"Er, just step across here for a moment, would you Brian, there's a good chap," said Singleton easily, and Hales mentally touched his cap to the man. He had sang-froid, if nothing else.

"Pleased," he said, and walked easily over to the group. He was cheered to see that several of them were looking distinctly uneasy, apparently disconcerted by his unconcerned manner.

"Please have a seat," said Singleton courteously, gesturing to an empty chair across from himself, in the centre of the unoccupied side of the row of tables. Hales seated himself in leisurely fashion, getting himself comfortable, jerking the chair back to give himself room to swing one ankle up to rest on the other knee. When he had got himself arranged precisely as he wished he looked up and gave the row of faces opposite a bright smile. "Having a judicial enquiry, are we?" he said, fighting down a powerful urge to laugh.

Glances were exchanged along the row of tables, and those present who had been looking disconcerted seemed to have been thrown still further off balance. Hales, realising that he might well be fighting for something, though he wasn't sure quite what, took that for good news. He settled himself in his casual posture on his chair, and waited.

"It's, ah, just after half past nine," said Singleton, consulting his watch. "Would you, ah, mind telling us where you've been this evening, Brian?"

He looked at his own watch to gain a little time, then looked mildly along the row of faces. The urge to laugh was stronger, becoming almost irresistible; for, oddly enough, they had chosen for their night to interrrogate him one of the nights when Eugen had been sent on duties that took him outside the camp, and he was by now up at the railway track, supervising the arrival of a train bringing a new intake of prisoners but also, it was hoped, some desperately needed medical and other supplies. He squirmed around on his hard chair to make himself infinitesimally more comfortable, and took his time.

When he sensed that the question was about to be put to him again, he finally replied. "Well," he said slowly. "I can't imagine by what conceivable right anyone should ask me where I've been or what I've been doing, still less why anyone should be in the remotest degree interested; but certainly, no, I don't *mind* telling you, if you really are interested." He sat silent, waiting.

There was a long, difficult pause. It was finally broken by Watts. "All right, then," he said impatiently. "You've said you don't mind telling us, so tell us, man. Where've you been to keep you out to this hour of the night?"

"Steady, the Buffs," said Hales soothingly, and heard a couple of ferocious harrumphs, valiantly suppressed, down the row of tables. Once again fighting down the demonic urge to titter, he said, easily, "I said just now, I don't know by what conceivable right you think you can question me, and if you want answers you can ask for them politely. But if you want to know where I've been this evening I'll tell you. I've been in the Russian compound."

This brought a long silence. Then, "Doing what?" demanded one of the inquisitors.

Once again he stretched the silence between question and answer to its fullest extent before speaking. "Doing... any... damn... thing... I... choose, is the plain answer to that," he said at last, leaving a heavily accentuated pause between words, "if I choose to take that position. As it is, as before, I'm willing to be more forthcoming, provided I'm asked politely. I've been indulging in pleasant conversation with my friend, Doctor Valeri Borisovitch Oblemov, and, when the opportunity presented itself, offering such minor assistance as I could give with his treatment of his patients." He sat back easily, happily aware that his answer was the unvarnished truth, and that the doctor and a dozen Russian prisoners who had required treatment that evening would testify to it if necessary. He surveyed blank looks, almost of stupefaction, on the faces of his questioners, and grinned involuntarily. They were utterly taken aback. Whether they had expected him to be reduced to confusion or dismay by being questioned he had no way of knowing; but he could read plainly in their speechless expressions that however they had expected him to respond, whatever they had expected him to say, they hadn't expected that. By this time almost feeling sorry for them, he drove home his advantage. "I often do," he said. "Actually."

They began to recover from the bombshell he had dropped so utterly unexpectedly to confound them; and some had not been confounded at all. "You know damn well the Russian compound is out of bounds," snapped Watts.

He waited once again, spinning out the silence for maximum effect before answering. "Ah," he then said. "I begin to see what this is in aid of. Well, of course I realised long ago that this was a pretty slack camp, as POW camps go. I see now. The guards, dissatisfied with their record here, have been wondering if a stiff ration of good old British bullshit will perhaps buck up our performance. They've called you in to stiffen our backs and put a bit of zing into us, eh?

Well, I'm all in favour of a bit of team spirit, but on this occasion I think you can count me out. Sorry, and all that, but..." He paused. When he spoke again it was in an entirely different tone, icy and crackling with hostility. "But I'll stop breaking camp rules, such as entering the Russian compound, when the guards tell me to, not before."

"You answer to us as well," snapped Watts. "We're all senior to you in rank here."

"There are no ranks here," he replied, equally sharply. "Or rather, there's only one rank: prisoner, and that we all are. I left the RAF when my kite went down," he went on icily, "and I'll rejoin it when I report back to my squadron. As long as I'm here I'll take on whatever rank, or duties, or pleasures, I feel like, provided only that they don't adversely affect the wellbeing of any other prisoner or provide tangible aid and comfort to an enemy power. If I choose to act as temporary and informal Russian medical orderly while I'm chatting to my good friend the doctor, I shall — unless you can show me a good reason why I shouldn't. And it'll have to be a *damned* good reason."

It was at this point that the soothing Lancastrian tones of Geoffrey Singleton made themselves heard once more. "Gentlemen, gentlemen," he murmured. "All this is beside the point. Let's calm ourselves, shall we?" He had the effect he usually had, of instantly calming everyone down. The questioners ceased muttering and glaring, and Hales felt the tightly-coiled belligerence ebbing slowly away.

"Brian," Singleton said, addressing him directly, in friendly, ordinary tones. "Please don't distress yourself. We're not in the least worried if you choose to spend your own time helping the Russian doctors, though I admit it came as something of a surprise. But that's not why we, ah, gathered tonight. We're rather more worried by your relationship with one of the German troops guarding this camp. *That's* what we're here to discuss, lad. You can understand that, I imagine?" He paused, giving Hales the chance to speak. When Hales made it clear that he had nothing to say at that moment, Singleton went on, speaking in the same gentle, amiable tone. "You've been seen, you see — with this young German guard. And it looked to the chap who saw you as if you were... pretty friendly with him. We're a bit concerned. that's all. We'd like you to reassure us."

The gentle, reassuring voice ceased. Hales realised that his explanation this time could be very important in its repercussions for himself. He thought rapidly. "I don't seek to conceal it," he said at length. "I *am* friends with him. But I don't see how that can possibly be dangerous to anyone here."

"What's the link?" asked someone. Hales thought it was the Dutchman. "How do you come to be friendly with one of the guards?"

"Music," said Hales simply. He noted the blank looks, and elaborated. "We're both very fond of music. We talk about it, all the time. We sing Schubert *Lieder* together. Also, I found that he teaches English in peacetime. I wanted to learn German, he wanted to improve his command of idiomatic English, and there you have it."

There was a silence as the half-a-dozen heads turned this way and that, exchanging glances. "Hmmm," murmured Singleton at last. "We've been told that there's a good deal more to it than that, to all appearances, at least." He snapped his fingers, the sound loud and vaguely menacing in the echoing quiet of the hut. A prisoner appeared from the shadows beyond the tribunal, and stepped into the small pool of dim light cast by the lamp they had rigged up behind them. He was a big, shambling fellow, whom Hales had never noticed before. He stood awkwardly at attention, after casting one glance at Hales. It was an eloquent glance, however, pregnant with contempt and disgust. Hales was instantly on his guard, thinking as fast as his mind would go. He was conscious of only one thought, one duty: he must protect his beloved, at any cost to himself.

Singleton signalled to the newcomer, who spoke up immediately. "I see 'em", he said, truculently. "They was comin' from over where the Russians are. Late at night. I see 'em where they separated. They was kissing each other." His voice was like his expression when he had looked across at Hales: he spoke as if his tongue was coated with slime, as if he wished he could suck it into a ball and gob it in Hales's face.

That was all. The heads all turned back to watch Hales, who sat motionless, his face registering nothing except a faint, icy disdain. The silence was broken once more by Singleton. "Well, Brian?" he said gently. "Would you like to comment?"

"Not particularly," said Hales quietly. "Except to say that I don't think your witness would last long in any known form of court of law. But since you'll clearly worry about it unless I reassure you, yes, I'm sure your informer here..." He paused to enjoy the various expressions of distaste at his choice of word, and saw the burly prisoner redden and restrain a convulsive movement towards him. Singleton, who appeared to have eyes in the back of his head, made a placatory, calming gesture behind him with his hand, and the man became quiet once more. Hales went on, "I'm sure your informer here did see what he's seen fit to report to you."

There was a *frisson* of surprised reaction down the tables. "You mean," asked Singleton in the same quiet tone, "that you were kissing this German soldier? Kissing him, let's be sure we know what we're saying?"

"Of course," said Hales easily. "It's a standard form of greeting or parting among many of the continental peoples. Among the French, for instance, the Russians, certainly, the Italians — and the Germans. I've exchanged kisses on the cheeks with him on many occasions. So I have with several of my closer friends among the Russians, if you come to that," he added, as the happy thought occurred to him that this was nothing more than the truth. Further inspiration came as he thought fast as he went along. "If you'd care to adjourn for a short period," he went on, pouring maximum sarcasm into his voice as he used the legal term, "I could pop across to the Russian compound and bring you a couple of witnesses. I think you'd find Doctor Oblemov, and Doctor Ustinov, and a couple of others I could produce, at least as impressive as this... as your friend here."

"They was snoggin' each other," snapped the witness without prompting. "And it wasn't no peck on the cheeks, neither. They was snoggin', on the mouf. Right on the lips. I see 'em plain."

"Right. Thank you," said Singleton, and at a further gesture from him the witness turned and disappeared back into the shadows beyond the light, directing a final glare of loathing and contempt at Hales as he went.

"I don't know what the truth of it is, but fortunately, it doesn't matter," said Singleton after another pause. "Personally I couldn't care less if you and this German boy are..."

"The German word is *Schwul*," offered Hales helpfully. "But I should guard with your left if you ever decide to put it to him." He sat in a meditative silence for a few moments. "He's fearfully Prussian in some ways, you know," he told them, reflecting as he said it that though it had never occurred to him before, it was in fact quite true: there was a strong streak of moral austerity about Eugen, a kind of bleak courage, which made him turn and face difficult or unpalatable facts, about himself, about the war, all manner of examples came crowding back into his mind from their long hours together. "Yes, that's the right word to use: he is very Prussian. Very conscious of his dignity..."

"Hmmm. I was going to say, if you and this German boy have got some sort of friendship going," murmured Singleton mildly after another pause, and Hales was compelled once again mentally to take his hat off to him for equanimity under heavy fire. "However," he went on, "as things are, I think I can see how the land lies. The point is, Brian, we aren't really all that concerned with whether you have some kind of relationship with this German, or what kind of relationship it is. Speaking for myself, if you tell me it's a friendship founded in a common love of music and nothing more, I accept that, and welcome. What we'd like to know is, are you willing to turn it to our advantage?" Hales stared at him, puzzled for the first time since he had walked back into the hut.

"Turn it to your advantage?" he repeated. "I'm afraid you have the better of me there."

Singleton looked at him across the table, a little wearily. "What we mean is, this boy is potentially very, very useful to us," he said, and Hales, as he began to understand, saw that Singleton, at least, knew perfectly well what the response would be.

"Go on," said Hales, outwardly as cold and composed as before, inwardly a seething inferno of indignation, indeed of outrage. To his own great surprise, the self-appointed tribunal had managed both to surprise and to enrage him. "Go on," he said again.

Singleton took a deep breath. "We're thinking in terms of the pressure you — or we, possibly acting through you, possibly not — could be in a position to exert on him. He could prove absolutely invaluable, as a source of information, possibly as a means of procuring invaluable items — parts for the wireless, that kind of thing. He must be a great deal better informed than we are of the progress of the war: that could be of inestimable value. The possibilities are almost endless. That, Brian, is what we wish you to think about. We'd like to know your thoughts. If there's anything you want to ask, please ask it now. But so far as we are concerned, we consider that your duty is quite clear. If you want time to consider, you shall have it: you can sleep on it. But that's the most we're willing to concede. We want your answer by *Appell* tomorrow — at the latest."

So there it was, he thought to himself. Out in the open. As neat and nasty a little plan as ever saw the light of day. They weren't out to crucify him for being what he was. Come to that, there were, he suddenly remembered, several notorious "benders", and even a few more or less openly "married" couples in the camp, and they aroused little interest or comment beyond the odd caustic or derisive joke or exclamation of mild disgust. No, the men round this ridiculous mock court of enquiry couldn't care less if he was queer, if Eugen was *schwul*; indeed, it was so much the better if he was, from their point of view and for their purposes. It provided them with that much more purchasing power, more leverage, a better position from which to bring pressure to bear. And so, armed with their information provided by the merest piece of mischance, here they were, calmly and cynically expecting him to exert blackmail and extortion on the man who meant more to him than the rest of life put together.

Oddly enough, it was not to Eugen that his mind immediately flew as he sat there considering it, but to Valeri Oblemov. Odder still, it was not out of revulsion at the proposition that had been put to him that he found himself recoiling in horror. He could understand why they had put it, even, in a way, sympathise with it and their motives. They felt they had to put the proposition, he supposed, and they put it; and that was an end of it. No, it was himself who he felt was defiled, from whom he recoiled. As he imagined Oblemov's sharp, hawkish face, further sharpened by unremitting toil and semi-starvation, yet still filled with a kindness and compassion great enough to reach out and embrace whole worlds, he wondered what the doctor would think of him, for putting himself and Eugen into such a position that they could be vulnerable to the kind of pressure now being exerted. And it was almost as if even Oblemov himself was sullied by his contact with the bearer of the plague. In that instant he could have killed himself, for having contaminated the two people he loved most in his small world. I ought to have to go about in a sheet with a bell, shouting "unclean", he thought.

And then the thought was gone, and all there was left was a problem to be solved. He knew, of course, what his answer must be, but he would consider the proposition in all its implications before he made his decision, delivered his verdict. The thought struck him that it was the others present who had constituted themselves into an absurd replica of a judicial tribunal, but it was he, Hales, who sat in the big chair, who had to deliver the verdict.

He decided to begin by playing for time. Judging by Singleton's tone the ploy was unlikely to work, but he thought he might buy himself a while to think ahead now, and that alone was a prize worth playing for. "I see," he said judicially. "So what it comes down to is this: I'm to go to my closest personal friend and without warning ask him to risk his life by acting as informer and black-market agent for you; and I'm to extort this by blackmailing him, using the very fact of his having become my friend as the thing to blackmail him with. Hmmm. You don't entertain a very high opinion of my personal morals, do you?"

"We don't hold a very high opinion of someone who holds himself aloof from most of his comrades and chooses one of the enemy for his closest personal friend," snapped Watts.

Hales chose to ignore that. "I suppose you know what would happen to him if he got caught passing information to you?" he said. "It wouldn't just be death, and you know it perfectly well. He'd be interrogated by the Gestapo, and you know very well what that would mean. Do you still ask me to ask him to do this?"

"We're not asking you to ask him," said Singleton sharply, losing his patience for the first time. "We shouldn't have to 'ask' you: you ought to recognise it as your clear and bounden duty. As for asking him, we're requiring you to secure what's wanted. How he does it is his business."

"It's also mine," snapped Hales, "since I'm the one you expect to act as extortionist and blackmailer for you. And also since he is my close friend."

"That's your problem," said Singleton. "It's no good your bleating about how you're being asked to do the dirty on your friend. If you'd used a little judgment and discretion in your choice of friends you wouldn't find yourself in this position now. But if you choose to make a friend of one of the enemy in wartime, you can expect squalls. Quite apart from anything else, what in God's name were you thinking about when you allowed yourself to make a friend of this German? We *are* at war with Germany, aren't we? We were last time I looked."

Hales narrowed his eyes and stared at him. "Are you questioning my patriotism?" he demanded softly. "Or my loyalty?" He waited for some time, but no one replied. He tapped his RAF jacket above the left breast pocket. "Because there's a DFM waiting for me at home, if they've found a bit of ribbon the right colour."

"It's not your bloody patriotism we're calling into question, man, it's your judgment," snapped Watts. "And we're giving you a chance to put previous errors of judgment right. If you do the right thing now, it washes out earlier lapses."

196

"And suppose my judgment of what's the right thing is at variance from yours?" asked Hales coldly.

"Then ours takes precedence," said Watts in tones just as frigid. "Understand this, Hales. We're not pussyfooting around, 'asking' you to do anything, even if Mr Singleton does wish to put it that way out of his natural courtesy. I don't suffer from natural courtesy, so I'll tell you straight. We're *ordering* you to do as we've set out, and that's an end of it."

"You're not in a position to give me orders."

"We're all your seniors here," retorted Watts, "and you'll get nowhere with rank insubordination, mark my words. We've been patient enough with you, and more than patient. It's high time you remembered where your responsibilities and your loyalties lie."

"Well, you've made it plain where *you* think they lie," Hales said curtly, "and you've also said I can sleep on it if I wish. Well, I do wish. I'll give you my decision here, tomorrow morning, after *Appell*. Just you, Singleton: I don't expect to see the whole gang of you."

He stood up, turned on his heel and strode to his bunk. He would have swung himself up and into bed without a word, but as he prepared to do so he felt a hand grasp him about the knee. He jumped almost painfully, then realised it was only Shepherd-McMurdo. He took it the Canadian Scotsman wanted to exchange banter or small talk, or to beg a light for one of the foul-smelling hand-rolled cigarettes he insisted on smoking in bed. Resigning himself to putting out of his mind the thoughts careering round it in a turmoil of anxiety and pain, he sighed faintly, and eased himself under his own bed to perch on the edge of Shepherd's.

He felt the entire structure shake as the giant levered himself into a sitting position. A pungent aroma of tobacco drifted round his head, and he felt Shepherd's face against his own. The bristles of his chin and cheeks scraped and scored his own face like coarse sandpaper. For a moment he thought the giant was trying to kiss him, and wondered if he had heard the muttered proceedings from the far side of the hut and decided to chance his arm on the strength of it. If so, Hales wondered, how in God's name might he fight off someone who could probably haul a double-decker bus a hundred yards by a rope held between his teeth? Then he felt Shepherd's large, hairy lips, not against his own, but against his *ear*, and heard him whisper in a tone fainter than he would have thought possible from someone of such unsubtle design and construction. "Dinnae tak yere buits off, son. Let yon fucken Boys' Brigade gae hoam, then we'll tak a wee walk. I've got suthen tae say tae ye." The face, steel-wool whiskers and the appalling miasma of tobacco were withdrawn, and Hales, was left to wonder what in the world Shepherd, Shepherd the self-styled Canadian Scotsman, whom he liked enormously as everyone did, but with whom he had never in the past exchanged more than idle, silly small talk and jokes, could possibly have to say to him that required these elaborate precautions. His mind boggling with curiosity, he heaved himself up onto his own bunk, and waited.

The faint glow from the far side of the hut was soon extinguished, and he lay for a while in darkness, listening to the faint clatterings as the members of the "tribunal" left to return to their own quarters. His thoughts strayed briefly to Eugen, picturing the well-loved face with its clear-cut, still boyish features, the wide-spaced blue eyes and the dusting of light freckles over the nose, the firm, hairless body, the fine, almost invisible golden down on his arms, legs and chest, and all the other delights to which he had been made so blesssedly privy over the past months. He wondered, with an ache that felt almost like a part of his own body, what Eugen was doing at that moment, what he was thinking, whether he was thinking of Hales. He thought he knew the answer to that one...

The next thing he knew was Shepherd's huge hand closing on his head where it rested, pillowed on his forearm. He awoke with a start, began to mutter something, then remembered and was silent. A faint "Shhh!" reached him in the dark. He slid down off his bunk and dropped soundlessly to the floor, where he could feel Shepherd's giant bulk beside him. The huge hand took his arm just above the elbow and steered him gently in the direction of the door. There Shepherd opened the door, gently shoved Hales to set him in motion, and followed, easing the door to after himself.

They strolled some way. Then they halted in the lee of a hut and stood sheltered from the wind. "Thus'll aye do," came Shepherd's voice. There were rustling sounds, followed shortly by the spark of Shepherd's lighter as he ignited one of his horrible cigarettes. Finally he spoke. "Ah have nae much tae say," he said, speaking more softly than Hales would have thought him capable of. "But I wanted to say it all the same. All I want to say is, don't let those bastards put the squeeze on you. If your laddie means as much tae ye as Ah think he does, jist ye stand yer ground, and tell yon bunch a gung-ho twats tae tak a flyin fuck. Ye wullnae hear a hard

198

wurrd aboot ut frae me."

Hales stood for some time, gazing at where the tip of Shepherd's cigarette punctuated the blackness, briefly illuminating his face with a dim red glow when he drew on it, considering the few words in great surprise. "It sounds to me as if you know a lot more about it than... well, than those others," he said lamely.

"Aye, Ah know," said Shepherd placidly. "Ah've seen ye often enough."

"You've seen us?"

There was a rumbling chuckle. "Aye, Ah've seen ye, right enough. Ye're nae the only yin tae have a fancy for wand'rin aboot the camp. Ah've watched ye headin off wi him, an Ah've watched ye comin back hours later. Ah don't know where ye go wi' him, nor want tae. I wudnae follow the two a ye — none a my business - though Ah've a guid idea. Ah know what ye get up tae wi him, though."

"You do?" said Hales faintly, no longer surprised by anything.

The chuckle was repeated. "Ah'm the closest tae ye in oor hut, by a guid distance," he said, his voice full of buried laughter. "Ye canna spend a whole day havin ut off wi someone an keep the fact tae yersel' — not unless ye can get a shower, anyway. Ye have tae pass within six inches a ma face when ye come creepin back in at night; an there's nothin wrong wi mah nose!"

"Christ!" said Hales, shocked. "And we thought we were being so clever. We really thought we had everybody fooled."

Shepherd chuckled again. "Och, dinna waste time worryin aboot ut. Most a the lamebrains in here cuidnae find their ane assholes wi both hands an a flamethrower for a fucken flashlight! Ye've naught to fash yersel' aboot wi them. An ye've none wi me, either. Like Ah said, all Ah wanted tae say was, don't let them bastards put the pressure on ye. You jist do what ye know's the right thing by yer laddie. An if ut ever comes tae a showdown, ye'll have me on your side, for one."

Just do what you know's the right thing... thought Hales. Immediately his mind echoed it: he thought of a worried old man in the village, writing immensely long letters in his carefully devised private code. Do your duty as you see it... He thought of innumerable small incidents when Eugen had shown the steely integrity that lay not far beneath the surface of the merry, affectionate boy and the lithe, willing lover. "I don't know if I could bring myself to kill anyone..."

He had known what his response had to be to the demands so suddenly made of him. His giant neighbour's still more unlooked-for encouragement stilled any last stirrings of doubt. "I never gave it a thought," he said at last. "I'd cut out my own tongue before I blackmailed him, especially with my own conduct as the blackmail. But I... I'm grateful for a bit of moral support, I can tell you. It's bloody good of you to take the trouble..."

"Son," rumbled Shepherd. "You listenin?"

"I am, yes, of course," said Hales, wondering what was coming next on this night of surprises.

"If we're fightin this fucken silly war aboot anything, it's aboot this," he said simply. "C'mon, let's get back in, it's too fucken cold tae be standin aboot like a pair a neds on a street corner waitin for somebodda tae hit on the heed." Hales felt the bulk of him moving past to head back for the hut, but he put a hand against him and encountered the giant mound of his stomach. He felt carefully along it until he found an arm, felt along that until he found the hand at the end of it, and slipped his own into it, the hand being almost engulfed in the huge paw, and shook it briefly. "Thanks, Bill," he said. "You don't know how good it feels to have... You know what I mean."

"Ah know," said Shepherd, leading the way back to their own quarters.

"There's only one thing I'd like to ask," ventured Hales as they walked back. "And I'm not sure how."

"Try the simplest way", said Shepherd. "Jist ask."

"All right. Did you do what you've just done for any special reason? I mean, any *other* reason? I mean... well, what I'm really asking is, was it because you're one of us?"

There was a momentary silence, and for a tremulous second or two Hales thought he had overstepped the limit, and wondered if daylight the following morning would disclose his mangled corpse where he had ventured to ask his question. Then, to his serious relief, the chuckle rumbled once more in the darkness. "Naw, son, that didnae come into ut. Ah've been a guid monny thungs in ma time, but never that yin." By now they were on the top step outside the door to their hut. Shepherd let them in without a sound. They removed their boots and crept noiselessly to their bunks. A minute and a half later Hales was asleep.

XVIII

HIS only thought when he got up and prepared for *Appell* the next morning was that he must see Eugen at the earliest possible moment, if only to warn him of what was afoot. He already knew what he was going to tell Singleton when he came for his decision after the roll call, and he knew that the sparks might fly at any time thereafter. He owed his young friend a warning to be ready for temporary separation, if nothing worse ensued. For Eugen, as much as for himself, their meetings had become more than a mere pleasure, more even than delight, but rather the keystone of his existence. They had both found increasingly in recent months, as the days had passed, that they only had any sense of reality in the precious moments when they were together. Between meetings they endured great tracts of mere time, which had by now become meaningless. Yes, Eugen must be told.

By a benevolent stroke of fortune it happened that it was Eugen's day off next day, so he made his plans accordingly.

He was up, washed and dressed early for *Appell.* The moment the parade was over he walked quickly back to F9 and made sure he was in the vanguard for breakfast. He had already finished when Singleton appeared at his shoulder, looking curiously at him and quite clearly trying to read his decision from his face. Hales said nothing, but jerked a thumb in the direction of the door and immediately strode that way himself, grim-faced.

Outside, they moved off by common instinct for privacy to the rear of the hut. There Hales turned and faced the other man, looking him squarely in the eyes. "I don't think you really need to ask me how I've decided," he said without preamble, "but I'll tell you anyway. I'm not willing to commit what I see as an act of betrayal, of the foulest kind." Singleton opened his mouth, but Hales motioned him to wait. "Let me finish, please. I don't know whether you'll see it, but this is important to me. Not just as a personal thing, but more than that. In fact, it seems to me to go to the heart of the reason why we're fighting this bloody war. From the very start we were told that this was not just a war, but a just war. We were told we were fighting to protect our way of life, our standards of tolerance, humanity and decency against barbarism. Well, maybe we were and maybe we weren't. But it seems to me that if I let you talk me into doing what you want me to do, or even if I just passively let you order me to do it and accept your orders, I shall be doing something just about as vile and unprincipled as anything I'm supposed to be fighting against. Not that I particularly see it that way. For me it's much simpler: you want me to be Judas Iscariot, and I won't do it. There's your answer, which you can take to your committee. I stand by it, and I'm ready to take the consequences." He gave Singleton a hard stare and waited to see what he had to say.

Singleton's face creased in a troubled frown. "You're piling up a lot of trouble for yourself," he said slowly. "Bad trouble. But... but I can't tell you I'm sorry you've given me this as your reply, because I'm not. In many ways I'd have been disappointed in you if you'd given any other. Not that I think you're right. I don't. I think you're a block-headed young donkey, and seriously misguided. But it's too late to worry about that. The misjudgment came when you allowed yourself to be blinded to your obvious duty and become friendly with this man in the first place. Personally, and I'm speaking personally, you understand, I don't see that you could have decided to act any other way now things have got this far. Don't expect Michael Watts and some of the others to think that way. They see life in simple terms: there is your duty, and here are you refusing to do it. Therefore, your head must roll. That's how they will present it when it all comes out in the wash when we get back home.

"Oh, yes," he went on as he saw Hales's raised eyebrows. "That's where you're stacking up trouble for yourself. They're going to throw the book at you when you get back to your unit — I beg your pardon, to your squadron. You'd better be prepared for a hard time. I shall be among those giving evidence against you. I shall have no alternative. But speaking as your friend — well, perhaps not quite that, but at any rate speaking as man to man, I do see how you're placed, and I understand your decision. I think you're in the wrong, I think you've busily dug your own grave and you will duly be buried in it, and, frankly, I haven't got much sympathy for you. But, for what it's worth, if it's any comfort to you, I do understand. Who knows, perhaps I'd have done the same thing in your shoes. In a way, I suppose I hope I would. Only *I* wouldn't have been bloody fool enough to have put myself in that position in the first place. There it is."

As Hales heard him out his grim, set face relaxed a little, and some of the bitterness faded from his brow. "You're a good fellow,

Singleton," he said at last. "It's good of you to take the trouble to say so. I hope you do see that there was nothing else I could do. You really left me no room to manoeuvre. But there's nothing personal. There never was. No hard feelings?"

"None here," said Singleton. Hales stuck out a hand, and after a moment's pause Singleton took it. They shook hands briefly. Then, without another word, Singleton turned and walked quickly out of sight round the corner of the hut. He did not look back. Hales hurried off to put into effect the plan he had sketched out earlier. He had a nagging feeling that he was somehow letting his side down by this feeling, but he felt a good deal better than he had expected to feel this morning. His feelings towards Singleton, at least, were considerably warmer than they had been the previous night, though towards the remainder of the group he still felt a smarting and unrelieved bitterness.

He threaded his way between the huts and took up station at his familiar post, from which he had listened morning after morning in the hope of hearing a few bars of music to brighten his day.

They had never been quite as naive as Singleton and his colleagues, with their predominating attitude of angry contempt and hostility, had regarded them. They had, in fact, foreseen long before that there was a serious risk of their being observed, and they had fully understood that, if they were seen at all, it was fairly long odds on its being by someone who would not be sympathetically disposed towards them. Accordingly they had taken such precautions as they could, and these included contingency measures for precisely the position in which they now found themselves. Thus they had long ago made an arrangement that whenever Eugen was in the barracks he would glance out of the window every little while in case his lover appeared. Now he waited, keeping a sharp lookout for any sign that he was watched or followed.

He had chosen his point of vantage particularly for its exposed position, and felt certain that no one would be able to follow or spy on him without showing himself, but he was sure that no one had observed him. He began to relax. When he had been there for less than ten minutes he saw Eugen's face appear briefly in the window. His heart gave a sharp pang of love, misery and apprehension as he saw the well-loved features. But there was no time for self-indulgence in feelings of any kind. He made a distinctive signal they had agreed on. It told Eugen that he had to see him at the earliest possible moment, that it was not a mere lovers' tryst but a matter of supreme urgency, to do with their safety, and that the one who made it would go to the prearranged meeting point and wait there for as long as he was able.

He watched closely until he saw Eugen make the agreed signal in reply, spared himself one last, loving gaze at his beloved's face, then turned and hurried off to be sure of being at the meeting place ready for whenever Eugen could get there. Eugen, for his part, gave him a quick but dazzling smile through the grimy window pane, then disappeared.

The meeting place was the shack where they had spent so many hours of joy in one another's passionate embrace, and so many more in the simpler delights of shared moments with a kindred spirit. They had agreed a secondary place against the faint possibility of finding the shack locked, or their being for some other reason unable to get there, but it proved unnecessary, and within a quarter of an hour of seeing that his signal had been seen and understood, Hales was lying on the mattress in the familiar hut with the light off. From the moment when he had left his place outside the barracks he had kept a watchful eye open for any sign of pursuit, and he had taken a circuitous route to the Russian compound, varying his pace, suddenly doubling back on himself and making use of every short cut he knew from his extensive wanderings round the camp, including several deliberate blind alleys and detours to throw off anyone who might be following. Once again he was confident that no one had been on his trail; but his heart was beating unpleasantly fast and he was sweating a rank sweat of nervous stress and fear as he waited for his lover to arrive.

Eugen was ten minutes behind him. He entered the hut quietly, switching on the light as he closed the door behind him. His face was grave, and he began speaking even as he dropped to the flooor and slid into Hales's arms. "It's happened, hasn't it?" he began. "Someone's found out about us, haven't they? And they're being troublesome."

"That's just about the size of it," assented Hales. And he told him in detail what had happened the night before and after *Appell* that morning. When he had finished Eugen lay staring up at the roof, deep in thought. Hales, who had a great respect for his friend's intelligence, remained silent, waiting until Eugen was ready to share his thoughts.

"I don't see what harm they can do us," he said at length. "Look. You've refused to do what they want. They can't harm you. They've said so. The worst they can do to you is make accusations against you when you are back in England. By then the war will be over, I shall be disappeared, somewhere in the ruins of Germany." Hales began to say something, but Eugen waved him into silence. "I know we were talking about me coming with you, but I could not come straight away. It would not be permitted, but besides, I could not think of coming to England with you until I had gone to my home and seen my parents.

"When this war comes to an end, everything will be in chaos. It will take years to make good the damage. Millions of people have been killed, millions more have lost their homes. Everything will have to be started up from nothing. In England, everything must be as it is here, geared up to war production, of armaments, ammunition, that sort of thing. It will all have to be dismantled to make all ready for the peace. No one is going to have time to waste considering whether you behaved honourably or not. Even if they do examine your case, you have said yourself that you are ready to accept the consequences of what you've done."

Hales nodded. "It's not me I'm worried about," he said. "What about you?"

"Well, what about me?" said Eugen calmly. "What can they do to me? Suppose they did the worst thing we can imagine, and somehow let my superiors know what they suspect about us. My superiors challenge me. I don't deny it. I'm not so stupid. Who knows who may have seen us together some time? No. I admit it: yes, I say, I know Sergeant Hales. He heard the music I play sometimes in the barracks, and asked me about it. Like me, he is a music lover. We spoke about it from time to time, and got to know each other. Did we do anything more than that? No, of course we didn't. What a ridiculous suggestion. Lovers? Were we lovers? What on earth gave you that idea?"

"Suppose... suppose the Gestapo got hold of the story?" asked Hales.

"That would be more dangerous," conceded Eugen. "But why should the Gestapo hear of it? Who's going to tell them? Whatever your people think of you, they have nothing to gain from bringing it to the ears of the Gestapo. It would be difficult for me, and very frightening, of course, but it would be a certain way of making sure that I never worked for them as they want, wouldn't it? And I can't believe that they would inform on me out of sheer spite. And there's another thing: if they somehow made sure it got to the Gestapo, they would know that they were condemning you to the same. Surely no English soldier would knowingly give a fellow Englishman into the hands of the *Schutzstaffel* or the Gestapo? No, Brian, there's little to fear, and I think you have more to fear than I do. So stop worrying, and get out of your clothes. I want to have as much of you as I can today. I think we should be much more — what's the word in English? Circumspect, that's it. I think we must be very circumspect for a while, very careful. Perhaps not meet for some time, and be much more careful than we have been when we do. Today may be our last time together like this for some time, so let's not spoil it, but make..." He paused, seeking the phrase.

"Make hay while the sun shines?" suggested Hales.

"That wasn't what I was trying to say, but it sounds right. It is a pleasant expression."

"Make the most of it?"

"Yes, that's what I was looking for. Make the most of it." As he spoke he was already slipping out from beneath the blankets, in which they had rolled themselves, for warmth as well as for companionship, rising to his feet and starting to strip off his clothes in the same supple movement. Hales rose more slowly, his face still shadowed with anxiety.

"I still don't like it," he muttered. But Eugen was already naked and reaching for him, and a moment later he fastened his mouth over Hales's and silenced him.

Hales's restless anxiety communicated itself to Eugen, however, and they ended up staying in the shack far less time than they had become accustomed to on Eugen's precious days off. When they parted it was with no more than a brief touch of hands and a few whispered words of affection and mutual comfort. Then they went to their separate quarters and spent separate miserable evenings wishing they had flung all caution to the four winds and stayed together until the last possible moment. Hales spent much of the evening playing crib for matchsticks with Shepherd. But his mind was not on the game, and when he owed rather more than three years' pay he gave it up and retreated to his bunk, where he tried to give his attention to a battered German grammar given to him by Eugen, because it brought him a little closer to his absent beloved.

* * *

Over the next few months autumn turned to winter, and it was a hard one. Rations, already dangerously low, became still more precarious, but their deteriorating physical condition was compensated for to some extent by the ever more heartening news of the war that filtered in from outside.

Hales and Eugen tortured themselves for some time, seeing one another less and staying together for far less time at most of their assignations. For some time also they ceased to make use of Oblemov's shack altogether. But as time crawled past and they heard nothing further about the plan to make use of Eugen they began to think they had taken alarm over nothing, and gradually began to drift back to their old ways.

Disaster came out of a clear sky one perishingly cold day in February. They had arranged to meet for their customary talk at a point on Eugen's patrol of the perimeter, but he had failed to appear. Hales was loitering where he could duck instantly out of sight if the trooper who was patrolling in his place came into sight, when a big, low-slung staff car drew up at the main camp gate. They virtually never had visitors in their lonely eyrie, so he watched curiously, and realised straightaway, from the sudden welter of heel-clicking and the instant and devoted attention it and its occupants received, that the visitors were either very important or greatly feared. He felt a sudden clutch of fear himself, settling like a lump of ice in his lower abdomen. It came to his mind that before his abortive watch where Eugen should have been on patrol he had already lurked near the barracks for over twenty minutes, which would normally have been more than enough for Eugen to have shown his face at the window. Yet he had seen no movement, no shadowy forms passing back and forth beyond the window, nothing at all. Acting on an impulse that he did not question, he prudently moved off and lounged about much nearer the gate.

As the car was bowed and scraped through the gate and whisked across the parade area to come to rest outside the Commandant's quarters, he squinted hard at it in an effort to see its occupant, but managed to see very little. When it pulled up, however, he could see more than enough, and his heart almost died within him as an icy wave of terror rolled over him. The driver, who waited outside leaning on the long, rakish bonnet of the car, was wearing the striking black, silver and scarlet of the SS. The two passengers, whom he ushered from the back of the big car and up to the Commandant's door, were smallish, anonymous-looking men in civilian dress of dark trousers, black raincoats and dark slouch hats. Hales had no doubt at all who they were, and fear rose up to swirl about him like a physical presence.

It was confirmed a few minutes later. The Commandant's door swung open, and the two anonymous visitors were ushered inside by unseen hands. A few minutes later they were already emerging once more. And this time they had another figure between them. They were holding him firmly by the elbows and hustling him along with them as they almost ran to their car. The figure was Eugen. Once at the car he heard raised voices, then witnessed the scene he had played over and over in his mind since he had first begun to fall a victim to Eugen's charm: the two mysterious and ominous-looking civilians hustled Eugen into the back of the car, one of them putting a hand on the top of his head and shoving it unceremoniously down to prevent Eugen from bumping it on the door surround as he was pushed in.

The SS driver slammed the doors closed and got back into the driver's seat, and the car immediately roared in a tight half-circle and back to the gate. There the barrier was raised with so little delay that it was ready before the car reached it. It shot through and went bouncing and jolting along the rough dirt road in the direction of the railway at a brisk twenty-five miles an hour.

So Eugen passed from Hales's sight. But while the sinister-looking civilians were inside the Commandant's quarters Hales had taken his opportunity to edge a fair bit closer to the gate than he had been before, with the result that as the car had come bucketing back across the frozen ruts and tussocks of the parade ground-cum sports area and out of the gate he had had a good view of its interior and its occupants. He had thus been able to get a last sight of the fair face of his young lover. Eugen had been wearing his upper lip stiff with all the Prussian hauteur and sang froid he could summon up: he was sitting bolt upright in the centre of the back seat, his face set in a haughty cast of defiance. But Hales, looking on in anguish with the eyes of love and true knowledge, could see clearly that it was a mask. He saw plainly the fear that underlay the determination to maintain his sang froid, saw too the merry, affectionate stripling beneath the proud, disdainful Prussian scion. He stared into the dark interior of the speeding car, desperate to keep sight of his beloved until the last possible moment. When it had disappeared from sight and the last faint reverberation of its engine had faded from earshot, he still saw in imagination his last glimpse of Eugen's set, still fair face. But he could derive no comfort from the memory of that sight. Eugen's had not been the face of one who goes to his death, but that of one who is already dead.

* * *

Later, when he was able to consider rationally the events of those last terrible days, and to relive to some extent the period immediately after Eugen was taken, Hales would conclude that at least for the remainder of that day he had not been fully sane.

After the staff car had vanished over a shoulder of the mountain, he had walked the camp for hours alone, speaking to no one and deaf and blind to anyone who may have spoken to him. He had a hazy recollection of squatting in some dark corner and weeping uncontrollably and unremittingly for a long time, then getting up, drying his eyes and resuming his plodding tramp, aimless but inexorable. And eventually, at some time so late in the short winter day that it was already dark, and thus at least six or seven hours after he had seen Eugen taken away, he found himself sitting in Oblemov's surgery, drinking hot Russian tea and being treated for some nasty gashes, apparently sustained by too close an encounter with the razor wire.

When Oblemov had cleaned the ugly straight gashes, rubbed some coarse ointment into them that made them smart abominably and then dressed them lightly, he had dismissed the orderly, going to the door of the hut with him and bolting it. Then he had returned and sat opposite Hales, fixed him with a steely gaze and said sternly, "You've got to pull yourself together, my lad."

The words, coming in a cold, hard tone that he had never heard from Oblemov before, for all his cynicism, his impatient, irascible front that he chose to present to the world, acted on Hales like a basinful of freezing water dashed in his face. Instinctively responding, more to the tone of voice than to the words themselves, he fought against the suffocating blanket of madness that had settled over him; and gradually, by degrees, he began to feel better.

"Good," said Oblemov, watching him closely and seeing the change stealing over him. "Now, then, tell me what happened."

Hales told him, striving to recall every detail of what he had seen that morning. "Take your cue from him," said Oblemov sternly. "They'll break him, probably have done so already. But he went to his end like a soldier. You must carry on living as he has gone to his death. You too are a soldier."

Hales stared at him. "A part-time one," he said miserably. "And not a very good one."

"Balls," snapped Oblemov. "You said yourself, when you told me about the fight you had with those colleagues of yours and their absurd games, that you pointed out to them there was a medal waiting for you when you got home. Presumably the English don't give them away like biscuits. Besides, it doesn't matter what sort of soldier you are: what matters is what kind of a soldier you seem to be. Being a soldier is all a matter of face, and which face you present to the world. You have the easier part in this: your duty is to go on living, and to show the world the same kind of face that your lad showed this morning."

"I don't know that I want to go on living," Hales snuffled wretchedly.

Oblemov made an incoherent sound in his throat that sounded, to Hales's astonished ears, like "Grrr." Then, "If you're going to snivel and whine like a woman, I don't want to hear it," he said. Hales, his head whipping round to stare at the doctor once again in astonishment, saw that his anger was unfeigned, and intense: he seemed to be in a genuine state of towering rage.

"God damn you, boy," he said, his voice quivering under the weight of a fury suppressed with an iron control. "There's your boy gone to unimaginable horrors in some cellar of the Gestapo, and here are you whining and grizzling like a courtesan's lapdog deprived of its biscuit. You've got to go on living, man, and smartish! Can't you see that?"

"Why?" said Hales, but his voice was stronger, and his own anger, beginning to rise, was already pumping new reserves of firmness and resolve into him.

"Because life bloody goes on," snapped Oblemov, throwing off the remnants of his control and roaring at him from his position a couple of feet away across the planed pine tabletop. "God, you'd have made a poor Russian! Life goes on, Brian. You have to accept the gift of life, because it's the only bloody gift you ever get in this miserable world. It's a gift, and a privilege, not some piece of frippery that's yours to do as you will with. It's God's one and only bloody gift to you, and you owe it to him, if not to yourself, to do something worthwhile with it. You must not crumple up the moment it goes sour on you, because you *may* not. You *owe* it, owe it to life itself, to keep going, and match it blow for blow. In this case, you had some wonderful times with this boy of yours — which in itself makes you one remarkably privileged among us. There won't be many going home from here who can boast any wonderful moments to remember their time here by. You're taking back the memory of many such. Now life has decided it's time to turn the cards against you for a while. Well, you accepted the wonderful times. Now you have a duty to accept the rough as you did the smooth, and do it with dignity and honour. Not to come grovelling and snivelling in here looking for a shoulder to grizzle on."

He sat back, exhausted. He was by this time so reduced by progressive privation and starvation that only his iron will was sustaining him, and even the effort of losing his temper was enough to sap his dwindling reserves of stamina.

Hales heard him in silence, until the storm had blown itself out. As the merciless castigation proceeded his head first dropped in shame, then rose again in a spirit of resolve. When the old man finally sat watching him through red-rimmed, bloodshot eyes over the rim of his tea glass, he looked him in the face and said, "You're quite right, of course, my beloved Valeri. I should be deeply, thoroughly ashamed of myself, and I am. I was halfway out of my mind, I think — you know, beside myself with fear and anxiety; but that's no excuse. If you hadn't given me that talking-to I might well have done something really foolish... I... I even thought about going and asking for an interview with the Commandant, and asking him what had happened to Eugen..."

"Well we can at least be thankful to providence that she didn't allow *that* to happen," said Oblemov drily, and Hales was overjoyed to see the customary twinkle coming back into his eyes. In that moment a sudden resolve came into his mind, and on impulse, without thinking, he decided he wanted to act on it. "Valeri Borisovitch," he said. "I want to come work for you. You mean more to me than anyone in the world now, now that... now that Eugen's... gone, and you're working yourself to death here. Anybody can see that. I want to come here and do whatever I can to help you, take some of the load off you. Will you let me do that, please? You said life must go on, and you're right. Well, I can't think of any better way to have it go on than by helping you to keep your people here alive, and working myself to help keep *you* alive."

Oblemov looked levelly across at him. "That's better," he said. "And yes, of course we shall be glad of the help. Start tomorrow, as soon after your breakfast as you can. If you can spare some of it —

your breakfast, that is — so much the better. Now it's high time you got back to your own quarters. You can use the basin in there" — he jerked a thumb in the direction of his cubby-hole — "to get cleaned up and wash the streaks off your face. You've got to show a strong front to that lot. Mustn't go in and show them you've been crying."

Hales looked across at him for a moment with love and grati- tude, then obediently followed his directions. A few minutes later he left and made his way through the camp to F9. Oblemov stood silhouetted against the light in the doorway of his surgery hut, watch- ing him until he was swallowed up in the darkness. He would not have allowed Hales to see it for worlds, but he was privately very pleased with him.

XIX

ON entering F9 he walked straight over to where he could see Singleton chatting to a couple of cronies over a desultory game of cards. They looked up as he loomed above them, surprised to see him approaching and apparently wishing to talk. "Got a minute?" he asked casually, looking at Singleton.

Singleton nodded, and motioned to him to draw up an extra chair, but he shook his head and jerked his head in the direction of the door. "In private, if it's all right by you." Singleton raised his eyebrows, but he nodded again. "Of course," he said quietly. He excused himself from his friends with an interrogative glance, re- ceived nods of assent, and followed Hales to the door of the hut with a puzzled look which was so obviously unfeigned that it had already exonerated its owner in Hales's mind from any responsibil- ity for Eugen's betrayal.

They went out and, as they had the previous time they had done the same thing, slipped silently round the corner of the hut. "We had visitors this morning," said Hales quietly.

"Oh?" Singleton questioned. His tone conveyed nothing to Hales, and further satisfied him that the man knew nothing of what had taken place. He had made up his mind to pursue it to the end, however, so he went on, "Yes. From the Gestapo." That did bring a reaction. Hales could hear his hissed intake of breath. "Go on," Sin- gleton said.

"They took someone away with them," Hales said evenly. "I

just wanted, for my own satisfaction, to be sure you didn't know anything about it."

When Singleton spoke next Hales could distinctly hear indignation contesting for supremacy with concern in his tone. "I see," was what he eventually said. "Was it..."

"Yes," said Hales flatly. "My friend. I don't know what they took him away for, but I can guess. Can't you?"

"It could have been all kinds of things," said Singleton reflectively; "but I imagine..." He left the rest unsaid.

"I just want to know," pursued Hales, "whether it was anything to do with you, or with your friends from that night months ago. I'm not thinking about revenge," he added. "It's for my own peace of mind. I only want to know."

"I had nothing to do with it," said Singleton. "And I'm quite sure I can speak for the others on that. None of us would dream of betraying anyone to the Gestapo, not even one of the guards. They're all ordinary squaddies, and by and large they've treated us decently. I'll have a word with the others, but you can take it from me that it was nothing to do with anyone who was there that night."

"That's what I thought," said Hales. "That's all I wanted to ask. Thanks." He half turned to go back inside, but Singleton put a restraining hand on his arm. "I'd just like to say one thing more," he said. "I'm sorry it's come to this for your... friend. I wouldn't have wished that on anyone."

"Okay," said Hales. "Thanks." They went gladly back into the warmth of the hut together, Singleton to resume his game with a faintly unhappy frown creasing his forehead, Hales to his bunk. On the way he ducked into the tobacco-reeking dark cavern of Shepherd's bunk, where he relayed the news of Eugen's taking. Shepherd offered his concern and sympathy in a stentorian whisper, and Hales was left still wondering who might have betrayed his beloved. He clambered into his own bunk and, against all his own expectations, slept like the dead.

The following morning he was up in good time and among the first few to drift to the parade area for *Appell*. Afterwards he was among those rostered to do breakfast. He hurried back to F9 and helped in the preparation of the pitifully meagre meal that they were all by now used to. While they were still polishing it off ravenously, chasing last crumbs round, licking plates and offering the usual ribald compliments to the chef, they became aware of a commotion somewhere in the direction of the main gate. There were cries, the repeated honking of horns, and then, stunning them all into instant silence and apprehension, the sound of shots.

There were only three or four, however, followed by an eerie dead silence. Then, suddenly, it was broken, and in a second washed entirely away as if it had never been, by a great wave of cheering. Wave on wave of it followed, swelling audibly by the second as more and more voices joined in.

Last crumbs were instantly forgotten. Plates went unlicked and tea was slopped everywhere as, to a man, they abandoned their breakfast and streamed to the door. The leaders dead-heated, and there was a moment of confusion as too many bodies strove to charge through at the same time and formed a temporary rugger scrum in the narrow doorway. Eventually they sorted themselves out, however, and burst out in a human tidal wave. Hales found himself running as wildly as any of them in the direction of the commotion, which was still gathering force as they ran.

They reached the parade area for the second time in half an hour; and then stopped dead in their tracks as if they had all run headlong into some gigantic invisible barrier. Ahead of them was an already fair-sized muster of prisoners. To the left, standing huddled in a disorderly group in front of the Commandant's quarters, were the majority of the camp guards, with, on the muddy grass in front of them, a huge heap of rifles and other weaponry. All this Hales took in in a single rapid glance. Then his eye swivelled to the main gate. His gasp of astonishment was lost in the identical sound coming from everyone else, when they all seemed to see it at the same moment: the two great gates themselves were lying, flattened as if by some kind of battering ram from without. Beside the guardhouse where incoming vehicles were halted and papers checked, the four guards who had been on sentry duty that morning were standing in a smaller replica of the dispirited-looking collection outside the Commandant's building. One of them was receiving attention from one of the camp medical officers, who appeared to be bandaging his arm and putting it in a sling.

And then, ranged in a semicircle just inside where the gates had been, were the unexpected guests who provided the real sensation: five Jeeps, each with a miniature pennant in the unmistakable pattern of the stars and stripes flying above its bonnet. And in the Jeeps, standing up to see as far into the compound as possible, soldiers in uniforms that were familiar yet not quite familiar: the colour slightly different from British khaki, the cut slightly different, pockets where there should have been none, the caps a slightly different shape, and, most assuredly, worn at an assortment of rakish angles that would have brought apoplectic howls of anguish from any British RSM. And then, running like water spreading through tissue paper, a murmur to begin with but swelling in moments to a whisper, then a rumble, a shout and finally a joyous, raucous, full-throated roar: "The Americans are here! It's the Yanks!"

Hales found himself howling the words, along with every man there. He turned to the man to his right, and saw that he, too had taken up the cry, and was repeating it over and over again like a chant. He glanced to his left, and saw the same thing, repeated many times as far as he could see into the crowd, which was increasing as new arrivals from the more distant huts came streaming up with every second that passed. He looked back at the man on his right, and saw that there were tears in his eyes — and only then became conscious of the tears in his own.

When the first, convulsive wave of semi-hysteria had dissipated, he dried his eyes unselfconsciously — it would have been absurd to feel selfconscious about it, when every man in sight for a hundred yards was doing the same thing — and took a more leisurely look about him. Outside the perimeter wire an enormous column of American troops were arriving and making preparations for what looked like a permanent stay. Hales watched as the camp Commandant approached the leading American Jeep. A much-decorated officer stepped down from the distinctive, snub-nosed little vehicle and exchanged salutes with him. Hales, watching in fascination, was amused to notice that he was, literally, breathless, having been holding his breath for some time without being aware that he was doing so.

The elderly German Colonel, he thought, looked more relieved than anything else. He had been too old for army service when the war began, and had been pressed into service when he should have been thinking about carpet slippers and dandling grandchildren on his knee, Hales thought. He was also reputed to be a gentlemanly, courteous man of the old school; he's probably glad they've lost, thought Hales to himself. But then he saw the old man's face sag as he turned away, and changed his mind. Even to those Germans who detested the Nazis and everything they represented, he supposed that the taste of defeat must still be bitter.

The reflection instantly brought a flood of thoughts of Eugen; and with them came a sudden, blinding explosion of hope. He dared not elaborate on it, or even to think about it consciously; but however he might try to keep it from his mind it had asserted its right to exist, and once it was in existence it could not be de-invented and cast into non-existence. If the Americans were here this morning, the thought declared, perhaps they were not far away yesterday. Perhaps they had even then penetrated to some point between here and wherever Eugen was being taken. In which case...

He forced the thought away, and turned back to see what was happening next. The Americans were moving inside the wire fence in numbers now, one party detailed to collect the German weapons; others, clearly medical teams, were filtering into the crowd, asking questions and collecting patients as they went. Yet others, by far the most numerous, were bringing parcels of food, crates of food, whole *vehicles* full of food, into the compound, and distributing it open-handedly, lavishly, almost recklessly. Hales was assailed by a sudden sharp pang of guilt, when he remembered that he had promised solemnly to work for Oblemov today. He wriggled through the press to where he could see the nearest food-distribution party. When he reached it he was greeted by a gum-chewing American soldier who gave him a large and friendly grin and invited him to help himself. "Do you mind if I take just a few things that are easy to digest?" he asked. "I've got a friend who's been starving himself half to death, and I'd like to take him something he'll be able to get down, and keep down."

"Sure," said the American. "Help yourself, bud." Hales gave him a grateful smile, and selected a few bland-looking items. He also seized a couple of delectable items for himself: a tin of peaches, a packet of sweet biscuits and a tin of sardines. He looked enquiringly at the American, wondering if he was purloining too much, and received another grin and an expansive wave of the hand. "Thanks very much indeed," he said, having to yell to be heard over the universal hubbub. "You're welcome," said the soldier, and then offered him a cigarette. It was so casual a gesture, made so naturally and unthinkingly, and yet was such a bombshell, that it practically reduced Hales to tears. His eyes, indeed, were wet as he accepted the cigarette and a light. The American saw them and smiled, understanding, and unobtrusively slipped his hand into his pocket and passed Hales the half-full packet. Hales, deeply moved, tried to stammer his gratitude. "Forget it, bud," said the soldier, and turned to serve his next customer with a final gesture of kindness, a laugh. Hales stuffed his collection into his pockets and started fighting his way, against the traffic, towards the back of the crowd. Almost everyone in the camp was now surging towards the parade area and the gates, but Hales had a bet with himself that the man he sought would be where he always was.

He won. When he reached the Russian compound he found it deserted, with only a few stragglers heading as fast as they could go in the direction of the noisy celebration at the far end of the camp. When Hales pushed the door of the surgery hut it was open, however, and when he slipped inside he saw Oblemov, sitting as usual behind the table at the far end. He sat down across from him as he had done so often before, and looked closely at him. The doctor was looking frailer, thinner and more pitifully weak and emaciated than Hales had ever seen him before, and it seemed all the more poignant to Hales, coming directly from noisy scenes of jubilation as he had.

"I've brought you something to eat, Valeri Borisovitch," he said after they had exchanged greetings, emptying his shopping from his various pockets onto the table. "And they're for *you*," he added firmly. "There's plenty for everyone now, so you've got no excuse to give yourself short rations. This is all for you, and I want to see you eat it." Oblemov's eyes glistened as he looked at the assortment of things Hales had turned out of his pockets. Slowly he reached out a hand to finger a packet of digestive biscuits. "I shall have to take this in gradual stages," he said, hesitantly. "I've been going without for so long..." But he managed to eat a little, and to keep it down, and they sat talking quietly while the uproar outside still gained in volume.

A little later Oblemov went to the cubby-hole and made tea for them. As they sipped it he said slowly, "This is perhaps the last time we shall sit and take tea together like this. It's been one of the pleasanter features of our life here, hasn't it?"

"It's been one of the things that have made life bearable," said Hales softly, speaking from the heart. "But it won't be the last time, surely? We'll be here for a day or so yet. And you must come to see me in England when we've all got home and got ourselves sorted out. And I'll come to see you, won't I? I want to see Mother Russia."

Oblemov studied his face carefully. "I'm afraid not. I don't think so," he said.

"Oh?" said Hales. "Why's that?"

Oblemov sighed. "I fear things are going to be very different after this war," he said sadly. "In particular, I'm afraid it won't be at all easy between Russia and the West."

"Explain," said Hales, adopting the brusque manner so often affected by his friend.

"Russia is weary," he said heavily. "Bone weary. In particular, weary of every European demagogue, dictator and psychopath fighting his wars to the last drop of Russia's blood; of having Europe's wars won over ramparts of Russian dead. Unless I'm greatly mistaken, Russia will not go to war again. That will be counted against her. I think Russia will go into her shell, and that it will be a very long time before she consents to come out of it again. It's not going to be a very pleasant world to live in, my friend, if my judgment's anything like correct. Especially for former friends such as you and me. So, no, I don't think we shall drink tea together again after we part here, batushka."

His use, for the first time, of the affectionate diminutive struck Hales like a physical blow. He looked across the rough old table at the old man, and a great surge of affection and love welled up in him. He looked at the bony, liver-spotted hand resting on the table; he stroked the back of the hand, with its prominent veins and long, sensitive musician's fingers with the tips of his own fingers for a few moments, then held it gently but tightly, as if willing some of the life of his own hand to flow into it, warming it and lending it some of his youth. "You have been my father here, Valeri Borisovitch," he said softly. "Thank you." And for once he saw that he had managed to confound all Oblemov's cynicism. The old man's eyes dropped, he turned and rose from his chair and went hastily towards his cubby-hole. "Have some more tea," he said over his shoulder.

XX

"LETTER for you, Mr. 'ales," said the clerk, popping his head round the door of the room Hales shared with the other two pupils. "Leicester postmark."

"Oh. Thanks Raymond. It'll be from Mother." Hales, frantically gathering up gown, wig, several heavy books, his brief and other impedimenta, not forgetting sandwiches and a book to read on the Underground, gestured at his royal-blue bag on the chipped, scored table in the middle of the room. "Just chuck it in my bag, would you. I'll read it on the tube, if I can get the cases to stick in my head first."

Raymond smiled indulgently. "You won't have no trouble, Mr. 'ales. Not you." He slipped the letter into Hales's bag as requested, and went back to his own lair, radiating benevolence.

"It's an outrage, the way he spoils you, Brian," grunted Arthur Cowell, the senior pupil. "I'm way senior to you, and I was commissioned, *and* I know some law — quite a bit, actually — and he doesn't talk to me in those nauseating tones of honeyed respect, the bloody old fraud."

"He doesn't make you work the way he makes me, either," said Hales over his shoulder, already leaving the room at a half-run. "You want to learn to count your blessings..." The last words floated back from the corridor, followed by the echo of his footsteps as he galloped for the door.

A 15 bus was providentially passing as he shot out into the Strand. He leaped aboard it and sat with his lips moving as he rehearsed his summing-up speech on behalf of the artistic long-term fraudster he was defending. In his mind's eye he saw the jury visibly moved and swayed by his impassioned oratory. Several women jurors were weeping openly as he concluded his peroration. He could see the reports in the evening papers: "Shades of Marshall Hall... ", "Not even the 'Marshall' in his heyday could have... ", "Move aside Birkett..." But a few moments of this heady stuff was enough; he prudently took out the volume of the Law Reports containing the case on which he was mainly relying, and spent the rest of the short bus ride desperately trying to commit the principal passages to memory.

At the Old Bailey he alighted from the bus in less spectacular style, crossed the road, robed, found that his case was on early, lost it but was on the whole very satisfied with his performance. The letter from his mother was buried beneath the books, gown, wig and other paraphernalia, and remained there for a week, until the next time he turned the bag out properly in an effort to make it a little lighter on his shoulder.

When he found it he turned the crumpled letter over in his hands, recognising his mother's well-known handwriting but wondering why the envelope was twice the usual size. "Best way to find out is opening it, I s'pose," he muttered to himself, and slit the envelope open with a miniature Japanese Samurai sword that served as the pupils' room paper knife.

The envelope contained a long letter from his mother, chatty, full of local gossip about people in the village whom he had hardly known before he moved away to start his own life, and could scarcely even remember as faces now. There was also a brief note from his father. It gave a brief report on the fortunes of the village cricket side, and then added, "The enclosed letter arrived yesterday, from the War Office. As you can see, it's been on its travels."

He took the final enclosure and studied it curiously. It was an ordinary letter, in a nondescript white envelope bearing a German stamp. It had been overstamped and scrawled on so often that there was hardly any of the original white surface still visible. There were numerous Royal Air Force and War Ministry rubber stamps, recommendations in a variety of hands both masculine and feminine to "try so-and-so", and more than one sticky label had been plastered over more scribbling to provide room for yet another try. But his own name still survived in the original writer's hand, and the moment Hales saw it he realised that he was trembling. The almost three years since he had returned home fell away, and he saw Eugen's face before his mind's eye as clearly as if they had last met the evening before.

He stood staring at the envelope for some moments before slitting it open. Then, without taking out the letter, he headed for the lavatory at a fast walk, scarcely suppressing the impulse to run. Once securely locked inside he sat down and with trembling fingers drew the letter from its envelope. It was in the clear, firm hand that he remembered perfectly, and at the sight of it he caught his breath, almost gasping in the unexpected pain it brought. He had to sit with his head down for a while, taking slow, deep breaths to bring the momentary feelings, almost of panic, under control.

At length he was able to straighten up and look at the letter again. Taking a deep breath he forced himself to be calm and began to read.

The letter bore a Berlin address and a date in June 1947. That meant it had spent almost a full year on its travels round the backwaters of the RAF and the Air and War Ministries before finally reaching him.

My dear Brian,

     I only realised when I sat down to write this that I never knew your address. So I'm sending it to the Royal Air Force, hoping that they will be able to send it on to you.

First of all, I know you will have been worrying about me after you saw me taken away on that terrible morning. So, first, please don't worry. As you see, I escaped. I realised that you could not have known, but I saw you as they took me away, and at that moment I truly thought that I was going to my death. Believe me, my dear Brian, I was thinking more about you than of myself. I always hoped that you would never be arrested. How they found out about us I don't know, and I don't suppose we shall ever know. I think it must have been one of the other prisoners who informed on us, but who, and why, I cannot begin to guess.

Anyhow, when the Gestapo drove off with me I had no idea what they would do with me. I half expected them to halt the car somewhere on the way and shoot me out of hand. But no, they took me to Freiburg, which was the nearest really big town to where we were.

However, we never got there, because a few kilometres before we reached the city, we ran straight into a large detachment of American troops. It was very lucky that we ran almost literally into them, because I found out afterwards that SS and Gestapo everywhere were shooting ordinary German soldiers like me and taking over their identities, to avoid being tried for war crimes — as I'm sure you have heard, they are being put on trial to this day for the most appalling activities. Do you remember we talked about those camps, where I said I'd heard rumours of Jews and others, including people such as you and me, being taken and slaughtered in huge numbers? Well, my God, it seems that they were all true, and that the numbers of the dead came to millions. I still find it impossible, sometimes when I try to think about it, to believe that such things could have happened, even though I know it must be true.

Anyway, we were all captured so quickly that the Gestapo people with me had no chance to do anything to me at all. I gave myself up to the Americans, who made me a prisoner but treated me very well. Not so the Gestapo. They were taken off one morning, with their

SS driver, and I never saw them again. Not that I was sorry about that!

Eventually I was released to the German civilian authorities, and after a lot of filling in of forms I was released. They tried to find out about my record, but it seems that someone burned all the files and records at our camp, so there was little they could do. I know the Americans liberated the camp very soon after I was taken away, and I suppose they asked the prisoners how we had treated them. I heard that poor Colonel Schumann shot himself, and I was very sorry to hear that. He was a gentle, kindly old man, far too old to be serving still. But then, we have heard such stories since the war ended that his is only one tiny tragedy among so many. I have heard stories from my own village and elsewhere of boys as young as fourteen being forced to join the army and go to try to hold up the final Russian advance on Berlin. They were slaughtered in their thousands, and they no more than children. I weep to hear these stories. But then, since I came home I have spent a great deal of time weeping — weeping for shame, for Germany's shame, for the misery and humiliation of defeat and more for the knowledge that it was a necessary and deserved defeat.

I've also wept for us, for not knowing if you were alive or dead, and for knowing that I probably shall not see you again.

I know that I cannot come to England, as we once talked about. There is too much to be done here. I am teaching again, and every time I teach my children certain expressions in English I remember where I learned them myself, and smile secretly to myself. But I must stay here, Brian, and I am sure you will understand that, you who understood me so much better than everyone, other than my father.

That brings me to another reason why I can not leave here. Poor Vati is still alive, but the war did much to break even his fine spirit, and the things we found out about that had gone on in the war did much, much more. Sometimes I hate Germany and Germans, and feel ashamed to be German myself, for what Germans did to my father. But I know that that is false reasoning, and that the only way to help put things right, to atone for what we Germans did, is by staying here and helping to make a better Germany in the place of the old one.

Do your duty as you see it, thought Hales in a bitter spasm of mingled regret, remorse and bright, vivid memory of bliss snatched, against all the odds, from echoing vistas of boredom, hunger and misery. And "He's fearfully Prussian," he heard himself saying.

So no trip to England for me; and I don't think, dear Brian, that it will be very possible for you to come here, either. There are very ominous things happening, and I think the map of Germany is about to be redrawn once again. The Russians are everywhere, and making themselves very objectionable. I have a terrible fear that we may one day soon find ourselves in some kind of annexed satellite of Russia, and the thought fills me with terror.

Now it was Oblemov's voice echoing dreamily around the cramped little lavatory cubicle: "It's not going to be a very pleasant world to live in my friend, especially for former friends such as you and me..."

But we put our trust in the Americans and, especially, the British, whom we trust to retain some sense of justice. But then I remember what you said one day as we talked in the camp, about the injustice of Versailles, and I wonder if *anyone* truly knows the meaning of the word "justice". Still, one must hope. Without hope, all else is pointless.

Now to smaller things, which yet seem larger, because they are things to do with us alone, not with great matters of state and the world. I was greatly comforted to find that you had written to me. It was those letters that made me feel fairly sure that at least you were still alive. Unfortunately I never read the letters, because Vati lost them. But he did read them first, and was able to tell me roughly what you had said. For a moment I was disappointed, and a little hurt, when I heard that you had said little, and that most of it was formal, with nothing of the love and affection that lay between us. But of course I quickly realised that that was only caution, and that you were leaving unsaid the most important things. I hope that was correct judgment, anyhow.

Hales broke off from reading and sat back, breathing hard. He was trembling again, and sweating profusely. All the long period of anguish, of sky-high hope gradually dying as no replies came to his letters, came back, his tangled emotions of the time starkly illuminated, as if by lightning, in a series of cameos of vivid recollection. He could remember exactly how he had felt when he had finally, reluctantly decided that no answering letters were ever going to arrive, and that he would in all probability never know if his beloved had lived or died that day in February 1945. He pulled himself together, and went back to the letter.

And that is all, really, my dearest Brian, except to say this. It does not seem that we are meant to be together. We are likely to find it difficult or impossible to meet for some very long time. I cannot come to England for the reasons I have explained here, which I am sure you will understand. You will, I fear, find it impossible to come to see me; and even if you could come, I don't think it would be a very happy way of meeting once again, if we had to be restrained and formal, unable to express anything of the love there is between us. Since as things are at present we cannot even write openly and without pretence. I think we must accept that it is the judgment of fate, and bow before that judgment.

In other words, we must try to forget each other, and make ourselves busy with other things. I know I am suggesting something so difficult that it is almost impossible, and asking a great deal of frail human flesh and blood. But I truly think it is for the best that we try to do this. I think also that if we busy ourselves with other things, as I have said, other people will come into our lives also.

And so, mein Geliebter, this is the last time I shall know the joy of calling you that: mein Geliebter. It's an

old-fashioned word, but I chose it because it seems
somehow right for you. I expect that this letter from me
will bring sorrow rather than joy, but please try to
remember the good things we have to remember, the
joy we somehow salvaged from the miseries of the war
and the prison camp. Remember also that I loved you
from the beginning, and know that I still love you now,
even if we are now doomed to spend our remaining time
apart and unable to see each other. I always hope that
my mother is right, and my beloved Vati is wrong: it's
not likely, but I hope it is so, because if it is, we are
destined to meet again, in another life. I hope it is so.
Meanwhile, du bist mein Schatz, und mein Geliebter.
Ich liebe dich, jetzt und ewig,

Eugen

* * *

By the time he had finished reading the letter through Hales had
forgotten where he was, and groaned aloud. At once a voice, concerned, came from outside the cubicle. "Who's that? Are you all
right?"

Hales came stumblingly back to himself. "Eh? Oh, yes, I'm
okay."

"Brian? Is that you? Are you all right, man?" came the voice
again, which he now identified as that of Cowell.

"Yes, yes, I'm all right," he called desperately. "Bit of tum trouble, that's all."

"Right-ho," came Cowell's voice again. "I'll be looking something out for you, to settle it down."

"Thanks, old man," he said with difficulty. The sound of footsteps dwindled away down the passage. Hales sighed with relief, and
went back to his letter. After reading it through a second time, he
folded it carefully, pushed it deep into the largest unoccupied pocket
of his wallet, and finally quit the cubicle and went back to his room.

* * *

Over the next forty years Hales busied himself with the law. He
built up a large practice, making a speciality of defence work and
lost causes. He allowed himself to be persuaded to take silk when he

had been at the bar for eighteen years; but he steadfastly refused the many invitations he received to ascend to the bench, and the still more numerous requests to take a Recordership. His grounds for refusing were simplicity itself, but since he never once disclosed them his persistent refusals drove his colleagues, the Lord Chancellor's office and most of all his wide circle of friends, to distracted protests. "All right, Brian, we know you *won't* take it. But for God's sake *why* won't you take it?" they would demand after his latest refusal. And he would murmur something about not feeling entitled to sit in judgment on others, who might well be stronger, worthier or more upright or deserving than he himself. The friends went away feeling certain there was something more to it underneath but, as always, frustrated by his immovably obstinate refusal to elaborate or explain.

A great many of his closer friends were perfectly well aware of his homosexuality, and one or two of the more thoughtful among them had a strong suspicion that it might have something to do with his rejection of judicial office. "But there've been dozens of judges who were gay, Brian," said one of his closest friends heatedly on one occasion after he had refused an invitation to the High Court bench. "You've never tried to make a secret of it, although you've never advertised or made a big thing of it. Clearly the LC doesn't think it matters. Christ, does *anybody* think it matters, these days?"

"The tabloid press would enjoy themselves for a day or so, I should imagine," murmured Hales with a faint smile.

"Even the uttermost and guttermost would think twice before damning a red judge merely for being gay," expostulated the friend, still over-heated. But Hales merely murmured soothing inconsequentialities until he had blown himself out, and never, then or at any other time, divulged that his reason lay in a remark of his own, almost forty years before, when he had said that someone was "really very Prussian," and came from a determination that he would never, lawyer or no lawyer, run the risk of having to pass sentence on others for being only that which he was himself.

During those forty years, as Eugen had ventured tentively to prophesy, other people did come into Hales's life, and ten years after he had seen Eugen pushed into a car and watched him driven off across a mountainside, he began living with a young doctor, in a harmonious partnership that was only to be dissolved when the doctor died, in the fourth year of Hales's retirement.

One day in 1994, six years after Hales had retired and two after the death of his beloved friend, he had collected the mail and was seated at the kitchen table, a large mug of tea at his elbow, sorting the junk from the meaningful. Only one envelope puzzled him. It was a large manila envelope, of a distinctive legal shape and size, and clearly contained something fairly bulky; and it bore the name of a well-known firm of London solicitors.

He slit the envelope open and drew from it a sheaf of papers. On top was a letter from the solicitors — he smiled wryly to himself as he observed that his standing was still high enough to merit a senior partner. It was brief, informing him that the firm had an arrangement with a leading law firm in Berlin, who had asked them to trace him, inform him that he was a beneficiary under the will of a recently deceased German citizen, and to forward to him the enclosed documents, which they begged to do therewith. It ended with various formalities he was required to complete, and a deferential personal note of conclusion from the partner.

He tossed the letter with its grandiosities impatiently aside, and found a large, stout, sealed envelope. He recognised the hand-writing instantly, and felt his heart leap skittishly for a moment. His stomach contracted, and he thought for a moment that he was going to be sick. Then he got control of himself, and tore the envelope open. Inside was a thin booklet, with a wad of writing paper clipped to the front.

Mein Geliebter,

I imagine you will still remember me, even after all this time. The very fact that I remember you in such indelibly vivid detail makes me feel that you cannot have completely forgotten me, either.

There's not a lot to tell. After I wrote to you, recommending that we should accept the judgment of providence and forget about one another, I spent forty years proving perfectly unable to follow my own excellent advice — which leads me to suspect that perhaps it wasn't so excellent after all! However, I expect it was right. It seemed the only thing to do at the time.

Well, in due course I married, and had children. It was not a happy marriage, which will not, I imagine, come as a surprise to you, and Helga and I parted after a few years. I went back to the way of life I was made for, and I have no complaints. It has been a fair life, all in all. I have spent many years now with someone who made me tolerably happy, and whom I was fortunately able to make happy in my turn. If he was happier than I, that was no fault of his, and he never even knew what lay in my past which made it so difficult for me to attain any true contentment or peace. It was, of course, you, and the knowledge that I had by my own pig-headedness denied myself the true consolation that might have come from a life by your side. I say "might" only because I have not, I fear, proved to be a very easy man to live with, and I wonder, in my darker moments, whether even you would have been able to put up with me. All I do know is that if anyone could have made my life truly happy, it would have been you or no one.

Anyhow, mein Geliebter, to come to the point, my partner died some years ago, leaving me alone; and I could not find either the energy or the goodwill to attempt any kind of return to my family. And now, I am dying. I have been told that I have very little time left, and I shall make sure that by the time you receive this I am safely dead: God knows how tempted I have been to try to effect a reunion; but every time I feared what tranquility of yours I might be breaking up, and quickly decided that it would be the most monstrous selfishness to risk disturbing your peace of mind for what could never be more than a brief, passing glimpse into a past that, for all I know, you may have already forgotten, or wish to leave to rest undisturbed. One should not move stones that have rested too long in the same place, for fear of what squirming things may be disclosed underneath. And yet... and yet, how I was tempted. Just a sight of your face might have done so much... but then, of course, there is no way of knowing if I would even have recognised you if I had seen you.

I am not going to insult you by leaving my money to you — there isn't much, anyway, and what there is will go to those who have the right to it, so far as there is any right in such a matter — that is, to my children, and after them, if any survives, to my grandson. To you, my beloved Brian, I have only three things to bequeath: this letter, in which at last I tell you the truth about my feelings for you; the enclosed small gift; and one other.

I hope the little gift will bring back good memories of me, of us and of the time we had together, so brief, so strange in the way it happened, but so endlessly wonderful — I say endlessly because I am discovering only now, as I write this at the end of my life, how the bond between us, which held us together and sustained us in the camp, truly *was* endless. I feel it holding as strongly as ever even now. This is my truth, and holds good even if you no longer feel it binding you as I feel it binding me. Anyway, as I say, I hope the small token which is all I leave to you will be a small but brightly shining beacon, to light up the journey of memory into the past, and that you will look at it and remember, with affection at least and perhaps — as I pray that it may be — with some of the old love.

I said there was a third thing I had to bequeathe to you. That is, of course, quite simply, my undying love. Believe me, mein Lieber, there was never anyone but you. I know that now, and wish I had known it earlier, when there was time.

Go in peace and happiness, my dear friend, and think of me sometimes, with love if you can find it in your heart.

Your loving friend, Eugen

The signature below was as firm and decisive as ever. Hales made himself read the letter to the end before looking at the "small gift". When he turned to it he gazed at it in wonder for some moments. It was only four pages thick, printed in old-fashioned, fussy German style on thin paper. It was a score of Schubert's song, "Das Lied im Grünen". On the front cover, in a boyish version of Eugen's hand, in faded purple ink, was his name. On the back cover was a scribbled note, clearly done much more recently. Hales could barely see the writing through the tears that had welled up in his eyes. He dabbed at them angrily, but they kept coming. Squinting, he read:

"This is the score I had in the camp. I always kept it carefully, and no one but me has ever laid a hand on it. Keep it, and remember me. Ich liebe dich. Eugen."

Epilogue: Full Circle

Epilogue: Full Circle

Hales had done all the sightseeing he could deal with. The moment had come, and he still could not decide whether he was looking forward to it with keen curiosity or with dread. He supposed he was about to find out, in retrospect and the hard way.

He stepped off the kerb and hailed a taxi, and watched the changing surroundings as it took him far from the centre of the city and into a well-to-do neighbourhood of quiet, spacious avenues lined with trees, with big houses tucked discreetly away in clumps of cedars and birches, limes and monkey puzzles.

At last the driver turned into a broad, curving driveway and deposited him before a house which, though large, was none the less smaller than many in the neighbourhood, and somehow dwarfed by its own driveway, gardens and towering trees. He watched the taxi disappear back into the street in a puff of blue exhaust, then turned to ring the bell. He had been seen, though, because the heavy wooden door swung open to admit him as he raised his hand to the bell-push.

Inside a pretty woman in middle age with large, gentle grey eyes waited for him. "You are Sir Brian Hales, yes?" she said. "Please come inside. It is such an honour to meet someone who was friendly with my father..."

He went into a pleasant, uncluttered living room, and was introduced to her husband. It was all going, he thought, quite remarkably painlessly. He began to dismiss the innumerable reservations he'd had about making the visit as unfounded.

Tea came, and biscuits. They made pressing invitations to dinner that evening, or to other meals on subsequent days, but he declined them all. "I do apologise," he told them, "but I was determined to make this only the very briefest of visits, just a few minutes to introduce ourselves. Later on, perhaps, yes, I'm sure, later on, we can have dinner, though I should be glad if you would permit me to take you somewhere in Berlin. But this time, well, I was very apprehensive, I had no idea whether I was being wise or quite inconceivably foolish to suggest this visit. It was for that reason that

I deliberately made it impossible for us to spend very long together. Indeed, I must be preparing to go now. I asked my taxi-driver to return in half an hour, and I see to my horror that it has almost passed already. Just one final thing: if I might perhaps just see your son, just for long enough to introduce myself."

"Of course," Eugen Schumacher's daughter told him, and not for the first time during the few minutes he had been in the house, he felt the unreality of the situation wash over him. She led him out into the large hallway, and indicated the stairs. "Up there, and Friedrich's room is on the right." She called up the stairs, and Hales heard a pleasant, youthful voice call "Ja, Mutti." He turned to begin climbing the elegant, sweeping staircase, but she took him by the arm and detained him for a moment. "You should be prepared, Sir Brian," she said, and he saw anxiety clearly in her eyes. It was not only anxiety for him, he felt vaguely, but some deeper worry, a worry she felt for herself. "He's... he's not, I think, quite as... as you may be expecting him to be..." she said falteringly.

He paused. "Is he..." He wondered how he could possibly ask if the boy was crippled or deformed. "Is he... er... is he ill?" he asked gently.

"No, no," she said with a nervous laugh. "Nothing like that. Only... Perhaps you'd better just go and see him," she tailed off. He stared down at her for a moment longer, then turned and went up the stairs.

The youth was waiting for him at the top, where a corridor ran off to both sides of a spacious landing. "Sir Brian Hales?" said the boy. Hales nodded courteously, at the same time scrutinising him closely. He was a tall, well-made boy of sixteen, with blond hair — not the burnished cream of his grandfather, Hales observed, but a coarser, straw-coloured blond. But there was nothing wrong with him, that Hales could see. The boy was already starting along the corridor. Mystified, he followed.

* * *

Ten minutes later he was sitting in his taxi on the way back to his hotel. He still felt sick with shock and horror, and did not even hear the chatter of the driver, who lapsed into silence after receiving no reply to half-a-dozen attempts at conversation. The Berlin suburbs flew past unnoticed, and when they reached the hotel the driver had to shake him vigorously to rouse him from his dark private reflections, which had coiled upwards like smoke until they loomed over him like monstrous shadowy forms of menace.

"You're English," the boy had been saying to him in tones of unmistakable enthusiasm as Hales followed him along the passage to his room. "Now there's a people for you! If only we'd had the sense to make them our allies and have them fighting alongside us, we'd have carried the whole world before us. With a man like Churchill at his side, the Fuehrer could not have faltered. What a man! What a partnership that would have been! If only there were such men in the world now. *Then* we could have driven out these bastard Turks, and the Czechs and the Yugoslav riff-raff, and all the other parasites that want to suck Germany's life blood. Truly, the only mistake the Fuehrer ever made was in making enemies out of the English. You must tell me how you came to be friends with my grandfather in the Fuehrer's heroic war..." But before turning to invite his guest to tell him his story he had swung round, the light of adoration blazing in his light blue eyes, and given the Nazi salute to the centrepiece of the room. Backing the enormous dressing-table, draped on either side by silks in red, black and silver, stood a portrait, fully three feet high by eighteen inches broad, of Adolf Hitler.

— THE END —

other books by Mike Seabrook from The Gay Men's Press:

Mike Seabrook
OUT OF BOUNDS

When handsome seventeen-year-old Stephen Hill joined the cricket club, it was only a matter of time before young schoolmaster Graham Curtis fell head over heels in love. Their passionate affair intensified until the threat of exposure became too great. For safety they decide to part temporarily — but their commitment is tested more than they imagined, when Stephen is courted by his clever, irresistible friend Richard, while Graham is blackmailed by a jealous former lover.

ISBN 0 85449 177 5
UK £8.95 US $14.95 AUS $19.95

Mike Seabrook
CONDUCT UNBECOMING

Bright, idealistic, and a touch naive, 23-year-old Bob Chambers seems launched on a succesful career in the Metropolitan Police. But one day he is assigned to the importuning squad, trusted with surveillance — and more —in public toilets. The drama that unfolds shows a complex conflict of loyalties, leading from Bob's operation as agent provocateur to unsuspected discoveries about his own sexuality and the inevitable conflict with his superiors.

"A psychologically spot-on thriller" — *Gay Times*, London

ISBN 0 85449 147 3
UK £7.95 US $12.95 AUS $19.95

Mike Seabrook
UNNATURAL RELATIONS

For Jamie Potten, burdened at fifteen with a bullying father and an uncaring mother, his encounter with nineteen-year-old Chris brings solace and joy. Chris's love for Jamie, however, leads to his prosecution for 'buggery with a minor', with the threat of a heavy prison sentence. In this gripping yet tender story of two young people facing together a brutal assault on their human rights, Mike Seabrook highlights the iniquitous position of gay teenagers under English law.

"I loved the book" — Jilly Cooper
"Sensitive, masterful, fascinating" —Joseph Wambaugh

ISBN 0 85449 116 3
UK £8.95 US $14.95 AUS $19.95

Other World War II adventures from The Gay Men's Press:

Noel Currer-Briggs
YOUNG MEN AT WAR

Anthony Arthur Kildwick, born in 1919 to a well-to-do English
family, finds the love of his life in a German exchange student at his
private school. When Manfred returns to Germany he is seduced by
Hitler's nationalist rhetoric, while Tony meets the outbreak of war
as a conscientious objector. Yet as the Nazi regime shows itself ever
more demonic, Tony decides he must fight, and is parachuted into
southern France to work with the Resistance. He discovers Manfred
is now an officer with the occupying forces, and their paths cross
again in dramatic circumstances.

Based largely on the author's own experience, this fascinating story
conveys a vivid sense of the conflicts of the 1930s, and the interplay
betwen friendship and internationalism, homosexuality and pacifism, patriotism and democracy, that was characteristic of those years.

ISBN 0 85449 236 4
UK £9.95 US $14.95 AUS $19.95

Rudi van Dantzig
FOR A LOST SOLDIER

During the winter of 1944 in occupied Amsterdam, eleven-year-old Jeroen is evacuated to a tiny fishing village community on the desolate coast of Friesland, where he meets Walt, a young Canadian soldier with the liberating forces. Their relationship immerses the young boy in a tumultuous world of emotional and sexual experience, suddenly curtailed when the Allies move on and Walt goes away. Back home in Amsterdam, a city in the throes of liberation fever, Jeroen searches for the soldier he has lost. A child's fears and confused emotions have rarely been described with such depth of understanding, and seen as it is from the boy's viewpoint it invites total empathy.

This novel by the artistic director of the Dutch National Ballet appeared successfully in hardback in 1991, and was made into a prize-winning film.

"A beautifully chronicled document of wartime life"
— *Gay Times*, London

"I was filled with admiration for the way in which Rudi van Dantzig has transformed a difficult and unusual autobiographical theme into a compelling literary work" — *Times Literary Supplement*, London

ISBN 0 85449 237 2
UK £9.95 US $14.95 AUS $19.95

Send for our free catalogue to GMP Publishers Ltd,
P O Box 247, Swaffham, Norfolk PE37 8PA, England

Gay Men's Press books can be ordered from any bookshop in the
UK, North America and Australia, and from
specialised bookshops elsewhere.

Our distributors whose addresses are given in the front pages of
this book can also supply individual customers by mail order.
Send retail price as given plus 10% for postage and packing.

*For payment by Mastercard/American Express/Visa, please give
number, expiry date and signature.*

_____

_____

Name and address in block letters please:

Name
_____

Address
_____

_____

_____